4

YET
SC
CS
DV
CS   AUG ' - 2019
RT   FEB 2020
WV   Feb 22

THE LAST SPYMASTER

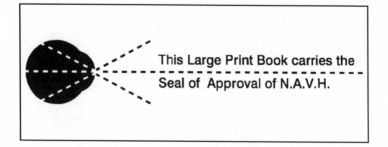

This Large Print Book carries the
Seal of Approval of N.A.V.H.

THE LAST SPYMASTER

GAYLE LYNDS

WHEELER PUBLISHING
An imprint of Thomson Gale, a part of The Thomson Corporation

THOMSON
━━━*━━━ ™
GALE

Detroit • New York • San Francisco • New Haven, Conn. • Waterville, Maine • London • Munich

LIBRARY OF CONGRESS CATALOGING-IN-PUBLICATION DATA

Lynds, Gayle.
    The last spymaster / by Gayle Lynds.
      p. cm.
    ISBN 1-59722-351-4 (alk. paper)
    I. Title.
PS3562.Y442L96 2006b
813'.54—dc22   2006021378

ISBN 13: 978-1-59722-351-5

Published in 2006 by arrangement with St. Martin's Press, LLC.

Printed in the United States of America on permanent paper
10 9 8 7 6 5 4 3 2 1

LT
LYND

For my stepdaughter, Katie Lynds, radiant with life, a beacon in the darkest night

ACKNOWLEDGMENTS

I'm deeply indebted to a remarkable crew of experts who shared ideas, anecdotes, and varied experiences in and out of the covert world. Foremost is Robert Kresge, fellow novelist and founding member of the CIA's Counterterrorism Unit. Others who gave unstinting research help are Julia Stone; Paul Stone, J.D.; Katrina Baum, Ph.D.; Deirdre Lynds; Katie Lynds; Philip Shelton; Theil Shelton; Kathleen Sharp; Lucy Jo Palladino, Ph.D.; Katherine Neville; Melodie Johnson Howe; Bones Howe; Raelynn Hillhouse, Ph.D.; Walter Davies; Julia Cunningham; Liz Bush; Matthias Bogucki; Ray Briare; Vicki Allen; and Joe Allen, J.D.

Toward the end of my finishing *The Last Spymaster,* my husband, novelist Dennis Lynds, died after a lengthy illness. He was my friend, my confidant, my private editor, my collaborator, and my love. His touch is evident on every page. I'm grateful for the years we had.

My respect for St. Martin's Press only increases. Editor extraordinaire Keith Kahla read, edited, and brainstormed through several drafts with me. I will always be deeply appreciative not only for his publishing savvy and warmth, but for that of Sally Richardson, Matthew Shear, Matthew Baldacci, Joan Higgins, John Murphy, Christina Harcar, Ronni Stolzenberg, Brian Heller, John Karle, Harriet Seltzer, and Gregory Gestner. Because of them, I am a very fortunate author.

My domestic literary agent, Henry Morrison, is an anchor in a swirling sea of change. My international literary agent, Danny Baror, speaks many languages, including those of the heart. My personal promotions guru, Deirdre Lynds, is a trailblazer and creative force and beloved stepdaughter. My webmaster, Greg Stephens, blends graphics and technology as only an artist of his sterling caliber can. My personal publicist, Sarie Morrell-Sanchez, is an entrepreneurial genius. My personal assistant, Barbara Toohey, is so adroit and smart that she makes getting organized fun — a true challenge.

In the middle of all of this, I somehow ended up cofounding International Thriller Writers Inc. (ITW) with grandmaster David

Morrell. The board of directors and committee heads are a close team. We cover for one another during deadlines, tours, and unexpected interruptions. I'm proud to call them friends. Besides David and me (co-presidents), other ITW board members are David Dun, vice president; Lee Child; Tess Gerritsen; and M. J. Rose. Committee chairs are Steve Berry, Grant Blackwood, Lincoln Child, David Hewson, Raelynn Hillhouse, Gregg Hurwitz, Douglas Preston, James Rollins, and M. Diane Vogt.

Thank you, one and all. You enrich my life.

PROLOGUE

November 16, 1985
Glienicke Bridge, between West Berlin and East Germany

The darkness seemed colder, more bitter, at Glienicke Bridge when a spy exchange was about to begin. Jay Tice shoved his hands deep into his topcoat pockets in a futile attempt to warm them as he scanned the forested hills and the steel-and-iron bridge, black and forbidding in the first rays of dawn.

Dusted with snow, two stone centaurs flanked the long expanse, towering over Tice's armored sedan and the two battered U.S. Army trucks. On high alert, a dozen soldiers carrying M-16s and wearing pistols over their belted overcoats moved like shadows across the road and among the skeletal trees. The night's snowfall had been light; still, it muffled the sounds of distant traffic.

Tice missed nothing, not the tension in his people's faces, certainly not the Kalashnikov-toting East German soldiers on the far side of the bridge, who patrolled slowly, menacingly, in the gray light. They guarded Pavel Abendroth, the renowned dissident and Jewish refusenik, and his warden — Stasi officer Raina Manhardt.

Tice moved his gaze away. He was a rumpled man of thirty-four, just shy of six feet tall. His nose was straight, his hair brown and of average length, his mouth wide and implacable. Depending on the light, his eyes were blue or brown. His one distinctive feature was the deep cleft that notched his chin, which was dramatic. Still, Tice had perfected the art of appearing almost bloodless, clearly boring. Seldom did anyone remember him or his cleft chin — unless he wanted them to.

"Issa'a kaem?" the voice beside him demanded.

With a sharp movement of his head, Tice peered at his half of the predawn swap — Faisal al-Hadi, a twenty-year-old Muslim militant caught in an arms deal Tice had busted. Standing motionless and straight as a knife, he was Tice's height but narrow, with a high-bridged nose and bony features, dressed in American jeans and a duffel coat.

12

According to his dossier, he spoke English, but no one in the command had heard him use it. Oddly, al-Hadi had yet to look at the bridge. Those waiting to be traded tended to stare across it with raw hunger.

Tice checked his wristwatch. *"Issa'a 5:12. Da'ayi' hidashar."* The trade must begin in just eleven minutes so it would be finished by 5:42 A.M. — sunrise.

This was Glienicker Brücke, "Bridge of Spies," witness to many of the Cold War's most crucial exchanges. It was a bridge leading nowhere, unused except for the infrequent official vehicle on a military mission between the Free West and the Communist East and the occasional vital spy swap. Some exchanges were notorious and covered by the press; others were secret, as was this one.

Before al-Hadi could respond, a car's motor pierced the silence. Tice spun. Rifles lashed around. The engine was a deep purr — large and expensive, its timing impeccable. A Mercedes. As soon as Tice read the license plate, he waved an arm backward in a wide swing that those on both sides of the bridge could see, signaling everyone to stand down.

Wearing a camel-hair overcoat, Palmer Westwood stepped from the luxury car. His

13

hair was thick and pepper gray, his features angular and grave. Fifty-two years old, Westwood was the CIA's new Associate Deputy Director of Operations, the ADDO, just in from Langley. He was late.

As Westwood hurried toward them, he pulled out his pocket watch. The fob was a small gold triangle — flat, with two jagged edges. He checked the time then glanced at the terrorist. "Any trouble?"

"Quiet so far," Tice told him. "We should go."

Westwood nodded, and Tice signaled. The soldiers closed in. They advanced as a group, passing the sign that warned ominously in four languages: YOU ARE LEAVING THE AMERICAN SECTOR. The old steel bridge was radiant, ablaze in arc lights, stretching ahead more than four hundred feet.

For the first time, al-Hadi looked across. Then he stared as if he could not tear his gaze away, his black eyes burning with fury he could no longer hide. As Tice followed his line of sight, he began to understand the terrorist's silence and apparent lack of interest.

"Come over here," Tice ordered as they stopped at the edge. "Stay on my left." The terrorist was right-handed.

Tice turned away so al-Hadi could not see as he unbuttoned his coat, pulled his pistol from the holster, and slid it into his waistband. He put another item into his left pocket. When he turned back, al-Hadi was in place. On either side, the dark forest was hushed, still, almost predatory.

Tice checked his watch again and gazed across just as Raina Manhardt peered up from hers. They nodded and stepped forward alone, two enemy intelligence officers doing their duty. Al-Hadi caught up with Tice, while Raina Manhardt slowed for Abendroth to join her. Jailed nine years in the gulag, the Jewish doctor had lost a third of his body weight from starvation rations and illness. Dressed in baggy clothes, he pressed his earmuffs close and smiled as he matched Manhardt's steps.

The walk had begun. As an icy wind gusted off the river, Tice moved close to al-Hadi and spoke in English: "You're damn lucky. If Dr. Abendroth weren't a cause célèbre, you wouldn't be going home."

Al-Hadi's eyes snapped. His molten gaze was locked on the small man in the distance. He said nothing.

"That's it, isn't it," Tice said softly. "A Jew is saving your life. Worse, a human-rights Jewish activist the West reveres."

"Mabahibish khanzeereen." Al-Hadi sneered. His right hand twitched.

Immediately, Tice used both hands to slap a handcuff on the wrist and squeeze it tight enough to inhibit circulation. "Keep walking. Now I've got a gun pointed at you under my coat, too. Dammit, don't pull away. You don't want anyone to see this. *Ala tool. Ala ikobri.*"

"*Kufr.* Infidels! The Jews are the enemies of Islam. Jews are the source of all conflicts! They are liars. *Murderers.* If I am defending my home, no one can call *me* a terrorist. All infidels must die!"

"If you hadn't behaved yourself in lockup, I never would've been able to talk Langley into letting you go — even for someone of Abendroth's stature. Up to now, you've been smart. But you'll never make it home alive if you don't drop whatever you're carrying in your right hand."

Al-Hadi's head jerked around. "What? How did you know?" His pinched face showed the pain caused by the handcuff.

For the past month, ever since his capture in the shoot-out in West Berlin, al-Hadi had tried to hide his intelligence behind a mask of indifference. But Tice had noted his watchful gaze, the small advantages he created for himself, and his ability to perceive

16

routine in an apparently randomized interrogation schedule. His intelligence would
argue against self-destruction.

"Experience. Keep walking." Tice tightened the handcuff. "Get rid of the weapon,
or you'll never see Damascus again."

For the first time, doubt flickered in the
young man's face.

"Drop it, son," Tice said. "You'd be insane
not to want to go home, and this is the only
chance you'll get. Drop it."

The fire that had burned so feverishly in
al-Hadi's eyes died. His fingers opened, and
a razored metal file fell silently into the
snow, a weapon of close assassination. Al-
Hadi peered away, but not before Tice saw
his humiliation. He had failed.

Then al-Hadi's lips thinned. He seemed
to gather himself. "Release me!" he ordered.

Tice considered then reached over and
unlocked the handcuff.

Al-Hadi gave no acknowledgment. Instead, he lifted his chin defiantly. Neither
spoke as they closed in on the bridge's
center. A gust of bitter wind needled Tice's
face. Following protocol, he stopped a yard
from the four-inch-wide white line that
marked the border between West and East.
But his prisoner bolted toward it.

"Halt!" Tice made a show of grabbing for his arm.

"La'a!" Without a glance at Dr. Abendroth, al-Hadi hurtled past.

As clouds of brittle snow exploded from the youth's heels, Tice focused on Raina Manhardt. A half-head taller than the diminutive doctor, she wore a fur hat and a stern expression.

"I wish I could say it was a pleasure." He spoke in German.

The Stasi officer's eyes flashed. She responded in English with a perfect American accent: "So we meet again, Comrade Tice." She spun on her boot heel and followed her charge.

Tice stared after her a few seconds then greeted Dr. Abendroth. "It's an honor, sir."

"Spaseeba!" Abendroth was excited. He took two large steps into the West and pumped Tice's hand. "My knees ache, or I would fall down and kiss this old bridge."

They turned in unison and strode off. The cold seemed to settle into Tice's bones. He inhaled a deep breath.

"You were worried?" Dr. Abendroth asked curiously. He had the wrinkled skin of a seventy-year-old, although he was only in his forties.

"Of course. And you?"

"I gave that up long ago." The dissident's smile deepened. "I prefer to think of pleasant things."

The return trip seemed longer to Tice. Ahead, the dawn rose slowly, almost reluctantly, above the bleak hills. The waiting party of armed Americans resembled a still life from some military album. Only Palmer Westwood seemed real. In his camel-hair overcoat, he stalked back and forth, furiously smoking a cigarette.

As soon as they stepped onto land, Tice introduced the two men.

The small, shabby pediatrician took the hand of the tall, genteel CIA official. "You came just to welcome me, Mr. Westwood? You are so civilized. I have shaken no one's hand in friendship in years, other than another prisoner's. And now I have done it twice within minutes." He gestured toward the stately Mercedes, where the driver stood at the open rear door, waiting. "My chariot?"

Tice gazed at it. "Yes."

With a crisp nod, Dr. Abendroth marched off alone, his head turning as if he were memorizing the world. While Palmer Westwood followed, Tice paused and glanced over his shoulder. On the other end of the bridge, Raina Manhardt and al-Hadi were

19

approaching their Zil limousine.

When Tice looked back, Westwood had stopped to grind out his cigarette beneath the toe of his wing tip. Tice shifted his focus to Abendroth, monitoring his approach to the open door of the sedan. It was time. Taking a small step backward, Tice squared his shoulders and gave an almost imperceptible nod.

The percussive noise of a single rifle shot splintered the quiet. Blood and bone fragments exploded into the air, and Pavel Abendroth pitched forward, the back of his skull shattered by the bullet. His right arm bounced off the doorframe and landed hard inside the sedan.

For an instant, the escort of American soldiers froze, their faces stunned. Then their rifles slashed up and moved violently, searching for a target. At the same time, Raina Manhardt shoved a grinning Faisal al-Hadi into the limo and dove in after him.

Tice ran to Abendroth, bellowing at his people to alert headquarters and find the sniper. With the stench of hot blood filling his nostrils, Tice crouched. The pediatrician lay crumpled on a patch of dirty snow. Tice picked up the hand that had fallen inside the car. Thick calluses and ragged scars covered the palm, showing the brutal labor and torture Abendroth had endured.

Tice found a faint pulse in the frail wrist, growing weaker. When it stopped, he closed the dead man's staring eyes and lifted his head to watch across the length of Glienicke Bridge. Tires spinning on the snow, the Communist limo shot off toward East Berlin.

■ ■ ■ ■

PART ONE

■ ■ ■ ■

I grew accustomed to walking on a knife's edge and could imagine no other life.
— Soviet General Dmitri Polyakov
For eighteen years, he was a U.S. mole code-named Tophat, until Soviet mole Robert Hanssen betrayed him.

1

April 2005
Chaux de Mont, Switzerland
All days should be like this. All moments.
Gerhard Shoutens hurtled down an expert
ski run that paralleled a razorback ridge,
following his friend Kristoph Maas. Sunlight
drenched the snow-mantled Alps, and the
wide sky was a vault of sapphire blue.

Gerhard reveled in the soaring exhilaration of speeding through the crisp new
powder. *"Das ist Wahnsinn!"* he shouted into
the wind.

Kristoph whooped in agreement. *"Super!
Toll!"*

They flashed through a hushed stand of
pines and into an open area, their velocity
increasing, their skis hissing as the trail took
them along the winding rim of a couloir.
On one side spread a slope of pristine snow.
Gerhard glanced down the other — a spec-
tacular gorge so deep that house-size boul-

ders at the bottom appeared to be mere pebbles. It was breathtaking.

"Sieh dir das mal an!" he yelled.

But before his friend could admire the view, his entire body seemed to recoil as if he had struck some obstacle hidden in the snow. He gave an outraged bellow, his skis lifted off the track, and he was airborne. Gerhard leaned low into his skis, frantically trying to reach him. But Kristoph shot off the edge and into the void.

Two days later
Allenwood Federal Correctional Complex
Allenwood, Pennsylvania

At 6:40 A.M., ten minutes past morning call at the crowded federal penitentiary in the Susquehanna Valley, a stranger in civilian clothes marched down a gray cellblock, staring straight ahead. A Bureau of Prisons lieutenant led; two guards followed. All looked uneasy.

The man paused at a cell. As soon as the door opened, he moved inside and glared down at the solitary cot. The blanket had been yanked aside to reveal blue prison trousers and shirt stuffed with crumpled newspapers and arranged to mimic a man lying on his side. There was also a fake wood arm covered with flesh-colored upholstery

26

from the prison factory. With the pillow pounded high as if it covered a head, and the blanket on top exposing part of the arm, not even the obligatory flash of a guard's light during nighttime checks would reveal that no one slept there.

"Clever bastard." The stranger jerked a cell phone from his pocket. He punched in a number and kept his voice low: "He's gone, all right. I'm in his cell now. I'll —"

"Seal it off," the voice on the other end of the line ordered. "No one's to search it, understand? And for God's sake, make sure no one tells the press that Jay Tice has escaped!"

Langley, Virginia

At 9:06 A.M. Laurence Litchfield, the CIA's Deputy Director of Operations — the DDO — hand-carried a sealed white envelope down from the seventh floor to the Staff Operations Center, the SOC, which was responsible for case-management support to colleagues in the field. In his mid-forties, Litchfield was lean, with a runner's wiry body and a lanky gait. His eyes were carved deep into his face. Above them, wide brows formed an ink-black line across his forehead.

The SOC chief looked up from her desk.

"Good morning, Mr. Litchfield. We got some overnight requests from our people in Yemen and Qatar. I was going to memo you about our progress with the intelligence summit, but I can fill you in now."

"First I need to talk to one of your people — Elaine Cunningham."

She noted the envelope in his hand. "Cunningham? You know she's sidelined."

"I know. Show me where she is."

She nodded and led him out the door and down two long corridors and into a room crammed with gray modular cubicles, which someone long ago had cynically dubbed the Parking Lot. Here a glacially changing landscape of some three dozen field officers waited like used cars collecting dust, futures uncertain. Their covers had been irrevocably blown, or they had proved inept, or they had run into Langley politics. For many, the next stop was the tedium of personnel or recruitment or curriculum — or, worst case, dismissal.

The chief pointed out Cunningham's cubicle among the maze, and Litchfield thanked her. "Go up to my office. I'll meet you there."

She left, and he turned down the narrow aisle and found Elaine Cunningham in her cramped enclosure, marching back and forth beside her desk, arms crossed, her shoulder propping her phone against her ear as she talked quietly into it. She was a small woman, twenty-nine years old and blond, dressed in an unbuttoned black jacket, white T-shirt, and belted black pants.

As he leaned against the frame of her cubicle to study her, she glanced up and recognized him. She winked one large blue eye in greeting.

And continued talking into the phone: "So, your missing source is a broker in Brussels. He's a morose Dane, unmarried, follows soccer. He didn't show up for a blind date yesterday and missed the alternate meet this morning. Now you have word he's in the wind, and Copenhagen can't find him." She pursed her lips. Her pace quickened. "All Scandinavians tend to be stereotyped as morose, but there are real national differences. It's the Swedes who are mostly angst-ridden, while the Danes are more happy-go-lucky. So your morose Dane may actually be Swedish, and if he's driving home, he probably didn't stop in Copenhagen but took the Øresund Fixed Link across the sound into Malmö. When amateurs change identities, they usually create legends based on what they already know. If he's Swedish — especially if he comes from the Malmö area — it's possible he knows Copenhagen well enough to fake it as his hometown, and if he does, it's a good bet he speaks Danish like a native."

Cunningham paused, listening. "My pleasure. No, this is the end of the Langley road for me. Hey, it's been great working with you, too. You always give me interesting questions." As she hung up, she grabbed the single sheet of paper in her printer tray. "Morning, Mr. Litchfield. This is my lucky day. Who would've thought I'd get to resign to the DDO himself. Just to make it official, here's my letter."

Litchfield was unsurprised. "You'll make your psychologist happy." He took the letter, folded it into his pocket, and sat in the only side chair.

"That's what I'm all about — making CIA clinicians happy." Her smile did not involve her eyes.

"I suspect you don't really want to quit. People who excel seldom do."

As Litchfield continued to watch, she blinked then sank into her desk chair. Dressed in her simple black and white clothes, her hair smoothed back into a ponytail at the nape of her neck, and wearing little makeup, she could pass as a cop or the leader of a gang of thieves. This flexibility of affect would be easier for her than for some, because she was neither beautiful nor ugly. Still, she was pretty enough that she could use her looks: Her face was slender, her cheekbones good, her classic features slightly irregular, and her golden hair shone. Litchfield had studied her file. Now he had seen her. So far, she was perfect.

"What you say has a certain truth to it," she acknowledged. "But I've also heard it said that a rut is just like a grave — only longer. I'm in a rut. I'm not doing Langley any good, and I'm not doing myself any good. It's time to get on with my life, such as it is." She gazed at the white envelope in his hand then peered up at him curiously. "But I think you have something else in mind."

He inclined his head. "I have a job tailored to your talents . . . and to your limitations. To do it, you'll be in the field alone, which you seem to prefer anyway."

"Not necessarily. It's just that the bodies Langley kept sending to partner with me turned out to be less than stellar."

"You don't trust anyone, do you?"

"My mother. I'm fond of my mother. I trust her. Unfortunately, she lives far away, in California."

"You trusted your husband, too. But he's dead. Afghanistan, right?"

For a moment she appeared speechless. She seemed to shrink, grow calcified, as hard as a tombstone.

He pushed her again: "You've had a problem working with people since he died. Your psychologist has recommended Langley let you go."

Instead of exploding, she nodded. Her expression was grim.

"You were one of our best hunters," Litchfield said. "Right now I need the best." As a hunter, her specialty was locating missing spies, assets gone to ground, "lost" foreign agents, anyone in the covert world of interest to Langley who had vanished — and doing it in such a way that the public never knew.

He watched a reflective look cross her face. It was time to change the subject: "Why do you think you were so successful?"

"Probably because I simply have a knack for it," she said. "I steep myself in the psychology of my target until the physical evidence and clues take on new meaning. That's all there is to it."

For the first time, he smiled. "No, there's far more than that." She was modest, and she had not lost her temper. All things considered, she was clearly his best choice.

Eyeing him speculatively, she said, "When the DDO comes to call, I figure something important has happened. And when I'm on the verge of being fired and he still comes to call, I figure it could be crucial. So let me help you out — if you think I can do the job, tell me what it is, and I'll tell you whether I can or want to take it on."

He looked around. "Not here. The assignment is with one of our special units. And it's M-classified." "M" indicated an extraordinarily sensitive covert operation. Among the highest the United States bestowed, single-letter security clearances meant the information was so secret it could be referred to only by initials.

Her blue eyes snapped with excitement. It had been a long time since she'd had such an opportunity. "Give me back my resignation letter. As long as I don't have to mommy fools, I'll deliver."

He handed it to her along with his envelope. "Here's the address and the name of your contact, plus my phone number. It's the usual protocol — you hunt, our regular people capture. Read, memorize, then shred everything, including my number. Good luck."

The Catoctin Mountains, Maryland

Dense forests flowed dark and primeval down the ridged sides of the Maryland mountains to where a roadside stop had been built on a green basin of land off busy Highway 15. A cool breeze typical of the early hour at this time of year blew around the two-pump gas station and parking lot and café.

Jay Tice stood utterly still in shadows. His bloody clothes announced he should be considered dangerous, but there was something else about him that was perhaps even more sinister: It was in his aging face, where intelligence and violence warred just beneath the skin. His hair was short, the color of iron shavings. Two crevices curved down from either side of his nose to his mouth. His chin was as firm as ever, marked by the dramatic cleft.

He moved off through the trees. At the rear of the café, he dropped to his haunches. There were four windows on the back wall — one was opaque glass, two displayed customers eating, and the fourth, next to the doorway, showed a desk and file cabinets. That was the office, just where he remembered. The back door was open. From it drifted the greasy odors of fried sausage and bacon. Tice looked around then sprinted to the doorway. He peered cautiously inside.

"Two eggs, easy!" A voice yelled from the end of the cluttered hall. "Half stack!"

Within seconds he slipped unnoticed into the office. He locked the door and activated the computer and, while it booted up, opened the window. From somewhere inside the café, a newscast described a terrorist bombing by a group thought to be connected to al-Qaeda. He sat down at the computer and created a new Yahoo! e-mail account from which he opened a blank e-mail, addressed it, and typed into the message window:

Dog's run away. Call home.

As soon as he hit SEND, he addressed another e-mail with a different message:

Unexpected storm forced evacuation. In touch soon.

Deleting all copies saved to the computer, he turned it off. He slid out the window, stifling a groan as his hip grazed the lip, furious that he was not as agile as he once was. He closed the window and seconds

later was in the forest again, moving swiftly
away.

2

Washington, D.C.

Controlling her excitement, Elaine Cunningham drove her Jaguar S-Type Sport 3.0 — red, sleek, and sumptuous — across the Potomac River and into the District. As the beat of Headshear's "Walking Tapestry" pounded from her speakers, she reveled in the Jag's power and balance, the seventeen-inch Herakles alloy wheels, the bird's-eye maple dashboard, and the softer-than-skin leather upholstery. She knew her love affair with this lump of luxury was shallow, and she did not care. It whispered when it cruised, and it growled when poked awake. Who could resist that?

Dupont Circle was just a mile northwest of the White House. As she drove around it, she maintained her usual second-stage alert, studying buildings, the mass of cars, the mobs of pedestrians. A towering water fountain sparkled in the center of the park-like circle, while beneath it people jogged, drank caffe lattes, and played chess. The world looked safe and innocent. But it was not, which was why she always carried a weapon since Rafe's death.

She turned the Jag up a hilly street, its gears sweetly adjusting, and found the address of the special unit — an old two-story Victorian with a wide front porch. A brass plate proclaimed:

INSTITUTE OF INTERNATIONAL
CONCERNS
A THINK TANK FOR THE NEW
MILLENNIUM

It was a busy neighborhood. People filled the sidewalks and cars lined the curbs. Dupont's parking was nearly impossible; only Georgetown's was worse. She rounded streets until she found a slot in which to wedge the Jag. Carrying her shoulder bag, she headed back, wondering again what was so vital that the DDO himself had personally interviewed her.

As she hurried up the Victorian's brick walk, the front door opened, and an old woman stepped out. She was slumped and lined. Silver hair wreathed her wrinkles. She wore a black dress, opaque support hose, and Hush Puppies.

"Welcome. We've been expecting you." The woman's voice carried easily, a tremor in it, convincing to anyone passing by.

"Thanks. Good to be here. I'm looking forward to working at the Institute."

Cunningham climbed the steps to the porch, noting the woman's hair was a wig and the cobweb of wrinkles only makeup, so finely done that only an expert would know. Passing the woman, she moved indoors and in a single, practiced sweep took in the needle-nose cameras embedded almost invisibly in the ceiling and the pinhead-size spots on the flocked wallpaper indicating motion detectors. As expected, the security was well cloaked and impressive. She felt herself relax, and yet her alertness increased.

She turned. "You're Hannah Barculo?" According to her assignment letter from Litchfield, her contact was Barculo, chief of unit. The unit was code-named Whippet.

"I am. This hornet's nest has been mine for five years." The woman closed the door. A series of firm clicks sounded, indicating electronic locks had snapped into place. "Our gatekeeper's on assignment. Sorry for the getup, but I've been working. Just got in. Let's go to my office."

As they strode through a long foyer decorated with fake antiques, Barculo's posture straightened, and her movements grew fluid and athletic. She was a good thirty years younger than she first appeared, probably in her mid-forties.

"Litchfield says you're good to go," Barculo said. "That right?"

Cunningham felt her chest tighten. Then she shook it off. "Absolutely."

"I'll be frank. I didn't want you." Barculo's expression was worried.

Cunningham had not expected to be greeted with open arms. "I'll be frank, too. We both know the hunters considered first-tier are on assignment overseas. But now there's some big emergency here. That means I'm the best choice of the lesser lot. If there were someone else without my checkered history, the DDO would've chosen him or her."

Barculo nodded. "Litchfield said we needed someone who could think without a book. In this case, that's you. It's also one of the qualities our quarry's known for."

They turned down a hall. All doors were shut, and no one was in sight. As their footsteps sounded on the hardwood floor, the old house creaked. Otherwise, it seemed eerily quiet, but safe headquarters were sometimes soundproofed completely.

Barculo opened an unmarked door. As she walked through, she sighed, peeled off her wig, and shook out her short walnut-brown hair. She sat behind a massive desk, where two steaming ceramic mugs waited. The rich aroma of freshly brewed coffee filled the office. It was spacious, with an elegant cove ceiling arching above. There were chairs, side tables, shelves of books, and a TV. In another era, it had probably been a sitting room.

As Cunningham closed the door, Barculo said, "Grab some caffeine and a seat."

Cunningham took a mug and chose a weathered armchair. She dropped her shoulder bag. "Anytime you're ready, I'd like to know what's going on."

Barculo stirred her coffee, gazing into it. When she looked up, she appeared to have reconciled something in her mind. "Did you ever meet Charles Jay Tice?"

"I heard him talk, but I was never close enough to be introduced. Does this have to do with one of his old operations?"

"Maybe. What do you remember?"

"He was a Cold War icon, of course. A legend in the Company. Supposed to have been a genius at running individuals and teams."

"Right. One way or another, he had a hand in a lot of our most critical actions in Europe. You must've studied some of them at the Farm."

"We never knew which were his. But I was told he was so devious he could outwit even Markus Wolf." She asked curiously, "Is that true?"

"I have no direct knowledge, but I wouldn't be surprised."

"I also heard that one of the moles Moscow executed had intel that might've stopped 9/11, but because of Tice's betrayal, it died with him." The words alone appalled her.

"True."

Cunningham digested that. "I read about his million-dollar numbered account in Switzerland and the lie-detector tests he failed, but in my experience there's always more. How was he really uncovered?"

"After we got Rick Ames in '94, and the FBI arrested Bob Hanssen in '01, there was a feeling we were safe from traitors, because we'd put away our top two. But Langley wanted to be certain. So we invited the FBI to help us create a computerized master grid of known and suspected leaks and breaches dating back into the early eighties. The grid's deep black, by the way, its existence not to be repeated."

"And the program turned up Tice?" Cunningham drank coffee.

"Exactly. Some of the worst violations couldn't be attributed to either Ames or Hanssen or any of the 'lesser' traitors we'd uncovered. So we fed in the names of officers, assignments, and schedules. Tice's name came up red-flagged. Remember that blank between 1991 and 1999 when Russian intelligence had no record of Hanssen spying for them at all? By then, Tice was selling out the store."

Even after the Cold War and the intense ideological rivalry ended, the Kremlin's primary espionage target remained the United States. As she sipped coffee, she thought about Jay Tice. When he was arrested in 2002, he was DDO — second in power only to the Director of Central Intelligence, the DCI. He had access to many of the nation's most closely held secrets. His arrest had exploded in a spy scandal of global proportions, blaring from headlines around the world for a year.

Adrenaline shot through her. "Wait a minute. You need a hunter. It's an emergency. For *Tice?*"

Barculo sighed worriedly and sat back. "He escaped from prison early today with

43

an inmate named Frank Theosopholis. Because this is national security, the U.S. Marshals have no jurisdiction. The DCI cut a deal with the FBI so it still gets to conduct the prison investigation, but the CIA gets apprehension responsibility. The DCI handed it off to Laurence Litchfield, and Litchfield assigned it to us — Whippet. We have a high success rate in under-the-table missions, plus we're so covert we're not even listed in Langley's directories. We've got only two days — that's it. If we fail, the FBI takes over. We *must* put Tice and Theosopholis back behind bars quickly and quietly."

"Only two days!"

"God knows what damage Tice can do now that he's out again. And Langley needs no more black eyes with the public or Congress."

"Agreed." Cunningham put confidence into her voice. "We'll have to meet the deadline. Sooner would be better. What have you done so far?"

"I've sent people to surveil the Russian embassy and Tice's old haunts. We're watching airports and train stations and car rental agencies. We've staked out the storage locker he rented for the things he kept after he sold his house, and we're monitoring his last

44

remaining bank account. We're following the same protocols for Theosopholis."

"Theosopholis isn't a familiar name. Someone Tice turned overseas?"

"He's not in any of our active databases. I've sent a request for copies of the old discs. Theosopholis has been serving time for killing a DEA asset. As soon as we have a dossier on Theosopholis, you'll get a copy. Here's Jay Tice's." She slid a fat file folder across the desk.

"How did they escape from Allenwood?"

"We don't know yet. All we've got is that their prison cells were empty, and both were missing. They slipped past the guards, the security cameras, and the gates without tripping a single damn alarm."

The folder was two inches thick. Cunningham opened it. Inside were printouts, photos, and copies of clippings. There was also a CD with Tice's name on it. "Both of them would've had phone access. What about our Ferret and Rhyolite satellites? The Keyhole satellites?"

Orbiting several thousand miles above the planet, the football field–size antennae of the Ferret and Rhyolite satellites picked up talk flowing through ground lines all over the globe. Keyhole satellites could read a newspaper's headlines from outer space, as well as the thermal signatures of cars, tanks, buildings, and people. Some had imaging lasers and could produce three-dimensional replicas of what was on the ground, right down to a wristwatch — or a flight ticket.

"We'll have those reports today," Barculo assured her.

"If one of the Keyholes had an orbit in the right position, we might have images of them bunking out of Allenwood."

"We can hope, but we can't wait. I've got a plane standing by at Andrews to fly you there."

"Good. Do you have ForeTell?" Based on PROMIS software created in the late 1970s, ForeTell was revolutionary — the most sophisticated organizing and tracking and analytic program on the planet. Highly secret and possessed only by U.S. intelligence and the military, it could collate data at a speed beyond human capacity, eliminate superfluous lines of inquiry then group it into patterns for analysis.

"We do."

"I need to get some analysis started before I leave."

"No. Go to Allenwood first." Barculo frowned. "We've lost enough time."

Hunters were independents, a difficult concept for some who were accustomed to issuing orders. Controlling her irritation, Cunningham stood up and said calmly, "I understand, and thanks for the advice. Nevertheless, my first stop has to be data analysis."

Hannah Barculo remained behind her desk a full ten seconds. Then she slapped the flats of her hands onto the top and pushed herself erect. "All right. I'll take you."

The hallway was still deserted, and the house silent. Cunningham peered at the closed, unmarked doors. "Is the unit out looking for Tice and Theosopholis, or is the whole place soundproofed?"

"Both." Barculo indicated a wide staircase. "Your office is on the second floor. The last single-occupancy. I figured you'd want to be alone."

She ignored the remark. "Did you know Tice?"

The Whippet chief glanced at her, surprised. "As a matter of fact, I did. A long time ago — in the mid-eighties in West Berlin. My first overseas assignment."

"What did you think of him?"

"He was a hard one. I never did meet anyone who felt like he truly knew him. Of course, many of our people admired him, really enjoyed him. He had a way about him that was pure charm. At the same time, there were those who hated him." She hesitated then confided: "He could be unreasonably demanding. He always thought he knew best. I have no idea how his poor wife put up with him." She opened a door. "This is it."

The room was as large as Barculo's office. A continuous shelflike desk rimmed three walls. On it were phones and keyboards and flat-screen monitors. Only one person was at work, a man in his thirties, wearing wire-rimmed glasses and dressed in casual shirt and pants. He peeled off headphones and looked up with a friendly smile.

Barculo introduced them. "Elaine Cunningham, meet Mark Silliphant."

"You're the hunter?" he asked.

"Sure am. And I need your help. Can you access Jay Tice's personnel records?" She set her purse and the dossier on the desk beside him.

As he started to shake his head, Barculo said, "I'll authorize it." She leaned over his shoulder and whispered instructions.

Silliphant's fingers drummed the keyboard as Cunningham paced across the parquet floor, arms crossed, planning.

At last he said, "Okay. I'm in."

She smiled. "Good." On the screen were

Jay Tice's name, photo, Social Security number, and Bureau of Prisons register number. "Extract every proper noun — names, cities, countries, buildings, corporations, that sort of thing — and their descriptors. Then cross-reference. Then organize by date and cross-reference. Organize by location and cross-reference again. I'm looking for connections. For instance, maybe Tice had a favorite café in Rome that's known for a certain dish or spice, but that café has moved to Richmond, Virginia, or he found a café in Richmond with that dish or spice. Next, isolate people, living or dead. Wherever Tice was, I want to know who was nearby but not necessarily, or apparently, in touch — and what they were doing, if possible. I especially want to know where they are now. And cross-reference again."

Silliphant did not look up. "I can sort for interactions they had on their own, too, away from Tice. If the information's available, that is."

"Please do. There should also be a list of the various government and public databases in which he or his missions appear. Integrate those." ForeTell could integrate innumerable databases without requiring reprogramming, no matter the code language used. She looked at Barculo. "Whatever you get on Theosopholis, I'd like Mark to run the same sort of questions about him." When Barculo nodded, she continued, "Do you have a wireless laptop I can borrow? That way, Mark can send me his results, and I can view the CD in Tice's file."

Barculo opened a closet and removed a notebook computer and a titanium case. She put the computer inside the case. "Anything else?"

"Thanks. That's it." Cunningham stowed the file folder on top and lowered the lid, keyed in a code, and locked it. "I wish I could stick around to work with Mark, but I agree with you — I should get to Allenwood."

Barculo's grave eyes softened. "I'll lead you out." They returned to the hall.

Cunningham had not forgotten their earlier conversation. She picked it up again: "Why exactly did people dislike Tice?"

Barculo thought about it. "Something happened in '83 that'll give you an idea. That summer he was running an undercover team I was on. One of the new men got a tip that Johannes Weinrich was up to something. In case you don't remember, Weinrich was one of Carlos's top lieutenants, and in those days Carlos the Jackal was the world's most wanted terrorist. He was Europe's Osama bin Laden."

"So a bloodbath was likely."

"Exactly." Barculo opened what looked like an ordinary office door, but inside was a deep broom closet, with a vacuum cleaner and shelves loaded with cleaning supplies. "Follow me." At the far end, she opened a second door and walked out onto a stairwell landing lit by a single bulb. The air smelled of mold and dust.

"So what happened?" Cunningham prodded.

"Our new man slipped across into East Berlin to follow Weinrich. But Tice got wind of it and chased him down in some alley. Tice didn't believe him, and he threatened to fire him for leaving without permission. Then he took him back to West Berlin, which left no one to keep tabs on Weinrich. A day later Weinrich picked up Nitropenta explosives and passed them on to two other terrorists. They planted them in the Maison de France in West Berlin. The blast was devastating. It was a miracle only one person was killed. The final tragedy was that the damn terrorists got away clean — they escaped back into East Berlin, where the Stasi protected them."

Cunningham stared. "Good God. How horrible."

"Yes. An outrageous attack on civilians. And the new man might've been able to stop it — if it hadn't been for Jay Tice." Barculo descended wood stairs into a dank cellar lined with brick.

Cunningham followed. "Who was the new man?"

At the bottom, Barculo turned. Nothing showed on her lined face. "Larry Litchfield."

"*Laurence* Litchfield? Our DDO?" The official who had assigned her to hunt down Jay Tice.

"It was a long time ago." Barculo shrugged. "Larry was furious and shaken. But he was also a damn fine operative. Obviously, it didn't kill his career." She cracked open a door, and a line of sunlight seeped in. "This is our backup entrance. Use it whenever possible. I've programmed a code for you, and you'll have to press your left thumb on the hidden keypad, too. Also, you'll need my cell number. I have yours, of course." She related both numbers and explained how to use the security system.

Cunningham memorized everything then asked, "Why do you think Tice turned?"

"Vanity," Barculo answered instantly. She

opened the door wider and leaned out. "Looks clear." She stepped aside.

Cunningham peered out at a cobbled alley rimmed by parked cars. The morning light bathed the vehicles and houses in a deceptively rosy glow.

"See you soon, Hannah."

There was the briefest of smiles. "I'd rather see Tice — back in prison. Don't try anything fancy, Elaine. Remember, you hunt. We capture. You're not trained to the degree we are, and we don't want you to get hurt. Find him fast. Then phone me."

Gripping the handle of the computer's carrying case, her purse slung over her shoulder, Elaine Cunningham nodded and looked around carefully. Pulse racing, she slipped outdoors and nonchalantly walked away.

3

Driving South through Virginia

As the heavy traffic of Interstate 95 surged around him, Jay Tice slouched low behind the wheel of a Geo Prizm, the brim of a Redskins cap pulled down to his sunglasses. He had reset his face, thickening his features until he appeared almost jowly. Impatiently he tuned from one news station to another on the car radio, finally settling on WTOP, Washington's only all-news channel. He heard not even a hint of his escape, which told him Langley had screwed the lid down tight.

In Stafford County, farmland spread out to the horizon. When Tice spotted the road he needed, he exited and drove along it then turned onto an isolated country lane that shot into thick forest. Eventually a towering pile of rocks rose into view. He passed it then parked on the shoulder near a seven-foot-high Civil War monument. In gray granite, it honored a forgotten skirmish of no military or political importance. Four years ago, using a charitable trust as a front, Tice had anonymously donated it to the county. It was one of the private "insurance policies" he had set up.

Listening and watching, he climbed out into the cloying scent of pine and walked cautiously toward the monument. Insects buzzed. A blue jay complained loudly, protecting the remains of a dead mouse it was eating. The granite memorial was a simple column that rose from an ornate base to a flat top. Crouching behind it, Tice probed the base until his fingers detected an oval-shaped rough patch. It was hardly noticeable to the eye, just part of the stone's natural texture, but his fingers had not forgotten. He pressed one edge until he felt a grudging click then pressed the opposite edge. A deep drawer glided out and stopped, mired in grass and weeds.

As he yanked out the vegetation, he heard the growling burr of a motorcycle engine. It was approaching fast. He slammed the drawer shut and bolted into the trees. When the noise moved away, he visualized the route he had driven from the frontage road. There were three intersecting roads and two long drives leading to farmhouses. It was possible the biker had turned onto one. It was also possible he had not. In the distance, the engine noise stopped.

Tice ran back to the monument and used both hands to plow up the weeds. Soil flew. The metal drawer slid out again, this time farther, but a divot of crabgrass was in the way. He jammed a heel into it, sent it flying, rebalanced, and yanked the drawer hard. As it fell onto the dirt, he felt more than heard footsteps on the road's grit.

He snatched a large hermetically sealed lockbox from the drawer and shoved the drawer back into the base. Tucking the box under his arm, he dashed back into the timber, weaving among poplars and oaks, his feet whispers on the duff. The memory of alleys in East Berlin and Rome and Vienna returned with sudden clarity. Stopping behind a big sycamore, he pulled his reading glasses from his shirt pocket, stuffed his sunglasses into the pocket, and slapped on the glasses.

He twirled the box's combination lock left and right and left again. But when he jerked on it, it refused to open. A twig snapped. Close. He peered warily around the trunk. Dressed in black, an opaque bubble helmet hiding his face, the motorcyclist had paused less than forty feet away. He expertly pivoted, holding in both hands a pistol equipped with a sound suppressor, searching for his target.

Tice did not need a second look to know who the biker was — a professional janitor, a well-trained killer sent to clean up someone's threat. He felt himself adjust, slide into an old familiar place. With a small, cool smile, he dropped back behind the tree and moved the lockbox so he could see the lock better. But a ray of sunlight bounced off the metal and arrowed off through the branches.

The response was immediate. *Pop.* A silenced gunshot whined past his head. Sycamore leaves exploded, staining the air green. *Pop.* Another shot detonated bark above his skull, spraying sharp particles that rained onto his Redskins cap.

As he heard the attacker break into a run, Tice leaped up, cursing under his breath, and sprinted. As the whine of silenced rounds followed, he dove into shadows, circled pines, loped past maples and oaks. Finally he ducked behind a bungalow-size boulder and hunched low against it, listening.

No birds sang. No small animals made scurrying sounds of retreat. The forest was silent, shocked by the violent intrusion. Tice focused and spun the box's lock again, working quickly. He tugged. The lock opened, and he lifted the lid. His hand went straight to the 9mm Browning wrapped in a chamois that lay on top. He flipped off the cloth, eased in a magazine, and jacked a round into the chamber. Automatically, he slipped the clip out again, inserted an extra round to replace the one in the chamber, and pushed the clip home.

Now he was the hunter. He yanked off his reading glasses and stood up, his back flat against the boulder, ready to ease out. As he returned his glasses to his pocket, he listened. Patience was key. Few of his enemies had been able to wait as long as he. The woodland would tell him what he needed to know.

Still, the quiet stretched. Finally, a few animals rustled off. Birds flew in fast bursts to test the absence of danger. When a pebble rattled, he frowned, straining for its location. The next noise was muted, like a rubber sole on stone. When it repeated, adrenaline flooded him — the janitor was on the other side of his sheltering boulder.

Tice stuck the pistol into his waistband and grabbed a stony ledge and pulled himself to the boulder's crown. Lying flat, he stared down the other side — directly at the top of the janitor's black helmet. Breathing slowly, he watched.

The man was standing on a dusty slab of sandstone a good fifteen feet below. His 9mm SIG Sauer was still in both hands, finger on the trigger, as he gracefully continued his deadly ballet, swiveling while advancing one careful step at a time.

Inwardly, Tice swore. His Browning was still in his waistband, trapped between his belly and the boulder. There was no room to roll to the side. As sweat dripped from his face, he thought about it. Finally, he filled his lungs with air, exhaled, and in a single motion pushed his torso up with one hand while the other drew the gun. The barrel cleared, but the tip glanced on the rock with an audible *clink.*

The janitor reacted instantly. Like a soccer player making a scissor kick, he threw himself up and back, his shoulders parallel to the ground, the front of his helmet facing the boulder's top. At the same time, his SIG Sauer fixed on Tice.

Tice had a split second. The two weapons fired in unison. The janitor's suppressed pistol made little noise, but the Browning's explosion was thunderous.

A bullet blistered past Tice's cheek and ripped off his baseball cap. At the same time, blood fountained up from the janitor's bullet-shattered helmet. As the reverberations of the shot faded through the timber, the man toppled, one leg twisted grotesquely beneath, gun still in hand.

When the killer did not move, and the forest's hush seemed to stretch into infinity, Tice slid down and kicked away the gun. Again he waited. At last he dropped to his heels and shoved his fingers under the helmet to the hot, wet throat.

No pulse. Frowning, he pulled off the helmet and studied the plain features, the thin mouth, the broad nose. He did not recognize the janitor. A search produced only a motorcycle key, extra ammo, and a flat wallet with cash but no credit cards or driver's license. The man had been sent out almost completely clean. No surprise.

Tice tossed the wallet deep into the trees and pocketed everything else. With the corpse unable to tell him more, he piled brush and leaves over it. As he worked, he tried to figure out how he had been found. No one knew about this place, and he was damn certain no one had followed him.

He finished hiding the body then patted himself down, looking for a tracker. Nothing. He scooped up the janitor's SIG Sauer. As he stripped off his shirt, he jogged back around the boulder to his metal lockbox, wet the shirt on dewy grass, and used it to clean himself. Waiting in the box was his holster and the rest of his "pocket litter" — cash, IDs, business cards, credit cards — plus navy trousers and a tan-colored shirt. He strapped the holster under his arm, slid in the SIG Sauer then dressed in the new clothes. The shirt pulled across his chest, reflecting his larger muscles, a result of working out at the penitentiary.

Moving quickly, he stuffed the IDs and other tradecraft items into his pockets and locked his bloodied prison clothes inside the box. Browning in one hand, box in the other, he doubled back to the road and hid inside the treeline. The sunny tableau was as he had left it: His car was still parked near the Civil War memorial. The blue jay was still dining on its mouse. Two cars and a pickup passed, their engines fading into the distance. None even slowed, telling him his assailant was likely alone.

He returned the lockbox to the monument's secret drawer and hurried to the Geo, checking up and down the road. The only sound was a fresh wind rising through the trees. At last he opened the trunk. A stench of blood and death drifted out. Frank Theosopholis lay in a fetal position on his left side, his knees pulled up, his arms crossed loosely at his chest, his nose pressed down into the old carpet. A stiletto protruded from his throat. Twenty years younger than Tice, he had carrot-red hair and a wrestler's build. With time for only a cursory search, Tice had found cash and the usual prison ID. Maybe he had missed something. He stared.

The wristwatch. He grabbed the hand. Rigor mortis had frozen the muscles. The shoulders and face were stiff, too. In a few more hours, the progressive rigidity would reach the feet. He worked the watch off — a digital Timex. He flipped it over twice and opened the battery compartment. Anger shot through him.

Inside the well was a highly miniaturized GPS tracker, no larger than the head of a finishing nail. So this was how he had been found. Furious, he wanted to grind the damn thing under his heel, destroy it.

Instead, he flicked the tracker onto his palm, closed the watch, and peered around. His gaze settled on the hungry blue jay, still eating. With a cold smile, he advanced. Shrieking, the bird flew off. He crouched. Where the bird had been pecking looked liked hamburger. He pressed the tracker into it.

"Think of it as dessert," he told the jay.

As he backed off, the bird landed again, cocked its head, and hopped back to its meal.

Tice trotted to the Geo. There was a rutted fire-control track ahead. He would conceal the car there and return on foot for the motorcycle. As he climbed in, he weighed the situation. Since the tracker was on Theosopholis, the logical deduction was that Theosopholis was the target. But as soon as the janitor saw Tice, he would have known he had the wrong man and should have withdrawn or attempted a live capture to find out where Theosopholis was. Instead, everything about his style announced wet job. He was assigned to liquidate Tice, and maybe only Tice.

Uneasily, Tice gunned the engine and accelerated away. Whoever had sent the bastard had impressive resources to have ferreted out the unknowable — while Tice still had too much to hide.

Maricopa County, Arizona

From the cab of the big 18-wheeler, Jerry Angelides surveyed the Sonoran Desert. It spread in all directions like a sea of powdered bones. The morning was cold, and the sunlight thin and uncertain. He tried to shake off a bad feeling. Something was going to happen. Brakes huffing, the truck turned and backed up to the warehouse. No other buildings were in sight, but then this area off Interstate 10 boasted far more Gila monsters and rattlesnakes than it did humans. All part of Mr. G's plan.

As he climbed out of the cab, he told his wheelman, "All you drivers stay put. Everybody else gets out but waits until I check around. Radio them."

"You got it, Jerry."

Jerry Angelides was a burly man with a bristle haircut and flat, steely eyes. He wore a sports jacket and dark trousers like always. As he headed for the warehouse, the two men who had been riding in the rear seat jumped out after him, carrying fully loaded Remington 870 pump-action shotguns. Other 18-wheelers backed up, and more men leaped out, cradling 870s. The sides of all of the trucks displayed big blue globes of the world with CROSS-GLOBAL TRANS-PORTATION arched above in blue and gold letters.

Angelides walked around the corner of the warehouse, head rotating, looking for anything unusual. He continued on over the hard-packed desert sand, past the cacti and the sun-baked rocks, past the rear of the warehouse, and around to the other side.

That was when he saw Mr. Lockyear's fancy white Cadillac. Mr. Lockyear himself was leaving the warehouse's side door. He was not supposed to be here unless invited. That was the agreement.

"It's real early for you, ain't it?" Mr. Lockyear was fat and sweating.

"I told you to stay away, Mr. Lockyear. You've been getting your monthlies, haven't you?" He sent the rent on the first of the month, FedEx, a thousand dollars cash, which FedEx would not like if they knew.

"Folks around here mind their own business, Jerry, but there're lines. Real lines. I take ownership seriously." Lockyear wore a straw hat. His sunglasses had metal frames that sat squarely on his bulging nose. "I think you maybe got things going on here that're a little fishy. That's why you don't mind paying more than usual. Shit, Jerry, it don't look good."

"You opened the crates?" Angelides reached inside his sports jacket.

"Well, now, just one crate. I had to, you see —" He froze as he saw the gun in Angelides's hand. "Wait a minute. I was just going to ask for more change each month. Maybe five hundred. Okay, three. I wasn't going to tell anyone —"

"Damn right you're not." Angelides

stepped back and pulled the trigger. The sound of the gunshot was percussive. The big 10mm bullet drilled a red hole right in the bridge of Mr. Lockyear's sunglasses. The dead man's face collapsed. There was a rattle in his throat, and he stepped back and fell like one of those carnival dolls.

Angelides sighed. He remembered he had not had a good feeling about this day. He hated it when people broke agreements. He leaned down and wiped blood from his gun hand onto Lockyear's white shirt. Then he returned the Colt to his shoulder holster. It was his favorite — just a little more than two pounds and only eight and a half inches long, still small enough to be concealable. It was also rechambered for serious 10mm bullets. People who knew anything knew he carried a good weapon.

His men tore around the corner, their shotguns ready. They stared.

"You okay?" one asked, peering at Angelides.

"Sure. Right as rain. That's the former Mr. Lockyear." Angelides pointed.

Another chuckled. "You're cold, Jerry. Real cold."

"It's not that I like it," Angelides explained. "It's necessary. You say to yourself, is this necessary? And if you have to say yes, then you do it. He won't cook for a while 'cause he's in the shade. When you finish loading, put him in his Cadillac and drive him over into that ravine. Now get on round front and open up the trucks."

He unlocked the side door and went inside to the power panel, where he pushed buttons. The mammoth doors rolled. He hurried out to watch the boys. They stood in a line, staring pizza-eyed at what seemed to be small lightweight dune buggies packed nose-to-tail deep into the shadows. Though they were accustomed to moving stolen goods of all sorts, especially arms and drugs, this was a new one. Two whistled in appreciation.

"They're called LandFlyers," Angelides explained, smiling. Each had a skinny little frame on top of four big wheels, plus seats and a cargo platform and a gun mount.

"Jesus," one said.

"No shit, Jerry. We're damn far away for a day at the beach!"

As the others laughed, a third man decided, "They must be military."

"That they are," Angelides confirmed. "But Uncle Sam hasn't got anything but prototypes yet. This is the first real shipment."

"Hey, there's gun mounts!" said a fourth

man. "What do they shoot, Jerry?"

"Fifty-caliber," he told them. Now they were really impressed.

The man standing next to Angelides shook his head. "There's too many. No way we can pack that many into the trucks."

"LandFlyers stack," Angelides told him. "Like LEGO blocks. That's why there are truck lifts. See 'em? You're gonna use the lifts to stack 'em. Now look off to the side — those wood crates. That's where the fifty-calibers are. Everything goes into the trucks, including the lifts. We leave nothing behind. Got it? *Nothing.*"

"Except the dead man."

Angelides's head whipped around. "Who said that?"

The men laughed. Angelides shrugged. "Load 'em and weep. You've got a long ways to drive, and you gotta keep to the schedule. Keys are in the ignitions."

Several of the LandFlyers' diesel engines fired up, and Angelides watched as they glided toward the ramps that led up into the big rigs. LandFlyers could blast across a desert at sixty-five miles an hour, hump over chongo rocks at thirty without going ass over teakettle, and do hairpin turns so sharp they would topple any other all-terrain vehicle. They could even keep running on

68

three wheels if the fourth got shot off. Land-Flyers weighed half as much as big-ass Humvees and were a lot shorter and narrower, too, but they carried just as much cargo. They were what the military called light-strike vehicles. He loved American engineering.

Angelides walked away from the noise and dialed his cell. Mr. G was a busy man, so it rang a few times. "Hello, Mr. Ghranditti," he said respectfully. "The buggies and weapons will be on the road soon. A smooth operation. Like silk." No point in worrying the boss about the little detail of Mr. Lockyear's demise. It was handled.

"Well done, Mr. Angelides," Martin Ghranditti told him. "It's good to work with a professional such as yourself. You'll be heading east to help me on this end?"

"You bet. The jet's waiting in Phoenix. Wouldn't miss it for the world."

4

New York City

As he said good-bye to Jerry Angelides, Martin Ghranditti paced across his Berber carpet. He was a large man of forty-nine, robust in health, well over six feet tall. Cosmopolitan by birth and inclination, he wore tailored ten-thousand-dollar suits — today's was dark charcoal gray with 22-karat-gold pinstripes. With his perpetual tan and threads of silver in his ebony hair, he looked sophisticated and multicultural, easily passing as the high-powered financial investor and philanthropist he advertised himself to be.

In truth, he was far more: He moved seamlessly from the dirty underbelly of illegal weapons sales to glittering national politics, from business deals with Western tycoons to corporate arrangements with hard-core terrorists training in Oregon and the Sudan. Recently he was a guest at a summit of Islamic militants in Beirut that included al-Qaeda and a secret new umbrella group that was revolutionizing the way the religious fanatics operated. Soon he would attend the National Prayer Breakfast in Washington with lobbyists and senators and the president.

He had been on his cell phone an hour, closing the deal for an island in the South Pacific. It had been a headache of international red tape, but the transaction was finished now, and his wife would be pleased. Pleasing her was everything.

He dialed again. "Did you send your man after Theosopholis?"

"Yes, but he's missing, too." There was worry in the voice. "So I sent a team to find both of them, but the GPS signal turned out to be in a tree. Then a bird flew off, and the signal went with it."

Ghranditti frowned. "What does a bird have to do with Theosopholis and Tice?"

The voice hesitated. "We think Tice must've found the tracker and somehow attached it to the bird. Theosopholis isn't that smart."

"What!"

"We think Tice must've —"

"No, no! *Stop.*" Ghranditti grimaced, barely controlling his bitter hatred of Tice.

71

"So you're telling me that not only did Tice and Theosopholis break out, the man you sent to find them is gone, too. And you've wasted one hell of a lot of time chasing a goddamned bird!"

"It wasn't like that —"

"Yes, it was! Tice is mocking you. Daring you. *Laughing* at you! I'll tell you where your man is — he's *dead.* Tice has *liquidated* him. Otherwise, you would've heard from him. I warned you, but you thought it'd be easy because of Theosopholis. Never underestimate Tice. Never! I don't care what it costs, or how many people you need. *Find Tice!*"

Aloft, Flying North to Pennsylvania

The air was dry and cool, the ventilation system breathy in the aging Gulfstream II. Elaine Cunningham sat beside a window, the only passenger in the twelve-seat turbojet, waiting impatiently. The moment the plane was safely airborne, she opened her computer and checked for an e-mail from Mark Silliphant. There was one:

Am working fast, but this is going to take some time.

Not unexpected. She set the computer aside and picked up Jay Tice's dossier —

then stopped. He was no drunk or spend-thrift like Rick Ames, no pious malcontent like Bob Hanssen. In fact, just the opposite. She opened the file folder and reread the top sheet — a short, unsigned analysis:

Jay Tice was known for doing it all. He was a brilliant strategist, tactician, and superspy. As a spymaster, he was one of the Cold War's top recruiters and runners of networks of spies, agents, assets, and moles. The CIA awarded him six medals, and three presidents honored him with four covert citations. . . .

She remembered vividly how his arrest had shocked the intelligence community: If the best of the best was a traitor, whom could you trust? Maybe not your boss. Maybe not your partner. Morale plunged, and politicians, pundits, and the press closed in for the media kill, blasting the CIA as a stumbling mastodon, humiliatingly inept. There had been no place to hide, no salve.

What Tice had done to the country still enraged her, but a good hunter began with no preconceptions, no judgments. Nothing to inhibit seeing the smallest detail for what it was, uncolored by emotion or attitude. As the turbojet sliced through the azure sky, she calmed herself. Moscow had paid Tice some $2 million for his treachery, but in her experience, vanity or greed was usually too simple an answer to be useful.

She flipped through printouts, reading. Finding an old report written when Tice joined the CIA, she highlighted a section that struck her as important.

. . . born August 6, 1951. His father, George, owned a Ford dealership in Denver. His mother, Ruth, was a homemaker. He had one sibling, a younger brother, Aaron. The family lived in Cherry Creek, an expensive Denver suburb. The boys attended private schools.

Beginning in elementary school, Tice had increasingly low marks, finally failing his junior year in high school. But when he repeated it, he made straight A's. That year, for the first time, he took up extracurricular activities. The next year his grades were again all A's, and he led debate and track teams to state championships.

He served one tour in Vietnam in the Marine Corps, earning a Silver Star and three Purple Hearts, then was admitted to Stanford University but on academic probation because of his early low grades.

Again he outperformed, graduating summa cum laude while debating, acting in plays, and running track. He set records in the 100 and 400.

His brother enlisted in the U.S. Army and was killed in the DMZ between North and South Korea. Tice's parents died subsequently of natural causes.

Tice was recruited at Yale while studying for a master's degree in international affairs.

Curious about Tice's early low grades, she studied a health questionnaire he had filled out about his childhood. It included a list of broken bones and emergency trips to a variety of doctors and hospitals throughout Denver. Seldom did he see the same doctor twice. She wondered whether he had been abused, which would help to explain his problems in school. As it turned out, his first CIA interviewer had confronted Tice with the same question:

Tice: My father had a temper, and he drank. It was the usual boring story. As I recall, Sophocles wrote in *Oedipus Rex,* "God keep you from the knowledge of who you are." [Interviewer's note: Quotation is accurate.] That was my father. He was a mean, little man who made a lot of money because it was the thing to do. But it didn't make him happy. He took it out on my mother, my brother, and me. Mother thought Aaron and I could accomplish anything. She always said we were the hope of the family. Aaron and I got out as soon as we could. She didn't live long after Aaron died.

Elaine put aside her sympathy for Tice's troubled childhood. At the same time, the abuse had to be factored into his profile. CIA recruits who reported fearing for their lives in childhood because of trauma such as abuse, severe illness, or war often struggled with ordinary survival tests at the Farm. On the other hand, when life-or-death stakes or threats of torture were incorporated, their attitude tended to become "If I survive this, I can survive anything." Ultimately, they often proved more resilient and higher-performing than other recruits and ended up being especially fine covert operatives.

She laid the printout on her lap and sat back, mulling. Jay Tice had translated his early difficulties into a drive to excel, which meant he shared characteristics with others who had the drive: When they failed at something they felt crucial, they often set higher goals the next time, hoping to erase the past with telling, even inspiring success. They were realistic in crisis, not blindly optimistic. They analyzed their disasters and made changes. They searched for meaning in results. And they were usually the family's nominee as the hope for the future. She reread: "we were the hope of the family." And finally, not only could they act on what others had to teach — they looked for mentors.

She pulled out her cell and dialed Hannah Barculo. "Any progress, Hannah?"

"A few leads. We're developing them. What about you?"

"I'm working through Tice's file, building a profile in my mind. I've just run into something that might be useful. Did Tice have a mentor?"

"Palmer Westwood," she said instantly. "He trained Jay in the field, and they stayed close. I don't know of anyone else, at least not over the long term. I've already got Westwood's house under surveillance. He lives in Chevy Chase, but he hasn't showed up, and there's been no sign of Tice, either. Westwood used to travel a lot. I'll put extra people on finding him."

"Good. How's Mark doing?"

"Still at his keyboard. That was a lot of work you gave him."

As she said good-bye, Cunningham wondered when Tice's treachery began. She turned to the first abstract of the reports that detailed his activities as a mole:

November 16, 1985. The Exchange of Dr. Pavel Abendroth and Faisal al-Hadi at Glienicke Bridge, Germany.

The exchange was arranged by CIA officer Jay Tice and Stasi officer Raina Manhardt. . . .

Raina Manhardt? That was interesting. During the Cold War's bleak 1980s, Manhardt had been a mole at the heart of the dreaded Stasi, spying for the BND — Bundesnachrichtendienst, or Federal Intelligence Agency — the CIA's equivalent agency in West Germany. With a miniature camera hidden in a tube of lipstick, she had photographed so many secret Communist documents that they had filled ten file drawers. Her intel had stopped assassinations and invasions, and if the Stasi had caught her, they would have shot her in the back of the head at close range, as they had a dozen other Western moles. Her daring story had been revealed after the Berlin Wall fell. The excited press had dubbed her the Cleopatra Spy.

Elaine thought about Manhardt, trying to imagine how difficult it must have been for her to be both Stasi spy and BND mole. Of course, Jay Tice had done the same thing, but not for democracy. With a frown, she resumed reading.

The U.S. and West Germany supported the exchange as a means to free Dr. Abendroth. They gave permission for al-Hadi to be swapped because he had behaved well in custody and had no previous record of arms activity.

East Germany wanted the exchange because its treasury was deeply in debt, and al-Hadi's family offered to pay $1.5 million for his safe return.

The Soviet Union's motive was to eliminate Dr. Abendroth, because Tice had a plan.

Background: In those days, the Politburo's top priority was halting ideological subversion and proving communism superior. So when an East Bloc dissident was mentioned as a front-runner for the Nobel Peace Prize, he or she was usually charged with espionage. This happened to Abendroth. After several years in Gulag

Perm 35, international pressure built until he was transferred in 1985 to house arrest in East Berlin. But at the same time, Moscow secretly ordered the Stasi to find a way to eliminate him.

Tice arranged the exchange not only to assassinate Abendroth, but so that America would be blamed for it. When it proved successful, Moscow opened a numbered Swiss account for Tice and deposited $50,000. This was his first active measure against America.

Elaine's throat tightened. Anger surged through her. *Damn Tice.*

A disembodied voice sounded from the turbojet's speakers. "Ms. Cunningham, you asked to be alerted when we got close to landing. Figure ten minutes."

Clutching the printout, she took a deep breath and peered down through the window at the rural Susquehanna Valley. Even from above, Allenwood Federal Correctional Complex gave off a grim, fortresslike air. Some four thousand prisoners were housed there in a minimum-security camp, a medium-security lockup, and the high-security penitentiary. Armed guards patrolled. Double rows of barbed wire topped by coils of razor wire secured

the perimeter. Still, somehow, Jay Tice had
escaped.

5

Along the North River, North Carolina

The Great Dismal Swamp spread dark and wild on either side of the raised road. The air was moist, thick with the peppery odors of relentless growth. Paved driveways sliced into the swamp, ending at modern houses on lush lawns. Jay Tice only glanced at them as he hurtled down the road, riding the motorcycle of the janitor sent to kill him.

The motorcycle, a Yamaha FJ1200, had yielded no clues, but at least it was new transportation. At the first shopping mall, he had stopped to switch license plates. At the second, he bought a full helmet to hide his face, then a waterproof zippered jacket that was tight at the waist and blousy around his chest to conceal his Browning and SIG Sauer. He could feel them now, substantial, reassuring. It had been a long time.

At the sign that announced Glimmer-woods, he cornered the Yamaha onto an asphalt drive and shot the motorcycle into the swamp's twilight. Above him, the treetops knitted together like thorns. "Glimmer" was the birth name of Palmer Westwood's mother, whose inheritance had enabled him to buy fifty prime acres in this pricey resort area where the residents prized an outdoors lifestyle and minding one's business, just as had the loggers, thieves, runaway slaves, and moonshiners who had claimed the swamp as their own for some three hundred years.

As soon as the antebellum manse came into view, Tice turned off his motor and coasted to a stop inside the swamp. He removed his helmet. Bathed in the Carolina sunshine, the white house with its porticoes and Grecian columns stood on a green knoll, the picture of Old South charm. The garage was open, showing a big Mercedes, always the old spy's favorite car. Fishing poles leaned against a wall — freshwater poles for the streams that fed the North River, and sturdier casting poles for Currituck Sound and the ocean. The buildings faced the river, where a canoe was tethered upside down on a dock. The swamp forest encircled all of it like the muscled antennae of a Medusa.

Something was wrong. It was not instinct that told Tice this, but a lifetime of watchfulness. He peered into the swamp, at last spotting a bicycle propped against a maple on a raised hub of land. A veil of vines was draped over it, rendering it almost invisible. But he could see one black fender. No dust — the bike had been left very recently. He lifted his head, listening. Birds called. A frog sang a banjo twang. But there was also a faint sloshing sound. Someone was moving through the water.

He slid out his Browning and sprinted onto Westwood's lawn, hugging the swamp. Ahead was a tall stake topped by a fluttering white flag. He pulled it up. The wood was barely damp — inserted within the hour. It marked the spot where someone had entered. He shoved it in again and hurried down into the wet bog. Calf-high water filled his shoes and plastered his pants to his skin, instantly chilling him. He moved forward. Wherever he looked, the vegetation repeated itself, endlessly varied while predictably the same. Without a compass or a clear view of the sun, the unskilled who ventured too far into the Great Dismal often never returned.

He held his gun in both hands at chest level, pointing up, and slogged onward, memorizing landmarks — deformed trees and massive boulders and clutches of weedy saplings. Sunlight filtered down in strawlike rays. The minutes stretched. Just as he had a sense he had gone too far, he saw ripples flowing from his left. He moved into them, searching for their source, deeper into the swamp until he neared a juniper. His lungs tightened. He turned in a circle, searching for a landmark. But everything looked alike — green striving hungering dizzying growth. He had no damn idea where he was.

He wiped a sleeve over his sweaty face and pushed into the ripples again, easing between the juniper and a boulder. When he emerged, a bush blocked him. As he reached for it, a gun barrel pressed into the back of his neck.

He froze then started to turn, but the gun dug deeper. He grew detached. Whoever had caused the ripples had ambushed him.

"Turn slowly." The voice was a commanding whisper from behind.

He rotated. A muzzle pointed at his forehead. On the other end was Palmer Westwood, eyes narrowed through a parted curtain of Spanish moss from where he sat on a low branch of the juniper. Westwood pressed a finger to his lips and pulled back the M-16 and disappeared.

Tice sighed. He kept watch as the old man slid down the trunk and his hip boots knifed into the water. Seventy-two years old, Westwood rose erect, lean, and bone-hard, his shoulders square. A "swamper" since childhood, he wore a long-sleeved shirt buttoned up to his chin and cotton pants tucked into the boots. Thick snow-white hair crowned his sharp, wrinkled features, tanned to a deep acorn brown. He had always been tirelessly active, yet he gave off a faint odor of cigarettes. He still smoked.

"What are you doing here, Jay?" he whispered again. "Was it all a mistake? Did they let you out?"

"Not exactly. Don't worry, I just want to ask a couple of questions."

Fury flashed across Westwood's face, but he kept his voice low. "You escaped! And now you want me to help you. You can forget about that!"

"Looks to me like you're the one who needs help. I saw a bike. You chasing an intruder?"

Westwood glared at Tice a moment and slowly nodded agreement. With hand signals and whispers, he delivered a plan to capture the man. As soon as Tice nodded in response, Westwood headed off, sliding his feet to lessen the wash.

Tice followed, scanning alertly. Bending low, Westwood hugged his M-16 close and scrambled under a fallen trunk. When Tice caught up, Westwood signaled the direction he was to take and climbed up onto a mound beside a cypress.

Tice slogged to the right, where a low table of land covered by switch cane became visible some thirty feet ahead. He spotted the beaver dam Westwood had described, wide and deep. He crawled up the slope, parting the cane with his free hand. At the top, he stood erect, noting the dam's channel extended deep into the swamp. That was a hell of a lot of water. Browning tucked against his pectoral muscle, he peered through the twilight. Standing like a sentinel beside the cypress, Westwood gave a brisk go-ahead nod and blended back, cloaking himself in moss again.

Tice fired into the dam. Mud and twigs exploded. High above, a battalion of birds burst from leafy hiding places.

Tice bellowed, "Where are you, you asshole?"

His voice seemed to float a few seconds then evaporate. When there was no response, he tucked the gun into his waistband, knelt over the dam, and used both hands to pull out debris. Cakes of mud flew.

A tide of water rolled over the top.

He stood again and roared, "Over here, you coward!" He waved his arms.

The interloper was probably not a real swamper, or he would have tried to take Westwood right away. On the other hand, if Tice were a real swamper, Westwood would have wanted a more direct course of action.

Tice peered down. The dark flow was increasing. "Come on!" he taunted, waving his arms again. "Are you lost? *Come on!*"

A bullet exploded into the soil near Tice's shoes, followed by a second, blasting past his thigh. Tice crouched and shot at what appeared to be a figure hunched near a bush. The plan was working: The man was now between Westwood and him.

Staying low, Tice shoved a heel hard into a log lodged at the dam's crest. The log gave not a millimeter. Grunting, he pushed again. A fusillade of bullets shattered the cane, hurling stinging pieces into the air. Tice dropped lower.

Westwood should react. He was supposed to threaten the interloper to give himself up. They wanted the man alive.

Scowling, Tice rose cautiously. The armed man was moving toward him. With each stride, dark waves splashed up and surged off into the shadows. Tice ducked again as another volley slashed past, shattering more cane. Needlelike pieces soared.

He shouted at Westwood, "At least cover me, dammit!"

The water spilling over the dam had slowed to a useless trickle. No time to lose. As the man's gunfire burned overhead, Tice rammed his heel into the log again and again. With a mighty heave, he slammed both feet, straining. The log only sighed, while the wet noises of the man's approach grew louder.

Tice jerked around. They were only fifteen feet apart. The intruder was young, his skull long and narrow, his expression determined.

The man also got a good look at Tice. Eyes widening with recognition, he aimed. Tice aimed. At this distance, neither would miss.

Brilliant light suddenly exploded. There was the sound of a small detonation. Instantly, night was day. Trees and bushes radiated neon green. Deeper in the swamp, gray shadows had become inky black, impenetrable. The killer's head whipped around. Tice stared, too. Near the big cypress where Westwood hid, a flaming torch glowed upward some eighteen feet. Impossibly, it seemed to rise directly from the boggy lake. The sight was spellbinding.

Tice threw every bit of muscle into kicking the log free. From the corners of his eyes, he saw the man turn back, gun raised. Tice gave one last violent heave with both heels. Finally, the log groaned and popped out then vanished, chased by a blast of spitting water. The roar was thunderous. The dam disintegrated. Icy spray stung Tice's face. Columns of brown water spouted like geysers. The torrent was like mighty hands — breaking shoving forcing physical respect upon everything in its path.

The stranger had no chance against such power. His scream punctured the air, and the mad deluge swept him away. He had dared trespass onto Palmer Westwood's land but probably had little idea whom he was challenging. With Westwood, few did.

In the eerie light, Tice gulped air. His pants clung, cold and clammy. There were only two good things in this mess — the chill was an anesthetic to his sore muscles, and his jacket was waterproof, so his weapons and IDs and tradecraft items were safe. At last he stood up.

As the water level lowered, Westwood wove toward him. He cradled the M-16 like a favored child.

"You're a goddamned showboat, Palmer," Tice growled.

"Liked my fox fire, did you?"

"So that's what you call it."

"There's a rotting stump that crests above the surface. Nearly impossible to see. Methane gas builds up and leaks. When I come in here sometimes, it's burning because of natural combustion. This time, I helped it."

"Let me guess. You turned on your cigarette lighter and tossed it."

"I did. Fox fire's an interesting phenomenon. Generally, it can mean any mystifying light or fire in the swamp. Sometimes it turns out to be luminous fungus or smoldering peat. Other times it's just a swarm of fireflies."

Standing motionless on the rise, Tice was silent, looking down at the old spy.

Westwood stopped ten feet away. Dry in his hip boots, he rolled easily with the lake's surges. "Of course, some people think fox fire is caused by demons or ghosts. They're the type who blame other people for everything. But you're not like that, are you, Jay? You believe in responsibility. Honor. Decency."

Now Tice understood. "You should've created a cross fire for me as soon as he started shooting. He might well be dead. And I could be, too."

Westwood nodded. "But that wouldn't be such a tragic loss, now, would it?" He snapped up his M-16 and aimed it at Tice. "You goddamned traitor!"

6

**Allenwood Federal Correctional Complex
Allenwood, Pennsylvania**

The rural Pennsylvania air was heavy and motionless around the quiet U.S. federal penitentiary. Incarceration, administration, and support buildings stood with military precision on the manicured grounds. At the exercise yard, uniformed guards watched prisoners raking gravel. Most inmates were in their cells or at their prison jobs — everything from food preparation to laundry and an upholstery factory.

Elaine studied the layout as she walked toward Lieutenant David Oxley, Bureau of Prisons. Slight but tall, he had a large nose and weary black eyes that brushed over her. There was a look about him of fine furniture that had grown worn, comfortable, and tired with the years. She guessed he was close to sixty.

He extended his hand. "The CIA has arrived."

"And the BOP is waiting." Elaine smiled and shook the hand. "Good to meet you." As they walked off together, she asked, "Has the FBI figured out yet how Tice and Theosopholis escaped?"

"Not yet. I take it the CIA hasn't found them."

"Not yet. But we will."

"See those pole lights?" There were some two dozen, so tall they towered over the buildings. "You might guess they give off a lot of light since this is a prison and security's an issue, and you'd be right. They're so powerful that locals complain. In fact, one of my guards says he can spot his black spaniel at more than five hundred feet in the dead of night. Still, no one seems to have seen the prisoners escape."

"You think they got out on their own?"

"It's always the first question. The FBI's finished interviewing the six security officers who were working that part of the building, and they're as baffled as the FBI. I kept them here for you. They're pretty whipped, though. They've been up all night."

"I'll meet them first. If Tice and Theosopholis had outside help, maybe it was someone who wasn't scheduled to work the shift. He — or they — could've come back to make the breakout happen."

"Doubt it. The president's new budget hit the BOP hard again, and that means some things don't get done. But you can count on our keeping a perfect record of who checks in and out. Only one employee came back last night — to pick up his books for a class he's taking, and he was gone by midnight."

"Maybe a private car or truck's been stolen from one of the parking lots. Are any missing?"

Lieutenant Oxley peered at her glumly and shook his head. "I wish."

She nodded to herself. She was getting nowhere, and figuring out how the men escaped was not her job. But who they were, their relationship, and especially their contacts with the outside world were.

"What about e-mail, snail mail, and phone calls?" she asked.

"Inmates don't have e-mail access," he told her, "and by law we can't touch anything between them and their lawyers. Theosopholis has family in Atlanta that he exchanges letters with. Some have visited him, but not often. But then, Atlanta's a long bus ride away. We gave that information to your people for follow-up."

"And Tice?"

"He gets the usual hate letters and marriage proposals. He throws them away. The media still ask for interviews, but he always turns them down. He's never made any 'general' phone calls or gotten any 'general' mail to speak of. And the only person he ever put on his visitor list was his attorney. But the case is basically inactive, so the lawyer hasn't been to see him in months."

"Did anyone request a visit or a phone call with Tice recently?"

As the lieutenant led her past flowers planted in rigid rows, he shook his head. "Tice's isolation isn't unusual. Some cons' only outside contacts are junk mail and catalogs. Sometimes it's because everyone's turned against them. Other times it's because they just want to be left alone."

At the mess hall, Lieutenant Oxley reached to open the door for her. She noted a long scar on his wrist — old and faded but marked by ugly welts.

"That must've hurt." She nodded at it.

He glanced at it, surprised, as if he had forgotten about it. "That's from a pipe cut. They can be nasty." He gave a wry smile. "Take my advice. Never be a plumber."

The mess hall was hard-edged, with linoleum flooring, tall colorless walls, and security windows. There was a lingering stink of grease that even the heavy odor of industrial disinfectant did not hide.

FBI Special Agent Gary Mayhew met her at the door. He had a thin look to his eyes, and square-tipped fingers that kept brushing his sports jacket as if looking for a pack of cigarettes. He glanced at the six security officers sprawled in chairs on the far side of the big room then told her in a low voice, "I'll cut to the chase. The only thing we're sure about is the cameras in the section where the two escapees were housed went haywire for eleven minutes at 3:31 this morning — that's when we figure they broke out. The cameras started working again soon enough afterward that the guards thought it was just a malfunction, but our IT people say it was programmed into the system from the building's main computer. Whoever did it used the control code of a female employee who left for Florida on vacation a couple of days ago."

"So Theosopholis, Tice, or someone else stole or bought it before she left, or maybe she did the programming herself, then took off."

Mayhew nodded grimly. "A lot of possibilities. We've informed your people how to find her." He led her to a table where floor plans were laid out. "This is where Theosopholis and Tice were housed. All the gates are electronic. To go anywhere — from section to section, floor to floor — you have to get past gates. The codes are changed in random patterns chosen by the computer, and some gates have more than one code. During the eleven minutes without video, Theosopholis and Tice would've had to get past a minimum of four guards and five gates, depending on which route they took." He traced two — one to the building's front entrance, the other to the rear.

"Were any of the security officers out of sight of the others?" she asked.

"In that eleven-minute period without cameras — all were. This would be a hell of a lot easier to figure out if Tice and Theosopholis had just used dynamite."

"Whoever masterminded it knew what he was doing."

"Sure looks like it." He handed her a copy of patrol schedules and a list of people who had entered and left throughout the night.

As she put them into her purse, she marched past rows of barren dining tables to the guards, who sat in identical plastic chairs. Two had crossed their arms, heads nodding. At the sound of her steps, they looked up. All watched her cautiously.

"Thanks for staying," she told them. As Lieutenant Oxley leaned against a wall, and Special Agent Mayhew sat on the end of a table, she pulled up a chair and smiled. "You're the ones who work there, so you may know more about Tice and Theosopholis than they know about themselves. My job is to find them, not to blame anyone for anything. Educate me. What are they like? Are they close?"

They glanced at one another. From the wall, the FBI man said, "Theosopholis apparently made friends here, but we couldn't find a one who'd admit to hearing about any escape plans."

She gazed at the security officers again. "Is that right? Was he a friendly guy?"

A man to her right inclined his head. "He was a talker, and he liked TV. There was a group of them that watched every night, nine to eleven, talking the whole time. It was like a religion."

"He mentioned getting out a lot," said a second. "He'd been plea-bargained down to manslaughter, so he had a chance to get parole next year. It was stupid to bust out now, but no con's a brain trust, or he wouldn't be here. He can forget parole for another ten years at least."

"I never thought he and Tice were friends," said a third man.

"Yeah, 'friends' is pushing it," the second guard said. "Still, Theosopholis was one of the few inmates who made an effort with Tice."

"They didn't have to be friends," the first man said logically. "They're both felons doing heavy time, and they ended up here. Plus their cells are next to each other. For a breakout, that's plenty of reason to partner."

The six nodded in unison.

"What about Tice?" she asked. "Who were his friends?"

The guard on her far left snorted. "Hell, Tice was never going to have friends in any joint. The other inmates hate traitors. They can be rapists or serial killers — doesn't matter. To a man, cons consider themselves loyal Americans. They hassle anyone who so much as passes the time of day with Tice or Ames or Walker." Rick Ames and John A. Walker were also doing natural life at Allenwood. Walker was the notorious former U.S. Navy communications officer who recruited his family to spy for the Soviets.

Another of the men explained, "The reason Theosopholis got away with it was because he was well liked — and he was a bruiser. Muscles like San Quentin."

"What did all of you think of Tice?"

Lieutenant Oxley peeled away from the wall. For a moment, exhaustion filled his face. Then his eyes shot fire. "Finks like him should be shot, like the Soviets did to the people he ratted out. Just my personal opinion."

The security officers looked at one another and nodded agreement.

"Can't believe you're still standing, Oxley," one of the guards observed.

"I was on duty last night, too," he told her, "but just a couple of minutes in their building — a long time before the escape."

At the end of the table, the FBI special agent unsnapped his cell phone from his belt and walked off, listening into it intently.

She asked the men, "What did Tice do to pass the time?"

The guard on her right answered. "He clerked in the law library seven and a half hours a day, five days a week — one of our best jobs for prisoners. He worked out in the gym and in the yard almost every day. And he jogged."

She looked at Lieutenant Oxley. "I'll want to talk to the other prisoners and staff and see Tice's and Theosopholis's cells."

"Of course," he said.

"I've got news." The FBI man was striding back, his expression purposeful as he rehooked his cell phone to his belt. As everyone focused on him, he announced, "We've got Theosopholis!"

"No shit!" one of the security officers said.

"Thank the Lord," said another. "How'd you do it?"

"Not the way we wanted," the FBI man cautioned. "Some hikers found an abandoned car on a fire road in Virginia and called the state police. Turns out it was a Geo Prizm stolen from the Wal-Mart lot in Lewisburg sometime early this morning. The police found Theosopholis inside the trunk, dead."

"Murdered?" Elaine asked instantly.

He gave a brisk nod. "Stabbed to death with a shank made out of a wood ruler. Enough letters were on the back that they could just make out 'USP Allenwood.'"

"The library," she said. "Jay Tice."

7

Along the North River, North Carolina

On the muddy bank, Jay Tice towered over Westwood. His hands hung open at his sides, his wet legs stood akimbo, and his expression was neutral as he stared down through the ghostly light at the old spy standing in hip boots in the swamp's choppy water.

Westwood glared up, his M-16 pointing steadily.

Tice made no move. "So that's the way it is. You serious about shooting me?"

"You're goddamned right I am!"

Tice nodded. He peered out, quickly analyzing shapes and colors. "I see your intruder. He's lying on a log. He's either unconscious or dead."

Giving Westwood no time to respond, Tice jumped down, splashing a dirty wave up onto Westwood's shirt and face. As Westwood swore and backed away, shaking water off the M-16, Tice pushed into the swamp. The water was like refrigerated flannel, thick with debris, even more difficult to slog through. Everything stank of decay.

"Damn you, Jay." Westwood fell in beside him. "Go back. Turn yourself in. They've got to be looking for you."

"I imagine they are."

"You *bastard.* All those years we worked together . . . All those times I trusted you to cover my ass . . . All the people who counted on you . . . How could you have done it? You betrayed all of us! Langley. *America!*"

"I always protected you."

"I never knew you. I swear to God, I never suspected. *Never!* I suppose I'm damn lucky to be alive."

"We're all lucky to be alive. Have you had any other visitors besides this one?"

Westwood scowled. "And if I have?"

"Your trespasser was not only armed, he recognized me. That's when he really wanted to terminate me. A few hours ago another one tried, too."

Westwood stared. "What happened to him?"

"I'm alive," Tice said grimly.

The trespasser lay on his back on top of an uprooted tree, eyes closed, arms and legs limp. Now that Tice was close, he saw how young he was, probably not much more than twenty-five. His square face was ashen, the skin blue beneath his black stubble. Black silt covered his clothes. His gun was nowhere in sight.

"Do you recognize him?" Tice asked.

"Never saw him before. What about you?"

"I don't know him." He checked. "He's dead."

"Too bad. But what could he expect — coming in here the way he did, trying to wipe us." With the M-16 in one hand, Westwood used the other to fish through the man's pockets. He brought out a wallet, a tube of ChapStick, an unopened package of M&M's, and a cell phone. Everything was sodden.

Tice took the cell. Water flowed from it. He touched the power button. It was as dead as its owner.

Westwood opened the wallet. "Some cash, but that's all." He pocketed it.

"How did you know he was here?"

"Surveillance cameras," Westwood told him. "After he'd been loitering a couple of hours, I walked out to chat. Of course, I took my M-16 and my flag marker —"

"The one stuck in the grass."

He nodded. "I don't need it, but he could've been some tourist whose curiosity had overtaken his common sense. When he faded into the Dismal, I went after him. He pulled a gun, and that changed everything. We did a nasty bit of dancing after that."

"What do you want to do with him?" Tice asked.

"Might as well leave him. The bobcats or bear will take care of him."

Allenwood Federal Correctional Complex Allenwood, Pennsylvania

The FBI and CIA jointly agreed to keep Frank Theosopholis's murder quiet for the time being, so Elaine continued her probe into both Tice and Theosopholis as if Theosopholis were still alive. She questioned some fifty inmates and prison personnel alone and in groups. The picture she developed of Theosopholis was of a hobbyist. Besides his nightly TV date, he entered sweepstakes and planned get-rich-quick schemes that went nowhere.

His bunkmate told her, "Hell, I slept through the whole thing. I didn't know he was gone until the guard kicked my ass outta bed. I hope Theo makes it!"

They had a standard nine-by-six-foot cell. The steel double bunk was anchored to the floor. Bolted to a wall was a thirty-by-eighteen-inch steel desk with an attached backless stool. There was a metal sink, an open metal toilet, and a small slit high in the wall from which they could see the sky if they stretched their necks. It was designed for functionality and minimum human needs, but it was clean and modern.

Looking for clues to where Theosopholis had planned to go, she read correspondence with his family and copies of letters to his lawyer begging for help to force a new trial. He also kept a stationery box of neatly packed notes about which games and sweepstakes he had entered. He would have been likely to get in touch with his family, if only to ask for money — if he had lived long enough.

Tice's profile was not only of a loner but of a model prisoner. He obeyed rules slavishly, and he made no effort to rehabilitate himself with other inmates.

"Hell, the asshole wouldn't even look you in the eye," one inmate told her.

She heard the same comment from both prisoners and staff. Tice's cell was larger but still cramped. Instead of a bunk, he had a wide cot. The covers were tossed back to reveal a dummy fashioned out of prison clothes and an arm-shaped piece of wood covered with skin-colored fabric. Besides the usual toilet and sink, he had a TV, a bookcase loaded with books, and a reading chair with a lamp and footstool.

She frowned. "How'd he manage to land in a private cell with amenities?"

Lieutenant Oxley shrugged. "I heard Tice was so cooperative in his debriefings that he got concessions. He knows how to take care of himself."

Tice's books — histories and biographies — were arranged by author surnames, no alphabetical errors. In the desk drawer were pencils, stationery, a dictionary, and a few other items. An AM-FM radio sat on top. Everything was neat, painfully tidy.

As the lieutenant waited patiently, she searched the drawer and found two color photos. One was a candid of a younger Tice and an older man — Palmer Westwood — taken in front of the Trevi Fountain in Rome probably in the mid-1980s, judging by their clothes. Both wore open-necked shirts. Hanging from Tice's neck was a gold chain and some kind of gold triangle. She studied their postures. They stood about eighteen inches apart, their gazes leveled on the camera's lens while their shoulders leaned slightly toward each other, their weight shifted to give a sense of closeness. Body language tended to be more honest and difficult to alter for deception than were words.

"Who's that with Tice?" Oxley asked, looking over her shoulder.

"A friend." She showed him the second picture. "This is his family."

It was a formal portrait, the same one she had seen in his file. It appeared to be from the mid-1980s, too. Tice's wife was a stunning platinum blonde. Her eyes were an unusual gemlike green. But there was something else about them, too, something haunted — and haunting. Tice and his wife sat on chairs. Their little boy stood between and behind, looking proud, while the girl, older than the boy, rested her forearms on her mother's lap and gazed up adoringly at Tice. But Tice and his wife leaned apart, signaling some kind of rift. Elaine recalled Hannah's comment — she had not envied the wife. The woman had a vacant gaze, as if she had spent too many years on a runway or checking her makeup, had been told too many times how dazzlingly, boringly gorgeous she was.

"I didn't know he had a family," Oxley said.

"Odd that they never visited." She wondered where the wife and children were. She still had that part of his biography to read.

She continued through the drawer. In a back corner, she found a gold chain. She compared it with the one in the photo in which Tice wore an open-necked shirt.

"Doesn't look like the one in the picture," Oxley observed.

"You may be right." She searched for the gold bangle. Nothing.

She dropped the chain into her pocket, put the photos into her purse, and went to the sink. As she checked the toiletries, sadness swept through her. There was something about a man's soap and shaving lotion that always got her. Probably memories of Rafe, she decided, and turned away.

Two newspapers from the day before — *USA Today* and the *International Herald Tribune* — were stacked on the floor beside the desk. The front section of the *Herald Tribune* was missing. Oxley helped her pull the squashed newspapers from inside the dummy, but none was from the missing section.

She walked to the door, turned, and pondered the claustrophobic room. Despite the comfy-looking chair and TV, it was unnervingly sterile. She imagined herself to be Tice and felt a sudden oppressive futility. Tice had never really been here, she concluded. It contained little of him, despite his being locked up in Allenwood for three years and knowing he was sentenced to life.

"Ready?" Oxley asked.

She nodded, and they retraced their path through the gray prisonscape of cells, bars, electronic gates, and institutional hush. Outdoors, the long shadows of afternoon had spread across the antiseptic buildings and meticulous grounds. In the distance, the foothills of the northern Allegheny Mountains rose in deceptively soft shapes, blood-red in the waning light.

"So what do you think?" Oxley asked as they walked back to her rental car.

"Tice is a man who leaves little to chance," she told him thoughtfully. "But I'm beginning to get a strong sense of him. One way or another, I'll find him."

Omaha, Nebraska

Over the past year the loading foreman had lost so much at the slots in Council Bluffs that his wife wanted a divorce. So when an anonymous offer came, sweetened with an advance of five thousand dollars in cash, he said a fast yes before his anonymous benefactor changed his mind.

The shipment in question contained cutting-edge satellite phones developed for Uncle Sam. Impact-resistant and waterproof, they united accessories never found in one place. Among them were wireless e-mail and Internet access and highly sophisticated GPS readers — and all used scrambled signals that cloaked tracking.

Plus, the sat phones could shoot megapixel photos or video with more than a million points of resolution — four times the quality of most cam phones. Officers could see what their soldiers saw and advise them instantly. On top of that, they were multiband, offering seamless mobility anywhere in the world. Military and government users could fly from Europe to the United States and Japan and China and Russia with a dozen stops in between and still never have to change phones or risk losing the data stored inside.

When the big truck finished loading, the foreman left the bay open and gave his people a break. They hurried indoors to the coffeepot, while he strolled around to the driver and handed him a cigar. They stood there talking for fifteen minutes.

When he returned, crates had been moved around, but nothing seemed missing. Best of all, his bowling bag was sitting on the lip; he brought it to work the days he planned to roll a few. He peered around the deserted loading area, then ahead at the security kiosk, where a guard — one of his gambling buddies — was waving a van out.

He snapped open the bag. A smile spread across his face as he stared at the neat stacks of hundred-dollar bills. His heart light, he closed and locked the bay doors, then stepped out to where he was visible in the driver's side-view mirror. As soon as he waved, the truck rolled off. He stood there watching, grinning, holding the bag tightly. No bowling tonight, he decided. He would make one last trip to the slots at friendly Harrah's for old time's sake. Then he would quit. After tonight, he would quit for sure.

Seattle, Washington

From where he sat at his computer, the traffic manager at the assembly factory sent shipments around the globe every day. With a few drumbeats of his fingertips, he doled out tens of millions of dollars' worth of equipment to governments and businesses. So when the offer came for more cash than he earned in a year, he thought about it that way: Instead of the usual keys on his keyboard, he would just tap others. And the diverted merchandise would go to Kansas City. That was important, too. Kansas City was far from the dangerous regimes of Iran or North Korea or Syria or any of the other

113

countries on the Department of Commerce's list of embargoed nations.

With a flicker of his eyes, and an appeased conscience, he spotted the first consignments of TuffBoss — a brand-new, cutting-edge notebook computer so rugged its magnesium-alloy case stopped bullets. Only four pounds in weight, the TuffBoss also boasted a spill-resistant keyboard as well as a disk drive mounted in a stainless-steel case and packed in a special protective gel. You could run a truck over it, and it would still work. Waterproof, vaporproof, and shockproof, a TuffBoss cranked so much memory it easily operated huge programs, which was why these first ones were going to emergency-response teams, soldiers in the field, and FBI bomb squads.

He hit the keys and redirected three of the shipments to Kansas City. The NYPD antiterrorist unit would just have to wait.

Santa Barbara, California

The day was foggy and cold. Seagulls sailed over the tall palms that dotted the grounds of the research institute in the heart of the Silicon Coast. Dressed in a standard UPS uniform, a man paused in the delivery entry of the stylish modern building. As expected, three wood boxes were waiting. There was no one around, although the hot music of Parliament's "Flashlight" drifted from a glassed-in office at the far end of the warehouse-size room, so loud he could hear it despite the door's being firmly closed.

He carried a box out to the UPS van he had just commandeered. The driver was in the rear, drugged. When he awoke, he would have a blistering headache and no idea his uniform and vehicle had been used for a quick but very lucrative robbery.

The thief slid the box into the van and hurried back for the next, because UPS drivers always hurried. A professional, he had taken the wrong product many years ago, which had put him in the dangerous situation of returning it and snatching the correct one. Now he always knew what he was supposed to grab. These boxes should contain thousands of StarDusts, subminiature computers in development for more than a decade. So miniaturized it was not much larger than a grain of sand, each Star-Dust was fueled by tiny solar batteries and capable of only two or three elementary jobs. But together, they could establish wireless connections among themselves and create powerful networks that could blanket anything that moved, grew, made noise, or gave off heat or odor.

He shoved the box next to the first and headed back for the third. StarDusts could be scattered like flower seeds across farms and cities or tossed onto trucks or planes or trains that shipped matériel and people. Wherever they were, their networks would send detailed data about ordinary people or squads of soldiers or scientists in clandestine weapons labs back to control centers where high-octane computers would collate the information and turn it over to whoever needed it. Designed for the government, they would not be available to the public for years.

Back in the van with the third and final box, he stopped long enough to open each. All contained little Bubble Wrapped bundles. Inside the bundles were dozens of the simple computers, each in its own plastic packet. Shaking his head in awe over the impossibly small size, he repacked everything and drove off toward the security kiosk. The guard looked at his uniform, not at his face, and waved him through.

8

Along the North River, North Carolina

Palmer Westwood's security center was in the cellar of his pre–Civil War manse. Dripping mud, Tice and he entered from outside, down indoor stairs. Tice checked the array of monitors that surveilled the compound's perimeter. Everything looked quiet. He focused on the room. A second flight of steps led up into the house. A TV hung from a wall. On a second were cabinets, wet bar, refrigerator, and a glass case of arms. There were chairs, a daybed, and a coffee table. The air was odorless, the ventilation system running quietly. If the place was stocked with food and water, as it no doubt was, Westwood was equipped for a small siege. The careful arrangements were typical.

Westwood sat at the desk, which held a wireless computer and telephone and short-wave radio. He stripped off his hip boots. Standing, Tice skinned off his wet clothes.

Westwood showed him the bathroom and a walk-in closet of clothing and disguises. Glancing frequently at the security monitors, they dried off and dressed quickly. Tice put on jeans, a denim shirt, tennis shoes, and a light jacket.

Westwood changed into a blue-checkered shirt and jeans and canvas shoes. Then he grabbed his M-16 and returned to the staircase that led outdoors.

He raised the rifle, and his face darkened. "Get out of here, Jay. You've got clean clothes. This is your last chance. I'll give you a head start before I report you, but only because we used to be friends."

Tice studied the old Cold Warrior then reached into his pocket.

"Careful," Westwood warned.

Tice nodded and withdrew his hand. He opened his fingers.

Westwood's posture sagged. "You've kept it all these years?"

Tice looked at it, too — a triangle of gold, jagged on two sides, lying on his palm. He let it slide onto the desktop. The gold caught the overhead light and glittered. "It wasn't so long ago, not for us. Let's see your watch. And don't pretend you don't have the fob. You couldn't turn your back on what happened any more than I could."

Westwood sighed and gave an almost imperceptible nod. As he walked toward Tice, he took out his watch and chain. He removed the fob and laid it next to Tice's gold piece. With a touch of his fingers, Tice slid the two triangles together. Each had a toothy side that fit the other's perfectly.

Westwood fell heavily into his desk chair. The crevices on his face deepened into canyons. Abruptly he looked all of his seven decades.

He and Tice peered into each other's eyes then quickly away.

"What do you want?" Westwood asked.

"Have you heard anything from Raina Manhardt?"

"Raina? Not in years."

From his shirt pocket, Tice took the clipping he had torn from yesterday's *International Herald Tribune* and silently passed it over. Westwood laid it on the desk and bent over it, his shoulders hunched. Tice stared at it, too:

RAINA MANHARDT'S SON DIES IN ALPINE SKIING ACCIDENT

As Westwood read, Tice studied the two photos that accompanied the piece. One showed Kristoph, his hair sun-streaked, his grin breezy. That was the way Tice remembered him, full of energy and intelligence. He was Raina's only child. The second was a close-up of their two-story house in Potsdam. A black funeral wreath hung on the door. The article quoted a press release issued by the BND conveying Frau Manhardt's gratitude to the public for their outpouring of sympathy and announcing she was taking an official leave of absence. The agency asked the public to respect her privacy and allow her time to grieve. It concluded with a firm statement that the young man's death was a tragic accident with no relation to his mother's work.

"So, he was nineteen," Westwood murmured. "How swiftly the years pass. It's been at least ten since I saw either of them. Berlin, of course. Did you see him often?"

"No."

"Did he know you were his father?"

"No."

"I can understand why his name wasn't Tice. After all, you never married her. But why didn't he have her name? It should've been Manhardt."

"About five years ago he got fed up with being the child of a legend. He said as long as he was Raina Manhardt's son, he was never sure whether his good marks, the awards he won, the advantages that came his way, the people he thought were his friends, were his because of himself — or because of his mother. Raina was never easy with her fame anyway, so she had the surname on all of his records changed to Maas. Then she transferred him to a new school."

"She became Frau Maas?"

"For anything that had to do with him, yes. By then the Cold War was old news, and the BND didn't need her in the spotlight anymore. She was able to live quietly. When he went off to university, they officially made him an orphan. She told me they laughed about that, but I think it hurt her, too."

Westwood stared. "What did you think?"

"I had no vote."

Westwood seemed to consider that. His eyes narrowed. "She must've been shocked as hell to find out you were spying for the East during the Cold War while she was risking everything to spy against it."

Tice looked away. "It just gave her one more reason to hate me."

Westwood separated the gold triangles. With one finger, he spun his on the desk. "I'm sorry about the boy, Jay. A tragedy. Now I know why you asked if she'd been in touch. The article doesn't say where she's gone. You'd probably like to talk to her."

"It's more than that. See the photo of her house? That's a statue of Icarus in the picture window in front of the drapes. It's a signal to me — one that we agreed on years ago. It tells me something's happened, and she wants help."

Westwood frowned. "That doesn't make sense. How could she expect any paper to print that exact photo? How could she know you'd see it? Maybe she left the statue there by accident, and the picture was taken and published with no ulterior motive."

"No. There's an editor there, a former East German. Raina helped him escape the Stasi. Without her, he'd be dead, and he knows it. We've had other signals over the years, but Allenwood has no e-mail for prisoners, and regular mail takes days from Europe. Besides, my mail was read before I got it. I told Raina I'd keep my *Herald Tribune* subscription, so all she had to do was ask him to print it, and she knew I'd see it. In any case, whatever's happened has to be very bad for her to ask for my help. Since the photo goes with the article about Kristoph, I have to figure it involves him."

"Maybe his death was no accident." Westwood returned the clipping.

Tice nodded. He folded it and slid it into his pocket and changed the subject. "What's Moses up to these days?"

"Good God, that monster? I haven't heard his name in years. He must be dead or in some dungeon — or spending his millions living the high life. Do you think his hand is in this?" Before Tice could answer, a curse exploded from Westwood. "Damn! We have company!" He stared over Tice's shoulder at the monitors.

Tice checked quickly. Two ordinary-looking vans were parked in the drive. A dozen men and women were jumping out, crouching, handguns raised. Dressed in casual clothes, they were spreading out, circling the house and dashing into the garage.

"You have another way out?" Tice scooped up his gold piece.

"Damn right I do!" Westwood grabbed his and ran to the bookcase. He yanked out a book and pressed something inside. "Come here and help me!"

Tice seized the case's edge and dragged. As a damp stink burst into the room, he peered around the bookcase into a black tunnel.

"There's a light switch just inside." Westwood snatched up his M-16. "You first."

Tice pulled out his Browning and flicked the switch. Lightbulbs glowed along an overhead line, showing a dirt tunnel that curved ahead, low and narrow, very old but supported by recent timbers. He plunged in, the soles of his shoes making a sucking sound as they hit the muddy floor. Westwood followed, and the bookcase shut behind.

"The house was on the Underground Railroad?" Tice asked.

"Hundreds of slaves escaped this way. Always have an exit strategy, right?"

They ran in single file, backs bent, dodging the lightbulbs. Soon the boggy reek was overpowering, like a closed grave. Tice listened for pursuit, but the only sound was the fast *slap-suck* of their footfalls. Then the tunnel became solid concrete, paved on all four sides to keep out swamp water.

"Watch for a white X painted on the right." Westwood's breath rasped.

Tice said nothing. His heart was pounding. He did not want to emerge breathless. God knew who or what would be waiting. Back aching from running crouched, he slowed the pace, and Westwood did not complain. Tice lifted his head, watching for the sign. The tunnel seemed to extend endlessly.

They passed another lightbulb. Behind him, Tice could hear Westwood gulp air. He turned to look, but Westwood gave him a weary nod, indicating they should go on. Two lightbulbs later, Tice finally saw the white mark in the distance.

"Not much farther," he told Westwood.

"Thank God. That'll make three-quarters of a mile."

At the X, Tice sank back against the rough wall. Westwood plodded up to him, sweat dripping from his face.

"You okay?" Tice asked.

Westwood lifted his head and let it fall. He leaned farther over, almost double. The M-16 dangled from one hand; the other gripped his thigh so the arm could support his torso. His tan looked gray.

"We'd better wait here awhile," Tice decided.

But after only a minute, Westwood said, "Above you is a trapdoor."

Tice saw it. He stuck his gun into his waistband and shoved the wood panel. It gave slightly. He straightened his back and used his leg muscles to push again. The door lifted free. Dirt rained down. The noises and odors of the swamp assaulted him. He slid the door outside and straightened until his eyes rose above ground level.

They were at the edge of a logging road. Bald cypresses loomed along it, their roots sunk deep into the coffee-colored swamp, their big branches a canopy.

Tice sprang up and pulled himself out. He looked around carefully. "It's clear." He leaned back inside and offered his hand.

Westwood took it. Tice pulled. As Westwood scrambled out, gratitude shone in his eyes then was gone. Tice smiled at him and crab-walked off, staying low, thinking he had heard something. Westwood sat on the hole's lip, legs dangling inside. He cocked his head, listening. Insects and frogs and birds made a ceaseless racket.

When an owl suddenly hooted and lumbered into flight, Westwood jumped to his feet. "They're here."

Tice swore. Now he heard the unmistakable sound of people running lightly on dirt. He looked back toward the house.

"Not just on the road — in the swamp, too. They're trying to surround us!" Westwood raised his M-16 and sprayed a fusillade.

"Not yet!" Tice grabbed the old spy's arm. "We can't even see them!"

But his voice was drowned out by a return volley. They dove for cover. Before Tice could stop him, Westwood opened fire again. This time Tice spotted a figure moving among the vines. He squeezed off two quick shots. A strangled cry greeted his effort. That should slow them.

As the return fire died off, Tice whispered, "We've got to get out of here."

Westwood nodded. "This way."

They dashed into the tangled growth. Hulking trees and jungly vegetation closed in. As voices shouted from behind, they settled into rhythmic slides through the water, weaving around obstacles. The wilderness fell into suspicious silence. They clambered up onto a weedy berm and ran. The gloom deepened. Breathing hard, at last they emerged at the sun-drenched North River.

Now he saw Westwood's goal. To their left, a dock extended out, then paralleled the bank, tucked in where the river had carved an indentation. Tethered to the dock was a high-wing Cessna Caravan floatplane rising and falling with the river's undulations. The white craft glistened, a sporty maroon stripe extending nose to tail. Beside it, branches overhung the steep bank, which plunged straight into the river.

"A welcome sight, isn't she?" Westwood said.

Tice loped onto the dock. "Hurry. They

can't be far behind." He untied the lines.

Pulling keys out, Westwood unlocked the cockpit door and scrambled over into the pilot's seat. As he flicked on the power, Tice jumped into the copilot's spot and closed the door. Westwood touched switches and dials. Tice turned around and rested the Browning on his forearm, aiming at the trailhead.

"No time to warm her up thoroughly, dammit." Westwood revved the engine.

"Just get us out of here!"

Westwood revved it again, adjusting instruments. The propeller turned over. The engine coughed, then took hold. The plane bounced eagerly as the propeller spun faster. Westwood moved the throttle, and the aircraft coasted from the dock, heading toward the center of the water. The backwash shimmered like mercury.

But as Westwood nudged the plane around to face the breeze, a gunman materialized on the riverbank. He hesitated, apparently stunned by the sudden open vista and dazzling sunshine.

"They're arriving," Tice said.

"I'll take your word for it."

As two more appeared, Westwood continued to work the instruments and increase pressure on the throttle. The propeller spun faster, invisibly. But as the plane picked up speed, a bullet slammed into the tail with an explosive *bang.* He cursed loudly, watching readings, inching the throttle toward lift-off. More shots crashed into the river and thudded into the tail. As the aircraft shook from a sudden fusillade, he moved the throttle with a strong stroke.

Miraculously, the nose lifted, the pontoons slapped the surface, and suddenly they were skimming away over the water, the gunfire falling behind. As the plane climbed toward the cloudless sky, Tice looked around and down. They were flying smoothly. The only sound was the engine's sweet hum. He dropped back into his seat and took a deep breath.

"Still some juice left in the old boy, right?" Westwood said, pleased with himself.

Tice gazed at him. "If they didn't before, whoever's behind all of this is going to assume now that you're with me — or know where I'm heading. Is there someplace safe you can go?"

"There is. I'm taking us to a friend's house on Chesapeake Bay. He's abroad, but I have a key. I'll be fine." He paused, then resumed gravely, "So this is about Raina and the boy. You know, Jay, I'm still somewhat in the game. Let me help."

"And get yourself killed? I don't think so."

"At least tell me what you're planning. Someone should know, in case of the worst. If Raina needs help, I can step in."

Tice paused, staring straight ahead, his face impassive. At last he shook his head once. "Bad plan. What's your cell number? I'll try to check in when I can."

Palmer's lips thinned in frustration, but he gave him the number.

Tice memorized it. "You still miss the work, don't you?"

"Damn right I do. Take my advice, Jay — as soon as you and Raina are finished with this business, throw yourself on the government's mercy. Go back to prison. That way you may survive."

Tice did not respond.

Westwood stared searchingly. At last he nodded and looked away. "You're right, Jay. I'll never understand what happened to you."

Tice's thoughts were elsewhere. He twisted around and studied the dock, small but still visible at the edge of the swamp. One of the men was talking into a cell phone.

"Circle back," he said.

"What?" Westwood said. "Are you crazy?"

"I want to see what they look like."

"Ah." Westwood banked, and they returned in a graceful curve.

Along the river, a scattering of the curious and the horrified had appeared on other private piers to stare at the clustered men and women, whose guns hung from their hands. The black orbs of their sunglasses peered up at the plane.

Tice studied the angry faces, adjusting for the years he had been locked away.

"Recognize any?" Westwood wanted to know.

Tice sat back and glanced at Westwood. Betraying no emotion, he lied. "No. Nothing but strangers."

9

Washington, D.C.

Martin Ghranditti advanced across the vestibule of his penthouse near Lincoln Park, his footsteps silent on the lush carpeting. He sniffed, inhaling the expensive scent of his fine furnishings. Although he'd had a busy day, he was still dressed impeccably in his charcoal suit. Rolling an unlit Cohiba cigar between his fingers, he contemplated his new paradise in the South Pacific. The excitement of that and his new weapons deal invigorated him. He was eager to learn what progress had been made. Ahead, the elevator door opened. As expected, Jerry Angelides waited inside.

"Hello, Mr. Ghranditti."

"On time as usual, Mr. Angelides."

Without breaking stride, Ghranditti stepped onto the elevator and turned. The vestibule's lights were already dimming. His penthouse was "smart," outfitted with the latest in electronic luxury. As the doors closed and his private elevator sank soundlessly, he considered Angelides, a man of moderate height and girth but who gave the appearance of a fierce Miura bull, from his clipped hair and broad shoulders to his substantial feet. As always, Angelides wore a sports jacket and trousers. He had never seen his employee in jeans or in formal attire, and he was certain he never would.

"Would you like me to fire that up for you, sir?" Angelides held out a Bic lighter.

"No. Have you checked into your hotel?"

"Yes, sir, I have. I like it. There's a great view of the Jefferson Memorial, and the refrigerator's jam-packed. I can get the History Channel and HBO, too. Thank you very much. And I just got off my cell, finding out the latest about the shipment. Just about everything's on the road or in the air, right on schedule. Looks to me like all you're gonna have to do is give the say-so."

Ghranditti smiled. "Very good. What's the status of the search for Tice?"

"Well, that's not such good news. They lost him in North Carolina. He and Palmer Westwood escaped in a floatplane, so they couldn't follow. They screwed up big-time. But they got a good description of the floatplane, and they're looking hard for it.

They're right — it's gotta land some-wheres."

"That damn Tice!" He stuck the unlit cigar into his mouth and clamped down.

"Yes, sir. I agree."

"What about this new woman, the professional hunter, Elaine Cunningham?"

"She flew up to Allenwood today. She's supposed to've been a real hotshot a couple years ago, the kind that could find anyone anywheres. Then she went wacky, and nobody would work with her."

"What do you think?"

Angelides shrugged. "You can never tell. Maybe it'd take someone like her to nail Tice. It's not like she's stuck in the same groove as the rest of them Langley suits."

The elevator door opened onto an expanse of polished brass, carved wood, and black enameled pillars. Ghranditti strode out, bearing down on the massive glass entry. There was a flurry of genteel activity as he closed in. The valet appeared with a gold cigarette lighter. Ghranditti waved him off. The doorman opened the door, and Ghranditti marched through, Angelides at his heels. His Cadillac limousine materialized at the curb, and the chauffeur was out and around, opening the rear door.

But Ghranditti stopped on the sidewalk

and turned. Everyone backed off. He pulled his cigar from his teeth and stared at Angelides, who approached. He said quietly, "You said Cunningham flew. Find out what airport. Have her followed. She's one lead we haven't covered. Besides, we don't want her mucking up our plans."

"Right you are, Mr. Ghranditti. You can count on me." Angelides smiled.

Ghranditti gave an abrupt nod and stepped into the limo. Within seconds, the long black luxury car was cruising off.

Aloft, flying south to Andrews Air Force Base, Maryland

Elaine peeled off her jacket and tossed it across the aisle, worrying what Tice was doing, whom he would harm next. She fell back against her seat and gazed out the window at a slick of clouds slicing the sky. Suddenly she saw herself as a teenager sitting with her mother in the front row at the federal courthouse in Los Angeles.

Her father stood behind the defense table, a big-ticket attorney at each of his tailored shoulders. He was buffed and polished in his suit, striped shirt, and red power tie, wearing that commanding look he wore. But then, he knew he had a secret $100 million stash in Liechtenstein and a mistress waiting in Paris, and once the judge pounded his gavel, only four years to serve in Lompoc's white-collar federal camp.

Why was she thinking about him? She felt good. She had longed to be back at work, to be useful again, to contribute. Langley was important to her. Helping the country was even more important, especially now. Plus she was dealing well with people, the way she used to. Then there was the hunt itself, against the most highly skilled quarry of her life. While Tice appalled her, she also found him fascinating — the ultimate challenge.

Excitement surged through her, instantly followed by a profound sense of responsibility. She must find Tice. She *would* find him. And now, after her work with his dossier and at Allenwood, she was starting to feel a resonance, a connection. Each assignment was like crawling inside someone else's scales and living with them until they became skin — *her* skin.

As she mulled that, she remembered a section in Tice's file that analyzed his success as a spymaster. She opened the file folder and settled back. Tice had used human manipulation like a subversive weapon, calling his approach the BAR Code — Befriend, Assess, Recruit. She flipped through the pages until she found it:

. . . Tice was unusually persuasive, with a huge talent for displaying warmth and compassion. When a recruiter reported a potential mole or asset or agent was resistant, Tice would have a personal meeting arranged. By the time the potential arrived, Tice had steeped himself in every detail of his or her life. Tice asked questions, listened intently, and showed deep interest in the person's concerns and worries for the future. Soon the potential began to believe he cared.

Tice met with them as many times as needed until they agreed to do the job. After they completed it, they were compromised — and he owned their souls.

His signature touch was deceptively simple: When they entered the door for the first meeting, he would already be walking toward them, his hand outstretched, smiling. He would introduce himself, disarming them and setting the stage for what was to follow: "Let's dispense with formalities. My friends call me Jay." . . .

The description was chilling. Great spymasters like Tice learned to pretend loyalty while actually being disloyal. Some authorities believed all were self-absorbed and egocentric, even narcissistic. Tice was so skillful that he must have known exactly what he was doing — manipulating people like puppets. This pattern of divided loyalties would have paved the way for his plunge down the slippery slope to treason.

As the plane bounced on a pocket of air, she took out her cell and dialed. "I'm in the plane, flying back, Hannah. Were the satellites useful?"

"They were overhead, but no help at all — yet. The FBI got a schedule of guard patrols and personnel assignments at Allenwood, and the NRO checked it against the satellites' digitized reports. The satellites didn't spot either Theosopholis or Tice, and everyone out in the open from one to five A.M. was accounted for. There were some deliveries, but all were expected and have been checked." She sounded frustrated. "I've ordered blowups of the sat photos. I want to look at them myself. Maybe all of that cutting-edge technology missed something."

"Good idea. Are there any new developments?"

"As a matter of fact, yes. You were right about Palmer Westwood. Once we really focused on him, we discovered he had a secret hideaway in the Great Dismal Swamp. The problem was, by the time my people got there, Tice and Westwood were long gone."

"They're together now?" She felt her heart rate accelerate. "What happened!"

"Witnesses reported that Westwood was flying Tice away in his pontoon plane when some strangers came out of the swamp and fired volleys at them. It sounded bad. The plane took a lot of hits, and maybe Westwood and Tice did, too. No way to be sure. We're searching everywhere for the plane. I've notified the Coast Guard on down. There was no sign of the shooters by the time we got there."

"Who are the witnesses?"

"Neighbors along the river. Our people interviewed them, and their stories matched well enough that we have to believe it's true. Some of them know Westwood, and the descriptions of the other man match Tice. Plus, we identified Tice's prints in the house's cellar and on a motorcycle left in the driveway."

"So, someone else is looking for him, and it sure doesn't sound as if they're going for a live capture." She paused, mulling rapidly.

"How could they have found out he escaped?"

Hannah sounded angry. "I wish I knew. No matter how well we buttoned down on this, there's the prison grapevine, and word could've leaked out. We're staying on top of it, believe me." She paused. "That was a hell of a good idea to check into Westwood. You have anything else to suggest?"

"I need to think about what I've learned first."

"Okay. Will you drive straight here from Andrews?"

"One stop." She described the missing section of the *Herald Tribune*. "I thought about checking the newspaper's Web site, but the same stories and articles don't necessarily appear in both the online and print versions. Besides, the smart thing is to look at what Tice himself saw."

"Where will you find the paper?"

"A bookstore-café on Fourteenth Street — the Reading Room. It holds on to old newspapers and magazines as a service to regulars."

"Be careful, Elaine. The killers chasing Tice have added a complication we don't need. If you close in on him, they could be there, too. And if they think you're in their way, you could find yourself at a lethal ground zero."

She had already thought of that. Still, she was suddenly uneasy. "Thanks. I appreciate the warning."

As the turbojet's engines thrummed, they said good-bye, and she turned on her computer. There was an e-mail from Mark Silliphant:

I've finished. ForeTell has found, sorted, cross-checked, and analyzed. But the results are in too big a file to send in one attachment. I can e-mail it in small batches, or you can have it all in one piece on a CD when you get back to Whippet.

She replied:

Thanks. I still have a lot of other work to do. Put it on a CD. I found a photo of Tice from the mid '80s in which he's wearing a gold triangle-shaped pendant hanging from a neck chain. I'm interested in the pendant. Send a new query through all of your data. Maybe you can locate it.

As she waited for his response, she wrote a reminder to herself to visit Tice's storage locker. Then she loaded the JAY TICE CD and discovered it contained video clips of

141

speeches at Langley beginning in 1994. She muted the audio so she could concentrate on his physical traits first. She inspected the oval face and refined features of a decade ago, the creases, the cheekbones, the chin — and watched him age. But even in the most recent talks, he rolled off the pads of his feet like an athlete. She turned on the sound and returned to the beginning. Two pieces of his advice struck her:

"Always have a good backup strategy and an even better way out."

"Do the unexpected. As Goethe wrote, 'Boldness has genius, power, and magic in it.' Being bold can be safer and yield greater results."

Tice was a compelling subject. When he spoke to staff, he was down-to-earth and approachable while projecting wisdom and leadership. When politicians or high officials were listening, the skin on his face tightened to the bones, chiseling his features. His voice deepened, and he grew striking, aristocratic, while communicating a sense of unassailable authority. From covert op to spymaster and intelligence chief, he was a chameleon, tailoring himself to his audience.

Still, she recalled hearing him tell a group of recruits, "To be memorable at the wrong time could be your death sentence." She moved her gaze away and tried to describe him but found herself unsure. He was a man of flesh, bone, and quicksilver.

She set the computer on the seat beside her where she could glance at the screen and continue to absorb Jay Tice. As she picked up his dossier, an e-mail arrived from Silliphant:

Will do. If I find anything about the triangle pendant, it'll be on the CD.

She opened Tice's file and paused at a recap of his CIA service. During the Cold War, he had worked throughout Europe, a month here, six months there — Paris, Vienna, Rome, West Berlin, Madrid, other places both large and small. The list was chronological and two pages long. Most overseas spies operated out of embassies, pretending to be diplomats, but Tice had been a nonofficial cover operative — a NOC. It was Langley's most hazardous line of work, not only because the assignments could be dicey, but because NOCs had no diplomatic immunity. If caught for spying, they usually ended up in prison, and some countries executed them. Tice was never caught.

Finally, in October 1985, Tice came in from the cold to head the West Berlin station. As she noted the date, she realized his first act of betrayal — Dr. Abendroth's assassination — occurred a few weeks later. Was there something about his being station chief that had instigated a sellout to the Soviets?

She found the file photo of Tice and his family, then flipped through his biography, noting his marriage to Marie Dillon in 1975 and the birth of their two children in 1976 and 1978. Then:

December 15, 1985

Jay Tice was late leaving that morning to go to the embassy. His BMW was parked at the end of the drive, blocking Marie Tice's car, which she needed to take Mariette and Aaron to school. While the children waited, Marie got into the BMW to move it. She turned on the ignition, which triggered a bomb planted beneath, killing her instantly. The children never regained consciousness and died in the hospital several hours later from injuries.

Tice was believed to have been the actual target. He was offered compassionate leave but refused. A week later he asked for personal time, which was granted. He was gone four days. The bombers were never found, but there were rumors at the time — although there was no evidence — that Tice knew who they were and terminated them. He had a reputation for going after anyone who attacked him.

Note: Three weeks earlier, on November 23, Mrs. Tice reported a dependency on prescription drugs to government doctors and filed an application for custodial medical care. The application had just been approved at the time of her death.

Elaine lowered the report, trying to absorb the tragedy. Tice's wife and two children. All of them. Gone. Dead.

She focused on the son's name — Aaron. He might have been named for Tice's brother, who was killed in the DMZ between North and South Korea. Maybe "Mariette" was chosen as a variation of "Marie." Whatever differences Tice had with Marie, the savage murder of her and their children must have hit him hard.

She skimmed the rest but saw nothing more about the bombing. She returned to the report: "A week later he asked for personal time . . . Tice knew who they were and terminated them." She would believe that now. From everything she had read and heard, Tice struck her as someone who did not forget who crossed him. He would do whatever it took to stop them — including wiping them.

But other sentences also stood out: "Jay Tice was late leaving that morning to go to the embassy. . . . He was offered compassionate leave but refused. . . . The bombers were never found . . ."

Had Marie known Tice was a KGB mole? If so, he might have feared she would reveal his treachery, or perhaps she had already threatened that. After his family's murder, Tice betrayed at least a dozen U.S. moles. There was no way he would not have known what their fates would be. In effect, he murdered them, which made it seem possible he had asked the KGB to liquidate Marie, too. He might have delayed leaving so she would be the one to move his car. To him, the children might have been simply collateral damage.

Frowning, she jotted a reminder to check Marie's family. She turned the page:

. . . Tice continued his work with his usual high degree of success, transferring back to Washington for a year in 1987, then returning to run the West Berlin station and the stations in Rome and London, then West Berlin again. After Ames's arrest in 1994, he returned to Langley to take over the Directorate of Operations.

Among his duties was digging out moles who might have burrowed into U.S. security. The irony was that he was in charge of finding himself.

He never remarried. He was considered a gentleman spymaster of the old school, popular and respected among colleagues and government officials and in demand socially.

Despite his being "popular and respected" and "in demand socially," he apparently had no real friends, since no one had stood by him after his arrest, although in other high-profile espionage cases, including Rick Ames's and Bob Hanssen's, at least a few friends had showed up to give moral support. Isolation was a contributing factor to turning against one's own. The infamous MI6 turncoat Kim Philby once said, "To betray, you must first belong. I never belonged."

And Tice was driven to excel, to exceed others' expectations. He had done that in high school and in college and in the CIA.

But when you reach the top, what else do you do, where else do you go? Tice had answered the question by taking on an even tougher challenge, one where the cost of failure was higher — working for first Soviet then Russian intelligence against the United States.

A clear understanding of the inner forces that drove him would help her to know where he would go, what he would do, what he wanted now. He could be performing for someone or something again. But for whom or what? With that answer, she would know how to find him.

10

Washington, D.C.
The last golden rays of sunlight spread
across the teeming capital city, showing it at
its best just before the small death of
nightfall. In the Reading Room, customers
prowled the aisles of books and filled the
chairs around the café's tables. The rich
aroma of coffee perfumed the air. In less
than five minutes, the owner produced the
back copy of the *Herald Tribune* that Elaine
wanted.

Carrying a cup of steaming espresso,
Elaine found a table, too impatient to wait
until she reached Whippet to read. She swallowed espresso and checked the headlines
— a contentious EU vote in Brussels, more
terrorist attacks in Europe, more violent
upheaval in the Middle East. . . .

She flipped through to the end and returned to the beginning, turning pages
slowly, until:

RAINA MANHARDT'S SON DIES IN ALPINE SKIING ACCIDENT

She frowned. The illustrious Raina Manhardt again. She pored through the paper one more time, but nothing else seemed connected to Tice. She read the news story:

Berlin, Germany — Kristoph Maas, the 19-year-old son of Cold War heroine Raina Manhardt, died yesterday in a skiing accident outside Chaux de Mont, Switzerland.

According to a BND spokesman, Maas was a software programmer living and working in Geneva. Skiing with him was a childhood friend, Gerhard Shoutens, also a programmer originally from Berlin. Shoutens said he saw Maas's skis strike something in the snow near the edge of a cliff. Maas lost his balance and plunged some 750 feet to his death.

The BND reports an autopsy showed he died from massive brain and internal injuries from the high-impact fall. . . .

Skiing was a high-risk sport in which accident and death happened more often than most people realized. Elaine suspected the prime reason the *Herald Tribune* had run the story was Manhardt's celebrity. Odd that her son had a different last name.

As she finished her espresso, Elaine pulled out the abstracts of Tice's missions, searching for Raina Manhardt's name — as an enemy operative during the Cold War or on the other end of a CIA exchange as she had been when Dr. Pavel Abendroth was assassinated. Nothing. Still, Tice and Manhardt had lived in the Berlin area off and on for at least a decade, working for both sides, but because of security it was likely neither knew that about the other. After the Berlin Wall crumbled, it would have been inevitable that the two — since they were highly placed intelligence officers of friendly agencies — would see each other on official business and rub shoulders at embassy parties. By then Manhardt would have been serving only one master, the BND, while Tice continued to work for both the CIA and Russian intelligence.

Had this news piece triggered Tice to escape, or was it merely coincidence? She noted Kristoph's age. He was born after the Abendroth exchange, after the murder of Tice's family, after Raina Manhardt became a mole for the BND, after Jay Tice sold out to the KGB.

Elaine decided that when she returned to Whippet, she would ask Mark to isolate all mentions of Raina Manhardt in the CIA databank. She rolled the newspaper section and stuck it into her shoulder bag. Her mind was already back at Whippet, wondering what Mark had found about Tice.

Traffic was thick, and pedestrians mobbed the sidewalks, jackets off, striding along. The air was humid, smelling of engine exhaust and cooling concrete. As Elaine walked north on Fourteenth Street toward where her Jaguar was parked, she considered what she knew about Jay Tice — until she crossed H Street and the skin on the back of her neck tightened. She shook off a shiver, feeling more than knowing she was being followed. As a hunter, she was seldom prey. Who could it be?

She clamped her shoulder bag to her side and angled her head so her peripheral vision swept back. The number of pedestrians advancing through the gritty light had thinned. There were a couple dozen, but none she recognized.

She hurried onward. When she checked again, she thought she saw a tall man slip hastily into a doorway. Then she was almost sure a woman abruptly turned to stare into a store window. Sweat slid down her spine. She was not only nervous about her own welfare; more important, no one must follow her to Whippet's secret Victorian.

On the other hand, if she handled the situation right, she might get a good look at her tail or tails and identify them.

At Eye Street, she peeled off into Franklin Square, frequent site of protests and rallies, hoping for a crowd. One advantage of her small size was she could lose herself more easily than most. The park was spacious and open, with shallow steps and sloping sidewalks — but no large gathering. An elderly couple walked a pair of leashed dachshunds. A woman dressed in Muslim *hijab* — veil, scarf, and long coat — held the hand of a little boy as they strolled toward Thirteenth. A teenage boy in baggy shorts and a skullcap soared past on Rollerblades. Homeless people lounged on benches.

In the glowing light of an old-fashioned lamppost, Elaine paused near the fountain, her nerves on fire as she remembered Hannah's ominous warning about the group that had attacked Jay Tice and Palmer Westwood: "If they think you're in their way, you could find yourself at a lethal ground zero." Abruptly the bright area was deserted except for a woman in a business suit, gripping a fat briefcase, who had stopped at the fountain, apparently to enjoy the jetting spray, and another woman, this one wearing a blousy caftan, who was lying down on her side on a park bench, hugging a battered book bag as her eyelids lowered into sleep. A public park was an unlikely venue for a professional to try to snatch or kill her, although not unheard-of, especially if the perpetrators were rogue or amateur.

Her heart seemed to stop. There was a sound, faint but sharp, like a child's hand slapping a leather cushion. Automatically, she dropped to the grass. Something slashed past, brushing her hair. Soundless. There and gone. Instantly, the muted sound sang again. As if by magic, a dart quivered in the KEEP OFF THE GRASS near her.

She rolled left, pulling the Walther PPK and sound suppressor from her bag. She abandoned the bag and switched course, rolling again as she screwed on the suppressor. As she crouched behind a tree, she surveyed the park. Facing her, the woman in the caftan slept. At the same time, the businesswoman with the briefcase remained in profile, still apparently enjoying the fountain. No one else was in sight. One of the women had to be the assassin.

Again the horrible sound. A dart sank into the bark above her head. As Elaine dodged left, wood fragments stung her cheek. But she had seen the book bag move. The shooter was the woman in the caftan. Again the sound, and a dart hissed past her temple. The book bag resettled high against the woman's chest.

Heart thundering, Elaine threw herself forward onto her belly behind a bush and carefully aimed the Walther up from underneath. As the book bag adjusted once more, she squeezed the trigger. *Pop.* Almost simultaneously, a dart sliced into the grass near her elbow. She waited.

People ambled toward the fountain. A suit jacket slung over his shoulder, a man joined the businesswoman there. They embraced, while the woman in the caftan lay unmoving, still on her side. Elaine held her breath. Finally, the lower arm that gripped the bag slid off and dangled limply, the knuckles touching the sidewalk.

Elaine looked around then grabbed her purse. She ripped three pages from one of Tice's printouts and rolled them into a funnel, bending the tip so nothing could slide through. Carefully she picked up one of the darts by its flight and dropped it inside. She did the same with the others. Killing with darts was almost impossible — unless the tips held poison. She folded the top and put the deadly package in one of her purse's zippered pockets. Controlling her emotions, she sauntered toward the janitor, a casual smile on her face.

Scanning, Elaine pressed the woman over onto her back. Blood had soaked a corner of the book bag scarlet. The bullet had entered at an angle through the belly and apparently up through the heart. The carotid artery had no pulse. In the shadowy light, she studied the woman's straight nose, round cheeks and chin, and wide mouth. Her hair was brown, cut in a simple bob. She looked as if she were in her early thirties, had no distinguishing characteristics, wore no rings, and carried no purse. Elaine did not recognize her.

She picked up the bag. Beneath was an air gun. She stuffed it inside and arranged the woman's arms across her ample chest as if she really were asleep. Both arms were quickly bloody. She felt a little sick. This was not her kind of work. She did not *do* this kind of work. She was a *hunter.* The only reason she was still alive was she'd had a clear view of the killer, while the killer had not had one of her. No one in her right mind depended on that kind of good fortune.

As she walked away, she opened the book bag. Inside were not only the air gun and ammo but a silenced 9mm Beretta, a backup weapon. Plus there was a phone book, which had given the bag the heft that had made it appear legitimate — an old tradecraft trick. The woman was a pro.

Elaine inhaled. Exhaled. Inhaled. Walked. And scrutinized the area. The killer had entered the park after her, so she was likely the tail Elaine had sensed. Still, there easily could be others, if only spotters.

At Fourteenth Street, red taillights and glowing headlights hurtled past, streams of garish light in the deepening dusk. Ahead her Jaguar was in sight now. She hurried toward it as she dialed Hannah. She wanted the janitor picked up as soon as possible. With luck, the woman could be identified.

But Hannah was not "available." She considered, then left a message. Hannah had said she would be at Whippet HQ, waiting for her. She looked around once more then climbed into the Jag.

Smoking his Cohiba cigar, Martin Ghranditti relaxed in the rear seat of his limousine as it cruised U Street. As he savored the smooth taste of the fine tobacco, he studied the jiggling laughing fast-talking half-clothed hordes, attracted by the city's nightlife, as mindless as moths to flames. He smoked and wondered what they wanted. In what did they believe? If they were any indication, the last standing superpower was well on its way to ruin. He nodded to himself, recognizing the destination and the path. And he would profit from it. Everyone had a talent; this was his.

The driver pulled to the curb, and a man in Bermuda shorts and a Hawaiian shirt, apparently drinking and partying, abruptly sobered and jumped in next to Ghranditti. The big limo immediately reentered traffic.

Without even the courtesy of a "good evening," the man demanded, "You have it?" He had a ferret's face and a restless, unpleasant gaze.

Ghranditti sighed and picked up a backpack from the floor. "Your fifty thousand dollars."

"You said a hundred thousand!" The man opened it and saw the bundles of bills. "Those sat phones are worth seven and a half million retail!"

Ghranditti smiled coldly. "You were planning to stand on the Mall to sell them?"

"Never again. This is it!" The man shoved his hand deep inside to make certain all were greenbacks.

"For you, there is always a next time," Ghranditti said knowingly. He tapped the glass that separated him from his driver, and the limo moved to the curb again. The man was a fool; he worked only for money.

"What does anyone want ten thousand cells for?" he complained. "I was almost caught when I set up —"

Ghranditti interrupted, "Being caught could be fatal. Get out."

The man stared, seeing something in Ghranditti that made him turn away quickly. Gripping his loot, he scrambled from the limo and slammed the door and ran.

Ghranditti grimaced then inhaled his cigar. As he contemplated the baseness of *Homo sapiens,* his cell phone rang. Fortunately, it was Jerry Angelides. Angelides had two qualities Ghranditti prized — a cheerful nature and consistency. Angelides failed so seldom that Ghranditti considered him a platinum-plated member of his permanent staff. Unlike the slob who had just taken fifty thousand for a hundred-thousand-dollar job, Angelides had honest pride in his work.

"Well, I have to hand it to you, Mr. Ghranditti," Angelides said. "You were right as usual. Good thing you told me to send somebody after that hunter, Elaine Cunningham. She almost got whacked by an operator from that organization you wanted me to keep tabs on."

Ghranditti swore loudly. "Tell me!"

"The shooter used one of those dart guns. The way I figure it, why bother unless the darts were loaded with poison? But Cunningham did good. She had a gun and a silencer. She whacked the shooter so quiet nobody noticed."

Enraged, Ghranditti sat up straight. He had been deceived. No one lied to Martin Ghranditti. His big shoulders squared. He did not hesitate. "This is what I want you to do. . . ."

11

As Washington's clogged traffic growled around her, Elaine drove the city's boulevards, angling quickly onto side streets, rounding Logan Circle six times, and cruising over the hopscotch bridge behind the Amtrak station and back again. Several times she managed sudden U-turns. As she dry-cleaned, she continued to try to reach Hannah, with no success.

When she was certain she had no tail, Elaine sped the car to the Dupont area and found a place to park. Troubled that Hannah had not called back, she hurried into the alley, stopped at Whippet's rear entrance, tapped in her code, and pressed her left thumb on the scanner. The door swung open, and she stepped inside, locked it, and listened. At last she ran lightly upstairs and through the broom closet.

She cracked open the door to the hall and listened again. The silence was profound, somehow even deeper than this morning. Something was wrong. She took out her Walther and pulled the door open wider. A thick draft rolled past, heavy with a raw, metallic stink. She recognized the primal odor immediately — fresh blood.

On high alert, she slipped soundlessly through the doorway and swallowed a gasp. Six men and a woman lay sprawled in the corridor a few feet away. Glazed eyes stared. Red flesh gaped. Blood shimmered in lakes on the floor. It dripped from the walls. The house emanated the hot stench of violent death.

Shocked, she tried to detect any sound, any motion, any sign of life. Were the killers still here? But after a full minute, the hush seemed only to grow heavier. She whipped out her cell and speed-dialed Langley's emergency number.

As soon as a voice answered, she said quietly, "This is Elaine Cunningham. I'm at one of our secret units. It's been attacked." She filled in details and described what she saw.

In cool, rote tones, the CIA officer asked: "Can you leave safely?"

"I believe so."

"Then get out of there. We'll have a team at the scene in under ten minutes."

"Make it faster."

She hit the OFF button and focused again on the carnage in the corridor. She took three quick steps and hunched beside the closest man and checked for a pulse. There was none. No surprise. He lay on his side, an exit wound in his chest. He had been shot from behind, probably while trying to escape. A bullet had shattered his temple, fired at close range — an execution after the first bullet knocked him down.

She knelt beside the next man, hoping for a pulse. Again, none. She recognized him from an assignment in Paris four years ago. His name was Harry Brillie, and he was regular DO then, or at least presented himself that way. His lean face held an expression of fury and surprise. Wounds bloodied his legs and throat. Blood splatters along the walls showed he had managed to stagger five feet before falling. Where the blood began was where his pistol lay.

Elaine lifted her head, analyzing the stillness. The house felt like a sarcophagus. Despite the orders to leave, she could not make herself. Someone might still have a thread of life, and she wanted to know who in hell had done this. She sped from one person to the next, checking, looking for Hannah's walnut-colored hair, for Mark's wire-rimmed glasses. Her fingers grew bloody searching for pulses. *Don't think,* she told herself. *Don't.*

Lungs tight, she ran down the hall to two crumpled men and a woman. Blood stained the wainscoting above them. She crouched. They had died where they had fallen. She backtracked and opened an office door. There were two bodies on the floor. They appeared to have been shot while rising from their chairs and turning toward the door. Both still had weapons in their hands.

She checked other offices. All were empty, except Mark Silliphant's. He was killed while sitting in his chair, a bullet neatly through the back of his skull. His head had crashed forward onto his keyboard. His glasses were crushed into his boyish face.

She returned to the corridor and ran again, still listening while opening more doors, finding more corpses. The attack had been intimate and savage and swift. So far, it was a slaughter.

At the other end of the hall was Hannah's office. The door was wide-open. Elaine rushed inside, but the room was empty. Hannah was not lying behind the desk. She turned to go, then noticed that the newspaper on the desktop was folded back to display the story and photos chronicling

Kristoph Maas's death. Hannah must have been too eager to wait; she had sent someone for the *Herald Tribune,* too, and she had settled on the same article that Elaine had as the one that would have interested Jay Tice.

Elaine hurried out and across the corridor. She opened the last door — and froze, stunned. Lying on the desk was the woman in the caftan from the park. The woman who had tried to scrub her.

Elaine sprinted, not believing. But there was no doubt — the same straight nose, same round cheeks and chin, same brown hair — and same bloody wound to the belly. What was the corpse doing here? She dropped to her heels before a clutter of items. Someone had swept everything off the desk to make room for the corpse. Her hand went instantly to a framed photo of a man and a girl. She recognized neither. Then to a photo of a woman with the same man and girl. This time she stared. And knew.

She jumped up and felt the corpse's hair, then ripped it off — a wig. The female janitor was the man in the photos. A Whippet operative. The realization that he was Whippet struck her like a body blow. She swallowed rage. Fought back terror. For some reason, Whippet had tried to wipe her. Now she remembered Hannah's supposedly innocent question: "Will you drive straight here from Andrews?" This had to be why she had been unable to reach Hannah. What the hell was going on!

And where was Hannah? She raced across the room and again into the hallway, moving swiftly but with an even more concentrated effort at silence. Suddenly, as if from a great distance, she heard the tiny clicks of the front door's closing, the same as when Hannah shut it after her arrival this morning.

Forcing herself to breathe, Elaine gripped her Walther in both hands and continued cautiously on. If someone had just arrived, they had two options — stay in the foyer or move into the house. She stared down the corridor, waiting for the person to appear. Beneath her, the old Victorian's floorboards creaked. She bit back a curse.

At the corner, she raised her Walther. She exhaled then peered around past the fake antiques, past the hidden security — to a body that lay sprawled just inside the front door. She had found Hannah Barculo at last.

And the answer to at least one question — whoever had closed the door had been leaving. Elaine padded to the Whippet chief, who lay on her back, mouth open in surprise, hand gripping her gun. The barrel was still warm. On the opposite wall was a bullet hole. There were three shots to her chest, the black fabric burned from close range. Hannah was dead, but she had fought back and not gone down easily.

Elaine inspected the door. There was no sign it was forced. She looked around quickly. Someone had sent a Whippet team to wipe her in the park. And now more Langley troops were headed here. Their orders could be to liquidate her, too. Sweat drenched her forehead. Her only choice was to get as far away as possible. She had to find out what in hell was going on.

The front door was her closest escape route. Pulse throbbing, she turned out the light and inched open the door. The outside carriage lamp was shattered, glass lying in a spray on the porch. She slid into the darkness, alert for any watchers, and closed her black jacket over her T-shirt, which suddenly seemed glaringly white. Night spread before her, dense and threatening, while traffic cruised the street as if nothing had happened. People strolled the sidewalk, past the lit houses.

She crossed the porch and descended,

studying pedestrians. Across the street a small family attracted her attention. Leading was a young couple, the man pushing a baby stroller. Forced by the narrowness of the sidewalk to follow was an older man, smiling fondly at them. An uncle? A grandfather? He wore a slouched cap and thick eyeglasses, and his expression was doting. Most people would never give him a second thought. But her gaze kept returning.

She dropped behind bushes, looking for surveillance. When she saw none, she joined the flow on the sidewalk on the Victorian's side of the street, paralleling the anomalous man. There was something about him — not the couple, but him — that held her notice. Then she knew. He was playing a role.

His hands curled at his sides, giving the impression of being relaxed, but the wrists were stationary. His eyes, which appeared kindly, periodically surveyed like a predatory hawk's. His gait was slow but far from elderly — he rolled off the pads of his feet like a professional runner. As he passed under a streetlamp, she saw clipped gray hair beneath his cap. Noted the furrows that curved down from his nose to his mouth. Stared at the cleft that marked the center of his chin.

168

Shock jolted her. She could have missed him easily. Should have missed him. He was that good. A grim smile spread across her face. She had found her target at last. The man was Jay Tice.

12

Georgetown

The ivory table linen shone, and the sterling gleamed. The drinks were generous, and the wine Longoria's finest. Embassy officials, politicians, and media stars surrounded the long dinner table at the home of a former Secretary of State. The party was one of those swank affairs Laurence Litchfield made a point to attend. As the Deputy Director of Operations, he did quiet public relations whenever possible, and the VIPs sitting in the candlelight were very important members of "the public."

Known for his incisive intellect, the French ambassador was an athletic man with a receding hairline. "Our Muslim population comes mostly from Morocco and Algeria," he explained. "A violent sect called Takfir wal-Hijra has been operating religious schools in both countries for years. They steep the kids in doctrine and call in hardened al-Qaeda veterans to train them to kill. This is brilliant planning, of course, because a lot of poor parents send their children to these schools just for the free meals. Then when the budding terrorists grow up, the Takfirs export them to my country."

"It's tragic," added the wife of the British ambassador. "If those young people ever knew what common human values are, they've forgotten. You can't reason with them. They spout memorized rhetoric. They don't want to talk to you anyway." One of four Muslims at the table, she was an economics professor at Georgetown and also owned a popular Middle Eastern restaurant. "Nowadays, jihad and immigration to the West go together. The thinking is that jihad can't be achieved without it."

For a moment, no one spoke. Immigration laws around the globe had long been used as a vehicle for invasion, but in today's circumstances it was chilling to remember that. The subject of terrorism had been holding the party in thrall, and Litchfield had listened quietly to the usual complaints that the CIA did little but bumble. He despaired that people were too often and too easily comforted by their shared, if uninformed, misery. In fact, before leaving

Langley tonight, he had gone down to the Global Response Center on the sixth floor. Another two hundred threats had arrived in the past twelve hours. Probably all would prove empty — but each would be checked in detail.

Now the topic changed again. "What the CIA does that nobody else does is talk their way into, or break into, or suborn an employee in some foreign office so they can steal secrets." Speaking was a young reporter with a photogenic face recently hired by a major network for nearly a million dollars annually. To this group, his pronouncement was hardly news, but he was too ignorant to know that. "Or in a president's office, if they're really good."

The hostess was kind; she played along. "Or eavesdrop on some diplomat's calls to find out whether he's lying to the White House. Isn't that right, Laurence?" Famed for her power salons, she was unrivaled at putting guests at ease, then teasing out revelations. Years ago Litchfield had decided she would have made a damn fine spy.

"All of it's useful." Litchfield gave a wry smile, glad for a lighter topic. "George Washington himself submitted a bill for nearly twenty thousand dollars to pay for his army's spies. Both Alexander the Great and Hannibal relied on espionage, too. The history of espionage is long, if not always illustrious. For instance, President Nixon took national security so seriously he even classified some White House menus."

As laughter rippled around the table, Litchfield felt his disposable cell phone vibrate. With relief, he excused himself and strode out of the elegant dining room. Once outdoors, he stuck his pipe between his teeth and moved lightly away from the house. In his mid-forties, he had a runner's wiry body. His tuxedo fit impeccably, but then he'd had it made for him on Savile Row. He stopped beside a box hedge and studied the garden. He had an aquiline nose, a square chin, and eyebrows that cut across his forehead in a black line. Satisfied no one was nearby, he listened to the message on his cell. His deep-set eyes clouded. It was from the DCI.

He dialed. "Bobbye? It sounds bad. What's happened?"

The DCI's usual honeyed tones rasped with outrage. "It's Whippet. Someone's taken them out."

"What! The whole unit? Are you certain?"

"Most of the ones here in D.C., yes. Four are still breathing, but only because they were out on assignment. One is Elaine Cunningham. She called in the report. Who in hell has the goddamned balls and is stupid enough to do such a thing?"

Litchfield froze, thinking. "Tice might've learned Whippet was assigned to find him." He swore loudly. "The unit's address is the same as when Tice headed ops. It was scheduled for a name and location change later this year."

Bobbye Johnson was not pleased. "Obviously it's time you shortened the resettlement schedules of our special units."

But Litchfield's mind was elsewhere, making plans. Edgy and field-smart, he had been the Associate Deputy Director under Tice — Tice's number two. When Tice was arrested, he was promoted to the throne of all clandestine activities. Following a legend like Tice, even a tainted legend, was hardly easy. Still, his tenure had been highly successful. Bobbye Johnson's had, too, but she got little credit for it. As DCI, she was a lightning rod for all that was wrong or perceived wrong with Langley. Washington thrived on gossip, and the latest was that she would be asked to resign. Litchfield was pleased that his name topped the rumor list of those likely to replace her, but this situation with Whippet and Tice could hurt him.

"Don't concern yourself, Bobbye." His

tone was properly supportive. "You've got more than enough responsibilities. I'll personally find Tice and whoever scrubbed our people — if it wasn't Tice."

"You have damn little time before we have to turn the hunt over to the FBI. As for Whippet, since you aren't here, I've been handling things personally." There was just enough admonition in her tone to remind him she was still very much in charge. "I've activated all protocols to protect the unit's identity. Our dead will be named under their cover identities. Whippet house will be cleaned out in less than an hour. I've talked to the police, and they'll cooperate. I've got Justice to agree to tell the media that the institute is a think tank populated by independent researchers flown in to analyze stateless violence."

"We need to send our own people to look for witnesses."

"I've made the assignment. Also, the house's security cameras should've recorded the attack. I've ordered video copies for your desk and mine. Shall I tell my assistant to alert your staff you're coming in?"

"I'm leaving now."

"Keep me posted," she ordered.

Litchfield severed the connection and clasped his hands behind his back. Much was at stake, and he must make the right decisions. The assault on Whippet showed not only daring but information and power — the defining elements of a Jay Tice operation. Worried, he stood motionless in the moonlight, inscrutable, an urbane statue in black and white.

Washington, D.C.

Jay Tice did not vary from his casual stroll as Elaine followed him around corners and down blocks. One of the notations in his file echoed in her mind: "He had a reputation for going after anyone who attacked him." Somehow the bastard had learned about Whippet and butchered them.

As she slowed, letting a trio of middle-aged men feed into the pedestrian traffic between Tice and her, she considered the phantom group that had tried to purge Tice and Palmer Westwood. Then that Whippet had tried to scrub her, and now Tice had decimated Whippet. Jay Tice was not only her target, he was central to everything that had happened.

Vehicle noises increased, and voices filled the air. They had arrived at Dupont Circle. It was a typical April night in an atypical area, even for D.C. Dupont was a crowded hotbed of not only urban culture but counterculture.

Tice wove among the crowds, and she elbowed and pushed after. Skin colors ranged from pale ivory to dark eggplant. Nose rings sparkled. Tattoos flashed. Naked arms gleamed. She was losing Tice.

She ducked and slid sideways and shoved through the moving talking laughing sweating masses, always keeping him in sight. The aromas of Starbucks coffee and Krispy Kreme doughnuts and beer mixed in the humid air. Tice strode past the wedge-shaped Washington Club and paused at the intersection. She hurried to catch up. For cover, she fell into step with two young men.

"Well, hi," said the one closest to her.

"Hi back." She shot him a smile and peeled away.

Tice crossed the street and headed toward Jurys Washington Hotel — a good place to meet someone. She loped after, joining some tourists, and followed Tice's slouched cap and catlike walk into the spacious stone-framed lobby and through the milling crowd and along a hall, where he slipped in among a cluster of guests. He vanished around the corner with some of them.

She raced to catch up, rounded the corner, too, and stopped. A row of elevators, and a dead end. A half-dozen people were piling into the only open elevator. She sprinted and peered inside. They frowned and stared back. He was not with them.

As her heart palpitated, the door closed, and she spun around, checking the other elevators. All were on higher floors, coming down. How could she have missed him? She dashed back into the corridor, but Tice was nowhere in sight. She rushed into the lobby and dodged through the bar, with its slurred talk and clinking glasses. No Tice. She hurried into the lobby again and through all of the halls and the restaurant and the café, searching everywhere.

Puzzled, furious with herself, she paused, recalling advice from one of his speeches: "Always have a good backup strategy and an even better way out." If he had purposefully led her to this hotel, he must have spotted her.

She swore a long stream of silent oaths and returned to the elevators. A different one opened, and a couple strolled out. The man was not Tice. She paced, studying the walls. Moldings and panels decorated them. There were no hinges, no doorknobs. Then she saw it — so much a part of the overall design that it was almost invisible — a small molding-framed rectangle. She pressed it.

There was a creak, and a low door swung back. The fusty odor of a basement flowed up, accompanied by the whine of elevator gears and pulleys.

Disgusted that she had allowed herself to be fooled, she bent and stepped onto a webbed steel landing. Closing the door, she trotted down a long flight of steps to the hotel's engineering room, a large echoing space with a concrete floor and boxy metal housings for utilities. Pipes and cables formed a gaudy overhead net. Fluorescent lights glared. She looked behind every housing, every post, listening so hard her ears ached. Seldom did she lose anyone, but tonight of all nights she had lost this very crucial target.

Fuming, Elaine headed back across the room to a driveway that rose to the street. As the sounds of traffic floated down, she took out her Langley cell phone and dialed the number Laurence Litchfield had given her. It was busy.

She left a message: "I found and lost Tice. Whippet tried to scrub me. Call!"

She climbed the drive. Hotel employees stood on the sidewalk, smoking and talking. Watching for Tice, watching for a tail, haunted that Whippet and perhaps others wanted her terminated, she wound through

179

Dupont's colorful nightlife. The doors to bars swung open, sending bursts of raucous laughter into the night.

She tried Litchfield again, but there was still no answer. God knew where he was or what he was doing, but eventually he would receive her message. She considered what to do until then.

She had to assume the Whippet killers did not want Langley to find out about the wet job on her. At the same time, someone at Langley might have been conspiring with them. Her town house was a defensible space, a place she knew better than any attacker could, and it was fully protected by a security system. Plus she had more weapons there. She might as well go home.

When she reached her Jag, a parking ticket waited on her windshield. She ripped it out from under the wiper and inspected the car carefully for booby traps and explosive devices. Satisfied, she slammed inside, dropped her cell phone onto the passenger seat so she could answer it immediately, and threw her shoulder bag onto the floor. She ignited the engine and hit her CD player, tuning it to the pounding beat of Soundgarden's "Let Me Drown." As the music shook the air, she tore out of the parking space.

She lived in Silver Spring. As she sped the

Jag toward Maryland, she watched alertly for tails. Maybe there was a solid clue to Tice's whereabouts in the data Mark Silliphant had compiled for her, and Whippet's need for her was over. But that was still no reason to eliminate her.

She slammed her fist against the steering wheel. She had forgotten to look for Mark's CD! In her mind, she reconstructed his office, the sad sight of him collapsed dead at his desk. The poor bastard. There had been no CD on his desk, much less one with Jay Tice's or her name on it.

When she arrived at her neighborhood, she drove around the block three times, then pulled into a parking space. She dropped her cell into her bag, grabbed her Walther, and crawled out. Crouching beside the Jag, she scrutinized the street. Two-story town houses lined it. Children's toys lay scattered on small front yards, waiting for the next day of play. Somewhere a dog barked playfully.

At last she walked home, turning everything over in her mind. Why would Tice have stayed in the house after the others on his team left? Maybe he was looking for something. But what? On the other hand, by leading her to Jurys, where he could lose her, he had treated her as if she were a simple tail. Maybe he had made her somewhere on the street without connecting her to Whippet. Still, he would perceive any surveillance to be a dangerous loose end at best. So why had he not tried to scrub her?

She turned up her sidewalk. Studying the shadows, she headed into the side yard. All of her windows were dark, as they should be. None showed any sign of being broken into. Neither did the rear of the town house.

She returned to her front step, unlocked the door, and opened it. Instantly she was struck by the musky aroma of a burning cigar. Adrenaline shot to her brain. She slid low into the dark, silently pulling the door closed. The cigar's orange coal glowed from across her living room, from an ashtray beside her armchair. A silhouette sat in deep shadow in the chair, a pistol pointed at her.

"Don't turn on the light." It was a man's voice, from the chair.

Making no sound, she laid her purse on the carpet. Walther in hand, she crept swiftly behind her sofa and along the wall. Her chest taut with tension, she rose up behind her love seat and leveled her gun. The silhouette's pistol was still aimed at the small entryway. He had not guessed.

As the smoke of the cigar spiraled, she ordered grimly, "Lay your weapon on the table. If you don't, I'll shoot — and at this short distance, I won't miss."

Behind her, she heard the faint sound of a pistol being cocked. But before she could move, the same man's voice said, "I thought you might be suspicious."

Her throat went dry. She whirled on her heels.

He cracked open two slats of the venetian blinds. Moonlight slanted through, glinting off another pistol trained on her. Hers still pointed uselessly at the figure in the chair.

Her heart seemed to stop. She could see his face.

"Hello, Elaine," he told her, his voice warm. "My friends call me Jay."

■ ■ ■ ■

PART TWO

■ ■ ■ ■

When an intelligence officer smells flowers, he looks around for a coffin.
— Robert Gates
former director of the CIA

13

Geneva, Switzerland

In an old apartment building off rue Madeleine, Raina Manhardt stopped at the window of her son's dark flat and pushed back the curtain as bolts of silver lightning speared the distant Alps. Thunderheads billowed across the black night sky. The scent of ozone was oppressive.

Kristoph's room was on the fourth floor, overlooking the labyrinth of winding streets and steepled rooftops of Geneva's Old Town, the Vieille Ville, but Raina focused on the sleeping street below. Someone was staked out in the recessed doorway of the *fromage* shop. When he stepped forward to shift his position, she could see the toes of his shoes in the lamplight.

She checked her watch. Nearly three A.M. She had little time left. Perhaps by now he had given up. But when a rolling burst of thunder followed the lightning, shaking the night, a hand slid out, palm up, checking for rain. She breathed shallowly, watching. A head followed, and the man glanced up at the roiling heavens. But he was too far away and the light was too poor for her to see his features.

Frowning, she pulled on her red plaid overshirt and caught sight of herself in the window glass. Her gaze went hollow, unfocused, a woman lost. For years she had not known how or where to find herself, and as long as there was Kristoph to protect, she had not looked. Now she must. In the dark glass, wearing her battered jeans, brown wool sweater, and plaid overshirt, she appeared to be a woman of action, physical, certainly not introspective. She had cultivated that affect, an image that had grown into uncomfortable reality. Her blue eyes were vaguely familiar, as was the jet-black hair, but the features were too young, too smooth, a product of lotions and superficiality. Not only did she no longer know herself, she did not recognize herself.

She resumed pacing the dark room. She must leave, she told herself. But her steps slowed. For a moment, it seemed she heard Kristoph's voice in the silence, lively and flecked with laughter. She imagined his stepping from the shadows, grinning, his thick hair tousled. She could almost feel his arms around her, welcoming her.

Yesterday she had packed his things, pausing to hold, to feel, to recall. Everything had reminded her of him — of sun and adventure and excited youth. And now he was gone. He would never age and discover himself. He would never be whoever he was intended to be. His death was worse than a missing limb. It was as if her heart had been torn out.

With an angry swing of her shoulders, she scooped up her valise and headed for the door. Gripping the knob, she looked back one last time, stared into the gloom, as if in it she could find a different past. But there were only corners without form, the curtained window, a ringing emptiness. She inhaled sharply and closed the door and locked the flat for the last time. She had work to do, the most vital of her life — for Kristoph.

She hurried down the three flights of stairs, staying close to the wall, where the old wood steps were stabilized and did not creak. When she reached the lobby, she discovered the overhead light was still on. To turn it off would alert the surveillant. She crouched behind a side table and peered through the vertical pane of glass beside the front door, studying the cheese shop's entry, much closer now, only some thirty feet away. The shoes showed clearly; shadows cloaked the rest of the man. She set down her valise and took out her Walther. By feel, she checked the magazine.

She resumed her watch just as a ghostly mongrel dog appeared, trotting along the cobblestones. Lightning detonated directly overhead, followed immediately by an ear-piercing blast of thunder. The dog yelped and streaked off, tail between his legs. Peals of more thunder reverberated. She waited, hoping. Luck was with her: A hand extended again, palm up. The man's face appeared.

Fury shot through her, and her lips peeled back. She knew him. She jammed the pistol into her waistband, jerked open the door, and stalked across the street, her plaid over-shirt flapping. Chilly raindrops pelted her face.

"Was ist denn in dich gefahren, Volker?" Seething with outrage, she whispered angrily in German, "How dare you follow me!"

"Hallo, Raina." With a guilty shrug, Volker Rehwaldt straightened and walked down the shop's stone steps, making no effort to explain or apologize. He was her height, five-foot-eight, with a rough face and pocked skin. He was dressed in a tweed

jacket and slacks and carried an umbrella. Slender but tough-looking, he seemed more urban wolf than spy.

"Did Erich send you," she demanded, "or did you come on your own?"

She and Erich Eisner, the BND's powerful president, had a long history. During the Cold War, he had been her handler for the BND, protecting her, asking for intel, and picking up the secret rolls of microfilm she hid behind panels in the interzonal trains that ran between East and West.

"Erich and I talked," Volker admitted. "We were worried. We know how important Kristoph was to you."

She paused, controlling her anger. "I appreciate that. Really, I do." Volker must follow her no farther. "Tell Erich I'm fine, considering everything. Tell him I've just been wandering back through Kristoph's life, visiting his friends and favorite places. I'll be in touch when I'm ready to go back to work."

He raised his gaze. She saw the sharpness of his appraisal.

It made her uneasy. She said earnestly, "If you were me, you'd want to grieve privately and in your own way, too. Please go, Volker. Frankly, I need to be alone."

His hard expression collapsed. He grabbed

her and pulled her close and patted her back. "I'm very sorry about Kristoph, Raina." His voice was muffled with sorrow.

Abruptly, he released her and stalked away through the lamplit mist, in and out of the shadows, his shoulders rounded forward as if studying the cobblestones. She had never seen him display such emotion. For an instant, she was tempted to invite him back, reveal her suspicions, and ask his help. Old longings for companionship filled her.

But logic prevailed: She did not know enough yet. It appeared to her the company that had hired Kristoph — Milieu Software Technology — was a sham, and someone there had ordered his death. Kristoph had thought he was working for Germany's Ministry of Justice on an ultrasecret software project. Through discreet inquiries, she had learned the ministry was not involved. Still, another government arm might be. And if she were right that Kristoph had been liquidated, she could be as expendable as he. Her life was unimportant — but the truth of his was everything.

More thunder exploded. As she ran back and ducked under the apartment building's awning, the heavens bled cold gray rain. She looked for Volker. He had stopped on the sidewalk and turned, holding his umbrella open over him. Rainwater poured off it. A thick torrent rushed along the street, rising toward his sensible shoes. He looked brave and German, standing vigil there in defiance of common sense and the gods of nature just to ensure she arrived home safely.

Still, she scowled. He shrugged and pushed off, raising a cell to his ear.

She called, "Tell Erich you're on your way home."

"*Ja.* I am. *Gute Nacht.*" The rain-blackened buildings seemed to absorb his words and reflect back loneliness. But then he was a spy, and that was the nature of the work.

She stepped indoors and checked her watch. Urgency swept through her. She snapped open the metal jaws of her valise and quickly removed two identical boxes of Swiss chocolates — Avelines *assortis,* popular among locals and tourists. She chose the correct one by feel — a tiny puncture in the clear plastic wrapping on the end — and returned the other to the valise. Gripping the valise's handles and her umbrella, the candy box under her arm where it could be sighted easily, she hurried outside.

Volker was gone, and the cloudburst was easing. She buttoned her overshirt to her throat and opened her umbrella. Pulse pounding, she took off uphill, jumping puddles. She crisscrossed through the maze of streets, dove into alleys, and exited. As the dark night deepened toward dawn, the rain and thunder stopped.

When she finally arrived at the stately Cathédrale Saint-Pierre, she strolled casually along rue Saint-Léger and down the terrace to the place du Bourg-de-Four, where centuries-old buildings stood fang to jowl, looming around the medieval plaza. A cold mist clung to them.

Warmed by drink, ruddy-faced tourists and locals ambled past the fountain and green park benches and leafless trees. From the network of old side avenues sounded a weary American blues tune. A few pricey nightclubs were still open, but at this hour, most businesses were closed.

Ahead, a woolen cap rose from a sunken entry to a dark art gallery. It was Raoul Harmont. His eyes were large and nervous as he peered around then saw her. His gaze locked on the box of chocolates. With a flip of his wrist, he took off the cap and unsnapped the ear protectors then tugged the cap back onto his head, signaling he had the surveillance videos she wanted. He sank from sight. He was behaving exactly as planned. Still, he was an amateur. The most dangerous part of an operation was when information was exchanged, which was why dead drops were vital. Harmont had refused. He would not release the tapes until he had her one thousand Swiss francs.

Displaying no concern, she surveyed the plaza, looking for anyone who showed a hint of interest in her. When she was abreast of Harmont's hiding place, she trotted down the steps.

Harmont's eyes gleamed out of the dusky shadows. He took the box and ripped off the clear plastic and stared at the cash. *"Bon!"*

"Hurry!" she said.

He handed her an identical box. She hefted it once, feeling the weight of the tapes and the shift as they bumped the sides. She dropped it into her valise and took out the other Avelines box and tucked it under her arm. "Wait twenty minutes before you leave." She glanced at him sharply. "Be sure no one finds out about this."

He nodded. "I could lose my job." But his tone was cavalier.

"Or your life," she warned. "Milieu's owners could be drug runners, the Mafia, international criminals, terrorists. If they find out what you've done . . ."

His eyes widened, and his mouth fell open.

Five quick steps, and she was back up on the sidewalk. The plaza was emptying. Her next stop was her car. She turned up rue Etienne-Dumont, hurrying past Soda's hip downstairs bar and the Demi-Lune Café, both closed. The rue was lined by five- and six-story buildings whose walls rose so smoothly they seemed to lean across the narrow passageway toward one another. She was just beginning to feel safe when she rounded a bend and heard an odd tapping noise closing in from behind.

She pulled her Walther from her waistband and darted up steps into a doorway and peered back. The mist had turned into ground fog. Creeping across it was the black silhouette of a man wearing a long coat. The tapping came from his thick cane, which shot forward then struck the cobblestones, stabbed forward then hit the stones again to the beat of his climbing steps. She replayed her journey from Kristoph's flat, recalling the men she had observed. Most had worn raincoats. Some had carried closed umbrellas. Warily she studied the advancing silhouette.

He walked out through the fog as if he owned it. She fell back out of sight, his image in her mind. He was about her age, forty-four, very tall and broad. His face was square, his features bulky, his thin hair parted and combed smoothly. Besides a khaki raincoat, he wore dark flannel trousers and a turtleneck and leather walking shoes. He appeared to be the epitome of the New European, with the relaxed savoir faire that announced he was accustomed to elite boardrooms and private clubs and weekends of sweaty sport.

Silently she slid the chocolates inside her valise and set the valise at her feet. Her pistol ready, she listened, gauging his progress. Suddenly the tapping stopped. The lane seemed to shudder with emptiness. She frowned. Then recognized the old tradecraft ruse: He had accustomed her to his noise, expecting her to focus on the lack of it — not on his footsteps, which were continuing softly. His umbrella or cane could be a weapon — during the Cold War, the KGB and Bulgarian intelligence and other East Bloc agencies were known for using "umbrella guns" loaded with poisons like ricin.

She leveled her Walther just as he stopped directly across from her, still facing ahead. She studied his profile as he pulled a lighter and a long brown cigarette from his pocket. The flame snapped alive, and he cupped his hand around it, inhaling the cigarette into life. He was at least six-foot-five, broad and thick, an ox of a man. With three fingers, he slid the lighter back into his pocket.

"Ah, here you are." He spoke in German, still not looking at her. His voice was a cultured basso. "You've led me a pretty chase."

"What do you want?" A trickle of sweat slid down her spine. She had told no one where she was going. She was certain she had not been followed.

"The question is, what do *you* want? Your son's had an unfortunate accident and died. We extend our sympathies. You've sent his body and things home, yet you linger here in Geneva. And now you're out until almost dawn. It makes one wonder."

"I wonder about you. Who are you? I repeat, what do you *want?*"

He glanced around. When he saw her Walther, he seemed surprised. He focused up the street once more and continued in American-accented English, "Well, then, I suppose there's no avoiding it. My identification code is, 'It never rains inside a glass bubble.' You may call me Alec. You're officially reactivated, Glinda. After all this time, I'm sure you're delighted to hear again from our old Company."

14

Gravelly Point, Virginia

It was 9:14 P.M. when Martin Ghranditti arrived in his limousine for a *treff* — a covert meeting — at Gravelly Point, a spit of dark lawn and wetlands along the Potomac River. He lowered his window, and the scent of freshly cut grass wafted in. As expected at this late hour in midweek April, the tree-dotted park was empty. He climbed out, buttoned his suit jacket over his barrel chest, and checked the parking lot. There was only one other car — Laurence Litchfield's. Good. He had kept the bastard waiting.

He marched off, enjoying the notion he could keep governments, private buyers, and spy agencies — especially spy agencies — waiting. It was a small thing but pleasurable, and due to a simple fact: Like people, nations were stupid. During the Cold War he had made a fortune because ordinary

Americans and Soviets had been so worried about nuclear holocaust they had paid little attention to the regional wars through which the two superpowers were fighting for political supremacy. Nicaragua. Angola. Afghanistan. Others. To avoid stirring up the public, America had secretly paid a few top weapons merchants like himself to supply the guns and bullets. He chuckled. What a great year 1984 had been. Forty wars raged. America armed 130 of the world's 160 countries directly or indirectly. His profits were astronomical. But then, he delivered. That was why spy agencies had waited. And now the CIA waited again.

He found Litchfield standing on the grassy bank above the Potomac, hands clasped behind, backlit by the shimmering white monuments and buildings of Washington on the other shore. As Ghranditti joined him, a passenger jet hurtled through the air toward them, engines howling, hot wind baking their faces. There was no way they could talk, so they watched it pass overhead a bare hundred feet, so fast the Doppler effect made an audible *bang.* Percussive crackling trailed the jet across the river's black surface.

As it touched down and taxied south toward the Reagan National terminal,

Ghranditti said, "Dramatic, isn't it? Let's walk."

They advanced west along the inlet. Murky water slapped the marshy beach.

Litchfield spoke curtly around his pipe: "You're late. I need to get into Langley. What's this all about?" Dressed in a tuxedo, his wiry frame was a black needle in the night.

Ghranditti did not answer. Instead, he gestured above, where more jets circled, tiny lights winking. "They're landing every eight to ten minutes now. During peak times, it's every two or three minutes. I think you'd agree we Americans do this sort of thing well. Precision timing. Brute force. The spectacle of it energizes us." His words took on a warning tone: "And the alternative is far less attractive — violent death."

Litchfield had been checking his watch. He looked at Ghranditti. "You have a point?"

Rage churned up into Ghranditti's throat. Still, he controlled himself. "Hannah Barculo's people haven't caught Jay Tice yet, and she hasn't kept me informed. Now I know why. You've ordered her to tell me whatever she has to, to keep me quiet, because you want him wiped. I suspect you thought she could do it fast and make it look like he was resisting arrest. Something no one — including me — would question."

Litchfield pulled his pipe from his lips. "You don't know what you're saying."

"Like hell I don't! I had my people follow Elaine Cunningham. One of the men had binoculars on her when a Whippet operative tried to liquidate her. That's when I knew. No one kills a hunter when they want the hunt to succeed and the quarry alive." He detected a whiff of respect despite Litchfield's inscrutable expression. "What were you planning to do — pin the wet job on Tice? Hammer one more nail into his coffin?"

The CIA man stared at Ghranditti. Then he bristled. "Yes, dammit! I helped you by turning Theosopholis into our snitch, and now the poor bastard's dead because Tice scrubbed him. Tice must be terminated!" He locked his hands behind his back and accelerated, pulling out ahead.

At the same time, Ghranditti slowed. *"No. Jay Tice must be taken alive!"*

Litchfield turned, frowning, eyes narrowed beneath the black slash of his brows.

"You thought I wasn't serious?" Ghranditti stopped and planted his feet. "I want Tice back in prison! Every waking instant he's there he knows he's not only lost everything, he can't rebuild. His honors and medals are dust! His old friends are dead to him! Do you have any idea what that's like for a man like Tice? It's been destroying him. Eating him up!" A flush heated his face. "Kill him? *No!* That'd put him out of his misery. I want him to have a *very* long life — in prison!"

"Tice is a traitor, Ghranditti. Even you should be able to figure out he's worth less than a skin rash. Alive, he's a threat. His escape proves it."

"He's no threat to me!"

"Wrong." Litchfield strode off again.

Ghranditti stared a few seconds then hurried to catch up. As he matched Litchfield's stride, he demanded, "What haven't you told me?"

"Do you still want the software?" Litchfield countered, glancing at him.

"Of course. Only a lunatic would turn down three million dollars." He had found money was the key to Litchfield; governments were foolish to pay their best people so little.

Litchfield puffed worriedly on his pipe. "I told you the program required some work. That's finished. But to do it, we needed someone with expertise but not enough experience to understand the implications.

We found a young German whiz known in computer circles there. He was an orphan, according to his university records. We liked that. If anything went wrong and he had an 'accident,' there was no family to get upset and dig around. So we hired him and isolated him in Geneva."

"And?"

"He began to get suspicious. It turns out he wasn't an orphan, and his last name was changed. Originally, he was Kristoph Manhardt."

Ghranditti's fleshy lips parted. "Manhardt? Raina Manhardt's son?" Pain pulsed behind his eyes.

Now he understood Tice's breakout. Tice and Raina had had a fiery but covert Cold War affair. That was the way people lived then. When sex, lust, love erupted between East and West, it was always forbidden and usually volcanic and, for safety, very clandestine. Theirs had been so well hidden that he had not learned about it until much later.

To protect himself, he lied: "Raina Manhardt was formidable in her day. But I don't see how that impacts Tice."

"Raina and Jay shared a bed during the Cold War. Kristoph was the right age to be his son. Plus Cunningham discovered a section of Jay's *Herald Tribune* was missing — a section that had an article about the kid's death. You put it together. Cunningham was sure to make the connection between Raina and Jay."

Ghranditti massaged his temples, fighting a headache. "Tell me the rest."

"We didn't know who the kid was until the story ran, and by then we'd left Geneva. When we checked the records of his cell phone, we found out he called Raina that morning. My people are back in Geneva, but she's been there since he died — two days — probably sniffing around the whole time. We don't know what the kid told her, or what she's learned. If she or Tice finds out about the software, it could lead to me — then to you. And if they do it fast, they could send the shipment into the toilet."

Ghranditti looked off across the park, but what he saw was in his mind — the Jay Tice of twenty years ago, the remorseless drive, the chameleon personality. His gut clenched. At the least, Tice deserved to be hurled into boiling oil or whipped to bloody death. He glanced at Litchfield, a pragmatic man who merely wanted money. The world must seem simple to him and most of humanity; they dreamed of so little.

But now Litchfield had changed the game. As much as it galled Ghranditti to abandon

Tice's just punishment, the truth was that the future of his wife and family was far more important.

He heaved a sigh. "Very well. But Hannah's fumbled enough. My men will find and wipe Tice. It's just as well for you, too. You and Whippet will stay clean."

"It's too late for that. Most of Whippet's been purged. Worse, in their own house. The only ones who survived were out on assignment here or overseas."

"Hannah, too?" He gave no indication he already knew the answer.

Litchfield gave a mute nod.

Ghranditti let out a long stream of air and asked casually, "Who did it?"

"If Tice realized Whippet was after him, my bet is on him. His connections used to be deep, and he's probably got more than enough money stashed to pay for it." He slowed, his analytical gaze considering Ghranditti. "Can you guarantee your people are strong enough to terminate him?"

"Without question." Inwardly, Ghranditti smiled. "What about your hunter? Did Tice scrub her, too?"

"No, she arrived at the house afterward. In fact, she's the one who reported the massacre."

"I don't want her killed. She could lead

us to Tice."

"For the moment, I agree. I'll have Whippet's computers and files searched, and I'll find out what Cunningham's learned."

"I want her basic information now." Ghranditti already had it, but again Litchfield did not need to know that.

As traffic on the George Washington Parkway rumbled in the distance, the two men stopped, and Litchfield pulled out his cell phone and a fountain pen and a small pad. He turned away and spoke quietly. When he hung up, he tore off a sheet and gave it to Ghranditti. They walked off toward the parking lot.

Ghranditti mulled. "You said the software's finished. Do you have it?"

"It's on its way to me."

"I hope the route's fully secured."

The corners of Litchfield's mouth rose in a small smile. "Forget it, Ghranditti. You know I'm not going to give you details."

Another jet blasted toward them, booming, seeming to hang suspended in the air. Then it swooped past overhead, whining like a demon. At the parking lot, the men exchanged brisk nods and separated. Ghranditti's chauffeur was already opening the limo's rear door.

Ghranditti settled into the leather. As the

door closed, he weighed his meeting with Litchfield: He had lost, and he had won. But overall, he decided, he had won, because Litchfield was still ignorant about the extent of his knowledge. He needed Litchfield — his software was critical to the deal. At the same time, Litchfield needed him — as the broker, he had sole initial contact with the buyer. The only potential problems were Jay Tice and Raina Manhardt. But if Litchfield's people handled Manhardt in Geneva, and Jerry Angelides handled Tice here, all would be well.

As the limo glided off toward the parkway's northbound lanes, he dialed Jerry Angelides and announced, "I have a change of orders for you." He described the new development with Jay Tice, Raina Manhardt, and Kristoph Maas. "As you can see, Tice is suddenly a far larger danger than we realized. Therefore, your capture is canceled. Tice must be erased. Make sure he knows he's going to die. I want him to *know!*"

Langley, Virginia

The lights of CIA headquarters were ablaze in the dark Virginia night. Still in his tuxedo, DDO Laurence Litchfield strode along the seventh floor, hands clasped behind his back. Voices occasionally sounded from

208

behind closed doors. This floor contained the offices of the director, the executive director, the top three deputy directors, including him, and various other officials and support staff.

This was the soul of U.S. intelligence, where security was as integral as arteries. Seldom could anyone — even he — find fault. Windows were configured with state-of-the-art devices to prevent eavesdropping with laser beams. Special cipher locks sealed offices, recording each person who entered. If someone unauthorized managed to get in, heat sensors and motion detectors would trigger alarms that brought security running, weapons ready.

As he passed the closed doors and absorbed the atmosphere, he remembered the giants who had walked this storied floor — statesmen, presidents, kings, and of course the great Allen Dulles, although only after retirement. It made him feel taller, as if he were worthy of the long line of Litchfields who had led Massachusetts from wilderness to revolution. Espionage, too, was a profession for titans, or at least it once was.

But now the CIA was in trouble, ravaged on all sides — Congress, the president, the public. After the Cold War, the budget was slashed, and several DCIs fell in love with the Pentagon, ceding operations and budget and technical innovations like the great Predator drone to it. In that postwar atmosphere, human intelligence — HUMINT — was considered superfluous and unreliable, and the espionage community was ordered to put its money and resources into flyovers, satellites, and glitzy gizmos used in "technical" spying. It was a mistake both shocking and dangerous.

The daring and initiative that had been the CIA's hallmark grew rare, leading to even more risk aversion in a profession that required risk. In the past year he had almost quit because it had become apparent the White House wanted a more compliant CIA, one whose clandestine service was controlled by the Pentagon. If that happened, it would be the death of the sort of independent thinking and information gathering and clean analysis that was most useful to any nation, where ideas and facts were more important than rank. That was when he knew there was only one answer — he must strike out on his own. It was not enough to be right. Sometimes, if only to test one's will, one must prove one could still win.

As Litchfield tapped in his door code, Bobbye Johnson, the DCI, appeared in the corridor, walking toward him, a worried expression on her face. She was in her shirtsleeves and dark gray suit pants, her auburn mane of hair rumpled. The hollows on her broad face were deep, showing weariness.

He assumed a pleasant smile. "Hello, Bobbye. I thought you would've gone home by now."

"Too much going on. You just get in?" Her voice had the moderate tones of the well-bred, well-educated Midwesterner. Her father had been Robert ("Red") Sunday, a tough OSS operative who had served in the Burma theater during World War II. She had inherited his brains and courage but not his good luck. The political situation was stacked against her. She had a gift for ignoring it.

"Traffic was bumper-to-bumper," he told her. "You know how it is. Want to come in?" He opened his office door and turned on the light.

"Not tonight. I'm going to fill you in and leave." Still, she glanced inside. "Whenever I see it, I have to remind myself it's your office now — not Jay's."

He leaned against the doorframe, hiding his annoyance that he had to waste time with her. "If things ever slow down, I'll make some radical changes. You'll see." He surveyed the desk, once Tice's, and the tall-backed chair, also once Tice's. All of the furniture had been Tice's — side chairs, tables, lamps, credenza, and the easy chairs grouped around the coffee table near the windows. Tice had put his books into storage, but the massive shelves remained. Litchfield had remembered the titles and replaced those he wanted while adding others more to his taste. He enjoyed working in Tice's sandbox, coloring it with his scent. He would never change anything more.

Johnson was looking at him. "All of Whippet's files, secure computers, and papers are in-house now. I've ordered a search for anything that would hint at who hit Whippet and why. Did Hannah ever mention she was concerned that one of their operations had generated particularly bad heat?" She offered no apology for stepping onto his management turf. She did this sometimes, shifting gears to when she had been an operative and hands-on spymaster herself.

"Not a word. Have you discounted my theory that Tice did it?"

"I'm interested in the truth, whatever it is."

"Of course." He was unworried the probe would reveal Hannah's attempts to eliminate Tice — she would never have committed that to paper or e-mail.

"We took over forensics inside Whippet house," Bobbye continued. "The police are working the exterior and grounds. We found no unknown fingerprints. No hair, no bill-folds, no matchbooks conveniently publicizing some bar or motel. Too bad real life isn't a TV show where the perfect clue is left behind. We have hundreds of samples from the bloodbath. Everything's being checked. I've sent our bodies out to canvass the neighborhood for witnesses. So far all they've got is that one shot was heard. People thought the noise was a car backfiring. A grandma in her sixties was visiting down the block, and she saw a man leave — older, wearing a cap. He was fast. According to the timing, he must've exited after the massacre."

"Older? He was fast? That's it?"

"She said it was too dark to see more. What caught her attention was that he looked as if he were her age, but he moved as if he were considerably younger."

"Tice! He might've gone back for a final check. He wouldn't worry about any corpses calling the police on him."

She nodded. "If Cunningham hadn't reported the attack, we might not have known about it for hours. Okay, I've got to get back to work. I've had three calls from the Oval Office just since nine o'clock. We'll be answering a lot of questions in the morning. The joint intelligence committee will have the knives out for us."

Litchfield noted the "us." "We'll get it under control, Bobbye."

She started to leave, arms crossed, head bent in thought. She turned. "Have you heard anything at all about Moses, whether he's working again?"

"Not since you asked the last time — six months ago now?" When she shrugged, he continued. "The way I see it, his heyday's long over. He's retired or dead. Most of the new people don't even seem to know he existed. Why?"

"This nasty business with Jay Tice reminds me of him. I don't like it when major figures from our world disappear without even a rumor about what's happened to them or where they are. Jay's case is similar, except he's reappeared — and we don't know for sure how or why." Shaking her head worriedly, she marched back toward her office.

15

Silver Spring, Maryland

Amid the dense shadows of her living room, surrounded by the pungent odor of the burning cigar, Elaine stared at Jay Tice in the moonlight. His dowdy cap was gone, and so was his old-man's slouch. He stood apparently relaxed, but his knees were flexed and his feet were at shoulder width for maximum balance, ready to sprint or attack. As he let the slats of the blinds close, his words hammered her brain: *My friends call me Jay.* His warmth and charm were poisoned honey. He was already trying to manipulate her, while his gun never wavered from its aim at her heart.

"Hello, Jay." She stood up slowly, planning her words, keeping herself calm. He was a dozen feet away. "I'm glad to meet you at last. What can I say to convince you to return to Allenwood?" She glanced down at her gun, still pointed back at the chair.

The angle to swing it toward him was wide, at least ninety degrees —

There was a swift movement of air, and her Walther disappeared, leaving her fingers stinging. Her heart hammered as the muzzle of his Browning cut into her belly and he towered in front of her so close she could smell the scent of old blood on him. Her own gun dangled from his other hand. His entire body radiated danger. She was looking up at the real Jay Tice, a full head taller than she. At his strong features and lined face and piercing eyes. The impact was of power and some deep percolating rage that was capable of crushing anyone or anything in his path.

Then the threat evaporated in a smile. "My returning to Allenwood isn't going to happen. At least not yet." His tone was inviting, collegial, giving the sense of someone who appreciated the other's presence. The way he inclined his large head and looked at her had an aura of Continental, cuff-linked suavity, while his disarming frankness painted him as utterly honest. He was a chameleon.

And he was gone — across the room, silent and swift, this time to the front window, where he kept glancing at the street through the blind while keeping the Browning trained on her.

Act relaxed. Don't fuel his sense of control.
"Not yet?" she said. "That gives me hope. Glad you made yourself a drink. I could use one myself." *Keep talking. Keep him talking.* "What's on your mind?" She went to her liquor cabinet. The aim of his pistol followed smoothly.

As she opened the cabinet, a small interior light shone, illuminating glasses and bottles and flowing out in a dusky arc that showed the figure in the armchair was a dummy like the one in Tice's prison cell. Wearing her jeans and shirt, it was stuffed with crushed newspapers, too, the edges showing from the sleeves. On top was her bulbous glass vase, the size of an adult's head, turned upside down. Black electrician's tape held a SIG Sauer to the chair's arm, aimed at the door. On the table beside the smoldering cigar lay a miniature recorder-player. That explained the voice when she came in the door. He must have prerecorded "Don't turn on the light" and used a remote to activate the order. But what showed the supremacy of his tradecraft was the cigar. Its glowing orange coal drew the eye and subtly guaranteed that the shadowy figure was a living, breathing person.

"Why did Whippet want to wipe me?" He

217

enunciated each word slowly, clearly.

She opened a bottle of Ketel One vodka. "I don't know that they did."

"They tried at least once. Maybe twice. The second time I recognized two of the operatives when they came after a friend and me at his place. They were Whippet, and it was obviously a wet assignment."

"Your friend was Palmer Westwood?"

He nodded. "How did you know?"

Suddenly the Langley-issued cell phone in her shoulder bag rang. *Laurence Litchfield.* Its sound was distinctive from her personal cell. She stared longingly at the bag. It rang again.

"Your cell?" Tice asked.

When she nodded, he took three steps and picked up the bag and fished out the cell, never taking his gaze from her. He laid the cell on the floor. Then he rose up. As it rang again, he slammed his heel down with a violent motion. The ringing ceased. The plastic shattered in a loud cracking noise. She inhaled sharply. He dropped the remains into her purse.

She moistened her dry lips and said nothing, but all she could think about was escape. She had to get away and alert Litchfield. Tice must be stopped.

He returned to the window. "You were going to tell me how you knew I was with Palmer."

Her hands trembled. She moved them into the shadow to pour two fingers of vodka. "It was a guess. He was your mentor at one time, and you were close. It made sense you'd go to him." She drank the liquor. It burned from her throat to her belly, but she felt marginally better.

"Whippet must've thought so, too. They tried to wipe us." He described an armed man in the swamp who had tried to shoot him, then the arrival of more than a dozen who chased them to the river, where they barely escaped in Westwood's plane. That was when he had recognized the two operatives.

Cunningham was silent. Hannah had said Whippet arrived after the attack. Either Hannah or Tice was lying. Considering everything, more likely both were. "I have no reason to believe you. If Langley wanted a traitor dead, they could handle it quietly in Allenwood. A common prison shanking over some minor dispute. Happens often enough no one would question it."

"True. That's one of the reasons I'm certain my escape has triggered something. Or it's interfering with someone's plans. What happened at Whippet? Who hit them?"

Her head jerked up. "You did. *You* arranged it!"

"Why would I? No, no, Elaine. I had no reason to hit Whippet."

"Yes, you did! You just admitted you knew they were after you. You did them first, before they could do you!"

"I didn't want butchery. I wanted information."

She remembered hearing Whippet's front door close. "If you know they were hit, then it *was* you inside. You went in because you knew it was safe — everyone was dead."

He shrugged. "I went in carefully. I had to confirm the two men I saw in North Carolina were still with Whippet. They were. I found them — as you said, dead."

"What if the police had arrived?"

"Their sirens would've given me plenty of warning. Whippet was my best hope. My one link to find out what's going on. It was worth the risk."

She thought about that — and about how quickly he had taken the gun from her, how quickly he had moved off to the window. Quickly, silently, almost invisibly. And she had not heard him inside Whippet house, either — until he left.

"I'd been hiding across the street for ten minutes or so," he explained, his tones

220

persuasive. "I wanted to isolate one of the operatives and get some answers. But when the front door opened, a dozen men slipped out. At first I thought they were part of the unit. But the porch light was off, they moved fast and together, and I saw dark blotches on their hands. Even in the moonlight, it looked like blood. Plus most had that wild look one learns to recognize — crude, like punch-drunk fighters who want to beat the hell out of someone. When I see that, I know something bad's gone down."

The words escaped her lips: "You were right. It was a slaughter."

"They'd left the door ajar, which told me they wanted their work discovered — probably to make sure the message got wherever it was intended to go as fast as possible. I didn't find anyone alive." He sighed. "It reminded me of La Belle Discotheque when it was bombed. You're probably too young to remember. It was 1986, West Berlin. Our soldiers used to hang out there, which was why Libyan terrorists targeted it. A couple of people died, and more than two hundred were injured, many badly. Both places had the same sense of devastation."

"You've left out a key element — me. I was alive. And I heard you leave. You can't tell me you didn't see or hear me, because you're better at this than I am."

His voice dropped ten degrees. "I saw you." From across the room, his gun homed in on her heart. "I repeat, someone's worried enough to send Whippet to terminate me. And you're Whippet. The only reason I can see to let you live is if you tell me what in hell is going on!"

From the passenger seat of the midnight-blue BMW 530i, Jerry Angelides surveyed the narrow street in Silver Spring. It rose like a concrete snake, gray and shifty. The moonlight was bright, the air still warm. That would not last. The night was going to turn cold; Angelides knew it. Trees and cars and lit windows rimmed the street, announcing boring suburbia behind the dark bricks of town houses. They were built in pairs so they could share a wall. In between were pencil-thin side yards.

Angelides was a connoisseur of environments. You had to know about them. More specifically, you had to know how to get in — and out. As he peered around, he had one of his bad feelings. It was like an itch. Something was going to happen.

As the BMW's tires thrummed along the pavement, he told his driver, "That's it, Rink. That's Cunningham's place. Stop here then go find someplace to park. Make it legal. Don't want any cops."

Rink hit the brakes, and Angelides and Billy got out and walked around a dark Honda and crouched. Over the hood, they studied Cunningham's place as the BMW cruised off. Angelides noted her front yard was little, about the size of an old-fashioned matchbox.

"Hey, there's no light," Billy said. "It's awful early to go to bed. I'll bet she's not home."

Billy was a nice-looking guy, neat in his sports jacket and pants. Billy had short brown hair trimmed just a little longer than a military cut, like Angelides's gray hair. He also wore a black pearl earring in each ear, but then, he was young, like twenty-two.

"Maybe, maybe not," Angelides advised. "See that red Jag down the street? It's the right license plate, so it's hers. Mighty fine-looking piece of machinery."

"She might be visiting neighbors," Billy suggested. He pulled out his 10mm Colt semiautomatic, a duplicate of Angelides's.

"Uh-huh." Angelides took out his Colt and a GPS tracker. "Don't get too far ahead of yourself. That's always a mistake. You gotta think ahead, but don't jump ahead. Okay, you take the rear. If there's still no light, break in, but be careful. Anything looks hinky, give me a warning call on the cell. If you can't talk, it's okay. I'll see your number and know it's you and come around. Otherwise, I'll give you ten, then I'm going in the front. We're gonna learn all we can about this little lady. First thing, we look for her. Second thing, we look for stuff about Tice."

Elaine stared at Tice's weapon, fighting back fear. *Think.* "Somehow you've discovered I'm your hunter. Since you're here now, you probably heard me call into Langley at Whippet, too. You figured there wasn't going to be enough time to question me there, so you decided to wait for me here. How did you find out about me?"

"I have my sources." He checked outside and stiffened. His words snapped: "Close the cabinet. The light's small, but it's a hazard. We have to leave."

She frowned. "What do you mean?"

"Shut the doors," he ordered. "*Now.* You've got visitors. Come here and look."

His worry seemed real. She set her glass inside the cabinet and closed it and ran across the room. She tipped up a slat and stared.

"There are two," he said. "See them?"

The older of the pair marched down the sidewalk, while the other watched the street. Both held guns low to their sides, where they were less noticeable.

"There was no surveillance when I arrived," he told her, "and I wasn't followed." He hurried across the room, grabbed a backpack, stuffed her Walther into it, and stuck the lit cigar into the whiskey that remained in his glass, stopping the odor. "That means it's you they want."

Keeping hope from her voice, she said neutrally, "They could be Langley."

"If they were, I'd be out the back door by now."

"They could be yours. This could be a movie you're producing to fool me."

"Why would I bother? My smartest move is to leave you to entertain them while I get away." He snapped the SIG Sauer free from the armchair.

She peered outside again. The first man had stopped at her Jaguar. She tensed. "One of them looks as if he's planting something on my Jag. Right rear fender."

"That doesn't sound like Langley, does it?" When she was silent, he asked, "Large or small?"

"Can't tell. The other one's moving. It looks as if he's headed toward my side yard." She moistened her lips. "Who are they?"

"They were with the gang that massacred Whippet." He put the SIG Sauer into the backpack. "I'd say they've come to finish the job."

16

As Cunningham bolted through the shadows to the dummy and ripped out newspapers, Tice attached a wireless audio receiver to his tape recorder. Then he helped her ram the papers into the fireplace, leaving the area with no trace that anyone had been here recently — except for the lingering stench of the cigar. Nothing to be done about that.

He shoved the whiskey glass into her hand. "Dump it into the kitchen trash."

She slung her bag across her chest, and he led her at a trot through her dark living room and into the hall, carrying his Browning and the backpack. He slapped on his reading glasses, took a small box from the backpack, popped the box open, and removed what looked like a triangular kernel of corn, except that it was a dull black color.

"This is an audio transmitter," he told her. "It's got special adhesive on one side. Lick it, and it sticks like a bad debt to anything. Attaching it activates it. With luck, I'll be able to plant it."

"You have a plan?" Her voice was tight.

"I do. Grab a towel out of the bathroom. Take the dark one." He dropped the box into the backpack and slid the kernel into his pants pocket and returned his reading glasses to his shirt pocket.

She snatched the navy terry-cloth towel from the guest bath. "If I had my Walther, I could help."

He shook his head, barely acknowledging her words. In the tiny kitchen he grabbed a flare-legged barstool and laid it on its side some four feet from the outside door. It partially blocked the path to the rest of the town house.

"Always give them something to focus on besides you."

"I know." She dumped the glass of whiskey into a container under the sink.

He scanned the room. The door was so close to the wall that there was no way either one of them could hide behind it. White moonlight streamed in through the oversize window above the sink, leaving a black shadow on the kitchen's far side. Cast by the leafy tree in her rear yard, the shadow undulated with the wind.

He yanked her inside the shadow just as a face appeared at the glass, peering warily inside. It was the young man he had seen out front. With a quiet curse, she tugged her black jacket shut over her white T-shirt and adjusted her shoulder bag. The kitchen was so small that there was no way to escape deeper into darkness.

He put his mouth against her ear. "Move with the shadow. If we're stationary, we're more noticeable."

Side by side, they shifted with the rolling darkness. Her tension was palpable. From the window, the man inspected the interior for what seemed an interminable time. He had a cheeky face, young but watchful. Tice studied him for a sign he had seen her gesture. But at last the head disappeared. Tice kept himself loose. He glanced at Cunningham. She nodded. He sensed fear, but she remained composed.

There was the scratch of picklocks, and the door opened cautiously, hinges squeaking. A hefty Colt in his hand, the intruder stepped up and across the threshold into a rectangle of moonlight that illuminated the overturned stool. He closed the door. As Tice had expected, the man leaned over to move it out of his way. Tice touched Cunningham's arm and pointed and gestured.

She gave a single nod, and they sprinted. The intruder turned, his weapon in one hand, the stool in the other. She flung the towel over his head. As he grunted and jerked with surprise, blind and helpless, Tice crashed the side of his hand down hard onto the back of his neck. The barstool thudded to the floor, and the gunman collapsed to his knees.

Cunningham tore his Colt away as Tice kneed him in the chin. The intruder's head snapped back, cutting oxygen to his brain. The towel slid off. His eyes were open but abruptly blank. With a low groan, he pitched forward, resting on his cheek like an exhausted baby. His eyelids closed.

Tice knelt and emptied the man's pockets. "He'll be out for a while. Throw me my backpack. Do you have a key to your pantry?"

"I used to. I'll look." She ran to the backpack, tossed it to him, and in three quick steps was opening a kitchen drawer.

He heard her pawing through it. "Nothing useful here except his cell." He dropped it into his backpack.

He took out the kernel-shaped audio transmitter and licked it and stuck it to the underside of the man's shirt collar. He checked Cunningham. She was still digging through the drawer. The Colt was on the counter. He would deal with that later. She pulled out a short leather strap. The loop at the end was torn open, the key gone. She muttered angrily and resumed her search.

Tice rose stiffly and opened the pantry door. He dragged the unconscious man inside and dumped him beside a box of laundry detergent.

"How about that key?" He closed the door.

"I've got it." She ran toward him, the key in one hand, the Colt in the other, her expression determined. She would not give up the weapon easily.

He watched the Colt warily, but as long as there was another killer outside, he would make no move to take it.

"Lock the pantry," he ordered. "Keep the key."

She rushed around him as he returned the stool to its place beside the counter and slung his backpack over one shoulder. As the lock clicked into place, he studied the kitchen one last time. Nothing appeared disturbed. He opened the rear door just as he heard the front door open. His chest squeezed.

Her head was cocked, listening. "The other guy's here," she whispered. Her eyes flashed, and in them he saw rage, a deep sense of violation. This was her home, and three intruders had broken into it tonight.

"We're gone."

She nodded, and they slid outside. As she locked the door, he surveyed her postage-stamp lawn and the other rear yards. A black wind blew against his skin.

"The rest of the wet squad could be anywhere around here," he warned. "Truce? Otherwise, I take the Colt."

Her grip on the weapon tightened. "Like hell you will." Her eyes widened then narrowed. "Temporary truce."

"If you fire, you'll draw the man in the house and everyone else." He studied her for a moment, finally deciding she was smart enough to mean it. "This way."

They took off at a run toward the side yard, hugging the shadows. At the front he pressed against the wall. She slipped in next to him, her small face tense and alert. A midnight-blue BMW was pulling into a driveway across the street. He frowned and looked at her.

"It doesn't belong to any of the neighbors," she whispered.

A man got out, scanned both ways, and dashed toward her place.

"He was at Whippet, too." Tice kept his

voice low. "That makes three of them so far. My car's two blocks away. We'll take yours."

"I'll drive."

"Damn right you will." That left him free to use his weapons. He peered farther around the corner. The street was empty.

They ran again, quietly crossing her front yard and escaping down the sidewalk, watching everywhere. She pressed the door release on her key chain. Ahead, the Jaguar's lights flashed.

"Stand outside until I figure out what's been left on your car."

She started to object then nodded.

As she stood sentry, he searched under the right rear fender, running his hands over the grime. At last he found the lump, the size of a shirt button. He pried it off.

"It's a tracker." He held up the innocent-looking piece. "Get inside. Hurry."

They jumped in then let the heavy doors close softly. He looked for the Colt — she had slid it into the pocket of her door. The handle stuck up.

As the engine purred to life, she scrutinized the area and touched the accelerator, maneuvering expertly into a left turn. "Don't put on your seat belt yet." She backed up and turned left once more, inching out of the tight slot.

"What in hell do you think you're doing!"

"I have an idea." Her blue eyes were constricted and angry. "It won't take more than ten seconds." She backed up once more.

"You want to leave the tracker on their car?" he asked.

"A surprise gift."

"More like an insult. Good psychological warfare. And it will waste their time. You've given me an idea." As she swung a hard left into the street and pressed the gas pedal, he leaned across her lap and wrapped his hand around the big Colt.

"Hey!" She pounded a fist against his head. The Jag swerved.

Blinking, he jerked back into his seat.

She swore, kept checking the Colt. "I barely missed crashing the car!"

"But you did miss it." He took out his pocketknife and opened it then cocked the Colt's hammer. "You'll like this." He stuck his knife blade into the open space beneath the gun's hammer and broke off the tip. The small piece of metal was almost invisible inside the weapon. It would jam the first time anyone tried to fire it.

She breathed deeply, scowling. She glanced at her town house. "The lights are on. Both floors. Either they've found their friend and are searching for us, or they haven't found him and are about to give up. In any case, they'll be out the door any moment. What's your idea?" She braked the car at the end of the driveway where the BMW was parked.

He handed her the tracker. "It's got a magnetic attachment. Do your worst." He had no intention of letting her drive off as soon as he got out.

She stared at it then up into his eyes. He saw cool calculation, that she knew exactly what he was doing and why, and acknowledged his superiority only because he had the only operating gun. She snatched the tracker.

She left the engine running, and they got out swiftly, scanning the street. He dropped the Colt's finger loop over the BMW's antenna and yanked the antenna high. She planted the tracker under a fender. They ran back to the Jag. Inside, he turned and watched through the rear window as she floored the accelerator. With a low growl, the car shot off effortlessly. The G-force slammed him deep into the leather seat.

"Christ. Are you sure you know how to drive this thing?"

Her voice was hard. "Zero to sixty in less

than eight seconds. It's just a V6. A V8's faster — only six-point-six seconds."

"A V6 is impressive enough." They whipped up her street past trees and cars. He stiffened. "Here they come. There're two. They've seen your car's gone. They're running to theirs." The pair moved like well-oiled machinery, showing the same trained intelligence he had seen when the gang had slipped away from Whippet house.

With a squeal of tires, she tore the Jag around a corner. "Where to?"

"Just get us far away." He inhaled and faced forward again. "Hopefully we've got some conversation to listen to from the bug I planted on the guy we knocked out. Personally, I'd like to know who those bastards are and what in hell is really going on. I'll bet you'd like to know, too. We'll start with the live action." He took out his wireless audio receiver and hit the POWER button.

17

As Elaine Cunningham pushed the car onward through the city night, they listened for voices from the wireless receiver, but there were none — no cursing about the missing Jaguar, no complaints about finding the gun hooked over the antenna. Not even any ambient street noises. There was only silence.

"Is it broken?" she asked.

Jay Tice frowned. "I tested it. I know it works. Okay, I'll try the tape recorder. Maybe it picked up something earlier." He pulled it out and hit REWIND then PLAY.

Static crackled. Someone moaned weakly — the intruder who was locked in the pantry. With relief, they glanced at each other. Tice raised the volume. Footsteps. He fast-forwarded through more footsteps and occasional moans as she drove north. Finally there was the noise of a door opening. It made the same squeak as her town house's rear door.

A voice asked, "Billy?" Pause. Louder this time: "Billy, where the hell are you?" The door closed. The man's voice again: "Rink, you parked yet? Get here quick." There were noises of searching, more doors opening and closing, and shouts of "Billy!" A door handle rattled loudly, and the moaning resumed. "You in there, Billy? Dammit, answer me!" There was a noisy crash.

"There goes my pantry door." She spun the car through an intersection.

He paused the tape recorder as she kept pace with the traffic. They were perhaps two miles from her town house, probably in Bethesda now.

"Any sign of pursuit?"

She checked her rearview mirror. "Nothing so far."

"Good. Pull into Rite Aid. I've got one more way to throw them off so we'll have time to listen to this." He dropped the tape recorder into his backpack and took out two Virginia license plates and QuakeHold! putty adhesive.

As she cornered the car into the driveway next to the drugstore, she asked, "Where did you get that?"

"I scavenged the plates and bought the QuakeHold!"

He finished applying the pads of adhesive to the plates' backs as she cruised into the parking lot, which stretched behind a dozen strip-mall stores. Pole lamps showered surreal blue-white illumination. She stopped the car near overgrown bushes. The lot was half full.

"Turn off the headlights," he told her. "Put it in PARK, and keep the engine running. Lower your window so we can talk if we have to."

She did as he said, ordering her nerves to quiet. This might be her chance to escape. As soon as she was away, she could phone Litchfield to send a capture team.

Tice grabbed his backpack, gun, and license plates and opened the door. He got out and closed it. She watched him survey the lot and pad off. Turning her head fractionally, she saw him reach the car's tail. He would need two hands to attach the plates, which meant it would take him several seconds to retrieve his Browning and fire. Her rib cage was as tight as a tourniquet as she studied her mirror. At last he lowered himself to go to work.

Smiling grimly to herself, she looked down and quietly shifted back into gear.

"Bad plan."

The voice was hushed, yet both words

were enunciated so clearly, the threat in each so palpable, that a shudder shot through her. Her head lashed left, and she stared through her window into the barrel of Tice's Browning.

"I don't know what you're talking about," she told him coldly.

Tice smiled — but there was no hint of humor or goodwill in it this time. "You lie rather well," he told her, "but not to me. You'll be dead if you so much as roll those big Michelins of yours one inch."

Her heart hammered. "You're going to draw attention to us if you don't get those license plates changed." When he did not move, she returned the gear to PARK.

And he vanished. She heard small sounds at the rear of the car as he worked. Then he appeared at the hood and disappeared again. More noises, and he was back in the front passenger seat.

She flicked on the headlights. "I'll bet you thought I was sticking around just to see your pretty face again." As he closed his door, she was already rolling the car toward the lot's exit. "Turn on the player."

He fished it out of his backpack. "Get on the Beltway and head west. Find other Jags or BMWs or Mercedeses. Blend in. Okay, back to your pantry and your visitors." He touched PLAY. The noise of three quick footsteps sounded from the small machine.

"Jesus," said the same man as before.

"Hey, Jerry." Greetings from a weak voice.

There were shuffling sounds. "What in hell happened, Billy?" The words bristled with fury. They were from the man called Jerry. "Who did this to you?"

"I'm not sure. I smelled cigar smoke. I'm not sure."

"I told you to call if there was trouble. Why didn't you call? Shit — you don't have your cell phone. Where's your Colt? Your cell and gun are gone, Billy. What in fuck have you done!"

"Jerry, please. Hey, Jerry. Come on. It's not so bad. It could happen —"

"Tell me everything," Jerry demanded.

The second man — Billy — sounded tense and frightened and young. "I didn't screw up. He . . . they . . . somebody tricked me. I remember something over my head, then I got conked out. Maybe I got hit twice. There was a stool in the way, and I leaned over — and, yeah, that's what happened. I leaned over to move it, and somebody threw something over my head to blind me, and I got hit hard a couple of times."

"You don't even know how many guys did

this to you? You didn't see a face? You don't have one single name? Not even a sex? Could it have been Cunningham?"

"Gee, Jerry," the voice pleaded. "Yeah, sure, I think it was Cunningham. It must've been, right?"

"Cigar smoke, Billy. Does the broad smoke cigars? Of course you don't know. You weren't awake long enough to figure it out. So let me tell you. There's a cigar butt in the trash, soaked in whiskey. Someone put it out in a hurry. There's a wet drink glass in a folding bar — vodka-wet. From morning? I don't think so. With two different alcohols, odds on, it's two people. There's dust knocked off both ends of a venetian blind in the living room, like two somebodies was looking outside. Billy, I've got to conclude you fucked up. It's a sad thing to say, but you fucked up bad. I taught you better than this. You laid yourself wide-open to fuck up because you believed the broad was asleep or wasn't here because the place was dark. This caused you to hurry in without being properly concerned. I coulda walked into a trap, too, because you fucked up. Then where would Mr. G be? He's got that big deal, and no way he stands for these fuckups. He's relying on me, and I've been relying on you, and now I'm disturbed because you have seriously fucked up."

The other man gasped. "Please, Jerry —"

There was the faint sound of a third man's voice. "Where are you? Hey, Jerry. Where are you!"

Jerry bellowed, "In the kitchen pantry, goddammit! We've got a big problem, Rink. I had a bad feeling something was going to happen. Guess this was it. Okay, Billy, so here's the way I figure it. You got ambushed by two people. There's no sign of a break-in, so I figure one was probably Cunningham. It's possible the other was Tice. No direct evidence of him I can see, except for the cigar smoke and the fact you got tricked. Tice likes to do that, 'cause it demoralizes you. So he leaves a stool tipped over. Like a dummy, you picks it up, giving him a perfect opening. Then he's gone like a yanked tooth. So why didn't he wipe you? Or more likely, why didn't he take you with him so he could grill you?"

"I don't know, Jerry," Billy said, worried.

"What's going on?" said the third man.

"Shut up, Rink," Jerry snapped. "Shut up, and learn something. The reason is, Billy, because he wanted me to look around like an asshole then feel like a real jerk because I couldn't find you. And I waste a lot of time, too, so he can make a clean getaway.

Fortunately, there's a tracker on that Jag of hers, and they won't get far. But then I ask myself, is that all there is to it? Remember, this guy's real smart. He maybe thinks he's the smartest man in the world, he's so smart."

"He doesn't know you, Jerry," Rink said.

"Damn right he doesn't. So he's made a fool of you, Billy. And now he's trying to make a fool of me."

"But I —" Billy tried.

"Shut up! Let me think!"

There was a steady drumbeat of footsteps. The sound stopped.

"What are you doing?" Billy said. "Come on, Jerry. Stop looking like that! What're you *doing?*"

"I'm not doing, I'm thinking. I think this real smart genius might've booby-trapped you, Billy. You think you got a bomb on you?"

"Jerry!" The voice was terrified.

"But I woulda spotted a bomb, right? Nope, so what's he gonna do — ? *Shit!*" The word was a long, drawn-out bellow of sudden understanding. "It's on you some-wheres. I'd bet the bank on it. That guy . . . that *guy!*" The noises of rustling and movement. "Here it is! Look at this. Both of you, see this? This is a bug. You got yourself bugged, Billy, a little present from that asshole traitor. So he may've heard every goddamn word. . . . *Shit! Shit! Shit!* If he's listening, he knows I bugged the Jag!"

"Jerry!" Billy begged. "Please!"

"Aw, come on, Jerry. It's not so bad," Rink tried. "I'll bet Tice isn't listening. I'll bet —"

"Shut the fuck up." Jerry's voice was cold and frighteningly calm. "I treated you real good, Billy, and I tried to teach you. I guess you didn't understand the part where just because I'm a nice guy, I'm not some kind of sucker or dummy. 'Nice' doesn't mean a pussy. It means nice. Polite. I got manners. We got to live in this world, and nice manners is pleasant. Like being kind to animals and old ladies is pleasant. See, I'm still trying to teach you. I'm being pleasant. This is Cunningham's gun. Probably a backup. A real good 9mm Beretta. She kept it in a lockbox at the back of her closet. There was this magazine there, too. I brought everything, thinking there just might be a time they'd be useful. Like I said — think ahead, don't jump ahead."

"Jerry?" Billy whimpered.

"Come on, Jerry," the one called Rink said. "Come on —"

There was the clicking noise of a clip being shoved home. "And this is her sound suppressor." The light whine of metal being screwed into metal. "I just didn't figure it'd be so soon I'd need it. I hate it when people fuck up bad when they've had every opportunity to do things right. I also really hate it when they lie to me or they break agreements. You done only one of the three, Billy, and for that I will always have fond feelings for you. But you see the way it is. I can't let Tice get away with this. Otherwise, he won't respect me. He has to understand he's interfering with my responsibilities. I hope you're listening, Tice."

"Jerry!" The word was a scream. "Nooooo! I didn't fuck up! They —"

Rink said, "You're not going to —"

There was a loud *pop.*

"See how I did that, Rink? Right between the eyes. Not a speck of blood on either of us. Tice, I sure do hope you're listening. Now you got one more mighty big problem — you got yourself a killer on your hands. Oh, yeah. It won't take much for me to set Cunningham up. After all, it's her Beretta, right? Her fingerprints, right? Even if you're taping this, you can't exactly turn the tape over to the cops, now, can you? Of course, *she* could, but then your ass would be in an even tighter sling, which means you're not gonna let her anywheres near a cop. So you can't let her go, and if you keep her, pretty soon her name and photo are gonna be plastered all over newspapers and big wide-screen TVs, which we both know makes you even more vulnerable. I think you'd better kill her, Tice, don't you?"

The tape went dead.

18

Geneva, Switzerland

As thunderheads tumbled across the black sky, the narrow Old Town lane seemed to reverberate with the hulking profile of the man from Langley — "Alec." The fog coiled up around his calves, tentatively touching the hem of his khaki raincoat. He moved only one enormous hand, delivering a thin brown cigarette to his lips.

The acrid smoke drifted through the night's damp to where Raina Manhardt hid in the recessed doorway. She digested his presence, his words, and the message intended to make her his tool: *You're officially reactivated, Glinda.*

He continued in English in his low, hypnotic basso: "What? No comment? No expression of excitement? Now, now, you must be of good cheer, because I may be able to help. If you'd like to hear what I know, come walk with me." Without a glance at her, he resumed his stroll through the creeping mist, swinging his umbrella. "Oh, and do me a favor, will you?" His voice trailed back. "Put that damn gun away. I never embark on a friendly conversation when a weapon's pointed at me."

She looked around warily. She did not understand how he — how anyone — could have found her. Had he come alone? She saw no sign of CIA backup or, God forbid, Volker or anyone else from the BND. If the BND spotted Alec and her together and interpreted their relationship correctly, they would arrest her as a traitor, although she had never spied against the new Germany. Worse, she would be unable to find out who had killed her son.

He had baited his hook with the one lure that would attract her — information. And he was right — she wanted whatever he knew. At the same time, he was threatening her with exposure or worse. Just as she had done countless times, she must take the risk. As she decided that, she loosened her belt and slipped her Walther inside at the small of her back then stashed the candy box that contained the videotapes under her belt in front. She buttoned the bottom two buttons of her red plaid overshirt over them and distributed her car keys, passport, and other items into her pockets. Jay Tice had taught her long ago to prepare when there was a chance she would have to move quickly.

Carrying her valise, she strode out after Alec. When she caught up, he glanced down.

He gave her a smile. "Ah, how nice."

Effortlessly, she returned an equally fake smile. But although he had changed to English, she spoke in German, a reminder that he did not own the entire playing field.

"You have my attention," she told him.

Alec continued agreeably in German: "Indulge me. You began working for Tice in 1983, his secret mole. Are you surprised I know?"

She was silent, the past sweeping like a cold wind over her.

"You refused to be paid," he went on. "What I'm curious about is why." He offered a cigarette.

She shook her head. "The short answer is disillusionment. The year before, I was sent on my first assignment into the West — to Hanover." Markus Wolf had identified her as an officer he could promote: She spoke both American- and Oxbridge-accented English as well as Russian, and she had a gift for analytical observation and investigation. "I expected to find gangs and crime and drugs and terrible poverty. Instead, it was lovely. Tranquil. People had plenty to eat. They wore warm clothes and owned houses or lived in solid apartment buildings. Most could even afford cars."

"You were surprised?"

"Shocked. It was the opposite of what I — what everyone who grew up in East Germany — was told."

"Did you reveal your discovery to Wolf?"

"I was young but not stupid. And I certainly didn't have a death wish. I connected with some underground sources and started reading Western papers and books and listening to your political debates and watching demonstrations on TV. Free speech. Free movement. You had *rights.* That changed me. Then Jay spotted me in Lübeck, buying a forbidden magazine. He followed me, but I made him. One thing led to another, and he offered me work for something I could believe in — democracy. That's why I never wanted to be paid."

"A Company mole. Code name Glinda. From *The Wizard of Oz*?"

"Yes." Jay had chosen it for her, the Good Witch of the North.

"Was it your idea to also sign up with the BND?"

She frowned. "That's enough. You said you had information for me."

"I'm getting to it. Indulge me this one last time."

As they continued to climb, she told him, "It was two years later. Jay suggested I volunteer. Walk in." She remembered the worry in his voice: *Can you do it? It'll be a tightrope. By feeding intel to both me and a BND handler, you'll double the risk the Stasi will spot you.* His concern had been just as big a lie as the Stasi's description of the Free West. Still, the warning was accurate: In the brutish spy wars, national alliances did not always translate down to the shifting sands of the street. Her life could vaporize at the incensed twitch of not only a Stasi trigger finger but a BND one, too.

"So if the BND found out you were also spying for Langley," Alec said, driving home the point, "it wouldn't have mattered much to them we were allies."

"It was my chance to work directly for a free Germany, for democracy. For the future. Now tell me what you know about Kristoph's death." Ahead, traffic flowed through an intersection. She watched it alertly. Her car was within a block.

He ignored the demand, continuing to smoke languidly. "Let's back up a bit. From what you've just told me, you're a woman of conviction. You risked your life for what

America and West Germany stood for. Now the Company needs your help again. We're concerned Kristoph might've been involved in something sinister. What have you learned?"

She stared up at him. "You don't know anything."

"Your history tells me you're not the type to remain in Geneva for some superficial reason. You cross-examined the forensics man. You went to Milieu Software. Was Kristoph involved in something illegal? A software company could easily be a terrorist front. Or maybe they were washing money. What can I do to help you clear your boy's name?"

Her lips thinned, but she said neutrally, "Are you suggesting Kristoph himself was doing something criminal?"

He shrugged. "We have an expression in America — the apple doesn't fall far from the tree."

A flush of outrage heated her cheeks. She knew exactly what he meant: She was a sleeper, burrowed into the BND's highest echelons, apparently ready to spy against Germany. Therefore, according to Alec's logic, Kristoph would hardly be reluctant to break laws himself. But Kristoph knew

253

nothing about Langley, and he was not that way.

"You bastard. What do you really want?" she demanded.

"Did Kristoph suspect something about Milieu Software?"

Their breaths were white streams in the chill. Ahead, a gray dawn disturbed the sky, illuminating the cloudy remains of the night's thunderstorm. She glanced around and started to move away, but he gripped her arm. She glared down at his hand and then up at him. He released her and cleared his throat.

She walked onto the sidewalk, continuing toward the intersection. Toward her car and escape. "Tell me what *you* know about Milieu."

"We had intel they were developing a huge software program. Did Kristoph describe it?"

No working spy gave information without an ulterior motive. She frowned and lied, "Kristoph said nothing about his job. It was as if he were sworn to secrecy."

"Then who else did you talk to about it?"

"Stop interrogating me, Alec. You're looking for filth in a clean handkerchief. I'm still in Geneva because I'm mourning my son. I was restless tonight, so I decided to take a walk around Old Town. If you've never been sleepless, you're not human. Something has attracted Langley's interest in me — a great deal of interest, or you wouldn't be here. That something appears to be Milieu. You must know they moved out before Kristoph died. There was no way I was able to investigate. Your ruse of offering help has only irritated me and wasted both of our time."

His eyes grew dull, almost lifeless. He flicked his cigarette into the wet gutter. "Why would you be interested in my help if your boy's death were an accident? You know more than you're saying. And your lurking in that doorway back there with a gun shows you came out tonight prepared for trouble." Casually he slid his right hand inside a pocket. "Remember, Glinda — you're activated. I order you to reveal what you know about Milieu Software, whom you've been talking with, and what was said."

She saw the fingers flex as if squeezing something. A signal perhaps? She increased her pace. "I've told you everything."

Immediately he was in front of her, blocking her, looming over her. "Where's the box of candy?"

Raina stiffened as if someone had just

jerked on her spine. "What are you talking about?" There was no way she was going to give him her videotapes.

"You went to the place du Bourg-de-Four with the box under your arm. When you arrived, you still had it. You ran down a dark stairwell for no apparent reason. You were there a full two minutes. Then you took off up the rue. It's illogical to think you'd be carrying it for a social call at this hour. Therefore, I must conclude you did a switch or you put something else inside it. In any case, it doesn't hold chocolates. *I want that box.*"

Heart pounding, Raina stared and thought quickly. Making her hands tremble, she unzipped her valise and shot a cowering smile up at Alec. "Did you mean this?" She pulled the metal opening of the valise wide and lifted the valise so he could see the real Avelines *assortis* lying next to her umbrella.

At the same time, motor revving, a large Citroën sedan sped around the corner and screeched to an abrupt stop in the center of the lane. The stink of burned rubber rose in the air. The headlights died.

With an exhalation of pleasure, Alec reached inside the valise. He had not even glanced at the car; his lack of curiosity told her he had summoned it. Everything happened within seconds. She slammed the jaws of the valise shut on his hand — hard. He grunted, and she crashed her shoulder up into his chest. It was like hitting a mountain, but her two quick assaults had surprised him.

His balance quaked. He grabbed for the building. She rammed the point of her elbow deep into his side in a *yoko hiji-ate* strike, worsening his balance. He grunted again and swung an arm. She ducked. He reeled. *The bigger they are,* she thought bitterly.

As he stumbled, the sedan's doors swung open, and two men jumped out, weapons in hand. She spun on her heel and bolted downhill through the shadows. A silenced bullet shattered a cobblestone at her flying feet. Shards exploded.

"No shooting!" she heard Alec yell out behind her. "We want her alive!"

Thank God. She accelerated down the slope and into the low fog and around the bend and past the doorway where she had hidden. Her hammering footsteps echoed hollowly against the sheer walls of the old buildings as she sped toward the curve where she had first seen Alec. She rounded that and, sweating, pressed onward, muscles straining. She hurtled past stone doorsteps and hanging streetlamps. She ran as if the dark hounds of hell chased.

When she finally shot around a turn from which she could see a slice of the place du Bourg-de-Four, she gulped air and risked a look over her shoulder. They were not in sight yet. Had she hurt Alec more than she thought? She slowed to listen but heard no sound of pursuit, just the traffic behind her, growing fainter.

Counting her blessings, she resumed her hellbent pace, passing the Demi-Lune Café. As the fountain and plaza came into wider view, the rich aroma of hot coffee drifted from a *boulangerie.* Breathing hard, she passed Soda's bar and dashed into the plaza, scanning. The nightclubs were closed, their patrons gone. She turned right, heading for another rue that would take her back uphill toward —

"Stopp, Raina." The steely command in German was like a dagger in her back.

Startled, chest heaving, she skidded and turned, already reaching under her shirt for her gun.

The voice continued in German, "That would not be advisable." The dull gray barrel of his Walther leading, Volker Rehwaldt stepped out of the shadows of the building at the corner. His rough face looked dry, as if something inside him had withered and died. His umbrella was gone, but he still wore his tweed jacket and dark slacks. And there was his pistol, pointed at her.

Her eyes narrowed. Puzzled, she let her hand drift to her side. "No more hugs, Volker? What's this about?" She glanced at his weapon then quickly around again. In the windows above, a few lights glowed.

"You must go with them," Volker ordered.

"*Them?* What are you talking about!" There was a clatter of feet in the lane at last — hurrying but not running.

He lifted his head, listening, too, and leveled his gaze at her. "Leave with them quietly. It is best."

She frowned, trying to understand. "Have you told Erich what you're doing?"

"Me? This isn't about what *I'm* doing." His upper lip rose in disgust. "Erich sent me to help them, Raina — *Glinda!*"

She stared, speechless. He knew, and Erich knew — but only part of the story. Outrage swept through her, hot and angry. Then fear. "You're wrong, Volker. You don't understand. I'd never work against — !"

She stopped, realizing why Alec and his men were not rushing to catch her — they knew Volker was waiting. And Alec had found her through Volker's uncharacteristic hug. It was impossible but true — the CIA and BND were collaborating against her.

"How could you spy on us? *Against us!*" he accused.

"That's a lie! You and I've been together years. Listen to me. Hear me out!" Still talking, she stepped closer, her hands in front, palms up in a gesture pleading for understanding. But she also needed to be within striking distance. "You know me better than to believe their fiction. I had to buy time to raise Kristoph. If Langley had come to me before this, I would've told them no and taken the consequences. I told them no tonight!"

He stiffened, unsure. Conflict raged on his pitted face, but it was unlikely he would side with her against Erich.

"At least give me the chance to explain how the Company —," she tried anyway.

"Nein!"

Before he could finish giving his head an angry shake, she balanced back on her left foot and drove her right foot straight into his solar plexus in a brutal *kekomi* kick. With his expertise, she would get no second chances. His face stretched in surprise, and he doubled over, his lungs emptying. She followed with a powerful *mawashi-geri* roundhouse kick to the point of his jaw.

His head snapped, his Walther fell, and he sprawled. His skull hit the cobbles with a hollow *thwack*. His eyelids dropped, did not even twitch.

She scooped up his Walther and bolted. The noise of approaching feet was louder. She pushed away the shock of what all of this meant and, using both hands, ripped open her plaid overshirt as she dodged between two metal fence barriers. Her hip hit one, and it crashed over.

The pain hardly registered as she yanked off the shirt and leaped onto the sidewalk and slowed under the lamplight. She held up the shirt to examine the back where Volker had patted her during his commiserating hug.

Silently cursing, she found it — a clear piece of adhesive tape. In the center, between the tape and the shirt, was what appeared to be a small steel button. She recognized it immediately — a miniature tracker.

She snapped off the tape. As she picked off the tracker, she shot off again, hurdling a concrete planter, heading toward the center of the square. Using her momentum to power her arm, she lobbed the tiny device toward the distant shops. She must send Alec and the others someplace where she would not be, and this was her best hope.

Before it could land, she turned abruptly and raced away, barely avoiding a Vespa left outside a *galleria.* She turned up the narrow rue des Chaudronniers, tying the sleeves of her shirt around her waist to hide the box that contained her videotapes. The passageway roughly paralleled the rue Etienne-Dumont. Listening worriedly as the noise of angry male voices rose from the plaza behind her, she settled into an exhausting uphill run, praying she could vanish. She rounded the first bend still climbing, now slipping on the damp cobblestones in her haste. She passed more stone doorsteps, more hanging lamplights. When she arrived at last at the intersection with promenade de Saint-Antoine, she allowed herself one quick look back.

The lane was deserted. She felt a brief moment of triumph, but she did not slow. Covered with sweat, weary to the bone, she dashed across the street and into the city parking garage and downstairs into shadowy light. The underground lot stank of diesel and wet concrete. She had never seen a lovelier sight.

Gulping air, legs trembling, she took out her car keys and headed for her rented Opel. Locked inside the trunk was her small suitcase — priceless now. As soon as she had suspected Kristoph had been murdered, she pulled together tradecraft artifacts from her past. Fortunately, four of the passports in her home safe were current. By calling in old favors, she swiftly assembled disguises and pocket litter to support the passports. Everything was compacted into that suitcase.

Footsteps echoing in the emptiness, she stopped at the car and gazed cautiously around one more time. Slowly she smiled. It was not a kind smile, but an angry, knowing one. She was here; they were not. She banished her sore muscles and throbbing pulse and opened the door. With a quick gesture, she tossed her overshirt across the front seat and climbed in. The engine started immediately.

She drove up the exit ramp and paused to check the sidewalks and street. But as she steered the Opel into traffic, a sense of dread swept through her. It was an old feeling, something straight from her days as a dual mole, a warning. She concentrated, thinking, until tonight's events at last fit together with frightening perfection: The CIA had needed to find her before she uncovered whatever they were investigating — or hiding. That was where Erich Eisner became important. It would have been a small matter to blackmail him — a phone call from Langley, followed by a secret e-mail with encoded attachments documenting her years of Cold War espionage for the CIA and that she was now a sleeper. She was the legend Erich had created and with which he had not only saved the BND but made his career. If the truth were publicized, the BND's image would be tarnished, and he would be a laughingstock — if not worse. To buy the CIA's silence, he would send Volker Rehwaldt to locate her.

Afterward she would be not only worthless as a CIA sleeper but a ticking bomb for Erich. The two agencies would have to cooperate in cleaning up after themselves. But shooting her dead would cause questions, an official investigation.

Volker had told her to go with "them" — the CIA. They planned to take her someplace in the Citroën where her suicide could be faked. It would be believable — she was so heartbroken by the death of her only child that she could not go on living. With a forged suicide note, there would be no questions, no official inquiry.

Her lips parted, and she breathed shallowly. She was in terrible danger. Both agencies would continue to search for her. The CIA was obviously driving the operation, so Washington was her best destination. She had picked up Jay's message that he had broken out of the penitentiary. Now she would send a coded response.

She hit the gas pedal, accelerating through a stoplight. She had loathed Jay so long that working with him again seemed stupid, impossible. He had sold her out, just as he had his country.

As she turned her car toward the airport, she resumed analyzing. The CIA had kept her in reserve nearly fifteen years, although she had golden contacts all the way up to the chancellor himself. She was a major asset with the potential to deliver Germany's most closely held state secrets as well as national and international intelligence. Still, Langley had never contacted her — until now. And then it was to blow her cover and gain nothing but Germany's cooperation in finding and liquidating her.

The CIA had been willing to sacrifice her and everything she could provide in the future to stop her investigation into her son's death. Her grip on the steering wheel tightened. Whatever Milieu Software Technology was doing, the CIA was willing to

pay an extraordinary price to find out — or
keep it from her.

19

Bethesda, Maryland

Jerry Angelides was deeply pissed. As the BMW sped across the lit suburban streets, he sat rigidly in the passenger seat with Billy's Colt on his lap, the fingers of his left hand drumming the barrel. He did not like to think about finding it hooked over the antenna like somebody's dirty laundry.

Then there was the problem with the tracker he had planted on the Jag. When he turned on the reader, he found Jay Tice had gotten him again — the bastard stuck it onto the BMW somewhere. Disgusted, he turned the reader off right away. The damn tracker could stay glued so long it grew warts.

Rink cleared his throat. "You'd think that fancy car of hers wouldn't be so hard to find," he tried conversationally.

Angelides said nothing.

Rink glanced at him, worry in his pale eyes.

Angelides saw it.

Rink said loudly, "I've never fucked up, Jerry. I'd never break an agreement or lie to you, Jerry."

Angelides sighed. He told himself to cut it out. Being steamed was not going to help, and it was just what Jay Tice was counting on. When you got angry enough, your brain short-circuited. Well, Tice was not going to win that little battle or any other one. He had made an anonymous call to the police about the corpse in Cunningham's town house and had sent out a dozen cars looking for the Jag. With luck, one of his men would phone to say he had spotted it. It was going to be pure pleasure to turn Tice into one dead rat.

He brought his temper under control. "I know you wouldn't. You're not like Billy. You're my man."

"That's right, Jerry. That's right. I'm your man."

"We'll make sure Tice ends up hanging off a hook in a meat locker somewheres."

"Damn right we will." Rink nodded vigorously.

Rink was in his late thirties, a long, skinny guy with a brush cut and a broken nose that headed east, then west. It gave him a kind of distinguished look, like he might have been big in sports — baseball, or maybe a football quarterback. The only trouble was, Rink would never screw up even a little. If you did not sometimes screw up — not fuck up, there was a difference — you did not take chances, which meant you were never going to win when you went up against someone damn good, like Tice.

On the other hand, Rink was a hell of a shot and ruthless when necessary, and he could really drive. And he was loyal. There was a lot to be said for loyalty. For Angelides, it was right up there with being respectful.

He caught Rink looking at him again. "Just drive. It's okay. I'm thinking."

Rink gave a little grin and wheeled the BMW around the corner onto another busy street. Rink looked nice in his sports jacket and pants, Angelides decided. Neat and presentable. He liked the way Rink was watching all around. It gave him a good feeling about Rink and things in general, which meant it was time to face the music. He pulled out his cell. Then he stared at it.

"Are you going to call Mr. G?" Rink asked.

"I told you I was thinking, Rink."

Rink sealed his lips and nodded.

Angelides turned the cell on its side and in the outside light saw E911 printed in white on the black casing. He smiled. This was more like it. That was the code that said the cell contained a GPS chip. Of course, Billy had an identical cell.

He dialed. This time, Mr. G answered quickly. Angelides said soberly, "I got some business to discuss, Mr. Ghranditti. It's mostly good. The one bad part is I found Jay Tice, but he got away. But it's good, too, because he's got that hunter, Cunningham, with him. They were holed up at her town house. We had a little back-and-forth before they took off in her car, and the bottom line is, Cunningham's set up for the murder of one of my men. I left some fresh ID, so he's not gonna be traced back to us. Then I phoned in a tip. The cops are probably there now. Pretty soon her face is gonna be plastered everywhere." No point in bothering Mr. G about the tracker and Billy's gun, which was returned like an insult.

"And the purpose of that?" He did not sound happy.

"Pressure," Angelides said fast. "I pushed Tice deep into a corner. She's an anchor, a real heavy one, slowing him down. And Tice is just enough full of himself that he's helped us by lifting my man's cell, which has got that new GPS technology. Most people think it's only for emergencies — for when you dial nine-one-one and need an ambulance or the police to find you. But that's not true. The chip puts out a signal as long as the cell's turned on. I'm thinking that the hotshot CIA guy you're doing business with knows someone who could read us the cell's location off the satellite. Which means Tice's location." He related Billy's cell number. "If the cell's not on right now, Tice is gonna turn it on eventually. He won't be able to resist."

There was a smile in Mr. G's voice. "Very smart, Mr. Angelides. I congratulate you. Yes, I'll take care of it."

Angelides grinned and said good-bye and hung up. The man was classy. He never yelled or cussed you out. But then, he was also busy. He did not waste time. On the other hand, if you fucked up, he would order you whacked. That was the deal with Hannah Barculo — she had fucked up real bad. Mr. G could not trust her anymore.

Angelides felt a weird something. Fear, maybe. For a moment, his mind translated that into what could happen to him, but he was not going there. Jerry Angelides did not fuck up, and he was not going to — now or ever.

On the Beltway, Virginia

As Elaine drove south through the night, shocked silence filled the car. Billy's heartbreaking plea for his life rang in her ears. Vehicles whipped past at blinding speeds. Red taillights streamed ahead in a bloody river. She was driving too slowly. She pressed the accelerator, her hands gripping the steering wheel as if it were a life preserver. The Jag caught up with traffic, but she kept it in the slow outer lane. She looked everywhere for a Virginia State Police patrol car.

She watched Tice throw the recorder-player into his backpack. Her gaze lingered. The recording inside proved she did not erase Billy.

"That was tough to listen to." She watched the highway and controlled her voice. "It was almost as if we were in the same room while Jerry was murdering Billy. I kept having the feeling I could do something to stop it. I had to remind myself it was too late."

Tice studied her profile. Her mouth was set in a thin line, and her skin was pale. "Your prints are on your Beretta?"

She gave a curt nod. "I'm set up. Care to fill me in on your plans for me?"

"I have complete faith you're not going to give me trouble."

She was silent. She must find a way to escape or report in to Litchfield. "You're in worse trouble now, too," she told him. "Your prints are on the drink glasses. And on the venetian blinds, the doorknobs, the kitchen stool, and God knows what else you handled at my place."

"Your point?"

"You can bet Jerry or one of his people has phoned in a tip. The police will seal off my place and do forensics. They're going to discover you were there. Langley's been keeping your escape quiet, and they can probably control the local cops once they find out — but only for a while. It'd be better for you to turn yourself in now."

"Doubtful. Did you recognize any of the voices or names?"

"No. What about you?"

He shook his head. "Whoever Jerry is, he's not to be taken lightly. He said he reported to someone named Mr. G and that a big deal was going down. Did that mean anything to you?"

"Nothing." And if she knew, she would not tell him. "I suppose it could be drugs, knockoffs, or stolen merchandise of some kind. Or maybe it's perfectly legal. 'Mr. G' is a tantalizing bit of information but worthless without some context." She glanced at

273

him. His expression was thoughtful. "Where do you want me to drive?"

"We'll get to that later. Let's assume I'm telling the truth — that my goal all along has been information. I'll obviously get nothing from Whippet now. At the same time, I'll assume you're telling the truth that you have no idea what the real story is. That means I've got to look elsewhere, and the best candidates are Jerry and his pals. Not only did they know about a highly secret Langley unit, they had the skill to liquidate it and escape. Plus they knew you were hunting me, or they wouldn't have arrived at your place. Sounds to me as if they have a very well informed source somewhere inside the government — maybe inside Langley itself."

She tensed then nodded. It was one more reason to contact only Litchfield.

He seemed to make a decision. He reached into his backpack and removed a Timex wristwatch. He handed it to her. "There are two buttons on the left-hand side. Touch the top one."

She propped it on the steering wheel so she could look at it and watch the traffic. She pressed the button. The watch's face changed. "There's a long series of numbers."

"Right. Keep pushing it."

She did. More numbers. They changed eighteen times before the face returned to a regular LED reading of the hour and minutes.

"Okay, now hit the second button," he told her.

This time, words appeared — OPEN and LOCK. She alternated the buttons. "What does it mean?"

"That's Frank Theosopholis's watch."

She peered at him sharply. "You wiped Theosopholis. The body's been found."

"He followed me through the penitentiary's electronic gates and jumped me before I could get out of the building. I was unarmed. That's when training counts. He was carrying a shank, but I ended up using it on him. I couldn't figure out how he'd managed to come after me, until I examined the watch more closely. Each of those number series controls one of the gates, commanding it to open and relock. There's a subminiature wireless receiver in the watch, too. It looks to me as if the codes reset themselves automatically when the prison computer reset the locks. The other thing is, there was a tracker inside — that's how the first assassin found me. And finally,

Theosopholis was always in the cell next to mine."

"Why would he jump you? Didn't he want to escape, too?"

"He was trying to stop me. I think he'd been planted to keep an eye on me just in case I did try something." He fished in his backpack and this time brought out Billy's cell phone. He put on his glasses and turned it on. The LED light glowed. Pressing buttons, he scowled. "I've been away too long. I should be able to find his phone book in here, right?"

She held out her hand. "You're going to end up erasing whatever's in there."

He laid the cell on her palm and said dryly, "Fun, isn't it — the glamorous life of being on the run from the law."

"Yeah. About as much fun as getting a Brazilian bikini wax."

The corners of his lips twitched toward a smile.

She propped the cell on top of the steering wheel. Checking the traffic, she touched MENU and worked her way through options.

At last she shook her head and handed it back. "Billy may be too dumb to still be alive, but he was smart enough to have password-protected records."

As he took the cell, she peered at him. Traffic lights flashed across his stern features. The cleft in his chin seemed deeper, the planes and angles of his face more acute. His oddly compelling personality, which so easily could turn from warmth to violence, had somehow segued into sincerity. To say he was smooth was an understatement. She wondered why he had bothered to tell her so much — then she knew. He was "enlisting" her, a form of psychological seduction. As insurance, he wanted her on his side. But two could play at that game.

"Want a suggestion?" she said. "Hit REDIAL. That way you'll call whoever he tried to reach last."

"Good idea."

He touched the button and lifted the cell to his ear and gazed at her, his eyes radiating inclusiveness, but she did not believe it for a moment. She softened her face and grinned encouragingly. He was armed, and she was not.

"It's ringing," he told her.

"Good." She checked her rearview mirror, hoping again to spot a state police car.

"Yeah," a man answered.

Tice's pulse quickened — he recognized the voice. He raised his brows at her. "Hello, Jerry. This is your new friend, Jay Tice."

"Tice?" Jerry asked. "What the fuck? How did you — !"

"I know it's late," Tice said, "but I hope you're not too tired to talk." There was a stunned emptiness in Tice's ear.

The tones were suddenly hearty: "Sure, buddy. Great idea. Where are you? How about a drink? We can talk face-to-face. You've been on my mind a lot lately."

"It's mutual. Actually, I've been thinking about Mr. G, too. Sad that he's so pissed at me."

Again there was a pause, as if Jerry were trying to figure out how Tice knew the nickname of his boss, much less that he might have an attitude about Jay Tice. "Well, Jay — you don't mind if I call you Jay, do you? Sure seems like I know you well enough to call you Jay. That's it — Jay and Jerry. So, Jay, it's not like I'd say Mr. G is pissed. No, I wouldn't go that far at all. It's more like he's a busy man, so he has to turn over certain responsibilities to me. Right now, you're my responsibility. Bottom line, Mr. G's thoughts on the matter are none of your damn business. But, hey, I'm glad you called. How's Cunningham? You ice her yet?"

"Had to, Jerry," he lied. "Very sad. I know you understand. But as you pointed out, one has one's responsibilities. Couldn't let Cunningham live. Besides, you know the type. No respect."

She shot him a look.

"Boy oh boy!" Jerry sounded impressed. "Do I *ever* know the type. So now you're all alone?"

"You got it."

He remembered Jerry's words: *Then where would Mr. G be? He's got that big deal, and no way he stands for these fuckups.* In negotiation, a prime rule was to use what you knew and plumb for weakness.

Jerry was protective of his boss, so Tice made his voice sympathetic as he threw out bait: "What's this I hear about Mr. G's being in real serious financial trouble? A man like you, someone with your brains and ability, might want to consider looking for a new job. That new deal of his is all over the grapevine, you know. It's falling apart. It's going into the dumper fast, which means he's going into the dumper. And you'll go with him."

"Like hell it's going into the dumper," he said indignantly. "Mr. G's fine. Whatever made you think —"

Tice had hit a nerve. "We both know how hard it is to pull a deal like that together. The word's out he's an amateur."

"Not Mr. G! Who says that? He's been doing this for years. He's at the top. He's the best in the business." But there was a faint inflection of uncertainty.

"As I said, the word's out, Jerry. You've got a lousy hand. Mr. G's a loser. Your reputation's about to take a serious hit. Consider working for one of his competitors. In fact," Tice said casually, "consider working for me."

Jerry's voice was a growl, going on the offensive. "I heard you did a lot of shady business. I heard you sold out on a lot of things. Make a lot of money, Jay? Didn't do you any good, did it, 'cause you aren't good enough to stay out of the joint. *You* fucked up big-time. I'm getting the picture. Well, let me tell you, Mr. G's deal is closing tomorrow right on schedule, so you're way behind the curve. Guess you'd like to know where I am and how we know that right now you're on the Beltway real close to Falls Church. In fact, hey — not that I want to worry you — be sure to keep yourself alert, 'cause my boys will be there any second. My driver's on his cell right now with a guy who's got the scoop. I hate fuckups, Jay. I really do. They're disgusting no-goods who're wasting the planet's real estate. That's you. Be sure to wave hello to me and my boys. Thanks for calling. I'll let Mr. G know you send your worst. *Sayonara*, Jay. *Arrivederci*. Go to hell, *buddy*."

Silence filled Tice's ear, while he remembered "Mr. G's deal is closing tomorrow" and "He's been doing this for years. . . . He's the best in the business." Whoever the man was, and whatever the deal was, there might not be enough time to stop it. With a flick of his finger, he turned off the cell.

"What did he say?" Elaine asked instantly.

"Looks as if the deal's illegal, and it's closing tomorrow. No more details than that." Gun in hand, he swiveled to face her. "We may have trouble. Jerry claims he's got someone reading our location. He and his people are on their way. If that's true, how in hell did they manage it?"

"It makes no sense." Still, she checked her mirrors and floored the gas in a swift kick-down. The Jag shot forward like a missile, driving them into their seats. She looked eagerly around for a state police car.

"You can believe it now. We've got company." He angled so he could study more closely a black sedan — a powerful Lincoln — that had broken out of traffic and swung into the lane behind them. It was coming up fast.

She immediately moved the car left, into

the next lane. The Lincoln's nose made a sudden rush to squeeze in behind again. She swore loudly and braked. At the last second, the Lincoln swerved away, tires squealing, barely missing the Jag's fender.

"That was too close." She exhaled.

But already the Lincoln was speeding again, catching up. Tice lowered his window. As it opened, so did the driver's-side window of the other car. Fresh air blasted through the Jag. The sudden din of engines and churning tires was explosive.

Tice raised his voice to make sure she heard: "The guy's armed. He was part of the assassination squad that took out Whippet, too. Get us out of here!"

20

Elaine studied the rushing Beltway. There were so many cars that gunshots could cause a catastrophic multiple-car crash. As the muzzle of a pistol extended from the Lincoln, she spun the steering wheel, moving into the next lane and the next, increasing speed.

"Here comes another car!" Tice warned.

Pulse throbbing, Elaine whipped the Jaguar in and out of the lanes as the two janitors' cars jockeyed, following. The second car was a green Olds, about six years old but with a powerful engine. In her rearview mirror she spotted a third car.

Her breath caught in her throat. "There's the BMW. Jerry's here. Behind us."

"I see it. Now he'll know I lied about wiping you." His smile was arctic. "Guess he won't trust me anymore. I can see Jerry in the passenger seat. It's just him and the same guy who drove them to your place."

"The BMW's a fast car. Its speed is comparable to the Jag's."

Quickly she took stock. The Jag's computerized suspension felt elastic, as always, and the engine was running smooth and hushed, purring. It could be pushed hard and securely to its governed speed of 130 miles an hour, which meant she probably had a mechanical and horsepower edge over at least two of the cars. What she had hoped was to slip out of sight then find an open stretch and outrun all of them.

Checking her mirrors, she pulled the Jag in behind a Ford SUV, then over in front of a Dodge muscle pickup, accelerating to eighty miles an hour. The Jag's engine rose to a happy growl.

She could see none of the pursuing cars. "I'm going to move again."

As Tice scanned tensely, she paced the next lane, where a blocky Hummer was pulling away from a chic Lexus. She had been studying both. As soon as she slid the Jag into the pocket, the Lexus, which had been rolling along inattentively, its eight-cylinder engine hardly breaking a sweat, accelerated and closed in on the Jag's rear, protecting its tail as she had hoped. The Dodge pickup, which had been going much faster earlier, caught the competitive spirit and put on a burst of speed, riding the rear bumper of a new Chevy, which was to the right of the Jag's grille. A Volvo and a Mustang and a Mercedes protected the Jag's other side. The Hummer continued to lead, its blunt nose creating a ragged slipstream.

The pack of eight vehicles tore through the night at eighty-five miles an hour, a lethal cavalcade of rushing steel and glass. The Jag was in the center, concealed. The steering wheel felt alive in her hands.

"Jerry's found us again," Tice said sharply.

Her rib cage contracted. As if by magic, the BMW had reappeared. It was two lanes over, Rink peering around, angling for a clear shot or a way to break through. This was the second time she had hidden the Jag then been found.

"I can't shake him," she said worriedly. "Rink seems to know where we are no matter what I do."

"They've definitely tagged us. But how?" He grabbed the dead man's cell from his backpack. "This is the only thing I took from Billy. Could there be a tracker in it? Maybe Jerry put trackers in all of his men's cells to keep tabs on them."

"We don't need it anyway. Get rid of it!" Then she knew. "Wait a minute! Is E911 stamped anywhere on it? Is it turned on? Look fast!"

"Yes, the power's on." He flipped it over and saw the white lettering. "Here's E911. What does it mean?"

"It means we're screwed. Toss it!" As he lowered his window and flung it out, she described the chip inside that enabled satellite tracking. "I could disable it, but I'd need time to figure it out. And you're right — there could be a tracker in it, too. Either way, that's how they found us."

"Can you get us away again?"

"That's the plan."

The Hummer had peeled off and exited. Ahead was a Cadillac. She flicked on her high beams. As if whacked in the butt, the Cadillac shot forward. She touched her gas pedal, keeping pace. Now that they were running faster, space opened on her right again. She shifted lanes and hit her high beams and moved again. She was nearing ninety miles an hour.

"If we stay clean," she decided, "I'll get off at the Little River Turnpike exit. I don't see any of our tails, do you?"

He craned. "Maybe you lost them."

"Dammit, the BMW's back." She checked the side-view mirror on Tice's door. Fleet and aerodynamic, the BMW was in the next lane, back about thirty feet. Too close.

"We're getting near the exit ramp," he warned.

She urged the Jag onward, weaving from lane to lane again, praying the other drivers knew what they were doing. But no matter what she tried, the BMW stayed with her. Swearing, she hurtled past the exit.

An idea occurred to her. It was risky, but it might work. "The Braddock Road exit is next. I'm going to try something."

"What?"

"It's too complicated to explain." She changed lanes swiftly, easing over to where there were only two lanes between the Jag and the exit. She inhaled, hoping — no, dammit, the BMW was still following. She must wait, be patient. She touched the gas feed and lifted her foot, accelerating and decelerating as she studied the speed of the cars in the slower outer lanes.

"Elaine!"

His warning was too late. She had been watching for Beltway signs, ignoring the BMW. The bullet blasted through the support between the Jag's side windows. Bits of metal exploded. She ducked.

Don't think about it. There was the exit. "Brace yourself," she snapped.

Tice grabbed the handgrip above his head.

As a second bullet slammed through, she gazed right and turned the steering wheel hard, holding it. Like an arrow, the car shot across the lanes inches between vehicles, leaving a trail of screaming horns and squealing tires. At the last second she slammed the brakes and slid the car neatly sideways onto the Braddock Road ramp, tires screeching.

Tice whipped his head around. "I see him. You've outmaneuvered him."

Her adrenaline pulsed like lava. She glanced over. The BMW was fleeing helplessly onward, trapped in an inner lane.

"We're not safe yet," he said. "Jerry will tell his people where we got off."

She slowed the car as the first intersection appeared. Despite the red light, she checked both ways and turned left. The car swept past large trees and flowering bushes. A mile later she drove into a McDonald's parking lot and out the rear and into a mixed residential-commercial area, putting distance between them and main thoroughfares.

She checked him. Then stared. "You're bleeding." Blood trickled down his right cheek, probably from one of the flying metal shards.

"You're bleeding, too. It's beading along

strands of your hair." He stared down a side street. "There's a car with a California license plate back there. Go around the block and park. Jerry will have his men looking for plates from around here, not from the West Coast. Do you feel okay?"

"Absolutely." She circled the block, noting the street signs, and neatly parallel parked. A plan was forming in her mind.

"Hold still." He checked her eyes. "Pupil size is normal. No concussion. Turn your head." He parted her hair away from her scalp. "The cuts look superficial."

More enlistment — plus the added element of compassion. His tool bag of psychological tricks was bottomless. "Told you. Let me see you." The only cut was on his cheek. "It's a scratch. We both got off lucky." She hoped he remembered he had crushed her Langley cell phone and so would leave her shoulder bag in the car again when he got out. Since he had to remove plates before attaching them to the Jag, she should have time to make one fast call.

"Turn off the engine and give me the keys." He picked up his backpack. "I'll be right back."

She scowled. She wanted him to think he had caught on to her plan to drive off again — but at the same time she did not want to look as if she were eager to get rid of him. He stared at her. At last, she broke eye contact, killed the engine, and handed him the keys, making a show of doing it reluctantly.

He snatched them and got out.

From inside the dark car, she watched as he ran across the street, carrying his backpack, pocketing the keys. She dove into her shoulder bag. The cell phone he had destroyed was the one issued by Langley. She still had her personal cell zipped inside an interior pocket. By the time he was crouched at the other car's front license plate, she had retrieved it and taken a North Virginia road map from the glove compartment. She bent over the map, pretending to read it, as she punched in the numbers Laurence Litchfield had given her during their interview.

The phone rang three times before he picked up. Although the Jag was buffered for sound, she cupped her hand around the mouthpiece: "Mr. Litchfield, this is Elaine Cunningham."

"Cunningham!" His voice escalated from shock to excitement: "I tried to call earlier, but I couldn't get through. Where are you? Are you all right?"

"I don't have much time. I'm with Jay

Tice. The reason you couldn't reach me is he smashed my cell. First, I want you to know I didn't kill the man in my town house."

"I couldn't imagine you had. We'll straighten it out later. I'll send people for Tice. Where are you?"

She gave him the cross streets of the block. "He's armed — my Walther, his SIG Sauer, and a Browning. All nine-millimeter. We're in my car — a red Jaguar. It's going to have California license plates in about five minutes." She read the number to him just before Tice pulled off the front plate. "I drive. He rides in the passenger seat beside me. But there's something else. Whippet —"

"Hold on."

As the phone muted, she watched Tice jog around the California car and squat at the rear plate. Her hands were sweaty. She rubbed the palm of one then the other on her pants. *Hurry up. Hurry up.* She pressed the phone deeper into her ear.

At last Litchfield was back. "I ordered your location run through the computer. We've found a stretch of country road outside Manassas where there's farmland, no houses. We'll be able to capture him there without alerting the world. It'll be a drive for you, but I need time to get a team into place anyway. Arrive no sooner than an hour." He gave her directions.

She memorized them. "What will happen?"

"It's good that you're driving. If Tice notices our cars closing in, pretend to drive away, escape. But in the end, let our cars trap yours between them. He may have three guns, but he'll have only one free hand if he uses you as a shield. I'll send our best sharpshooters." He hesitated. "Can you handle it?"

Her throat was suddenly dry. She swallowed. "Of course. He has to be sent back to prison. But I'll warn you — he's as dangerous as he ever was."

"I believe you. I received your first message. Have you learned anything more?"

She watched Tice stand erect. He held two license plates in one hand, his backpack in the other. "A few things. Tice claims Whippet tried to scrub him and Palmer Westwood —" Tice broke into a jog, heading toward the Jag. "He's coming."

She cut the power and zipped the cell phone back inside her shoulder bag and bent again over the road map. As she listened to the small sounds of his attaching the new plates, she studied the map, following Litchfield's directions. They were good, and now she had them solidly in her mind. She checked her wristwatch for the exact time. With luck, soon Jay Tice would be in Langley custody.

21

Geneva, Switzerland

Raina Manhardt's last words of warning had shaken Raoul Harmont, and the dawn streets of Old Town had done nothing to dispel his unease. But now that he was safe in his study at the top of his narrow four-story house, he exulted. He counted his money again and leaned back with a satisfied smile, his hands folded over his paunch. Selling her the videotapes was the kind of business deal he liked — 100 percent profit.

He was so pleased that he laughed aloud. Then frowned. Had he heard the *click* of the latch to the door that opened onto his balcony?

Impossible. Still, he spun around in his desk chair. "Who . . . ? What . . . ?"

A man stepped inside, aiming a pistol with a very long sound suppressor. Harmont stared at the weapon, horrified, mesmerized.

"What was in the box of chocolates?" The man's French accent was excellent, but there was a slight American inflection.

Harmont licked his dry lips and looked up past the broad chest and the heavy shoulders to the muscular face.

"What . . . what chocolates?" Harmont tried.

But before he could move, the tall man took two swift steps and slashed the gun across his face. Blood spurted. Pain exploded.

"Stop!" Harmont shrieked and lifted his hands.

The man batted them aside and struck again.

A tooth shattered. Blood poured. "Tapes of the lobbies!" Harmont screamed. "Surveillance videos —"

"The entrances to the Milieu Software building?"

Harmont nodded frantically as his fingers smeared the blood across his cheeks. His mouth flamed with pain.

"Originals?"

"C-copies." His right eye was swelling shut.

"I'll take the originals. Where are they?"

Harmont felt a surge of hope. He squinted his good eye and opened his desk drawer.

"Here. She paid two thousand. The originals will cost you five."

The American laughed loudly. "Really?" Still laughing, he grabbed Harmont's collar and dragged him from his chair and out onto the balcony.

Terrified, Harmont struggled. "What are you doing? *No!* Just *one* thousand francs!" He felt his feet leave the balcony's floor. Felt himself thrust into space. "Take them!" he begged. "You can *have* them! Take them . . . *take them . . .* !"

Too late. Screeching, Harmont flailed and dropped through the air.

Langley, Virginia

Pleased with himself, Laurence Litchfield hurried down the quiet seventh-floor corridor. All of his carefully laid groundwork had paid off. Elaine Cunningham had finally called again, and now Martin Ghranditti's killers were on their way to a blood rendezvous with Cunningham and Jay Tice.

He savored the triumph as he turned into a small conference room where three analysts on the graveyard shift were sitting at the table, file folders and cans of diet soda at their elbows as they stared at the TV that hung from a wall. A sense of urgency mixed with camaraderie filled the room.

Tuned to the Qatar-based satellite channel al-Jazeera, the TV showed a woman wearing a *khimar,* a head scarf, sitting behind a desk as she read an editorial, each word radiating righteous anger. A translation streamed across the bottom of the screen: ". . . the Great Satan's goal is to occupy the Middle East. They started a cruel war to get our oil and expand their military empire, and now Allah's punishing them. They have created what they said they wanted to stop — outstretched hands among al-Qaeda and jihadists around the globe. Muslims who doubted us now fight with us. . . ."

"Nothing's changed on al-Jazeera, I see," Litchfield said cheerfully as he took the empty chair waiting for him at the head of the table. He stretched out his legs and crossed his ankles and smiled to himself.

Reg O'Toole raised a remote control and turned off the set. His black face was smoothly shaved, his eyes bright and alert. But then, it was daytime in half the world. "You'd think they'd be as bored with using 'Great Satan' as we are of hearing it," he grumbled. "I liked it when bin Laden started calling us a snake."

"You would," said Geraldine Genowicz. "No dignity. Hey, 'Great Satan' works like any known brand. We're Tide detergent. We're Ford cars. Of course they went back to using it. They ring the bell, and Pavlov's dog drools." She was in her early thirties, with braces on her teeth and freckles sprinkled across her nose.

"So what have you got for me?" Litchfield said, interrupting the exchange. Langley analysts and operatives were hired because they were among the best brains in the country, but along with that came a certain amount of anarchy.

"Some good intel," said David Quintano. In his early fifties, he was the senior of the three. He slid his reading glasses down from his forehead to his nose as he consulted his file folder. "As you know, one bomb exploded yesterday in front of the U.S. Embassy in London, killing two Brits and a U.S. Marine. A second bomb didn't — and that was a real break for us, because it was connected to a cell phone. We tracked the cell's SIM card to a Muslim bookstore in the East End. The owner had bought a whole box of SIMs. We didn't have him arrested, so he wouldn't know we were on to him. NSA has been tracking the SIMs, listening in on conversations."

Litchfield sat up straight. "That's interesting."

"There's more," Genowicz said. Her expression was sober, her freckles standing out like peppercorns against her rosy skin. "Pakistani intelligence arrested two men in Peshawar before they could destroy a half-dozen CDs, most made recently. The discs contain details about future operations as well as the usual how-to instructions for making bombs, acquiring passports, stealing credit cards, and so forth. Plus some phone numbers that've turned out to be important."

"My turn," O'Toole said. "Toronto Customs arrested a woman flying in from Hong Kong on a forged South African passport. We've been targeting those passport holders because hard-core jihadists are increasing enlistments of non-Arab recruits on the theory they're less suspicious. Then they give them forged South African passports so they'll have visa-free entry into a lot of countries. Her suitcase had a false lining, and inside it was a sheet of paper covered in coded text. It was a photocopy — I'm not kidding — probably made in a mud hut in the wilds between Afghanistan and Pakistan or China, but nevertheless a photocopy. NSA just finished decrypting it. It's from Osama bin Laden himself. He's quit using electronic communications because he's afraid we'll find him. That's why the courier."

The three glanced at one another.

"I'm waiting," Litchfield said impatiently. Then he knew: "The Majlis al-Sha'b?"

"Yes, sir," O'Toole said, his expression grim. "At last."

Over the past year, Litchfield's sources had picked up clues that a new umbrella network was forming. Called the Majlis al-Sha'b, it seemed to be an outgrowth of a threatening development — a new high command uniting the Shiite Muslims of Hezbollah and the Islamic Republic of Iran with the Sunnis of HAMAS and the Palestine Islamic Jihad. The Sunni-Shiite alliance, although uneasy and not all-inclusive, bridged a bitter historic divide as well as merging Arab nationalists with Jihad, Inc.

Quintano shoved his glasses back up to his forehead. "We've put together a clearer picture of what's going on. From the phone conversations NSA's been picking up off the cells with those SIM cards, it's clear al-Qaeda realizes it's failed to achieve its strategic goal of a real political uprising in the Islamic world — so far. Bin Laden's dream of a new caliphate is for all practical purposes on the back burner, and al-Qaeda's morale is tanking."

Litchfield nodded. "But the United States hasn't achieved our basic goal, either. We still can't guarantee our security against another attack. In fact, we still can't confirm whether or not al-Qaeda has weapons of mass destruction."

"Right," Quintano agreed. "But the momentum's with us. Because the Middle East believes we're obsessed with al-Qaeda, each country is worried we'll become obsessed with it, too — like we did with Afghanistan and Iraq. That's why Muslim intelligence agencies have been cooperating with us against al-Qaeda. That's why Syria capitulated publicly when we told them to get out of Lebanon. Of course, they still have huge intelligence resources there — they're just buried deeper. All of them think our bad mood's irrational, but it's made them very nervous about crossing us." He peered across the table to Genowicz.

"This is where I come in," she told Litchfield. "The CDs that the Pakistanis confiscated show the jihadists are finding it more and more difficult to mount another big assault. They've researched for years, and they've got the plans, but the West's security is tougher, and it's blanketing their top targets. NSA's been monitoring the active phone numbers listed on the CDs, too.

They've been hearing a lot of whining and asking Allah for help. So while we're closing in on our goal, al-Qaeda's falling behind in theirs. At the moment, they're losing the war." She peered at Quintano.

Quintano turned to Litchfield. "So bin Laden's decided to do something radical about it. As you know, a new breed of holy warrior emerged after 9/11 when we disrupted his control over al-Qaeda. According to the paper hidden in the woman's suitcase, bin Laden looked around and decided that of all the groups, the Majlis were strongest, largest, and most directed — and they'd take his vision to the next level. So the paper concludes with his statement officially passing leadership from al-Qaeda to them. He's sent a copy to each of the Majlis leaders, which means at least one must be hiding somewhere in Canada or the United States. We're searching now."

O'Toole warned, "The Majlis has mutated into a bigger movement more frightening than al-Qaeda. They're technologically more savvy, more worldly, more elusive, and younger. They've replaced a lot of bin Laden's religious and ideological restrictions with broader interpretations that target everyone who's not an Islamic fundamentalist. And that means fellow Muslims, too. At the same time, the Majlis are thoroughly trained to lead double lives. When they want to, they blend into Western culture smoothly."

"They've learned from al-Qaeda's mistakes while carrying on their strengths," Genowicz concluded, her voice low and worried.

The room was silent. Litchfield looked at the grave faces. "What's the organization of the Majlis like?"

"NSA's transcripts indicate it's not a council in the sense that they get up in the morning and have a conference call to figure out which civilians they're going to hit next," O'Toole said. "They're more like a cabal. They're going in the same direction, understand what direction they're going in, and work independently or together as needed. It really *is* a 'People's Assembly,' but not a democracy. Each of the leaders comes with his own network. Together, they call the shots. They want to keep the nature of their group amorphous so they can expand without us interfering."

Litchfield asked impatiently, "Where's their headquarters? How often do they meet? Exactly how many leaders and networks are there? *Who* are they?"

Around the table, shoulders slumped.

O'Toole looked Litchfield in the eye. "We don't know yet, but we will."

"They scare the crap out of us," Genowicz admitted.

Litchfield nodded to himself. One didn't need political influence or a superpower's financial resources or even military bases girdling the globe to plant bombs or take hostages or send commercial airliners into skyscrapers. Terrorism was a thinking man's game. An al-Qaeda squad of just twenty men armed with only box cutters had pulled off 9/11 in attacks so brilliantly conceived, scrupulously planned, and sensitive to the levers of global power that they had changed the world. If the Majlis were even smarter than al-Qaeda, God help everyone.

"Mr. Litchfield?" The voice came from the door. It was his assistant, Ron Wenceslao. Worry lines etched his forehead. "From what we can figure out, whoever wiped Whippet turned off the electricity, so we didn't get any video of the wet squad. But the upside is that Elaine Cunningham ordered a ForeTell assessment of Jay Tice." He flashed a CD. "It's all here, and some of it looks interesting."

Before Wenceslao had finished the sentence, Litchfield was on his feet. There was nothing more to learn here anyway.

"Thanks, Ron. I'll relieve you of that." He took the CD and peered back into the room. "Look harder. Let me know as soon as you have anything." Carrying the CD in an iron grip, he hurried off.

Paris, France

Since returning to Paris, Gerhard Shoutens had been unable to stop thinking about the awful moments before Kristoph skied off the sheer couloir at Chaux de Mont. He replayed the scene endlessly in his mind. The hiss of the snow under their skis, the bite of the cold air in the crystal sunlight, the soaring exhilaration as they flashed past tall firs and down the trail that rimmed the couloir. And then Kristoph's abrupt jerk and his enraged bellow as he flew off into the void.

Haunted by it all, Gerhard was hunched in his Windbreaker and still wandering the streets as the eastern sky brightened into morning. Cafés and shops opened, and vans disgorged fragrant baguettes and croissants. He walked aimlessly, his mind hundreds of miles away in the mountains of Switzerland with his doomed friend.

When Kristoph's loud bellow echoed through his mind for perhaps the ten thousandth time, it suddenly changed. Gerhard stopped in his tracks. He was on the Petit Pont, the "Little Bridge." Beneath his feet, the Seine flowed around pilings. He had no recollection of having arrived here.

What riveted him was the few seconds before Kristoph flew off the rim. In his mind, Gerhard listened and watched, concentrating as he stared blindly down at the dark waters. Then he knew: Kristoph had uttered a small surprised cry of pain before — by no more than a second, but definitely *before.* It was as if something had struck him. And his skis had not swerved to avoid an obstacle but lifted up and left the snow an inch or so, definitely airborne. Then came the bellow, overwhelming the small cry.

Gerhard stiffened. Kristoph's death had been no accident. He was sure now. Something had hit him that was so painful he cried out, so powerful it knocked him into the air. No wonder he was unable to stop his rush into the abyss. But what had caused it? There was no gunshot, nothing unusual at all.

He must phone Frau Manhardt to let her know. Patting his pockets, he cursed his absentmindedness and hurried back toward his apartment for his cell phone. Sickened, furious, he reached boulevard Saint-

Germain, hardly noticing the thunder of morning traffic.

As he rushed along the curb, his side abruptly exploded in pain. He cried out reflexively, and his feet left the sidewalk. It was almost as if a giant had driven a sledgehammer into him. Instantly he knew — this was what had happened to Kristoph. And he was just as helpless. With a furious yell, he dropped into the path of a city bus that had no room to swerve and no time to stop.

Blinding light erupted inside his mind. Horns blared. Brakes screamed. Too late. The bus hurtled into him, snapped his neck, and the darkness of death enveloped him.

Some twenty yards away, a tall man wearing a belted trench coat turned casually and ambled off, sliding what looked like a large flashlight into his pocket.

22

On the Road, Virginia

Controlling her nervousness, Elaine looked up from the road map as Tice slid in next to her. The suburban street remained quiet. Black shadows and bright moonlight created a high-contrast monochrome of parked cars, grassy lawns, and houses.

"Finished." Browning in hand, he closed the door and dropped his backpack at his feet. "The bullet holes in the car don't look too bad. Maybe we'll be able to pick up colored putty to make them less noticeable." He returned her car keys.

She started the engine. *Act natural.* "Jags consider putty sacrilegious. They like solid steel and burled hardwood."

He nodded noncommittally. "You did a damn good job of driving."

She nodded back. "You're welcome." She sped off and turned the car west.

She glanced at him as he arranged himself

in his seat so that his back was against the door again, his left leg up. He kept watch alertly. His short gray hair shone in the lights of a passing car.

Without making him suspicious, she must rendezvous with Litchfield's secret Langley team. She did not allow herself to think ahead to the peril of the pseudochase or to how Tice would react. For a moment she had a disorienting sense of remoteness, as if she were a stranger, some person she no longer knew, stepping off a precipitous brink.

"Correct me if I'm wrong," she said evenly, "but I've got a feeling there's someplace you want to go, and you'd probably like to be certain Jerry and his animals won't follow or find you there."

From the corners of her eyes, she watched him pin his keen gaze on her.

"So I figure I'll keep driving awhile to make sure we've really lost them," she continued, "then you can tell me where to take you."

He studied her profile. The photo e-mailed to him with her background information had been only a year old. In it, her hair was pulled back, probably in a ponytail low on her neck, like the one she wore now, but so tight against her scalp that she looked severe, puritanical, at best a mousy intellectual. There had been no hint of her sense of humor. In person, she was younger and far prettier. Of one thing he was sure — she did not trust him, which made it impossible for him to move swiftly and invisibly. He had to decide what to do about her.

"Good idea," he agreed, buying time.

She stopped the Jag at a red light and read the street signs. "Why did you do it, Jay?" she asked quietly.

His hand flexed on the grip of his Browning. Rage oozed from his pores. For an instant, the cool night air inside the car's steel skin felt molten.

"You don't conform to the usual profile," she went on. "You're no misfit or failure. There's no indication you needed or wanted more than your usual Langley salary. You spied for Russia, but you're not Russian, and you never indicated you thought their political system was better than ours. So how about indulging me? Help me to understand." Earlier he had masked his fury with a disarming smile. Not this time.

He could feel the tension in his jaw, the heat of his outrage in his stare. "After my arrest, I had to talk about it endlessly. There were reasons, and they're no one's damn business." Memories flashed through his mind, unhappy signposts in a dark, morally ambiguous past. "Years ago, a mentor told me operatives with too many regrets tended to end up dead. To be effective, you had to get on with it. So I did. But along the way I collected a Mount Everest of regrets — you can interpret that any way you want. There's an Italian proverb I like —'After the game, the king and the pawn go into the same box.' We all die — rich and poor, good or bad or indifferent. Until then, we have choices. I made choices, and now my future's limited. Don't look at me like that. It's reality. I've been marked by the people behind Jerry. I want my life to mean something again, but I may not have much time."

"What you're saying is you want your life to mean something to *you* again."

"That's right."

"It's a different truth."

"Fair enough." His wrath was easing. "This isn't about proving I'm better than anyone thinks. Frankly, I'd rather you weren't here, although you've shown you have your uses. But if we don't come to some kind of agreement, I'll have to drop you off, and the chances are good Jerry will find and scrub you. Or I'll let you stay, and something will happen, but you'll be in the way and get hurt because I can't trust you enough to inform you fully. This is my roundabout way of saying I'd like you to work with me instead of against me. At least until this mess is cleaned up. Another truce."

She remembered his file, everything she had learned about him. He not only manipulated human frailty, he used it as a lethal weapon. His "warmth and compassion" were "unusually persuasive," and he "steeped himself in every detail" of his target until the target "began to believe he cared." *B*efriend. *A*ssess. *R*ecruit. Then he owned you, or he did his damnedest to make sure you believed he did.

As soon as the light turned green, she hit the gas pedal, sending the Jaguar off again into the night.

Time passed. He waited patiently.

Finally she said neutrally, "You're asking a lot."

"Goddammit, Elaine!" he exploded. "If you still think you're going to capture me or get away long enough to report me, you're crazy! In the first place, you can count on Jerry's dirty pal inside the government — inside Langley, is my guess — already being on the alert for any contact from you. In the second place, there's no way they can let you live now, even if you and I aren't together. You've seen too much. There's no choice — they've got to scrub you. Here's the hard truth: I don't have time for a prisoner. Either you pull your weight, or I've got to get rid of you. Something big is going down. *Huge.* Someone needs to find out what that is!"

"I don't have a lot of reason to trust you." They would soon pass the outskirts of Fairfax Station. Still on track to the meet.

"I could easily have left you to Jerry's 'tender mercies' at your town house. I could've personally wiped you long ago."

"Okay, then. Let's run a test. Tell me about your escape. Allenwood's a fortress — more security than a beehive has stings. But when you slipped out, no one noticed. Your dossier shows you habitually premeditate and plan carefully. But you were a recluse in prison, except for the occasional communication with your lawyer. I'm inclined to think you found an angel — or a devil — inside."

He raised an eyebrow. "When you're undercover, you can't be sure when you'll need a safety net. Someday your life may depend on it. Decades ago, I set up small numbered accounts. Completely secret. I suggest you do the same."

"We had satellite photos of Allenwood.

You were never outdoors."

"Ah, yes. But if one moves from a building's loading door into a van's door in one step, one is exposed to overhead observation only a fraction of a second. And if one wears the driver's cap, there's no red flag to draw IMINT's attention."

She scowled. "There's a reason you escaped when you did — not next week or next month. It couldn't have been to uncover some government skunk or a big illegal deal, because you didn't know about either. Neither of us did. No, it was the death of Raina Manhardt's son. That's the trigger. But you haven't mentioned it."

He frowned, trying to figure out how she knew.

"You took the front section of the *Herald Tribune* with you," she told him. "Just the front section. There was only one article in it that connected to you."

Jesus. She did not miss much. "Okay, you're partly correct. I knew her in Berlin, and I was fond of her son. I suspect there's more to his skiing accident."

"You *suspect?* Come on, Jay. If I play, the first rule is you've got to level with me. No holding back. I want everything you know or deduce or guess. I need a lot of very compelling reasons to throw in my lot with a traitor. Tell me about Raina Manhardt."

"You say you expect me to play fair," he shot back. "Then it's your turn. A trade. Tell me about your husband and why you've been such a troublemaker since he died."

She stiffened.

"As I recall, he was in the Special Activities Division," he prompted. The CIA's elite undercover paramilitary could deploy faster than Army Special Forces. Just two weeks after 9/11, they slipped into Afghanistan. With greenbacks in saddlebags and large steel suitcases, they rode horses and rusty trucks into the backcountry to track down tribal warlords and trade bundles of cash for information about enemy troop positions, armaments, communications, and command structures. They had been remarkably successful.

She moistened her lips. "Yes. A paramilitary officer." In an instant, it was late November 2001. Snow veiled the steep slopes of the Tora Bora. Wiry and intense, Rafe was huddled with Afghan soldiers near a broken Soviet T-55 tank. In his thick beard, he looked just like them, his wool *pakol* hat pulled down to one ear in their dashing way. But when he spotted her, his windburned face opened in a smile that turned the gray, bitter day into summer and told her everything she needed to know — he was still her Rafe. She had just arrived to work on the critical hunt for Osama bin Laden.

She took a deep breath. "The day I got to the Tora Bora, we caught a *mujahid* who claimed to cook for bin Laden. He described the cave where bin Laden was holed up. It was consistent with our intel and only a half hour away, but the *muj* said bin Laden planned to move out by dusk. We had only a couple of hours. So I told Rafe and the Afghans to go ahead. I'd get Special Forces backup. At that point, there was no commander on the scene above the rank of lieutenant colonel."

He nodded. "I remember."

"So they took off on horseback. The Special Forces captain wanted to send support, but he didn't have a specific mission order. So he had to ask the light colonel, and the light colonel crawled up Central Command. No one made a decision. While I was yelling at them to help Rafe anyway, two Russian choppers flew in from the direction of Pakistan and landed near the cave. Within minutes they were back in the air, returning the way they'd come — loaded with people. I radioed Rafe to say it was too late — get the hell out of there —

but a hundred al-Qaeda had jumped them. I could hear the automatic fire across the slopes at the same time it was coming over the radio. It was . . . horrible. Then Rafe got shot. He was in a lot of pain, but he held on long enough to tell me a *muj* was saying we'd tortured the cook until he talked, but bin Laden had escaped because Allah had given him wings." It felt as if a shard of glass were caught in her throat. "Rafe was signing off when he was shot again. That bullet killed him. All of our Alliance Afghans were killed, too."

"And you're the one who told them to go ahead. You'd take care of everything."

She said nothing, continuing to drive, chin up, tears streaming down her cheeks.

He remembered a box of tissues. He fumbled around and dug it out from beside his seat. She grabbed a wad and dried her cheeks and swiped at her eyes.

He said, "You think one of the Eastern Alliance people warned al-Qaeda?"

She blew her nose. "The Afghans switched sides a lot, so yes, probably. If Command had backed us, we could've got bin Laden. And nobody tortured that cook. We fed him. We'd been able to cut off their food supplies, and he was hungry."

Tice was silent. Her eyes were puffy and

red. She seemed drained and terribly sad. She peered across at him as if to see whether he really had stuck it out with her. Their gazes met. Unexpectedly, vulnerability passed between them. It was only a moment, but the exposure was jarring.

They looked away quickly.

He sat motionless, unnerved. *What have you done?* The voice was inside his mind before he could stop it. It was always the same accusation. Marie. Mariette. Aaron. Kristoph. He could not bring himself to look at her.

The silence lengthened until finally he said, "It was arrogant of you to send them after bin Laden, but it was also their choice to go without official support. You showed confidence and an ability to see a job that needed to be done. You did the right thing. And now you're facing another tough decision — you know we've got to trust each other."

The car felt too small to her, claustrophobic. *He's pretending "warmth and compassion." He doesn't mean it.* She braked as they approached a stoplight. Ahead, farmland rolled off on one side of the black road where leafy trees made shadowy mounds in the fields. She read the intersection's signs and hid a cold smile. They were only ten miles from the Langley team.

"That's them!" Rink whacked the steering wheel in triumph. He turned on the BMW's engine. "Look! You can see the Jag plain as day. We've got them now!"

Jerry Angelides sat tensely while excitement prickled his skin. His two Colts — his and Billy's — waited in his lap. He had a funny feeling, like a spring sunburn. Like the traffic light turned red just so the Jag would have to stop and they could positively ID it. Things were looking up. His four cars were ready.

When the light turned green, and the Jag sped off, he snapped, "Don't lose her, but stay back!"

Rink pressed the gas pedal. As they followed, Angelides dialed his cell. He would put all of the cars on a conference call and coordinate the attack.

23

Miami, Florida

As Martin Ghranditti's private Falcon 2000 jet landed with a light bounce, he stared out into Miami's glitzy night. He could almost smell the frangipani and mango groves in the sultry air. It reminded him of the scent of his woman, the only one he had really loved, dead now nearly twenty years. He had been accused of having no heart, but he carried her there, wrapped in memories, her platinum hair a halo. As the jet's engines decelerated to a throb, and the craft cruised across the tarmac, he could feel the electricity of her touch. He unsnapped his seat belt and swayed toward the bar.

Armand appeared from nowhere. "Your usual Grey Goose, sir?" He was sixty years old, of moderate height and weight, with a sour face and mouse-gray hair so smooth it could be painted to his pasty skin. He spoke deferentially, the tone of a loyal servant

320

awaiting orders.

Occasionally Ghranditti wondered what Armand was really thinking, what any of them were thinking, but tonight he cared less than usual. "Yes. On the rocks." He marched to a plush sofa at the front of the jet and sat. He did not bother with a seat belt. They were rolling toward the hangar.

The vodka arrived, and Armand's hand extracted a side table and set down the glass and vanished. Ghranditti adjusted the glass and drank. He liked the light, clean nose. Even more, he liked the explosiveness of the taste. The vodka shot a mellow glow clear to his gut. He took a deep breath. For some reason, he was in a nostalgic mood. He did not quite approve, but as he had grown older he had allowed himself small indulgences.

He drank again, mourning the Cold War. His era. A great time to be alive. Longing for those days, he stared into his glass and felt a surge of grief. Afterward, the grand old Soviet Union had turned into a sorry New Russia — the munitions dump of the world, where everything was for sale. And worst of all, Russia and the United States quit financing their proxy wars, which killed the small, exclusive club of top weapons players to which he had belonged. The business erupted into chaos. Anyone could show up in Eastern Europe with an end-user certificate and make deals. One result was the new generation was both arrogant and ignorant. Despite the ease of making money in their petty little deals, and their ability to sound cutting-edge by talking e-mail and Web sites, they could not tell an Igla dummy missile from a real one.

Still, to them, he was out of step. An antique, a dinosaur. It had disgusted him so much that he finally retired. Like other Cold War arms titans, he was now off everyone's radar screen. He wondered whether the others resented it as much as he.

By the time he looked out the window, the jet had stopped inside the hangar. He drained his glass. What he wanted most was to go home to his family, but first he must meet his client.

He stepped from the jet onto the stairs. A stench of diesel and sweat stained the muggy air. As he straightened to his full height, a sense of purpose flowed through him, and he looked down to where a tall, trim man with stylishly unkempt hair stood gripping a Toys "R" Us shopping bag in his right hand. He had no beard and wore a Western two-button dark suit and fashionable wire-rimmed glasses on his large nose.

The glasses were a focal point, purposefully distracting from the flat cheeks and sharply angular face that could radiate a feral power that even Ghranditti found disconcerting, which was one reason he carried a 9mm Beretta in a shoulder holster. The client's name was Faisal al-Hadi.

"Assalaam alaykom, Sayed Faisal." Ignoring the handrail, not hurrying, Ghranditti walked down the steps.

"Alaykom assalaam, Sayed Martin," al-Hadi replied politely. *"Izzayak?"*

"I'm well, thank you," Ghranditti continued in Arabic. His two security men stood a few feet distant, holding the client's M-4 and handgun. Behind them waited Ghranditti's armored limo, the rear doors open. "I hope you'll ride with me," he continued. "It will be my pleasure to drop you at your hotel." This had already been decided, but making it a social pleasantry gave lip service to the lie of friendship. In business as in statecraft, there were no "friends," only interests.

They climbed into his black limousine. Ghranditti liked dealing with high-echelon Islamic terrorists; one had no illusions. They were smart and deadly and protective to the extreme. But then they lived in armed camps of the mind.

As the limo glided off and the air-conditioning cooled them, Ghranditti nodded at the toy-store bag. "I see you brought the payment."

"Yes, Martin. And when precisely do you expect to send off the shipment?" Faisal al-Hadi's gaze was as somber as an imam's.

"Late tomorrow. I'll phone with the exact time and place."

"We find it difficult to release another payment without more assurance."

"That's why you're dealing with Martin Ghranditti," he said easily. "My terms haven't changed since the old days. If something goes wrong on my end, you'll receive it back in full. Guaranteed."

A fraction of a smile played on al-Hadi's lips. "It's been a while since I've heard those words from you."

"Times change. Countries change. And the players change, but weapons are always needed. I was bored."

Al-Hadi laughed. For an instant, surprise flickered behind the wire-rimmed glasses, almost as if he were embarrassed by his display of good humor.

Ghranditti chuckled.

"It's your thirst for adventure," al-Hadi continued knowingly. "I have no illusions you're doing this because you've decided to return to Allah."

"I have a mission, too. You're trying to export a religion. I'm trying to save humanity."

Al-Hadi sobered. "By selling weapons and stolen government product? That makes no sense."

"Of course it does. It's shock therapy, a large dose of realism. Or perhaps all of you will simply kill each other off. That's where the planet's headed, isn't it?"

"And meanwhile you grow richer and richer," al-Hadi said sarcastically. "Oh, yes, I know you're still operating in the gray areas of the law. You stay anonymous by using wire transfers, front companies, and offshore accounts. You've never risked your life in a war zone. You've never had to look into the faces of the Muslim parents whose children your guns kill. Servants coddle you. Governments protect you. When our deal is completed, you'll slip like a gold-plated shadow back into luxury."

Ghranditti controlled himself. While terrorist leaders like al-Hadi ordered the faithful to live according to premodern times, they flew on jumbo jets and used Web sites to recruit and plan attacks. Their largest source of revenue was narcotics; their largest expense was weapons. Their dominant business partner in both endeavors was America.

Ghranditti despaired over the man's hypocrisy. "Money is how the world keeps score," he said calmly. "Terrorism is Big Business — three times the size of the U.S. money supply and growing. Both of us know money ensures you get the attention you want. Why else would you have targeted the World Trade Center? Why else would you be casing other nerve centers of global finance?"

Al-Hadi paused. He blinked slowly.

Ghranditti realized he might have gone too far. He softened his tones. "You've come a long way from the first time we met. Your first weapons buy. Nearly twenty years ago now. Do you remember?"

"Always." Al-Hadi's anthracite eyes continued to blink slowly, the only sign of his fury. "Jay Tice screwed us, then he 'saved' me by arranging to exchange me. I suppose I should be grateful. After all, I lived to execute many Jews. Many infidels."

Ghranditti looked away. What he recalled most vividly was that Jay Tice and a team of covert operators had uncovered the details of al-Hadi's enormous shipment. Ghranditti had lost a small fortune. It was the first time — and the last.

Outside the window, skyscrapers burnished by colorful floodlights told Ghranditti they were nearing Miami's business center. "We'll be at your hotel soon. Would you allow me to look at the payment now? Not that I don't trust you, either." From inside his jacket he removed the printout that listed the finalized shipment.

Al-Hadi took the printout and passed him the Toys "R" Us bag and asked casually, "Are you having problems acquiring any of the items?"

Ghranditti felt a warning stab. "Everything's on schedule. The miniature computers, the LandFlyers, the drones. All of it."

"You didn't mention the software."

"A simple memory lapse. Why?"

"When the great Ghranditti returns, I expect nothing less than perfection," he said neutrally and handed over a key.

As al-Hadi studied the printout, Ghranditti opened the bag and removed a small metal box. He unlocked the lid and lifted it, his expression unchanged, but his heart rate sped. As the headlamps of passing cars flashed into the limo, hundreds of uncut diamonds glittered, winked, and exploded with silver and blue lights. The mass of jewels was stunning. With a sense of awe, he pushed his index finger into them and stirred. The diamonds were cool and rough and beautiful, like life.

"Satisfactory," he said at last.

Al-Hadi looked up, irritated. "A half-million dollars' worth of diamonds are merely 'satisfactory'?"

"Ah, but you see, satisfaction is everything, isn't it?"

Near the Sheraton, the limo stopped in the mouth of an alley, blocking it. Ghranditti's two security guards immediately got out of the front seat, carrying al-Hadi's weapons. Their hard gazes probed traffic and the scattering of pedestrians as they faded back into the black shadows of the alley. Ghranditti's chauffeur climbed out from behind the wheel and hurried around to open al-Hadi's door.

Al-Hadi put one foot onto the concrete then stared back at Ghranditti. "Is Tice still in prison?"

"Yes, of course," Ghranditti lied smoothly. "Why do you ask?"

"I should've killed him long ago."

Ghranditti nodded, unsurprised, and watched as the dark alley swallowed the terrorist. The chauffeur returned to his steering wheel. The two security men slid into the front seat. And the limo rolled off.

Ghranditti sank back, smiling broadly to

himself. Everything he had told al-Hadi about why he had agreed to handle the job was true. But there was also another reason: The news of their unusual transaction would eventually leak out — six months from now, two years from now. It would restore his reputation with a comeback so big that even today's crop of gloating amateurs would have to acknowledge it. It would also establish his legacy as a pioneering weapons merchant. A legacy was timeless. He wanted — deserved — nothing less.

And now Ghranditti knew there would be no more problems — he had sent Jerry and his men to ambush Jay Tice and Elaine Cunningham based on fresh information supplied by Laurence Litchfield.

The limo crossed the MacArthur Causeway and dove into Miami Beach, one of the most expensive strips of real estate in the world. The landmark moderne hotels for which the oceanfront was known towered to the east, porcelain and gold above the sand. The street wound south. Soon high hedges and pastel-painted walls lined it. Ornate gates that were really security barricades sealed the driveways. On the far side stood mansions with the pedigrees of grand duchesses.

His Mediterranean villa was just ahead.

Its armed guards and electronic security system, which rivaled a bank's, gave him a sense of serenity, because his wife and young children must be protected at all costs. The big gates swung open, and the limo flowed through. He sighed, relaxing. At the portico, Karl jumped out and opened the rear door. Ghranditti emerged and strolled into the imposing foyer. The marble floor extended thirty feet in a half circle. Museum-quality antiques rimmed the room. Tropical plants and flowers in floor vases gave an air of natural beauty to what otherwise might be too austere.

"Is that you, Martin?" his wife called from the library. "Come have a drink with me. I thought you'd be home sooner."

"I'll look in on the children first, then I'll join you."

He climbed the marble staircase. Its gold rail shone, curving upward to the airy second floor. He had bought the villa ten years ago when he married, knowing it would be filled with children. Now they had three — first a son, then a daughter, then another son. The perfect number. He also bought homes for them in Rome, London, Sun Valley, and Saint Moritz. And this morning, he had closed the deal for the island.

He turned the knob of Aaron's bedroom door and stepped inside. The boy was asleep, his nose buried in his pillow. With a surge of bittersweet pride, Ghranditti smiled down. At the age of nine, Aaron had given up stuffed animals for the excitement of anything with wheels. Tonight he had a red fire truck possessively under his arm. For a moment, Ghranditti considered the tragedy of the world the boy would inherit unless something radical was done. He ran his fingertips lightly over Aaron's rumpled hair. He felt his responsibility to this child, to all of them, strongly.

He visited Mariette next. She was small for her age, seven years old, curled up with her dolls. Her long black hair was a mass of shiny ringlets on her pink pillow. A book lay open beside her. Precocious, she had been reading three years. Tonight it was her favorite — *Dear Rat* by Julia Cunningham. The air smelled of suntan lotion and orange blossoms.

Finally he padded into the baby's room — Kristoph, who was two. He had graduated to a bed, for which he had great enthusiasm. The frame was a mock racing car. Wrapped around his neck was his tattered baby blanket. He lay on his side, sucking his thumb as he slept. Ghranditti knelt

331

and reverently pulled up the sheet, tucking it around his little shoulders. He kissed Kristoph's warm forehead.

When he left, he had a feeling of peacefulness, of setting things right. He strode along the thick hall carpet and downstairs again.

Armand was leaving the library, looking happy with himself. Ghranditti frowned.

Armand saw his master's displeasure. "Madam says I may retire, sir," he explained. "Is there anything I can do for you first?" His head dipped in a servile nod. "Anything at all."

With a flick of his fingers, Ghranditti dismissed him. He strode past to join his wife, his Marie.

24

On the Road, Virginia

As the Jaguar cruised on through the rural night, air flowed in from the open moon-roof, thick with the aromas of plowed earth and sprouting vegetation. Tice glanced at Cunningham. She had given him no answer. He was going to have to decide quickly what to do about her.

"Now I understand about the operation in Rome — why you blew it."

She stiffened. "My big mistake was agreeing to work with the idiot." It had been her last assignment. After that, Langley brought her home to the Parking Lot and numbing visits with CIA shrinks.

"You're right," he agreed. "The man was a fool."

She shot him a surprised look.

"As I understand it, you were supposed to find an al-Qaeda mole who'd ditched out on his handlers. You and your partner located him at a cell meeting, but it was breaking up. You phoned in for a snatch squad. But your partner wouldn't wait."

"We'd had one hell of a time finding the guy. Took us weeks."

"So when he tried to go after them, you took him down and tied him up. He filed charges."

She bit back a smile. "Yeah, but he's still alive."

He nodded. "He's lucky you had the guts to do the smart thing." He had been watching behind. Now he straightened uneasily, adjusting the Browning in his hand. "We may have a tail. It's closing in on us for the third time. Looks big. It has those new blue-white headlamps."

She checked her rearview mirror. "I see it."

"I haven't been able to make out any other characteristics. Have you?"

She frowned as she glanced again. "Sorry. I didn't notice it."

He gave a brisk nod, wondering how she could have missed it. "There's a second car, too, farther back. But it looks to me as if it's starting to catch up."

"Probably just some kids out joyriding."

"Yeah, probably," he said neutrally.

She peered over her steering wheel.

"There's a crossroads ahead. It's pretty far away. I'll make a left when we get there. That'll force them into a wider turn radius if they follow. We'll be able to see what the car or cars look like better."

"Good idea."

No buildings were in sight. Only endless open space surrounded them, interrupted occasionally by patches of black woods that stretched deep into the fields. He had a sense of desolation, as if he were in an uninhabited country far away.

Again he gazed behind. "The second car's caught up. It's riding the first one's tail. They're holding the same speed as us. Pump up ours. Let's see what they do."

She pressed the accelerator. Within two minutes their two tails had caught up, resuming the same distance as before.

"You see?" he asked.

Her eyes were wide. "We're a caravan. This isn't normal."

"We're almost at the crossroads."

The roads intersected about a quarter mile away. Two highway lights towered above, faintly illuminating the bleak rolling landscape. There were still no houses, no other vehicles, not even any horses or cows. He alternately watched the cars behind and ahead. They were approaching the intersection fast.

"Hold on." Her voice was tight.

She braked hard then made a quick left-hand turn onto a blacktop road. It was narrow, no center line, not even any shoulders. She checked her rearview mirror.

"The second car's pulled in front. Maybe to confuse us," he said. But as the second wheeled around the corner, he recognized the sleek lines, the glossy ebony color. "Dammit all to hell!" By feel, he grabbed the SIG Sauer from his backpack. "It's the black Lincoln that chased us on the Beltway." He stared as the second car spun around the turn, too, its back tires skidding, almost as if showing off. He swore loudly again. "The one with the blue-white lights is Jerry's BMW!"

"What!" Her voice rose. "How could they have found us? Are you sure it's them!"

He glanced at her then stuffed the SIG Sauer into his waistband. "Damn right I'm sure. Can't make out any faces. Looks like two men in each car."

She accelerated to seventy miles an hour, trying to understand Jerry's appearance. It was unbelievable. But the CIA had to be somewhere close. This was the correct stretch of road, the place where they were supposed to act out their movie. She peered eagerly ahead, but there were no other vehicles.

The two cars caught up and resumed pacing them. She clutched the wheel so hard her hands hurt. Where was Langley!

Her voice snapped. "I'm going to outrun them. Does the map show anywhere we can duck and hide?"

"I'll look." He yanked the map from the glove compartment and turned on the small overhead map light.

She rammed the gas pedal to the floor. The Jag went into kickdown, sending them deep into their seats. She pushed it to eighty. The tires sang.

As the car settled into flight, he held up the map to read.

To ninety. Then ninety-five. The scattering of trees was a blur. In her mirrors, she saw the two cars were trying to catch up. To one hundred. She breathed deeply, forcing herself to trust the pliant strength of the Jag and her ability to control it. The asphalt road seemed needle-thin as it curved into the distance.

"I don't see a way off for at least seven miles," Tice told her grimly.

"There are two more cars. Ahead." Langley at last!

She stared hopefully through the windshield. The vehicles raced toward them around a bend, their headlamps shooting flickering light through pine trees. They appeared to be in tandem, too, maintaining a rigid distance from each other.

"It's almost as if they need to be close enough to each other so they can enact some plan." He glanced behind and ahead, keeping track of both pairs.

She did the same. "Oh, my God." Her voice was a dry whisper. "Look."

He whipped around just in time to see the two front vehicles were suddenly hurtling side by side toward them, their beams on high, blazing light. There was no shoulder on this road. The edge dropped off into weeds and grass and brush. The overbright row of headlights grew larger, more glaring, an assault.

He spun back and stared. "The BMW's making its move now."

With a graceful rush, the BMW pulled abreast of the Lincoln, creating another speeding wall of metal and glass. Their headlamps were on high beam, too, shattering the darkness. Side by side, the two sets of cars closed in relentlessly on the Jag.

"Now we have the answer," Tice said. "Why only one car was following for such a long time. Why Jerry hasn't tried anything. It's their plan. They've been waiting to spring a trap on us."

A bolt of fear shot through her, followed by indignation. *Stop lying to yourself.* Laurence Litchfield interviewed her for the job. Litchfield ran Whippet. Whippet tried to wipe her. Whippet tried to wipe Tice. She had been set up from the beginning. The only people keeping the rendezvous were Jerry and his wet squad.

In a gesture that spoke volumes, Tice laid her Walther on her lap. "No strings."

"What can we do?" She battled to control her emotions. The gun's dull metal shone, beckoned. She felt deep gratitude.

"Jerry's tasting victory now, so his edge isn't as sharp. He's got a lot of troops in play, but that makes his job harder, too. They're vicious, but they're city-based thugs. Those are our advantages. See the woods ahead?"

In the BMW, Rink leaned into the steering wheel eagerly. "We've got them now!"

Jerry started to nod. "Dammit! What in hell?"

The Jaguar had screeched to a sudden stop. It sat at the side of the road like a lump of red coal.

"They're giving up!" Rink said happily.

"Like hell they are. Not Tice. He's up to something. Move in fast!" As Rink hit the gas, Jerry barked into his cell, "Close in! Close in!"

The Jag's exterior lights died. Angelides strained to see what they were doing. No interior light showed. The front doors opened and closed so swiftly they hardly seemed to move.

"Jerry!" Rink said.

"I see 'em!"

Two shadows flitted out and plunged down off the road and up into woods that spread back through the farmland. Rink skewed the BMW sideways and screeched to a stop twenty feet from the silent Jaguar, his headlamps aimed at the timber. Within seconds the Lincoln stopped beside them, mimicking the slew. The dazzling headlights exposed the bark of tree trunks in detail while deepening the forest's shadows into black Rorschach blots, impenetrable.

There was no movement in the woods, no sign of Tice or Cunningham. But as Jerry and Rink opened their doors, bullets thudded into their car. The men slammed their doors, staying inside. As they ducked, the BMW rocked and sank.

"Shit!" Rink bellowed. "They shot out my tires!"

Jerry was getting pissed. He did not like to waste time on being pissed. "They blasted the Lincoln's, too. The bullets came from two directions. Guess now we know for sure Cunningham can shoot."

"How in hell are we supposed to drive out of here!"

"The Jag," Jerry said impatiently. "We'll whack them, then we'll take the Jag." He announced into the cell, "Into the trees. Move!"

But as Jerry and his three men leaped out and ran, there was another fusillade. Bullets smashed into metal, bit into asphalt. The men dove as the other two cars — an Oldsmobile and another Lincoln — swerved and halted nearby, their beams also trained on the forest. Two more firestorms erupted from the trees, shredding their tires, too.

"Damn you, Tice!" Jerry growled. "I'll get you for this. I'll get you!"

Abruptly everything was quiet. The night air was still, motionless. His men's tension was electric. Eyes sharp, he studied the woods. He listened. Finally, the noise of four more car doors opening broke the heavy silence.

"The rest of the boys are getting out,"

Rink whispered. "They must've figured it's safe."

Jerry nodded. Running footsteps pounded the asphalt. As the new quartet slid in, a shadow flickered among the vegetation and faded into the woods.

"That's them!" Jerry stabbed a finger. "Remember that spot. Walt, you and your men circle around. Cut 'em off." He motioned to the others. "The rest of us are gonna go after them head-on. Move!"

Beside an old-growth walnut tree, Tice stood balanced on the balls of both feet, his Browning in one hand, a fist-size rock in the other. He had returned the SIG Sauer to his shoulder holster. Sweat coated him. The forest was a sea of shadows.

The quiet oaths of the urban gunmen floated through the trees as they stumbled on roots and walked into low branches. Although they were having as many problems as he had hoped, it did not lessen their deadliness. He turned, tracking the group that was circling left in the time-honored flanking maneuver that Stonewall Jackson had used to win many victories here in his home state. The other group was heading for where he had last shot at them. Several hundred yards separated the two teams.

He had to give Cunningham time. He crouched and cracked the rock against a low boulder. Stone on stone.

A hoarse whisper drifted through the night: "Over there!"

He listened, forcing himself to be patient. When he was sure both sides were converging, he hurled the rock in the direction of the road. It landed with a crash and rolled noisily. The two teams adjusted to the new destination and accelerated, predators scenting blood.

He picked up a second rock and ran around the tree and slid under a leafy bush. He turned onto his side, pulling his knees to his chest, dropped the rock, and held the Browning ready. Twigs and sharp stones stabbed through his clothes. He peered out carefully. The flanking group was crossing far to his left, hurrying toward where the first rock had landed. The second team headed toward it from the right. They would pass close to him. Their footsteps grew louder.

They seemed to materialize out of the shadows, Jerry in the lead. His muscular body padded easily, like a dog in the wild but without the finesse. As expected, three men followed Jerry in single file. If this were an alley, they would peer around every

Dumpster, lift every lid, try all doors, miss nothing. They would find him. Sweat trickled off Tice's forehead, burning his eyes.

Instead, they passed his bush one by one, their eyes scanning, looking for the obvious. When the forest shadows swallowed them again, Tice released a long stream of air and crawled out, listening. As soon as he was certain of their location, he hurled the second rock. It landed with a loud *thump*, closer to Jerry's group.

A challenge rang out from them: "Hold it right there!"

Like a vicious echo, a single gunshot exploded. More followed from both sides. The air shook with the noise.

"Oh, shit!" someone bellowed.

"Walt's down! He's been hit!"

There were more curses.

"Hold fire!" Jerry shouted. "Stop it, dammit! *Stop* it. We're shooting each other, for chrissakes!"

With a cold smile, Tice melted into the timber, leaving them to their chaos. He wove among the trees, his feet light on the duff, skirting patches of moonlight. When he could no longer hear the janitors, he increased his speed. Dodged bushes. Darted past boulders. The scent of pine filled his head until he thought it would explode.

When he finally emerged onto a plowed field, he was breathing so hard his chest ached. On the horizon, cars slashed along a rise as if they were lit beads pulled on a string. He slowed and looked up eagerly and found the North Star. Oriented, he inhaled deeply, willing oxygen to his tired muscles. He loped off.

25

Carrying her Walther and shoulder bag, Elaine slithered out from under the Jag and crouched, her clothes filthy, her hair loose. Jerry's four vehicles blocked one lane, hunched like crippled beetles on the frames of their wheels, their headlights glaring sightless into the timber.

Watching the woods, she ran to Jerry's BMW. The band that tied her hair fell off. Cursing, she backtracked and snapped it up. And ran again and yanked open the BMW's passenger door and dove inside, closing it swiftly to minimize the amount of time the interior light showed. Shadows filled the car. It stank of cigarettes and old sandwiches.

She looked around then opened the glove compartment. There was no time to pick and choose. Jerry and his men could return anytime. Suddenly a volley of gunfire erupted. She fell flat on the seat, head hitting the armrest. Heart hammering, she listened. Waited. More gunshots followed. Too many. Was Jay all right?

Still, if someone returned now, she would be in serious trouble, too — trapped in Jerry's car. *Hurry, hurry.* As more bullets exploded, she scooped the contents of the glove compartment into a pocket in her shoulder bag. She ran her hands over the seat but found nothing. Frantically she felt the floor carpet, picking up matches and a crushed paper cigar ring and candy wrappers, and slammed them into her purse. At last she raised her head and peered out the window. The thick woods seemed silent, tranquil.

She opened the door and tumbled out onto weeds and reached up with both hands and pressed the door closed. Scanning for movement, she crouched and ran. Each footfall sounded like thunder to her ears.

At the Jag, she surveyed around then jumped inside and switched on the ignition. Lungs aching as she tried to catch her breath, she cruised the car quietly away, watching her rearview mirror.

She had been hiding in the woods when Tice began running back and forth, the Browning in one hand, the SIG Sauer in the other, shooting out the janitors' tires

347

from two positions. The point was to make them think both Tice and she were escaping. Then, while his volleys imprisoned the men low in their cars, she had dashed back and slid beneath the Jag.

She forced worry from her mind. When the collection of wounded cars behind her was out of sight, she floored the gas feed. Soon a little intersection came into view. She noted her odometer reading and turned right, rushing off onto a road that looped north. Precisely five miles later she pulled onto the shoulder and cut her lights. The engine thrummed. Tilled earth spread gray and dead-looking, interrupted only by the distant woods where Tice planned to lose the killers. She hoped he had lost them. She was sure he had.

When a knuckle tapped the passenger window, she jumped. Sweaty and disheveled, Tice stared soberly at her through the glass. The fine lines on his face had deepened into caverns. He was a beautiful sight. As she unlocked his door, he peered suspiciously back over his shoulder then dropped like a rock inside.

"Let's get the hell out of here." Gulping air, he closed the door and fell back against the seat. Twigs clung to his jacket. His hands were scratched. He rested them on his thighs. They quivered.

She checked her mirrors and again floored the accelerator. They soared off. "Are you okay?"

He nodded, his chest heaving. The warrior home from the fray. "Was it quiet when you left?"

"Like a tomb. Tell me what happened."

As he described the hunt, his deception tactics, and the response of Jerry's men, there was a small, strange smile on his face, a combination of triumph and knowing. She looked at him and found herself transfixed by strength she suddenly saw clearly.

When he finished telling her about his escape through the woods, he sat up and fell silent, resuming sentry duty. She checked him several times. He was a grand master from a mysterious world she realized she wanted to know. A sort of awe filled her. From the moment they had met, he had been educating her, mentoring her, everything from how to hide well within shadows to the importance of small numbered accounts and how partners could escape multiple pursuers with simple tools — guns, a car, a map, and their wits.

He caught her gazing at him. "You're looking at me oddly." For an instant he seemed puzzled. "You're very young," he decided. "You have a lot to learn."

She blinked slowly and studied the deserted road. "Of course I do."

"I don't mean tradecraft. What you're feeling has nothing to do with me. It's the situation. We're both pumped up on adrenaline, and adrenaline can make a flicker of an emotion or a thought seem momentous. But the only thing that's changed is that you've had to trust me, and I've had to trust you, and it worked. We did our jobs, had some good luck, and saved our own hides — and each other's. To let that escalate can lead to trouble."

She said nothing.

His voice softened. "Some operatives react by getting angry and resentful. Some feel a physical attraction. Others feel dependent. An array of emotional responses are possible — and all of them are strong. Look, Elaine, I'm going to make a leap here. Because of everything that's happened to you in the past, you've probably been feeling pretty isolated. And now, after many tense hours of my being your target, you've had to accept me as a partner. That's a huge reversal. It jerks one up short and shows how tissue-thin our most closely held beliefs can be. So, considering all of this, it's possible your emotions are telling you that I've got some kind of special wisdom. Not true. All I've got is experience. I paid attention, and I learned, but experience isn't the same as wisdom. In fact, I'd argue that I don't have an overabundance of wisdom, or I wouldn't be where I am in my life."

She sighed. He was right — something had changed in her when he climbed into the car, dirty and exhausted and jubilant, and told her how he had escaped. Some part of her wanted to give him superhuman qualities.

She straightened her spine. "You're right. But I still think you were terrific. I'm not going to change my mind. Okay, it's your turn. We made a deal. Remember? I told you about Rafe. Fill me in about Raina."

He paused. Then: "There's not that much to tell. The answer is, I fell in love with her in Germany. The affair complicated both of our lives — and our work. Then she fell out of love with me. But I never regretted any of it. Never. As I said, what I regret are the lousy choices I made."

She frowned, thinking about Kristoph's age. That would explain a lot. "Then, was Kristoph your son?"

His eyes closed. For a few seconds his sweaty face seemed bruised, as if the artist had pounded the living clay too hard. "You could say that. And you're right that the newspaper story activated my escape." He told her about Raina's signal and what little he knew.

She asked questions. He answered until finally he grew impatient.

"That's enough." He gave her a hard look. "When were you planning to tell me what you did?"

"What I . . . ?" Guilt washed through her.

His voice grew flinty. "You weren't surprised we had a tail. You expected one — but not that Jerry would be it. And you weren't surprised when two more cars showed up ahead of us. In fact, you were relieved — until you realized they were with Jerry, and all of them planned to ambush us." He stared. "What happened?"

She did not look at him. "I have another cell phone. My personal one. I called Laurence Litchfield."

At the name, Tice gave an almost imperceptible jerk. Then he stilled and settled back inside himself and assumed the mask she had come to know well — unobtrusive but very self-assured, his gray eyes impenetrable.

"Tell me everything," he demanded.

She repeated the conversation. "I hadn't gotten around to mentioning it, but Whippet tried to scrub me, too." She described the attack in Franklin Park then finding the assassin's corpse on the desk in Whippet house. "I hadn't connected any of it to Litchfield. But it makes sense now. He personally vetted me before he assigned me to hunt you. It didn't seem unusual at the time because it was such a special situation. Maybe he's not the inside source. It could be someone else in his office."

His mouth thinned into an angry line. "Just before I was arrested, I warned Larry about Hannah. I'd seen a few things that indicated she and her people might be skimming from their front companies. It sounds to me that instead of investigating, Larry threw in his lot with them. Years ago, he was a hotdogger, a real cowboy type. I thought that was behind him."

"What do you mean?" There was another lit intersection far ahead. Around it spread dark houses and stores.

"In the early eighties I sent him under-cover into East Berlin to chase a lead that Carlos the Jackal and Johannes Weinrich were up to something." The tip had come from Raina, one of her first. "Larry was new. He lost Weinrich on the street. I never got a good explanation about why, and of course experienced operatives lose rabbits, too. The problem was that Weinrich then handed off explosives that were used to bomb the Maison de France in West Berlin."

She frowned. "When I asked Hannah Barculo about you, she described the same event, but her version was very different. According to her, Litchfield said he developed the intel himself and followed up on his own initiative. You were the one who blew the operation — not him."

As she related Hannah's story, a cold wave of outrage rolled through Tice. Litchfield had been one of his protégés, and he was stunned by the lie. At last he sighed. There was nothing to be done about it now. "So Larry rewrote history. I suppose all of us do that occasionally, especially when we're young. Of course, I reamed him for screwing up, but my job was to develop talent, too, and he was very talented. Have you ever heard of an information broker named Moses? He peaked in the last few years of the Cold War."

"I vaguely recall the name." She caught him studying her again.

He looked away. "Moses kept a low profile and was very expensive. Without the knowledge of anyone, Moses tipped Larry that a major international figure was going to be assassinated, but he had two conditions before he'd reveal the details — Larry personally had to pay Moses's fee, and he had to work it alone, keep it secret so Moses's name wouldn't surface until it was resolved. Larry was ambitious, and his family had some money, so he paid and kept his mouth shut. As it turned out, Carlos had put a trio of Iranian Muslims through plastic surgery to make them look less Persian and more Italian and was having them trained to pass as Catholic priests."

She inhaled. "You said a major international figure — they were going to terminate the pope?"

"Yes, Pope John Paul the Second. He was a lightning rod for anti-Communists, especially in Poland. The Bulgarians had failed to assassinate him, so Carlos figured Moscow could pay him to do the job instead. The pope was home in Rome between trips to Liechtenstein and India. Good timing for Carlos. Larry scoped out the situation, then he slipped into East Berlin with one of our new miniature cameras and crawled through an air duct to where he could record the trainers talking the fake priests through the operation step by step. Larry showed he was daring and smart. With his evidence, we stopped the plot and informed the Vatican and used the intel in several vital ways. To my knowledge, Larry was never negligent again, and that operation launched his career. He got a raise and a promotion to the number two slot in Madrid."

"That was a hell of a tip. Moses must've been something."

He gave a casual nod and continued, "Hannah was in Berlin then, too. She and Larry worked together. When I think about it, she seemed to respect him a lot."

"That may explain some of it. But what does the rest mean? Whippet was taken out by Jerry. Now Jerry is working for Litchfield, or at least Litchfield is feeding him information. Does he know it was Jerry who hit Hannah and the unit? Are he and Mr. G partners in the 'big deal'? From the way Jerry talked about Mr. G, it sounds as if he's loyal to him, so I doubt he'd work for Litchfield without Mr. G's knowing about it."

"That's my analysis, too. And in some way, the situation — this deal — is connected to Raina or Kristoph or both. Otherwise, they wouldn't be coming after me." They were nearing the intersection. "Turn north. We're going to one of my oldest contacts. There aren't many people I trust. Even fewer who trust me these days. He's one."

She peeled off onto the road. "Who is he?"

"I'll let you discover that for yourself."

Again silence filled the car.

Occasionally he checked her solemn face. There was something about her that reminded him of his daughter, Mariette. It astounded him to think Mariette would be twenty-nine now, the same age as Elaine. She had been a beautiful child, willowy and bright as a rose, with a stimulating intelligence. Aaron would be twenty-seven. With a stab of pain, he wondered what his towheaded son would be like. Aaron had loved books and dinosaurs and soccer. When he allowed himself, he thought longingly of Mariette and Aaron and Kristoph. Three children. All dead. His chest ached. And poor Marie. Tragic Marie. It made no sense he was still alive.

At last he said, "Don't beat yourself up about Larry Litchfield. Of course you'd go to him. Right now, what matters is you acquired critical information. However it plays out, that's what you've got to remember."

With a smile, she looked at him. At the same moment, he peered at her. Their gazes met, and unspoken forgiveness passed between them.

She resumed watching the road, thinking.

After a while she made a decision: "You must've had extraordinary reasons to turn against us, Jay. It makes no damn sense to me, but I won't ask you about it again. Rest easy."

He nodded. "Some things can never be explained. This is one."

■ ■ ■ ■

PART THREE

■ ■ ■ ■

Intelligence stops when you pick up a gun.
— Oleg Tsarev
former KGB officer,
First Chief Directorate

26

Miami Beach, Florida

Miles Davis's "So What" played from a small stage where a saxophonist led a combo, his eyes closed, his expression drug-sweet. As Martin Ghranditti watched the performance on the plasma television in his elegant library, the camera panned back. In the TV audience, cigarette smoke and sweat and exhausted intentions fought with over-wrought gaiety.

Ghranditti looked away, smelling the stink in his mind. Marie was sitting relaxed on the other end of the sofa. Her eyes were closed, too, as she listened. A small smile played on her lips. For some reason he could not fathom, she liked jazz. Her long, platinum-blond hair was brushed back, as luxurious as silk, to display the fine architecture of her face. He studied the straight nose, the chiseled cheekbones, the high forehead. His gaze slid down the curves of her body, dressed tonight in some clinging black knit. A hot tide rolled through him. Her long legs were crossed at the knees. A sandal dangled precariously from the toes of her right foot, hinting at danger. She was hypnotic. He focused on her naked, gleaming legs.

When the music stopped, she opened her eyes and turned not just her head but her entire body, as if she knew he had been watching her, what he was thinking.

"I closed the deal for the island." He drank his Grey Goose, neat.

She stared. Her eyes were stunning, an unusual sea green — gemlike and emotional. "I don't want to move away," she said firmly. "I told you that. I'll travel with you, Martin — whenever and wherever you like. Business, vacation, whatever. With or without the children. But I don't want to move away permanently." She picked up her glass from the table beside her. Only ice cubes remained. She shook the glass, rattling the cubes. She tilted back her head and sipped the melt.

He watched the way her lips clung to the glass. "We have to move, Marie," he said reasonably.

"Why?" Again she stared at him, puzzled. "The children are happy. I'm planning to be happy myself. I've found a therapist."

"A therapist?" He felt a tendril of fear. "What kind of therapist?"

"A psychologist. I want to continue to see her." There was a tremor in her voice. "I want to find out who I am."

His heart thumped against his ribs. "You're Marie Ghranditti!" he thundered. "You're beautiful! Exquisite! You have everything any woman could want. Three healthy children. Wealth and status. You're safe and loved and admired. You're perfect!" And at last she had reached the exactly right age — thirty-one.

"I'm perfect to you," she said quietly. "That's been your goal. But somewhere along the way, *I* got lost."

He noted the stubbornness in her chin. It had been there for days, propelling him to rush closing the purchase of the island. "Did you take your medication? You get like this when you don't take your OxyContin. You *must* take it. You don't need any damn psychologist!"

As if his gaze were too much, she looked away. "I've been cutting back. You knew I've wanted to make some changes." She spoke to the long wall of books, to the rich leather bindings, the gold-leaf letters, the rococo designs. "I don't *think* anymore. I don't even remember what I look like really. It's been so long. Years and years. Do you remember what I look like? What I used to talk about? What I wanted? If you do, please tell me."

He glared at the back of her platinum head, horrified. "You ungrateful — !" His cell buzzed. He snatched it from his jacket and saw the number. It was Jerry Angelides. "I'll be back," he told her and rose to his feet, looming, waiting for her to cringe.

Instead, she looked up over her shoulder with those brilliant green eyes and shrugged. She did not know the power of those eyes.

"You really do work much too hard, Martin," she said.

Confused, he strode out of the library and across the foyer. As he slammed into his office, he punched the TALK button. "Did you get Tice and Cunningham?"

"We came close, Mr. Ghranditti."

"You phoned to say that!"

"It's like every time we get closer." Angelides's voice was strong, assured. "I've got the boys fanned out. We had some car trouble, so we're doubling up until everything's fixed. Tell your Langley man we need better tips. No more of this dumb crap of having to chase Tice all over the place. I figure now's a real good time for your source to nail where Tice is, because he and

Cunningham have gotta be flat on their asses. They've gotta go to ground to sleep. But the boys and I are fine. Rarin' to stay on the road, you might say."

Ghranditti took a deep breath, collecting himself, his mind still partly on Marie. She would listen to reason, he decided. Eventually she always did, and he would tell her doctor to increase her dosage. The immediate priority was the shipment. And Angelides might well be correct.

"I'll inform my source," Ghranditti told him. "Keep up the search. You have the manpower. Use it!"

Outside Herndon, Virginia

The narrow black ribbon of a road curled through the rolling Virginia countryside. The moon was low in the sky, its light thinning. Elaine wheeled the Jag onto an asphalt driveway where a sign announced PRIVATE PROPERTY — KEEP OUT and followed it across a stone bridge and through tangled woodland. Ahead she could see a glen where old stone buildings from the nineteenth century stood around a circular drive. Looking stately and solid, the two-story main house was at the far end, an upstairs window alight. On either side was a single-story cottage, but both were dark.

As the nose of the Jag entered the glen, floodlights burst on. Elaine drove around toward the big house and parked, but before she could turn off the ignition, Jay was out of the car.

As she hurried after him, the front door opened. She stared, surprised, and smiled grimly to herself: Now she knew who had enabled Jay's escape. In the doorway, holding a large, slender dog by her collar, was the Bureau of Prisons lieutenant who had escorted her around Allenwood — David Oxley. Barefoot and dressed in tight jeans and a T-shirt, he no longer seemed slight but wiry, and his black eyes were far from weary — they were steely and sharp. He surveyed the compound then disappeared indoors.

Jay was on his heels, and Elaine followed, locking the door behind. The place gave off a deserted air. They were in a large living room, where cardboard packing boxes were stacked high against a wall. Bedsheets covered sofas and chairs and what looked like a baby grand piano. To her left, on the far side of the room, was a closed door. To her right, a hall extended. On one side, an enclosed staircase rose to the next floor, the door open as if the owner had just run down. On the other side stood a stone fireplace.

Their host smiled. "The CIA has arrived."

"Indeed I have. And the inside man's waiting."

Jay glanced over at her. "Always have a good backup plan."

"You've sure proved that point." She studied Oxley. "So what's your real name?"

He gave a low chuckle. "Ben Kuhnert, at your service." He peered pointedly at Jay. "You look like field trash. What have you been rolling in?"

"Forest duff. But we got away clean."

"You got away dirty. You both need showers and clean clothes. Zahra's should fit Ms. Cunningham. Come here, Jay. You've got to meet Houri. She's an important member of the team. Let the nice man shake your paw, Houri."

The dog sat, her feathered tail whacking the floor, and Jay took the raised paw and shook it. "Smart dog. Isn't 'houri' what a beautiful young woman in paradise is called?"

"It is. And Houri's a beautiful dog. Also smart, as you say. It's the nature of her breed. In fact, she's so smart that her philosophy is *kul kalb yijji yoomo*." He translated the Arabic: " 'Each dog's day will come.' It usually means there'll be a reckoning, but she translates it literally."

Elaine walked to framed photographs standing on the fireplace mantel and picked up one. She looked across at Kuhnert. His cheeks and chin and prominent nose were broad and sturdy. His skin was neither pink nor dark but lightly golden. The array of pictures showed what looked like five generations, not only from the Middle East's windswept deserts and mosques to the green hills of Virginia and the Islamic Center on Massachusetts Avenue, but from Berlin's Brandenburg Gate and Town Hall to Washington's Capitol Building. No one was dressed in Bedouin robes or burqas, but some wore *hijab,* traditional clothing. From the photos, it looked to her that Kuhnert was Arabic on one side and German on the other — and Muslim on both.

"I hope you have good security." Jay surveyed the room.

"Motion sensors, floodlights, a few other tricks, and Houri. Among her many talents, she's an early-warning system. She let me know you were here before you were close enough to trigger the lights."

"Have you packed up your computer?"

"Not yet. It's in my office." Ben Kuhnert nodded across the living room, and Jay hurried toward the closed door.

Ben's office was about ten by fifteen feet and mostly bare — two dozen cardboard boxes were packed near the door. Tice strode past. There were two desks, one with a laptop and the other with a powerful desktop computer. Worrying about Raina, he sat at the PC, flicked it on, put on his reading glasses, and tapped the keyboard. It had been hours since he was last able to check for a message from her.

He called up Internet Explorer, typed in *www.iht.com,* and soon the online version of the *International Herald Tribune* appeared. He clicked CLASSIFIEDS and went to IN-TERNATIONAL REAL ESTATE MARKET-PLACE and then to PARIS AND SUBURBS. There were dozens of places listed for sale or rent. That was a good sign. His heart rate accelerated.

A voice interrupted from the doorway. "Elaine seems like a good one," Ben said.

"I wouldn't have brought her if she weren't. I'll be with you in a minute."

"Meet us in the kitchen when you're finished. I'm going to show Elaine where to hide her car." He vanished.

Jay leaned close, hoping. When he saw an ad signed "Billie B, owner," his breath caught in his throat. Billie Burke had played Glinda in *The Wizard of Oz.* The name was one of his and Raina's recognition codes. The Realtor in another was R. Bolger. Ray Bolger's role was the Scarecrow. When he found a third listing describing a villa with a "garland" of roses carved into each pillar, excitement coursed through him. He hit the PRINT button. Judy Garland had played Dorothy. He studied the three ads. Each related in code a different time and place to meet in the D.C. area.

Raina would try to go to all, and he would, too. If they missed each other, they would use the same schedule the next day, and the next if need be, until they connected. But if Mr. G's shipment went out today, and Raina and Kristoph were involved, tomorrow would be too late.

He sat back and lifted his chin and closed his eyes. Still, after eleven long years, he would see her again, talk to her, watch the way her nose crinkled when she laughed — and it would not be next week or next year, but very soon. If all went well.

Before he could stop it, the grief for Kristoph he had been forcing away shot through him, piercing as a stiletto, and he was back in Berlin during those grim days when his marriage imploded and he had fallen in love with and turned Raina. Three years later, after Marie and the children were killed, Kristoph was born. Kristoph had grown into a terrific kid, interesting, full of so many questions you thought you would lose your mind. But he had loved every minute he was able to be with Kristoph.

He remembered strolling through the Tiergarten when the boy was a lanky five-year-old, holding his hand. Odd how vulnerable a young hand was, and how strong. And how devastatingly brief childhood was. Years passed in the beat of a heart, and children were too old or too busy or too blasé. Or they were halfway around the planet, as Kristoph had been. He had looked over the boy's blond head that afternoon and into Raina's eyes, as blue and deep as the ocean, at the love brimming for both of them. He ached for the past, for them.

It was not good to dwell. In an act of iron will, he pushed aside his grief and checked the fake e-mail address he had created after escaping Allenwood. He paused and stared. Raina had sent a message. Excited, he leaned close and read:

K worked for Milieu Software. Our old Company is interested in purchasing it.

Tried to jog, but it's too hot out.

He inhaled sharply. So Kristoph had worked for Milieu, and Raina was being hunted. His chest tight, his gaze roamed the small office as he thought uneasily. Finally he decided there was only one thing to do — call his contact. He listened to the house's silence — Elaine and Ben were still outdoors. He took out one of his disposable cell phones and tapped in the number.

The sleepy voice was suspicious: "Yes?"

"It's me again." He watched the office door. "There's some kind of big deal going down today. Someone called Mr. G is one of the principals. His people took out Whippet, and now they're trying to erase Elaine Cunningham and me. Milieu Software and Larry Litchfield are involved — Kristoph worked for Milieu. Also, you should know Raina's coming in. She's hot, so she's probably using a legend. . . . Yes, dammit, I'm sure! Anything about Moses?"

"Still nothing."

Disappointment surged through him. "I've got to go. They'll be back any minute."

He hung up, turned off the computer, and stood. Feet firmly planted, he took a moment to center himself. This was the most critical operation of his life, and it was about to enter its final, perilous stage. He could not afford even the smallest mistake. Planning carefully, he strode to the door.

27

Milan, Italy

In her white wig and body padding, Raina Manhardt stepped out of the Alitalia tunnel with the last of the passengers from Geneva. Bent over, walking slowly on the blue-green carpet, she was in her persona of Melissa O'Dey. She carried her suitcase in one hand, listing toward it, infirm. She watched from the corners of her eyes as people hurried off to claim their baggage or check the monitors for their next flight. She checked her flight, too — it was on time. She had a one-hour layover.

As she moved away, her mind kept racing ahead to whether Jay would meet her in Washington. She had never expected to see him again. But now she hoped to, dreaded to. The conflict was nothing new. She remembered November and December 1985 — first Pavel Abendroth had been assassinated, then Jay's whole family was murdered in a car bombing. Jay and she met twice shortly afterward, but guilt about Dr. Abendroth loomed between them. Neither wanted to see the other again.

Then in late December her husband had visited, and they decided to divorce. He was a colonel in the Soviet Army. Six months later, in May, he was killed, too, in a skirmish with mujahideen outside Kabul. When Jay heard, he added a personal note to his usual coded packet. With an exchange of more messages, they arranged to meet far from anyone who might recognize them, in Dubrovnik, Yugoslavia.

Perched on cliffs above sapphire waters, Dubrovnik was a medieval port city on the Adriatic, with storybook houses and ancient battlements and limestone pavement polished to a smooth sheen by centuries of wear. Jay rented a small *pension* for them, with feather beds and rock fireplaces.

Nervous, unsure, she found him waiting in the rose garden. He jumped to his feet and froze, shocked, as he stared at her swollen belly. Then his eyes misted, and he was holding her, his arms locked around her, crushing her close.

His breath was warm against her neck. "I'm happy. Are you happy about this?"

"Very," she had whispered. "But I should

tell you that you're not —"

"Don't." His voice was husky with emotion. "You're here. A baby's coming. That's all I need to know."

The geography of love was mysterious and bewitching — until betrayed. As she thought about that in the Milan terminal, she forced her attention back to the crowds. A babel of languages filled the air. Boarding announcements sounded from the airport's speakers. She stopped at a currency-exchange booth to trade her euros and Swiss francs for dollars.

But as she walked off, her shoulders tightened. She had noticed abrupt movement to the side and behind. It was a man bending over to tie his shoelaces. He had been just slow enough for an experienced operative to make him.

She pretended to peer into the window of a Dufry store as he straightened up. Although handsome in a rough-hewn sort of way, he exuded a characterlessness that discouraged anyone from looking twice. Perhaps thirty years old, he wore dark pants, a knit shirt, and a loose sports jacket. There was a muted bulge under his left arm.

He had not flown in with her, nor did she recognize him from anywhere else. She stepped into a café and asked for a table.

The problem was serious — if he were tailing her, that meant the CIA or the BND or both would be waiting for her at Dulles. As she turned to be seated, she glanced back at the café's entryway, hoping she was wrong. Hoping he had continued down the concourse. Her hands were suddenly sweaty. There was someone else asking for a table — the man.

Outside Herndon, Virginia

It was the last few lonely hours before dawn, and the night felt like a black abyss. Following Ben's directions, Elaine drove the Jag around his big stone house, her headlamps off. Ben had deactivated the outside floodlights while they were outdoors, and darkness cloaked the car.

At last she saw him, waiting alertly beside the smaller of two stone-and-wood garages, Browning in hand, a silhouette visible only because of starlight. Houri circled him, then paced toward the house, her long nose raised, sniffing suspiciously. Elaine parked inside the garage, grabbed her SIG Sauer, and stepped out. She surveyed the drive and trees as she joined Ben.

He closed the garage door. "While we're here, I want to show you an escape route. With luck, you won't need it." He led her around to the rear, where he described the system he had invented.

As they walked back along the drive, she asked curiously, "Why have you been helping Jay?"

"A lot of reasons. One is that I owe him a large debt." He turned over his wrist. In the faint light, the scar he had told her in prison was the result of a pipe cut looked even uglier. He held up the backs of both arms. Welted scars indicating deep wounds began at his elbows and vanished up under the sleeves of his T-shirt. "I have them all over, courtesy of the KGB. They decided to test some experimental interrogation techniques on me. Jay got me out of that mess."

There was a lump in her throat. "How horrible for you."

He shrugged. "I worked with Jay off and on for years. Never met anyone I respected more. I retired from the DO a while ago, so when Jay was sentenced, I had the time to put together the documents I needed to go deep cover and get a job with the Bureau of Prisons. Then I arranged a transfer to Allenwood. Of course, the FBI will eventually figure out I was the one behind Jay's escape."

"That's why the house is packed up. And Zahra? Who's she?"

"My wife. Between shifts, I'd live here as Ben Kuhnert. I had an apartment near Allenwood where I was David Oxley. Zahra's found us a new place far away. Maybe someday we'll be able to come back." His gaze swept over the lawns and trees and old stone buildings with an intimacy that announced emotional claim. "Hope so, anyway."

"Maybe you can answer a question. . . . Why do you think Jay turned on America, Ben?"

He glanced at her, surprised. Then he nodded to himself. "You haven't worked with Jay enough yet to realize he's an enigma. He's capable of anything within reason — *his* reason. He's brilliant, witty, egotistical, impatient, and — above all — courageous. As a spymaster, he exuded an optimism that was contagious, and his people developed a sense of pride and an esprit de corps others envied. Partly that's because he's got such a strong sense of who he is that he doesn't bother much about what a bureaucracy's going to think. But that fed his reckless side, too. If he did sell us out to the Russians, he had a good reason — or thought he did."

"If?" It was the first time anyone outside her own mind had expressed doubt.

"There's always an 'if' in our world."

"But you don't know what that reason could be."

"I'll probably never know. That's where loyalty comes in. It reveals character, and it's a measure of whom one can trust enough for friendship and, ultimately, whether one can trust oneself. The Russians have a good saying — 'Tell me who your friend is, and I'll tell you who you are.'"

They turned onto a brick path beneath tall oaks and cut across the side lawn toward the kitchen. Houri ran ahead, feathered ears flying. As soon as they were indoors, Ben reactivated the floodlights, and Elaine hurried to the big kitchen window to keep watch. From there she had a complete view of the circular drive and the two stone houses on either side.

Ben took eggs and cheese from the refrigerator and put a frying pan on the gas stove. As he turned on the burner, he considered her. There was a forlorn quality to her as she stood against the dark glass in her dirty T-shirt and pants, gripping her weapon, staring out, her blond hair wild. A smudge of dirt streaked down her cheek.

"You like him," he decided, "but you're having a hard time getting past the idea that he's a traitor."

"I may never."

He nodded. "If it'll help, I believe he's a good man. Fair. Decent. And a hell of a liar. Intelligence systems are based on secrecy, so lying's necessary. You know that. But it does wear on you, change you, especially since you're doing it in hopes of creating a better world, and a better world can't be based on lies. If you're on the firing line long enough, you'll forget who you used to be, and then you won't care. Because if you care, you can't keep doing the work."

She peered at him, her pale blue eyes large, then she gazed back out the window into the daunting night. "I thought I understood that."

Ben raised his voice. "Hello, Jay. Aren't you tired of standing in the doorway? Come on in." He looked behind him.

Jay did not move. His skin was dark with grime, the bristle of his growing beard an iron-colored mat. He was studying Elaine, his eyes soft, not hiding his fondness for her. "The key is belief. You have to believe in something worth caring about. Something good. But first you have to figure out what that is for you."

She gave a small, unsure smile and nodded.

Ben noisily set a bowl of scrambled eggs

and a plate of whole-grain toast onto the wood trestle table. "Sit down and eat," he ordered. "Both of you." Sharp cheddar cheese blanketed the eggs, melting. The savory aromas filled the kitchen.

"Thanks, Ben." Elaine pulled out a chair and settled gratefully onto it.

When Jay said nothing, Elaine and Ben turned to watch as he padded toward them, his gait light, almost menacing. His face was more than sober, it was grim, and he radiated hyperwariness. He skinned off his jacket so that he was wearing only his shirt and his holstered Browning. The flap was open so he could pull the gun out quickly. He tossed the jacket onto a chair and put a hand into his jeans pocket and withdrew it.

Mystified, Elaine watched him open his fingers. Her breath caught in her throat — a triangle-shaped gold piece glittered on his palm. She remembered the photo she found in his cell in which he was wearing the piece as a pendant. Jay let it drop onto the table-top, where it spun like an arrow. She touched it, stopping the spin. She looked up at Ben, saw his expression had grown detached, cold.

Jay's hazel eyes were dark pits. "Ben?"

Ben stared at Jay a moment. Then he nodded. Never taking his gaze from Jay, he went to the fireplace mantel, picked up something small, and shot it in a fast slide across the table. It came to rest next to Jay. It was another gold triangle.

Ben announced, "In case you don't remember — Palmer's fits one side of yours. Mine fits the other."

Jay did not respond. He adjusted them until their toothy sides joined. He lifted his head and smiled widely.

Ben grinned back. "Okay, fill me in."

As the tension evaporated, Elaine exhaled: She had just witnessed something almost primitive.

Ben went to the kitchen window, taking over her post. Jay sat across from her and piled scrambled eggs onto his plate. But he did not eat. "I'll start at the beginning, Ben. The reason I asked you to break me out of Allenwood was a story in the *Herald Tribune* about the accidental death of Kristoph Maas." He hesitated. "He was Raina Manhardt's and my boy."

"You and Raina Manhardt? I had no idea. How long were you and she — ?"

"Not long enough." Again Jay hesitated. "I didn't see them after '94. Raina and I sometimes phoned. At Christmas she'd send photos." He almost smiled. Then he recalled how difficult it had been to have a normal conversation with her. The last time was the worst, when he told her about his arrest.

"I'm really sorry about the boy, Jay," Ben said. "Must be terrible for you."

"It hasn't been great," he admitted. He described the news story and photos that included Raina's signal that she needed help. "It seemed logical that whatever had happened, it involved Kristoph. I planned to lie low after you busted me out and wait for her to get in touch. Instead, Theosopholis tried to scrub me as I was leaving the prison, a janitor attacked when I stopped to pick up supplies, and another janitor was waiting at Palmer Westwood's place. He tried to wipe me, too. When a wet squad arrived, Palmer and I barely escaped. But that time I was in luck — I recognized two of the shooters. Both were Whippet." He paused. "Whippet is a Langley unit."

"Langley? No!"

"It gets worse." Jay picked up his fork. "Elaine?"

"My assignment to hunt Jay came through Whippet," she told Ben. "I was just starting to make progress when a janitor attacked me. I was able to wipe him, but when I got back to Whippet, I not only discovered everyone there had been liquidated, his corpse was lying on a desk. He was really a Whippet operative in disguise, which was strong evidence they'd tried to scrub me, too."

As Ben stared at her, Jay picked up the story: "I'd arrived earlier, just as the wet squad was leaving, and I got a good look at most. Later I spotted two outside Elaine's town house." He described knocking out Billy, taking his cell phone, and planting a bug on him. "So what we know from the recording and my conversation with Jerry is that some kind of big deal is going down today and that Jerry works for a Mr. G, who's the force behind it."

Ben said nothing, shaking his head gloomily.

"A few hours ago," Elaine went on, "we were attacked again. That's because I was able to sneak a phone call to Laurence Litchfield. He told me he'd send a team to capture Jay." She grimaced, feeling again the terror. "Instead, Jerry and his killers showed up. They ambushed us."

"Jesus Christ," Ben said. "Larry Litchfield, too?"

"The entanglement is deeper," Jay said. "Kristoph was a programmer. When he died, he was on a job for an outfit called Milieu Software. Milieu is a Whippet front company. Larry runs Whippet."

Ben swore loudly.

Jay leaned forward and clasped his hands. He looked down at them and then up at Ben. "Whippet was over in Geneva doing something that probably got Kristoph killed, so the deal isn't confined to the United States. Raina is being hunted, too. Whoever Mr. G is, he's got the resources to penetrate a high-security federal pen and plant Theosopholis. At the same time, Larry Litchfield wouldn't touch anything unless he understood exactly what was going on. Whatever the deal is, he must think it's failure-proof. Since he's been informing on us, he must be working directly with Mr. G, because he wouldn't bother with anyone lower. As for Mr. G, he's got steel nuts to order Whippet butchered."

Ben inhaled. "Holy shit. This deal must be *huge.*"

Jay nodded. "Huge and dangerous. We need to find out exactly what it is and stop it. That's going to take experienced operatives. Only the best will have a chance. I want the old team."

Ben peeled away from the window casing. "I'll phone them."

"Everyone but Palmer. He wanted to help because of Raina, but he's over seventy now.

I've already told him no."

Ben headed toward the hallway. "Understood. Finish eating and get your showers so you'll be ready when they get here."

Ben Kuhnert sat at the big computer in his office, and Houri laid her head in his lap. He petted her absentmindedly as he gathered himself, shaking off unease. Finally he tapped into his online address book and ordered the computer to dial out.

Frank Mesa lived thirty miles away. He answered quickly, but his voice was turgid with sleep. "Yeah?"

"This is Ben. I need you. Bring your piece of the medallion."

"Are you crazy?" The voice rose with indignation. "Go look at your goddamn clock!"

"Your gold piece — bring it," Ben said. "Come armed. We've got a situation."

There was a long pause. A noisy clearing of a throat. A defeated sigh. "Okay. But indulge me — I'm going to throw on some clothes first."

As soon as he heard the dial tone, Ben again went to his address book, and again the computer dialed.

Elijah Helprin was slower to respond, but he sounded fully awake. "Yes? Hello."

"This is Ben. I need you. Bring your part of the medallion."

There was a surprised hesitation. "What's happened?"

"I'll tell you when you get here. Come armed. Don't forget the gold piece."

"Give me a break, Ben. Tell me *now.*"

"Not until you're here. Are you coming or not?"

"Of course I'm coming," he said irritably. "It'll be thirty minutes."

"You're dressed?" Ben asked.

"I've got clothes on. Why — is it formal?" He sighed. "I said I'd be there."

After Ben and Houri left, Elaine studied the arrowhead-shaped pieces glowing in the kitchen's light. They formed two-fifths of a disc. Including Palmer Westwood's, that meant two were missing.

"Ben's making two phone calls," she told Jay.

He nodded, reached down the table, and snagged the remote control. The television was behind her, near the fireplace. He turned it on to a news station.

Suddenly she was exhausted. As reporters' voices droned, they ate in companionable silence. News from around the world included more terrorist bombings and attacks. She glanced at Jay occasionally, noting the dark circles under his eyes and the tired slouch in his shoulders. When they finished eating almost simultaneously, she looked up to smile and comment.

But his gaze was in a laser lock on the television. He snapped up the TV remote and increased the volume.

"Elaine," he ordered, "look!"

She slid around on her chair.

". . . According to a police spokesman, the murdered man was Victor Malone," the newscaster read. A photo showed on the screen.

"Oh, no," she breathed. "It's Billy!"

Jay's voice was tight. "Jerry seems to have done a damn good job of covering him with a legend."

". . . was a college student from Chicago," the newscaster was saying. "Until recently, he lived in a Takoma Park motel under another name. It's believed Ms. Cunningham employed him to do repair work. . . ."

She felt the color drain from her face as her CIA photo filled the screen — her expression somber, her hair pulled back into a ponytail. She was easily identifiable.

"Elaine Cunningham's nine-millimeter pistol was found in a neighbor's trash can.

She works for the CIA and is considered
dangerous. . . ."

28

Milan, Italy

The airport café was busy, most of the tables full. The constant hum of humanity on the move floated through the arcaded entrance to Raina's ears, while the odors of garlic and aromatic tomato sauces wafted from the rear with each swing of the kitchen door. She ate risotto alla Milanese, glancing occasionally at her tail who sat at a table near the entry and devoured his meal. It was better to know exactly where he was than to force the issue of a clear exit.

For a moment she felt terribly alone. Memories washed over her. She paused eating and was catapulted back to 1989, to November 9, to that unforgettable night when the volatile Berlins had combusted not into a nuclear World War III but into outrageous celebration. For the first time since 1961, Communist citizens crossed freely into West Berlin. Tens of thousands

391

from both sides converged on the hated Wall, laughing, hugging, climbing it, dancing on it, chipping away at the pitted concrete, wildly kissing complete strangers, and uncorking champagne bottles.

She had found a baby-sitter for Kristoph and used the pandemonium to steal over the border for a few rare hours with Jay in a little hostelry near the Lehrter S-Bahn station. It had been two months since they had been able to be together. As soon as he heard her in the hall, he opened the door.

At the sight of him, desire riveted her. Then she flung herself into his arms. He pulled her into the room and kissed her neck, her face, her ears, her mouth, and kicked the door shut. His mouth was hot and sensual, shooting electrical charges to her core. She wanted to devour him, crawl into him, be him. Nothing else mattered. Just Jay. Only Jay. She had to have him.

The sex was explosive. After an hour they peeled apart and lay side by side, panting, sweating, their naked skin pressed together. And they talked. With Jay in those days, talk was like sex — thrilling, incredibly satisfying.

That night she thought the world was theirs. Soon their work would be finished. Jay could retire and write about the history they had lived. She could quit the CIA and BND, dust off her easel, and return to the painting for which she yearned but no longer had the heart. They would put behind them the bad marriages and the awful spy games and their invisible wounds and be together at last, have a home, raise Kristoph, have more children. They would live the lives others took for granted.

With the promise of that glittering future, she folded herself back into his arms for more sex, this time slow, deliberate, building.

But life turned inside out after that. Although the Cold War was over, as long as she was BND and he was CIA, they could not live together, much less marry, because that would increase the odds her triple-agent past would be uncovered. She asked when he would resign. When she could resign. But Jay made excuses. Then Erich turned her into a national symbol, an icon of hope, and the spotlight on her intensified the risk. Still, if they were free of both agencies, they could pack up Kristoph and slip away, and no one — not Kristoph, not their countries, not them — would be hurt.

Finally she wrote a formal resignation to the CIA. She was through. Finished. Jay was still her handler, so she gave him the letter.

As soon as Langley officially confirmed her separation, she told him, she would leave the BND. He disappeared for a month. Now it was years later, and Kristoph was dead, and those dreams were scar tissue. There was no Jay and Raina, Raina and Jay. They were backstory, like the Cold War. Like their dead spouses and Pavel Abendroth. Yet she was still captive, trapped in another DMZ, because Jay had stayed with Langley, and he had refused to accept her resignation.

She blinked and peered around the café. She looked at her watch and paid her bill and picked up her suitcase. As she shuffled out, the skin on the back of her neck crawled. She could feel the man's hot gaze tracking her.

Moving through the terminal, she forced herself back to work. To the exterior world of suitcases and flight tickets and feet that hustled and flew. To the peril of a stranger with a gun and an assignment. She caught glimpses of him as he followed, nonchalantly finishing a piece of focaccia. As she approached her gate, she passed shops and restrooms and spotted his reflection in the glass of an information booth. She slowed to check on him.

He stuffed the last bit of bread into his mouth and licked his fingers and passed her without a look, removing an Alitalia ticket envelope from inside his jacket. Then he joined the mob waiting for her flight to be called. He already knew what plane she was taking, and he was going to be on it.

Staying calm, she stopped beside a family talking in Polish some twenty feet away from him. Only first and business class had been called; the mass of people waited restlessly. His gaze brushed over her, then he casually ignored her. When the loudspeaker blared more seat numbers, about a third of the throng rustled into action, flooding between them.

Before he could look at her again, she darted back to the ladies' room. Locked in a stall, she kicked off her shoes as she skinned off her wig and Melissa O'Dey dress and padding. She dropped everything to the floor. On the toilet seat, she popped open her suitcase. No motion wasted, she stepped into men's Levi's and zipped them shut. Yanked on a wig of black hair that swung to her shoulders. Slithered into a sports bra that flattened her breasts. Pulled on a man's blue work shirt. Took moist wipes and scrubbed away her wrinkles. And grabbed a large gym bag and shook it open, then stuffed the old-lady costume into the suitcase and closed it. Tugging and adjusting, she slid the suitcase inside the gym bag and zipped it tight. Breathing deeply, she put on her favorite running shoes and tied them.

And listened. A mother and daughter spoke Italian at the sinks. She heard footsteps, flushing toilets, but nothing that told her the restroom had been invaded by security or a crazed male spy who had lost his target.

Avoiding eye contact, she strolled out with no more than a casual glance from a few of the other supplicants. She did not return to the concourse. Instead, she shifted her emphasis of movement from hips to shoulders, from female to male, and crossed directly into the adjacent men's room. She garnered even less notice there.

Locked in another toilet stall, she tied her new black hair into a ragged male ponytail with a thick, dirty rubber band. Peering in a hand mirror, she stuck on a black mustache and a short, uncombed black beard. Shoved her arms into a Harley-Davidson stenciled denim jacket, and slapped on narrow, evil-looking sunglasses — "shades."

This was as good as it got. Fresh passport and ticket in hand, she shut the suitcase and gym bag and slouched across the restroom, gripping the bag, now drawing attention in her flamboyant new persona. "Gunnar Hamsun" was flying to London, where he would catch his connection to Dulles International. She would buy props for him in terminal stores.

When she emerged onto the concourse, the last call for Melissa's Alitalia flight to Dulles was sounding. In the distance, her shadow stood next to the boarding gate, shifting his weight from foot to foot, cell phone to ear, as he glanced at his watch and glared around the empty waiting area. There was no one at the gate but him and airline personnel.

As the flight attendant unhooked the door to close it, signaling no more passengers could board, the man's face reddened. He barked into his cell, snapped it closed, and dashed stiff-backed into the airline tunnel.

As Raina strode away, she smiled grimly to herself, her gaze wary, watchful.

Outside Herndon, Virginia

By the time a car's motor sounded out on the drive, Elaine had finished showering and thrown on jeans and a sweater she found in Zahra's bureau. She grabbed her Walther and ran downstairs.

"Stay in the kitchen, Jay," Ben called. "Elaine's got her pistol."

Carrying an M-16, Ben was striding out of his office, all sinew and wiry muscle. His Browning was visible in the shoulder holster, strapped over his T-shirt. Houri was beside him, heeling. Her eyes were bright and vigilant.

"Elaine, I'm going to give you instructions," Ben told her. "Do exactly as I say. Nothing more. Nothing less. Got it?"

When she nodded, surprised, he shot orders over his shoulder as he unlocked the front door but did not open it. He stepped back as the engine noise stopped. There was no sound of a car door closing.

Ben used hand motions to order Houri to the left side of the front door, where she would be quickly visible to anyone who walked in. Elaine was also to his left, between him and the kitchen. He leveled his weapon at the closed door and checked Elaine as she loosened her knees, found the right balance, lifted the Walther in both hands, and aimed at the door, too. He nodded approval.

When the bell rang, he raised his voice and said, "Come in."

The knob turned. The door opened. Stepping inside, backlit by the floodlights, was a short man with a full head of bushy gray hair.

He stopped, and the grin on his face vanished. He stared at the M-16 then across to the Walther and around to Houri. He had swarthy skin and black eyes and a stocky body encased in a crew-necked sweater and zippered jacket. His casual pants were pressed to a sharp military seam. He looked a decade younger than Jay and Ben.

"What in hell is going on!" he demanded.

"Continue in slowly," Ben ordered. "Keep your hands where I can see them."

"Have you lost your fucking mind?" The man started to leave.

Ben nodded at Houri. Instantly she was up on all paws, growling. Her lips rose, showing sharp fangs. Her rumble deepened, warning of imminent attack.

Ben told the stranger, "I wouldn't try that again. If I decide to be nice, I won't shoot. I'll let the dog take you down. On the other hand, she's trained to kill."

The short man glared at Ben.

His face impassive, Ben stared back.

The rising growl of the dog sent shudders along Elaine's spine.

The man's eyes shifted. He checked the dog again. His shoulders slumped. "What do you want?"

"Show me your gold piece. Carefully."

"Call off Houri first."

Ben nodded at her again. But the growls did not stop. She moved her nose, pointing behind the stranger out into the floodlit night.

Ben's finger tightened on the trigger. The muscles in his jaw worked. "Who's with you?"

Silently, an older man with thick white hair and a sun-wrinkled face with raptor features rolled around the doorjamb. Elaine recognized him instantly — Palmer Westwood.

Westwood ignored the dog and the weapons, and his old eyes glowed warmly at Ben. "It's been a long time, Ben. I expected a better welcome than this."

Ben paused, seeming to consider the implications of this unexpected visitor. Again he nodded at the dog. This time the menacing rumbles stopped.

"Do you have your gold piece?" Ben demanded.

"I do."

"I need to see yours, too."

In slow motion, the two men slid their hands into pockets and brought out similar gold triangles.

"Follow Elaine," Ben ordered.

She backed toward the short hallway, keeping her Walther trained on them. They started after her together, but Ben cocked his head. The dog moved between them, separating them. Ben locked the front door as Elaine continued to back up, leading them single file into the kitchen. The aroma of strong coffee percolating on the counter permeated the air. A fire hissed in the fireplace.

Their eyes widening with surprise, both men looked silently across the room to Jay, who stood at the window, his expression neutral. The muzzle of his Browning tracked their progress.

"You'll see where you need to put them." Ben spoke from behind.

They glanced around then headed toward the table and laid down their gold pieces. Palmer Westwood nudged his into the other side of Jay's, then the first man tucked his into Westwood's. Each piece fit perfectly. Elaine lowered her pistol. Jay holstered his and picked up a coffee mug from the windowsill.

Ben relaxed his M-16. "Stand down, Houri."

The dog shook herself all over, metamorphosing from killer to pet.

Watching, Palmer Westwood smiled, showing even white teeth. He turned and pumped Ben's hand. "It's even better to see you now, Ben."

"I agree." Ben smiled back.

The two men towered over the first one, who was grinning good-naturedly again. He shook Ben's hand next.

"*Shalom,* Elijah," Ben said.

"*Salam* yourself." Elijah leaned toward the dog. "Hello, Houri. Shake." She sat, tail wagging, for the greeting. He straightened and looked at Ben then Jay. "Palmer came by looking for you, Jay, and told me what he knew. We wondered whether we'd find you here. Ben never gave me a chance to ask." Then he glared at Elaine and demanded, "Who's she, Ben?"

"Jay's hunter — Elaine Cunningham. Elaine, meet Palmer Westwood and Elijah Helprin."

She shook their hands and exchanged pleasantries.

Palmer slid off his jacket and adjusted the weapon at the small of his back. "Glad to see you're still alive, Jay."

But Jay was frowning at Palmer. "I asked you to stay out of this."

Palmer straightened, hard and regal, and looked him in the eye. "I've been in the game long enough to know what I'm getting into. I smell caffeine. I'm going to have some."

As he marched to the percolator, Houri ran to Ben, her claws tapping a rapid tattoo on the linoleum. She silently nudged his arm.

"Our last visitor is here," he announced. "Stay in the kitchen, Elaine. I'll handle him. Come on, Houri."

As he and the dog left, the noise of a well-timed automobile engine became audible, approaching the house. Elijah joined Palmer at the coffeepot and poured himself a large mug. When the front door opened, Ben's commanding voice carried back, and another man responded angrily. Everyone watched the arch that led into the hall.

Houri stalked through it, glancing warily over her shoulder. A stranger followed, Ben close behind. The new man was in his mid-sixties, second in age to Palmer. Of moderate height and weight, he had mousy hair and bland coloring and a boring face made more so by horn-rimmed bifocals. He wore a zippered jacket and cotton chinos. There was nothing distinctive about him, yet one had the sense there could be.

When he saw Jay, the neutral facade shattered. "What are you doing here, you goddamned traitor!" Disgust and rage seethed from him.

He whirled to leave but was stopped

instantly by Ben's raised M-16. At the same time, Houri showed her teeth, and a threatening growl rose from her throat.

The man's back stiffened. He glanced at the dog then stared at Ben.

"You know the drill." Ben's tone was implacable.

They stood that way a few seconds longer, then the man turned back into the kitchen, his body still rigid. Without a glance at Jay, he checked around then walked angrily to the table. He dropped a gold triangle and poked it into place. The medallion was now complete. When he raised his head, his furious glare fixed again on Jay.

Before he could speak, Ben said, "Give Jay a chance. All of you have to hear what's happened anyway. Then if you still want out, Frank, you can go. Any of you can go. No hard feelings. All we ask is you don't say anything to anyone."

Frank tore his gaze from Jay but said nothing.

Jay spoke across the room, his voice expressionless, almost a monotone, in the code of undercover professionals relating nothing but the facts, as he began the story again, alternating with Elaine. When he explained how Jerry had killed Billy in cold blood, Frank seemed to lose his edginess.

When Elaine described the cars hurtling toward them, two from the front, two from the rear, and that Larry Litchfield had sent them, Frank heaved a sigh of resignation.

As Jay finished the story, Frank stared down at the gold pieces. "It's been a long time since we've seen this whole thing put together." He lifted his head, considering them where they sat and stood. Behind his horn-rimmed glasses, affection seeped into his sober eyes, then worry. "Okay, I'm in. Jay, I hope like hell you're not as guilty as I think you are, but even if you are, we've got to find out what Larry's up to. That arrogant SOB could fall into a cesspool and come up smelling like roses. I've got my BlackBerry with a list of contacts from the old days. My Uzi's in the car. I'm wearing my Browning." Then he swung around to study Elaine. "But what about her? Can we trust her? What do you really know about her?"

The men stared. She banished emotion from her face and looked at each, one at a time. "Jay will vouch for me. And I may have more information for you, but before I hand it over, it's your turn. Who are *you*? What's your relationship? What do the pieces of that gold medallion mean?"

"What information do you have?" Jay demanded.

"I cleaned out the front seat and glove compartment of Jerry's BMW after you drew them into the woods."

They looked at Jay for a decision. Their faces were wrinkled, the colors of their eyes dimming, but they exuded an informed electricity that was ageless.

Finally, Jay nodded at Palmer. "You tell her. You were in charge."

29

The atmosphere in Ben Kuhnert's kitchen was tense. Houri circled restlessly beneath the heavy-timbered ceiling. Palmer pulled out a chair and sat at the table, not even touching his coffee. His profile was almost inanimate. Whatever the events were, Elaine decided, they must have been momentous.

"It was 1985, the depths of the Cold War in West Berlin," Palmer began, his voice low, commanding. "The city was a political island, completely surrounded by the Wall. We were so close to East Germany, we could hear the Communists piss. They'd made themselves into a sanctuary for terrorists — but they called them revolutionaries — and there wasn't a damn thing we could do about it. The Stasi trained them and sold them guns. They even booked that butcher Carlos into a luxury hotel with other hard-currency guests. Then in February, Jay got a tip that an unusual group of Islamic fanatics had landed in East Berlin to make a big arms buy."

Ben paced the kitchen, his large nose and opinionated chin leading. "'Big' and 'unusual' got our attention fast. Terrorist attacks were soaring. There were more in Europe than today even."

"Palmer wasted no time." Jay was focused on his mentor. "He put together a black operation called DEADAIM to track the deal. There were nine of us NOCs."

"We bugged government supply offices and arms manufacturers," Frank told her, his thick body stiff. "Did black-bag jobs, too."

"We acted as go-betweens and fixers and looked for people to turn." Short and stocky, Elijah sat on the edge of a kitchen chair as if ready to spring into action. "We had the language skills, and we had Catholics and Muslims and Jews and Protestants and men and women, so we could talk the various talks and move in a lot of worlds."

"Then in March, Trent was kidnapped." Palmer shook his white head with the bad memory. "It took us four months and a fifty thousand dollars cash ransom to get him back."

The room fell into silence. They avoided one another's eyes.

"And?" Elaine prompted.

Palmer sighed. "By then, we'd been investigating five months. We knew the buyers were heads of a fledgling network of radical Islamic groups called al-Ahrar. Al-Ahrar means 'freedom.' They wanted a big deal to impress other extremist leaders to bring in their groups, too. It was a promising experiment for them — and could grow into a hell of a threat to our side. To finance it, they imported hash from the Bekaa Valley and sold it on the streets of Europe."

"Jay was sneaking into East Berlin and finally scored some photos." Like the others, Elijah had not touched his coffee since Palmer began the story. "We were able to identify some. The mastermind was a kid — a Syrian named Faisal al-Hadi. They were all so damn young that we were shocked."

Elaine said nothing, but she remembered al-Hadi's name. He was the other half of the exchange in which Jay had arranged Dr. Abendroth's assassination.

"Al-Hadi was only twenty," Jay told her from his post at the window, "but he was the oldest. They were the first wave of the diaper commandos we see heading terrorist cells now. But in those days, as my source said, it was highly unusual."

"This was when it got really obvious Jay

was a hotshot." Ben glanced at him.

"He was going places," Frank agreed. "I'll bet half the intel came from his work."

"Then Linda disappeared," Elijah said bitterly. "Cops found her body caught in reeds down the Havel, drowned. Sally was 'accidentally' killed by a hit-and-run driver on the Ku'damm. And Carlee died in her sleep of asphyxiation from a gas leak. It was all crap. Poor women. Three liquidations of our people in two days."

"At the same time, the six of us had near misses," Palmer said somberly.

"There had to be a leak, but it didn't make sense," Frank said. "Our security was tight, and we were close — handpicked for psychological makeup and expertise."

"Finally we got a break, but it was almost the end of us," Frank said. "An intel broker nobody had ever heard of phoned the consul general and gave a code name — Moses. He said his product was free this one time to prove his bona fides. So the consul general listened then burned the phone lines getting the chief of station to set up a *treff* with Palmer. Right, Palmer?"

The old spymaster's voice was hollow: "Moses claimed Trent wasn't Trent. He said the Stasi snatched our Trent and performed plastic surgery on a guy with Trent's coloring and body build and taught him to be Trent. Then they erased Trent and sent the double to infiltrate DEADAIM, screw it up, and move on to other missions and do the same thing. The corker was the bastard bit into a poison pill before we could get a damn thing out of him!"

Elaine inhaled. "How did the Stasi know about DEADAIM? You were *black*."

Frank grimaced. "Yeah, that was real bad. Our families and friends hadn't seen us. The only people in the loop were at Berlin Operations Base and, of course, Langley."

"It must've been someone there," she said. "So that's why you cut up the medallion. You needed to make sure no other double slipped in."

"It was Palmer's idea," Jay told her. "He bought a medallion at a carnival, and Frank used a jeweler's saw so no two pieces were the same. We added them to our pocket litter and went deeper undercover. No contact with the Berlin station or Langley at all. None. After that, we had no more problems."

"Not with that," Palmer agreed. "But we still hadn't identified the buyer, and it was September. There was enough money involved it could've been one of the big ones — Sarkis Soghanalian or Adnan Khashoggi or the Icelander, Loftur Johannesson."

"The street went silent," Elijah told her. "But we knew the deal had to go down soon. We were starting to sweat missiles — then Jay vanished."

"We were worried he'd been kidnapped like Trent," Frank rumbled. "Instead, he came home with a rabbit stuffed in his hat. You've got to understand about Jay. He never talked about his sources. He wouldn't tell you jack shit. He wouldn't tell Langley or Berlin, either. They'd get so mad they'd threaten to can him. But he wouldn't tell. So when he got back with that satisfied look on his face, I knew he'd been to one of his secret rendezvous — and he had the time and location."

Palmer nodded. "With that, we were back in business. The goal was a major news incident, so our people passed the intel to the German authorities and the international press. When al-Ahrar showed at the warehouse, our people were hiding. As soon as the kids started loading their trucks, we tried to arrest them. Instead, the dummies opened fire. We shot back. They wouldn't give up. Suddenly we had a bloodbath on our hands. In the end, most of their leaders died, which effectively killed the whole al-

Ahrar network. A big win for us in that way alone."

Frank's eyes shone through his horn-rimmed bifocals. "We got everything. They had some brand-new weapons straight out of Soviet factories that we'd never even heard of. When we told Ramstein what we were sending, they drooled on themselves."

"We also got a sack filled with nine million dollars in cash — al-Ahrar's last payment to their dealer. Whoever he was, he must've choked on the loss." Palmer's leathery face spread in a grin. "The incident made headlines for a month. Langley was ecstatic."

"They promoted Palmer to ADDO," Jay told her. "He thought he might like the job, and by God, Langley delivered."

"They did right by Jay, too," Ben said. "A newspaper blew his cover by printing his photo, which meant his days as a NOC were over. So Langley made him Berlin chief. Then he shot up the food chain even higher than Palmer and became DDO."

"And the Commies got the big wet kiss-off." Elijah chuckled.

Around the room, the men broke into relieved laughter. They caught one another's eyes and laughed harder. The kitchen rocked. It had been a terrifying time when

413

they lost nearly half their team to treachery, and yet not only did they persevere, but they triumphed completely. They reveled in the impossible accomplishment.

But then the laughter died. A chill seemed to settle over the room. They had crucial business to address. They stared at Elaine.

Before Jay could say a word, Elaine picked up her shoulder bag. "Let's see what I found in the BMW."

As Palmer, Elijah, and Frank leaned close, and Jay and Ben hovered, she dropped items onto the table — AAA maps, two books of Camel's matches, a crushed paper cigar ring, a recent issue of *Briare's Military and Intelligence Magazine,* sticky candy wrappers, a cracked plastic CD case without a label, three gel pens, assorted pencils, and a little Bubble Wrapped bundle. There was no car registration.

The operatives pushed through the plunder. Looking for notes, Jay checked the paper cigar ring, and Palmer inspected the matchbooks. Frank picked up the magazine and turned pages.

Elijah grabbed the Bubble Wrapped bundle. He ripped it open and dumped out little packets and peeled one open. "I'll be damned." His swarthy face darkened as he spilled out what appeared to be a fat grain of sand. "It's a StarDust computer!"

"A computer that miniaturized?" Jay said instantly. "What does it do?"

"*Submicro*miniaturized," Elijah corrected. "Shit! This is cutting-edge technology! How in hell did Jerry get it? The military's been experimenting with StarDusts secretly. So have we. They're not going to be on the market for years!" Worriedly, he glanced at Elaine. "I'm the only one here not retired. Still in the DO." He opened another packet, his expression grim. "These little babies are amazing. Tiny solar batteries fuel them. You program them to record two or three simple jobs like monitoring motion and temperature. They talk to each other and send their intel to a central computer that coordinates all of it. StarDust networks are powerful — they can blanket miles!"

"You say you've used them in operations?" Jay asked.

"A month ago we dropped some from a plane into an Afghanistan canyon and were able to track Taliban on horseback where we'd always lost them. We found their hidden tunnel, and that led us to a cell of al-Qaeda dug into a cave complex. Hell, we'd been trying to break that cell for a year!"

"Frank, you've got the *Briare's*," Jay said sharply. "Anything marked?"

He shook his head. "Not a damn thing."

Jay grabbed the magazine. "Okay, everyone, we're onto something. See what else you can find."

They examined the rest of the items closely for words, scribbles, numbers, anything. A new pile grew on the other end of the table where they tossed what they discarded.

"I'll be damned!" Jay flipped the magazine around and pointed to a dog-eared page. "Take a look at this." It was a photo of a small winged drone.

LETHAL GYROBIRD SOARS IN MILITARY'S ESTIMATION

"How the hell did I miss that?" Frank frowned. "What's a GyroBird?"

"A brand-new miniature drone — state-of-the-art," Jay told them. "Each weighs only seven ounces, and the wings fold back so soldiers can carry them in backpacks or hanging off their belts. The drones take still photos and stream live video day or night. That's standard. But two things make these particularly useful — they use ducted fan propulsion so they fly not only like a fixed-wing aircraft but hover and land like a helicopter, and each is loaded with a special high-blast explosive that'll take the top off a building."

Ben let out a long stream of air. "And this and the StarDusts are from the car Mr. G's janitors are using!"

"Neither's available to the public." Jay's face was grim as he pointed out, "And the only customer for both is the U.S. government. That means Mr. G's deal is not only big — it's dangerous as hell. An illegal arms transaction of this size can only mean one thing — terrorists."

30

Miami, Florida

Whispering prayers to himself, Faisal al-Hadi carried his gym bag along the Miami sidewalk, while in his mind he was in the sacred Damascus of his boyhood. He could almost hear cymbals clanging and water sellers calling, *"Atchan, taa Saubi!"* If you thirst, come to me! He imagined slipping into the great Umayyad Mosque and kneeling amid the cool marble tiles. *Thanks be to Allah.*

With a slow intake of breath, al-Hadi returned to the present and peered around. People strolled past without a second look, but then he appeared to be one of them, with his fashionable hair, smooth-shaved face, and Western clothes. As traffic flowed like a dirty river, he pushed in through Kinko's door. The artificial lights made his eyes ache. Squinting, he sat at a computer and

418

inserted a credit card under an assumed name.

He retyped Martin Ghranditti's printout, translating it into Arabic, then went online to PhotoHeat.com, an abomination of X-rated pictures. In the past, he had concealed text and photos and maps on Western sites promoting books, toys, cars, and sports. He had even penetrated eBay. But although spy agencies prowled the ether with detection software, they found only a fraction of the secret messages hidden in the Web's billions of Web sites and images.

With a dark smile, al-Hadi used a CD containing new encryption software to convert Ghranditti's manifest into ciphertext that looked like garbage — a mixture of symbols, numbers, and letters. Then he activated the CD's steganography program. All computer files — text, images, sound recordings — had unused or insignificant data areas where the program could hide material.

A series of Arabic-labeled buttons flashed onto his screen. Working quickly, he inputted the file path and added the location of his encrypted text. The program prompted him for a pass phrase. He typed in *iHna hena* — "we are here" — and clicked FINISH. Within seconds the data was invisibly integrated into the tenth photo on the obscene Web site. He activated the Internet trace destructor and exited.

Confident, he removed his credit card and CD and dropped them into his long gym bag, next to his M-4 and pistol. He stood erect, a silent man of moral rectitude, a warrior for Allah. Gym bag in hand, he drifted back outside into the godless crowds of glittering Miami, remembering the last time one of his messages had been discovered by the infidels.

They had been so baffled they'd had to send it to the National Security Agency, where their best mathematicians needed a supercomputer and a year of work to decode it. They did not have the luxury of a year now. He would own the shipment in hours.

Outside Herndon, Virginia

In Ben Kuhnert's country kitchen, the fire in the stone fireplace had burned down to nervous flames. Everyone was focused on Jay. Almost imperceptibly, the flesh of his face tightened against his bones just as Elaine had seen on the video. Jay looked aristocratic, radiating a confidence that made her want to believe anything he said, accept anything he decided. Even Palmer seemed riveted.

As if anointing them, Jay's eyes swept the team: "We need to uncover exactly what's in the deal, who's behind it, who's getting it, what it's intended for, and when and where it's going to change hands. And we need to do it fast — remember, it's happening today." As they nodded soberly, he looked at Elijah. "You know about the Star-Dusts. They were probably stolen somewhere along the line. Check into them."

"I'll find out who manufactured them and take it from there," Elijah said instantly.

Jay slid the *Briare's* across the table to Palmer. Palmer stopped it with a quick motion. "Same assignment, Palmer. You take on the drones."

Palmer's nod was so curt that Elaine was reminded he was accustomed to giving orders, not taking them — even from Jay.

"Today it's mostly Islamic or Arab terrorists who are buying illegally," Jay continued.

Ben interrupted, "Consider it handled."

"What about me?" Frank, the consummate gray operative with the bland countenance, had an eager glow to him.

"You still have sources among international traffickers?" Jay asked.

"I do. Some had such intimate relationships with Washington that they bought estates around here."

"Okay, your job is to find a Mr. G who employs a Jerry and a Rink. He'd have insider intel about Whippet and the power to pull in Larry Litchfield and put together a shipment that includes StarDusts and Gy-roBirds. Jerry said Mr. G's 'been doing this for years. He's at the top. He's the best in the business.'" He paused. "I remember several significant players whose last names began with G — Manucher Gorbanifar, Werner Glatt, Mark Allen Grady, Tim Gut-terman."

"There's a whole new crop since 9/11," Elijah assured him.

Jay nodded. "Before you go off, there are two more details. First, I told you Milieu Software hired Kristoph and that Milieu was a Whippet front. I don't know for sure why they chose him, but my guess is it was because he was something of a hotshot pro-grammer."

"He could've created some kind of special software to keep track of Mr. G's deal," Eli-jah said.

"Exactly," Jay agreed. "Raina's set up three alternate meets for today. If anything happens to me, someone has to find out what she knows and help her." He related the times and locations.

"We'll take care of her," Palmer assured

him. "What's the second detail?"

"Moses. Since he came up in the story about DEADAIM — have any of you heard anything about him? Is he still working?"

Palmer peered over his reading glasses at the others. "I told Jay it's been at least five years since anyone even mentioned the name to me."

"Sounds right," Elijah agreed. "I figured he'd retired. But then, I never got any of his famous calls promising intel in exchange for big bucks. He phone any of you?"

As they shook their heads, Jay asked, "Does anyone know his true identity?"

Again the men around the table shook their heads.

Ben looked puzzled. "What's this about, Jay? Have *you* heard from Moses?"

"Never. My interest's personal." Jay's face was a mask. He reached back and snared his backpack and changed the subject. "The people we're up against are more than good, and maybe not just because of the help Larry Litchfield's giving them. They fooled Elaine and me three times." He took out five new disposable cell phones and handed them out. "We can't take the risk you'll be tracked through your personal cells. I used a fake identity to buy these. Each phone has a hundred prepaid hours, and we can hold six-person conference calls."

"What's my assignment?" Elaine wanted to know.

"Too many people are looking for you, so you'll be low-key. You'll drive me."

"And I can watch your back," she said.

Ben looked up from examining his new cell phone. "I'll leave Houri here while you and Elaine get some sleep. If anyone moves out there, she'll let you know."

"We appreciate that. Turn on the cells," Jay ordered. "Figure out what your number is. We're going to have to memorize all of them, but they're sequential. I know I don't need to say it, but just to make sure we're clear — I'm relying on each of you to keep everything that's been said among ourselves. I'll sleep with my cell phone. Call as soon as you learn anything or you run into trouble."

"Just like the old days." Ben's eyes glittered with anticipation.

She watched as Jay looked at them with pride. In seconds they were on their feet, picking up their pieces of the medallion and exchanging numbers.

Jay slid his gold triangle into his pocket. "Our turn."

But she was already walking away, weary to the bone. Their rooms were adjacent on the second floor. As he followed her up the long staircase, their steps fell into rhythm. Beneath them, the voices of the operatives faded. The front door closed as Ben left to contact his Muslim source.

At the top of the stairs, she and Jay turned down the hall together. She lengthened her stride to match his. But then in the quiet, she heard Billy's voice again, his heartbreaking plea to Jerry to spare his life, and the muffled *pop* of the bullet that killed him. Her breath caught in her throat. She remembered the description of Pavel Abendroth's assassination in the CIA's list of Jay's treacheries — it had launched Jay's career as a mole.

She looked across at him and worked to keep her tone neutral. "Tell me about Dr. Abendroth."

"What about him?"

"Did you have him assassinated?"

As they continued on, she kept glancing at him.

His profile was granite. "And if I did?"

"I . . ." She was speechless. She had expected him to deny it. She wanted to shout, *Why!* The question ricocheted through her brain, but she had told him she would not ask why again.

And he did not offer. "Good night. Get

some sleep." He vanished into his room.

Northern Virginia

In the distance, traffic on Route 7 rumbled. Watching all around the lit parking lot, Ben Kuhnert ran to the mosque's porch, yanked off his shoes, and stepped inside, hoping he was not too late. He sped through the ritual washing of hands and face at the *hamam* then hurried to the imam's office and through to the private patio.

When he saw Imam Mustafa Nawwi, he exhaled with relief — the coffee and tea ceremony had not begun. He calmed himself, showing no sign of his worry that he could extract information from the imam about the identities of any terrorists involved in Mr. G's deal.

Surprised, Mustafa stared, the carafe in one hand. *"Salam, Binyamin. Ahlan wa-sahlan!"* It was a Bedouin expression: Our house is as open to you as the plain. "You're just in time. Let me serve you."

"Salam, Mustafa. It's good to see you, too." The spicy scent of the cardamom-flavored brew steamed in the cool dawn air.

Like a saint from the past, Mustafa Nawwi was cadaverous and dark-bearded, dressed in his usual long black robe. He took two cups from a cupboard above the high table,

426

poured, and handed coffee to Ben.

Because Mustafa had poured first, it was his responsibility to speak first: "I remember when we were boys, and your *khall* visited from Jerusalem. He's the one who taught us this tradition. We were such Americans."

"I'm still American, Mustafa," Ben said quietly. "But I'm also Muslim. If you don't feel American, why do you stay?" He knew the answer, and from it he hoped to build his argument.

"Ah, but I do feel very American. We have no disagreement, except that you want me to turn against some of my flock. But they're not accountable to me, Ben — only to Allah. I see now why you haven't been here in months. I'm saddened."

Following the imam's lead, Ben tipped back his head and drank. The coffee was as hot as the desert and as bitter as disappointment, cleansing the palate and the soul. Each step in the ritual had a purpose, each reflected a Bedouin philosophy of life. Many bloody fights on the sands had been averted in this way. By using the traditions of the ancient ceremony, Ben was gambling he could persuade his old friend to give him information about the arms deal.

It was Ben's turn. He poured and returned the imam's cup. Now he would speak first.

"Ideas are one thing. Actions entirely different. I've shown you evidence — all on the public record. They're fanatics claiming jihad as an excuse to murder anyone who won't follow them, while you and I know the truth is in the Koran — 'Thy task is only to exhort; thou cannot compel them to believe.'"

Mustafa's olive features were thoughtful. But then he frowned. "Still, it's not for me to judge their sincerity."

"Don't you think we have a responsibility to stop evil, old friend? You and I know the essence of Allah's laws is justice for all of humanity."

Mustafa looked at him sharply. "You didn't come here at this early hour to debate, Ben. What's happened?"

"I've been doing some contract work for State and stumbled onto an illegal weapons deal." The State Department was his longtime cover. "And it's in the District. The objective could be anywhere nearby. A block away. Even here at the mosque. You know they target nonextremist Muslims now."

As the imam's face sobered, Ben faced east, toward Mecca. The imam joined him, their shoulders touching, the physicality to remind them that humanity was a community, its diversity necessary and beautiful.

As they drank the last of the strong brew, Ben said a silent prayer that his argument had penetrated.

The imam set their cups aside and poured tea — sweet mint, symbolizing life itself — into two tiny cups. This was the only tea, and the end of the ritual. As they drank, Ben felt a chill of worry, wondering about Mustafa's decision. When their cups were empty, they set them on the high table and hugged, pounding each other's back.

It was the imam's turn to resume the conversation. As Ben watched anxiously, the cleric stepped back. He crossed his arms, his expression grave.

"As Bedouins, the sands of the desert run like blood through our veins," he said thoughtfully. "I spent quite a bit of time with our tribe when I was in Jordan. Their lives are hard, but they live in joy by praising Allah for what every moment brings. They feel showered by Allah's love — not hate." He hesitated, then nodded to himself. "You're right — we've allowed extremists to redefine Islam not just to the world but to too many of us." He squared his shoulders. "Stay for the prayer service, Ben. Afterward I'll give you the name of a person who may know something."

31

Washington, D.C.

Inside his redbrick Federalist house, Laurence Litchfield hurried downstairs through the morning's gloom. He turned on the lights in his office and sat at his desk. Behind him, his grandfather clock ticked softly. Above him, his wife and children slept. He liked the quiet, the lack of any activity but his own, the sense of complete ownership.

It had been one hell of a night, dismally capped with the news that Ghranditti's people had lost Jay Tice and Elaine Cunningham in rural Virginia, even though the ambush should have been a slam dunk. Every time he thought about it, he wanted to scrub them himself. Not only were the pair very much alive, Cunningham must realize his role in the failed trap, and if Jay were at his charming best, she might tell him.

Still, all was far from lost. Before he went to bed, he'd had a long talk with the Silver Spring police chief, who understood the importance of national security and would notify him the instant they found Cunningham.

The situation with Raina Manhardt was also hopeful. Her son's friend in Paris and the Genevois who gave her the security videos of the Milieu Software building had been eliminated. And with a list of her BND identities from Volker Rehwaldt, Alec discovered "Melissa O'Dey" had bought a plane ticket in Geneva. Then when they screened the video record of boarding passengers, Rehwaldt spotted her in disguise.

With a chilly smile, Litchfield turned on his computer and loaded the CD about Jay Tice that Cunningham had ordered compiled. He bypassed a file of e-mails and went straight to the meat — the data about Tice. It had been grouped into categories — people, places, years, missions, and so forth. He skimmed through, pausing occasionally to make a note.

He had just clicked onto Jay's operations when he heard vehicles pull into his drive. He whirled his chair around and peered out through his ivy-framed window, across the green lawn and the redbrick walks and the goldfish pond. Jaw clenched, he jumped to his feet, sped out of his office to the front door, and yanked it open.

Nate Harroldsen from Langley's Office of Security was standing on the brick stoop, hands clasped behind his back. "Good morning, Mr. Litchfield," he said cheerfully. He had pale blond hair and a broad pug nose. "I saw the light was on in your office, so I figured I wouldn't ring the bell. Didn't want to wake anyone else. She wants you to ride into Langley with her."

Litchfield put a smile on his face while inwardly cursing. In the driveway sat the DCI's armored black sedan. Behind it was an SUV — her chase car — its blue lights flashing. He smiled wider and nodded toward the sedan's darkened windows, acknowledging Bobbye Johnson's presence.

He told Harroldsen, "Give me a minute."

"She's in a hurry," Harroldsen warned.

"Got it," he said curtly.

He left the front door open and hurried back to his office, shutting that door. As he pulled the CD from his computer, he checked his cell for messages. There was one from Alec St. Ann. As he put the CD into his briefcase, he speed-dialed. While he was with Bobbye, it would be impossible to talk with either Alec or Martin Ghranditti.

His briefcase was fully packed, the electronic lock was activated, and his annoyance was escalating by the time Alec answered.

"Make it fast," Litchfield snapped. "The DCI's sitting in my driveway."

Alec had the audacity to chuckle. "Lucky you." Then his tones sobered. "Now I believe the stories about Raina Manhardt's Cold War escapades. She damn well vanished into thin air in the Milan terminal."

Litchfield swore loudly. "What happened?"

"I sent one of our local ops to make sure she boarded her flight then to ride along to keep an eye on her until we could snatch her in D.C. He picked her up easily, but while they were at the departure gate, she was there one minute and gone the next. He hunted but finally boarded, thinking she might've slipped on and was hiding. She wasn't. So when we got into Milan, my team searched the terminal while Volker and I checked airlines' manifests. None of her other BND identities is in use. Now we're in the air. I have no idea whether she's still flying into Dulles, but we are."

Before Litchfield could respond, his doorbell sounded. The underused power behind it annoyed him far more than the noise.

Alec heard it, too. "Bobbye Johnson again?"

Litchfield ignored him. He related the names and contact information for the three surviving local Whippet operatives. "I want one at Reagan, one at Dulles, and one at Baltimore. I'll feed you more people as I can take them off other assignments."

Without waiting for an answer, he broke the connection and plastered another smile on his face and left. He marched past Harroldsen, hurried down the walk, and slid in next to Bobbye. She handed him a Starbucks venti latte. It was what she drank — not what he liked. She wore a navy skirt suit today, not her usual suit jacket and pants. She had good legs, considering she was at least fifty. Her short auburn mane was perfect, not a hair out of place, swept back from her broad forehead.

He started to thank her for the coffee, but she was already talking: "We've got a command performance," she told him brusquely as the two vehicles backed out of the driveway and rolled away on the secluded street. "The joint intelligence committee is holding a closed session to focus on Jay Tice, Whippet, and Elaine Cunningham."

He ignored a tremor of worry. "Ah, yes. Just as you predicted."

She nodded with resignation and drank her latte. "Is there anything you want to tell me about Whippet, Larry?"

A warning sounded in his mind. "Has something else happened?"

"I'd appreciate a straight answer to my question." Her face was so neutral it was almost blank.

"Not that I can think of," he told her, infusing his words with sincerity.

"Interesting. I've already been in to Langley, getting myself up to speed in case I was correct that there'd be a committee hearing. A disturbing report was waiting on my desk. Our financial people went through Whippet's numbers. Imagine what they discovered. . . ." She drank again, her hands steady, waiting for his response.

He decided she was fishing, hoping he would either confirm what she thought she knew or reveal something she knew nothing about.

Resting his latte on his knee, he put a frown of concern on his face. "I'm sorry, Bobbye, but I can't think of a thing. Obviously something's on your mind. Tell me about it. Maybe I can help."

She stared. Then nodded to herself. "Whippet's been skimming from most of its front companies. You took the unit under your wing, made them your special team. How could you not have known that?"

He made his eyes radiate shock. "You're certain? Of course you are, or you wouldn't have brought it up. Are you saying Hannah was involved? Maybe that's why Whippet was hit —" He sank back and gazed out the window, thinking rapidly. He had known about the embezzlement from the beginning and had used it as both cudgel and candy to keep Hannah under his thumb.

"Get used to having me around, Larry," the DCI told him as they cruised past the White House. "Today, we're cemented at the hip. Something rancid is in the air, and you're going to help me uncover it."

Miami Beach, Florida

Marie Ghranditti stood at the plate-glass mirror that extended the length of her bathroom. Her eyes were blue. Not green — *blue.* With the snap of her wrist, she pulled the towel from her head. Slowly she smiled at herself. Her wet hair was dark brown, almost black now. She would never have the same nose or chin or cheekbones as before, but at least the dye had given her the hair color she remembered.

She turned her head, listening. Quiet terror flooded her. Martin had returned to

437

their bedroom. Quickly she wrapped the towel around her hair and put in her contacts. She looked away from the mirror. She could not bear to see "her" green eyes. They belonged to a dead woman.

"Marie!"

His voice resounded across the painful chasm of her memory, from the small town in Belarus where he had killed the men who had come to ship her sister and her to Hong Kong or Tokyo or Taipei. Her sister, Katya, had wanted to go, even though both had heard what happened to girls there. For Katya, anything was better than the hunger and violence of Belarus in 1990. Katya had been eighteen; she — Emmi — seventeen. Since then, Martin had supported Katya, who lived in Rome with her five children and never a husband.

"I'm coming, Martin. Just a moment, please."

He had left her morning OxyContin pill next to the sink. After her therapist had described the drug as a powerful narcotic, she had researched it at the library, then weaned herself off it, using melatonin at night to help her sleep, Immodium for the constant diarrhea, and herbal teas to calm her stomach. It had been six weeks of hell. She opened a box of Band-Aids and dropped the pill inside. She would need it later today.

She slid into her thick terry-cloth robe and cinched it. And opened the door, smiling brightly. "It's a lovely morning, isn't it? Will you be here today?" She knew he would not; Armand had said he was flying to Washington.

Armand exchanged a covert look with her then circled behind Martin and adjusted the shoulders of today's suit. It was the color of mink with a thin ruby stripe that matched Martin's silk tie. Breakfast — eggs Benedict, fresh grapefruit, and beignets — was waiting on the balcony that overlooked the pool and gave a sweeping view of the channel and Miami on the distant shore.

"Happy birthday, Marie." Martin smiled broadly, his dark eyes sparkling with mischief. "You'll see your gift on the table."

"Really? Oh, how good you are to me!" She brushed her lips across his mouth and clapped her hands like a child and ran to the table, behaving exactly as he wanted.

She had gone to him undernourished and uneducated, and he had raised her like a child, tutoring her until she learned his needs. She knew intimately not only his streaks of generosity but his rages and savage fists. That each gift came with a price.

As Armand left, gaze firmly downcast, Martin beamed at her across the bedroom's luxurious furnishings. His raven hair with the threads of white was arranged around his face. His tan — refreshed this morning in their home salon — glowed. His heavy features reflected a certainty that was sensual and disgusting.

She sat at the table and breathed the fresh ocean air, trying to enjoy the dozen perfect white roses in the priceless Ming dynasty vase that stood in the center. Her gaze lowered to the simple black enamel box beside her plate — Martin's birthday gift. Again she smiled up at him, waiting until he sat.

It was a job, she told herself. Living with Martin, learning what he wanted, becoming "Marie," marrying him, was simply a job, a better one than she could ever have found in Belarus. But now there were children to consider. For four months she had planned, hidden cash she acquired by returning the few clothes and gifts she dared, and tried to grow strong.

"The children are getting dressed," he told her. "I described the island ranch for them — the wide beaches and the forests and the sunny climate. It's a paradise — a real Shangri-la. I'll take the children sailing and fishing every day. There's a zoo with peacocks and giraffes and gazelle. There's even a village of natives. They speak pidgin English, but they're used to serving the 'big house.' I'm sure we can domesticate them. Open your gift, darling." His jowls quivered with anticipation.

"You're so good to us. I'm sure the children are terribly excited."

"You've changed your mind?" he asked. "You want to move, too?"

"Of course, Martin. Anything to be with you. I'm your Marie, aren't I?"

His hand covered hers, huge and perspiring. Inwardly she cringed; outwardly she smiled. He peered at her across the table, tears misting his eyes, seeing what he wanted to see. Whom he wanted to see — some long-ago woman named Marie Tice with platinum-colored hair and green eyes and a drug habit who died on her thirty-first birthday and whom he thought he had desperately loved, still desperately loved.

"This is a milestone, darling," he announced. "You're thirty-one now. I hope your birthday gift pleases you."

He released her hand, and she lifted the lid. Without thinking, she gasped as she stared down at a pebbled sea of uncut diamonds, each shining from an inner light that was almost lifelike. The effect was breathtaking. But more than that, in them she saw safety for the children.

"Martin!" she exclaimed. "Such beauty. How can I ever thank you!"

She left the lid open, glancing occasionally at the shimmering jewels as they ate. Wondering how much she could realize by selling them. Surely, with what she had already, that would be enough for the children and her to vanish so completely Martin Ghranditti and his army of homicidal goons would never find them.

But when he stood up to leave, he surprised her — he picked up the enameled box. Chilled, she saw suspicion in his eyes.

A small smile of sadistic pleasure played on his lips. He closed the lid by fractions, observing her, hoping she would react. "These gorgeous gems will be waiting for you on the island, darling," he vowed smoothly. "Think how glad you'll be to see them again."

When he left, the room seemed to exhale with relief. Weak with fear, she pushed herself up from the table, grasped the balcony rail, and peered across the aqua swimming pool to the estate's gates. The children and she were Martin's dream, and dreams for men like him could not survive in the real world. Once he moved them to his island "paradise," he would never let them go. She was certain now.

As his long black limo vanished, she heard a quiet tap on the door. She forced herself erect and ran into the bedroom.

"Come in."

Armand stepped inside and closed the door quickly. His eyes were full of worry for her. "Today?" he asked.

"Yes, Armand," she said firmly. *Today.*

32

Washington, D.C.

The conference room in the august Senate Building was hushed, the doors closed. Although the joint session of the intelligence committee was recorded, no press was allowed. Committee members filled the chairs around the polished mahogany table, their expressions alert. A grilling was always meaty, and they had a prominent victim this morning — the Director of Central Intelligence.

The voice of Senator Bradley Wrethford of Nevada boomed from the head of the table while his rheumy gaze fixed down its length to where DCI Bobbye Johnson sat composed at the end: "So you're telling us that Langley knows nothing. Mr. Litchfield knows nothing. And you know nothing." He was leaning so close to the microphone, he could kiss it. "How are we supposed to react other than with complete disbelief — or outrage that yet more scandals will erupt and bite our backsides?"

Laurence Litchfield did not like "Litchfield knows nothing." It had been a long hour in which the committee members had taken turns criticizing the CIA for the record. He knew the game. He also knew the worse Bobbye Johnson looked, the more quickly she would be forced out. His goal was to make certain that what happened today helped to solidify in everyone's minds that he was the right man to replace her.

Congresswoman Janet Deloitte of Alabama had soft cheeks and doe-brown eyes. She addressed the room in a polite Deep South drawl that did little to disguise her sharply honed survival skills: "So, y'all, our DCI hasn't found Tice or Cunningham. She's been keepin' on her payroll a borderline personality — Cunningham again — against whom an arrest warrant's been issued for killin' an innocent young man. And she has no information about the decimatin' assault on her secret unit. My thinkin' is that Mr. Litchfield is right — Tice knew it was assigned to find him, so he hired killers to make a preemptive strike. That makes the Agency look worse than stupid. These events are more instances of Mrs. Johnson's glarin' ineptness." She gave the DCI a hard smile.

"The evidence against Elaine Cunningham is circumstantial." The DCI spoke calmly. "There are no eyewitnesses. As for how Jay Tice escaped, that's the FBI's job. Ours is to find him. And we *will* find him." Her lips thinned. She did not look at Litchfield. "It's shortsighted to focus on Tice for the wet job on Whippet. To do so creates an environment of fait accompli. We must examine without prejudice all evidence, so the culprit can be identified, located, and brought to justice."

There was a ringing tone of idealism in her voice that Litchfield sensed touched some in the committee. That had to be stopped. "If I may speak," he said courteously, "I have a suggestion that might solve a lot of our short-term problems."

Wrethford checked his watch. "Go ahead, young man. I like solving problems."

Litchfield waited until he had everyone's attention. "These days, all of us try to avoid doing anything to shake confidence in America's security. So we agreed to make every effort to put Tice back behind bars before the public heard. No one could've predicted the developments with Cunningham and our unit." He smiled graciously at the DCI. Her eyes narrowed with suspicion. "The director has been protecting me. The truth is, our people have discovered Whippet was raking off its front companies."

An angry mutter rolled around the table. Eyes stared at Bobbye Johnson. He had expected her to look stunned, certainly angry that he had been the one to reveal this information. Still, she remained controlled, her hands folded neatly in her lap, her chin up. It made him oddly uneasy.

"In point of fact," she corrected, "just before we arrived, I was told the thefts date back to Jay Tice's tenure as DDO."

"In point of another fact," he added quickly, "Tice may have been in on it."

Wrethford threw down his pen and fumed, "That's a hell of a pot of fish!" He glared at Bobbye Johnson. "You should've told us yourself." He smiled at Litchfield: "Keep talking. I don't see much hope in this mess, but I'm willing to listen."

Timing was everything, Litchfield reflected. "In less than twenty-four hours, the CIA loses primacy and the FBI takes over. That means keeping the lid on Tice's escape will be harder, since more people will be involved. When one is faced with a public relations disaster, it's best to get out ahead of it." He noted the nodding heads. "That means we've got to go public about Tice's escape today, before it leaks and we have to counter charges of stonewalling or misleading the public. No one wants to put him back on the world stage, but there's an upside to it, too."

"I doubt that, Mr. Litchfield!" objected the senior senator from Utah.

"I want to hear what he has to say," the congresswoman from Ohio announced.

"Thank you, ma'am," Litchfield said sincerely. "If the CIA and FBI issue a joint press release, America will see its top two intelligence agencies working shoulder to shoulder, something we've been trying to impress on them since 9/11. We can bring in all of law enforcement, and Tice will be the talk of thousands of coffee shops and coffee rooms and online chat rooms. The pressure will be relentless. He'll make mistakes, and we'll capture him sooner." Again heads nodded. "Plus the news this week has been full of terrorist attacks. Tice's escape will siphon off some of the heat."

Fury oozed from the DCI's pores. She had been outmaneuvered, but she should have expected it — if not earlier, then now, and if not now, then later. Litchfield had no sympathy for losers. The best of intentions, the highest of goals, the most sacred of vows, were impossible when made by the ordinary, and Bobbye Johnson was ordinary.

The Blue Ridge Mountains, Virginia

The thick mountain forest shimmered like green neon as the morning sun climbed across the continent. On one side of the pine-scented clearing, four planks lay on blocks of wood in a learning square about fifteen by fifteen feet for an outdoor *madrassa*, a religious school. Ben Kuhnert passed it, escorted by three men pointing old but very lethal M-16 rifles and dressed in woodland camouflage uniforms. More joined from prefab huts hidden from overhead surveillance by the timber's thick canopy. Tall and sinewy, they had strong features and stony stares and handled their weapons with confidence. Despite the coolness of the morning, Ben was sweating. He was unarmed.

As the phalanx marched him toward a large hut, a man in his early thirties stepped out and onto the porch. The image of a regal Afghan warlord, he wore a flat-topped *pakol* cap and had a neatly trimmed black beard. From his hip hung a 9mm semiautomatic pistol. He carried an AK-47 casually in his right hand and a walkie-talkie in his left. His blue eyes were narrow slits in his smooth bronze skin as he studied Ben. He was Gul Shah, the director of this secret training camp.

Ben stopped, looking up to where Shah towered on the hut's top step, and greeted him in Pashtu. Then: "Imam Nawwi was kind enough to suggest that Gul Shah, my brother in Allah, might help me out with some information I need."

Shah raised a black eyebrow. In English, his accent scholarly Boston, he said, "You speak better Pashtu than I do. But you're no Pashtun."

"My mother's people were Bedouin. My father's were German. I'm Muslim. Both sides."

Gul Shah nodded. "What information are you looking for?"

Ben had come trusting not only that Mustafa would never send him into certain death, but that Shah and his men were true Pashtuns who lived by the five-thousand-year-old Pashtunwali code. Among its tenets were tolerance for all and an almost pathological respect for strangers and guests. But at the same time, Pashtuns were also notorious warriors. It was said that they were at peace only when they were at war.

"I've reason to believe a large consignment of contraband weapons and matériel is being transferred today somewhere near here," Ben told him. "Its destination could be anywhere, including international. What I'd like to know is who's buying, where it's going, and exactly when and where it'll change hands."

An angry murmur rumbled through the throng. Gul Shah allowed the menacing growl to escalate. His intense pale eyes fixed again on Ben, considering. Ben breathed evenly, quieting his racing pulse.

At last Shah raised his AK-47 high above his head and shook it. Instantly, the noise stopped. He addressed Ben: "Did Imam Nawwi say why he thought we'd have access to that, or why we'd give it to you if we did?"

"I doubt he knew," Ben admitted.

The warlord pursed his lips. There was something about the answer he liked. "What did he tell you about us?"

"You were born in this country or came as very young children. You're Americans. Pashtun Americans. That's all." Their people were from the wild and often lawless frontier that sprawled over both sides of the towering mountains between Afghanistan and Pakistan.

Gul Shah motioned to Ben's three escorts. "Bring him."

While the others watched the warlord and stranger disappear into the hut, one guerrilla melted back into the forest. He wore an ash-colored turban and carried a British Bullpup assault rifle. He crouched for a time in shadows until he was sure no one had followed, then he pulled a cell phone from the folds of his *shalwar* and dialed.

When his boss answered, the guerrilla gave his code name: "This is Methuselah."

"Report."

"Ben Kuhnert's resurfaced." He quoted Kuhnert's question about a shipment of arms. "No one in his right mind would walk unarmed into this camp unless it was critical — or he was nuts. Kuhnert's behaving very serious. Since you didn't warn me, my guess is he's not on your payroll."

"That's right, but the intel's interesting. Tell me more."

Since the response was slightly off point, Methuselah listened until he discerned the faint sounds of a keyboard's being tapped and a running car engine.

"You can't talk, can you?" Methuselah decided.

"Abu Dhabi is a good place to lay over.

452

Then where will you go?"

"Okay, got it. So you're saying Kuhnert's freelancing, and we don't know what he's up to. If Gul Shah catches Kuhnert in a lie, he'll make sure he's buried under the pines where no one will find him. You want me to make that happen?"

"Detained, I'd say."

"That could still get him scrubbed, Chief."

"Nevertheless."

"Understood." Methuselah turned off his cell and glided back through the trees.

33

Washington, D.C.

The morning's early clouds had vanished, leaving the sky a brittle blue. Old magnolia trees and oaks cast long shadows across the rolling lawns of Capitol Hill. Litchfield and Bobbye Johnson hurried through the shade toward her armored sedan.

"Tell me why I shouldn't fire you." Bobbye's mouth was a thin, ominous line.

Laurence Litchfield felt a wave of disquiet. The DCI was one of the few people in federal government who by law had unconditional authority to hire and fire without giving reason, to protect the security of the agency. He needed to survive only another day, then he would have the wherewithal to oust her.

"Because after what just happened, you'd look petty," he said kindly, feeling a moment of pity. "And because you already sleep with the dead. You know your time's up. Hell, it's all to your credit you've lasted as long as you have, especially considering Jay Tice was arrested after you took the helm, and that Defense has been swiping more and more of Langley's prerogatives while whispering bedroom promises in the Oval Office. You haven't been able to stop that or the constant insults to Langley's ability, integrity, and product. What I don't know is why you hang on."

Her driver stood at her rear door, holding it open. She climbed inside, while Litchfield hurried around and got in next to her.

She studied him appraisingly. "I stay because good-citizen backyard barbecuers like Aldrich Ames and Robert Hanssen lived lives of inestimable deceit. Because the politically ambitious wrap themselves in religion and use their god's name to justify their personal lust for power. Because until peace drapes itself over this sorry old world, independent intelligence and analysis are critical."

The sedan glided off, heading downhill toward the Potomac River. As she gazed away, he sensed a deep well of sadness, or perhaps disappointment.

She spoke to the world drifting past their windows: "And because someone whose only self-interest is three squares and a hot shower has to stand against the forces that look upon Langley as if it were a holiday roast, to be sliced and passed out to the greedy who buy places at the front of the line. Yes, Defense is on a campaign to militarize intelligence, but I'm holding them back better than anyone I know could — including you. Your sense of entitlement is bottomless, Larry. Trust me, the tide will turn, and someone like me needs to be at Langley's helm, as you put it, to make certain we help the ship of state right itself."

Taken aback, he said nothing. He busied himself by pulling out his laptop and reloading it with the Jay Tice CD. He had been working on it off and on, whenever there was a lull as they unearthed Whippet's black history. Once he had explained what he was doing, she did not interrupt again. He was convinced the answer to where Jay would go was in his relationships with operatives — and that meant it was probably on the CD somewhere.

"Your turn," she said sweetly.

But he was saved, at least for the moment — his cell rang. "Do you mind?"

"Fine. But we're not finished."

He nodded and answered the call.

"This is Methuselah," the voice announced.

Methuselah was one of the undercover operatives Litchfield had personally sent to infiltrate U.S. cells of Islamic extremists. The men reported directly to him and only to him. He had learned how crucial such a firewall was from Jay Tice, and the tactic had paid off. His spies not only survived, a year ago three had relayed intel that had led to his discovery of the Majlis al-Sha'b.

He glanced at Bobbye, who was watching him quizzically. But as soon as he said into the cell phone, "Report," she inclined her head, understanding.

The voice spoke coolly: "Ben Kuhnert's resurfaced."

Litchfield frowned. Ben Kuhnert was retired — what was he doing there? He listened closely as Methuselah repeated what Kuhnert had told Gul Shah about an arms shipment — it could easily be Ghranditti's deal. Litchfield thought fast. Kuhnert was one of the longtime NOCs who had worked with Jay in Europe. He typed the name into the laptop and ordered a search. Dozens of abstracts appeared of operations to which both had been assigned. He needed to narrow them. He ran another search, this time for missions that included Palmer Westwood. There were far fewer.

After Methuselah ended his report and

severed the connection, Litchfield continued to speak occasionally into the phone so Bobbye would not realize he was buying time. He checked the trio's joint missions — and stopped at DEADAIM. West Berlin, 1985. He had read the news reports at the time, but never the file. His gaze froze on "cut up a gold carnival medal so the five could identify one another."

In his mind, he could see the triangular pendant Jay used to wear on a chain under his shirt. He recalled thinking at the time it was important to Jay, and now that he had read about DEADAIM, he understood why. But did it still matter? Because if so, the other old men mattered, too.

Again he ran a search, this time for the addresses of Elijah Helprin, Ben Kuhnert, and Frank Mesa. He did not bother with Palmer Westwood, since Langley was looking for him. Information about the three appeared at once. Yes, all lived in Northern Virginia, where CIA retirees and employees peppered the landscape.

Litchfield said a brisk good-bye into the dial tone. He needed to call Ghranditti with the news, which meant he had to get rid of Bobbye.

She was studying him. "All right, Larry. What in God's name are you up to?"

He continued to scan the abstracts as if he found nothing compelling. "Right now, I'm working on that CD of information about Jay Tice. And I'm thinking it'd be a good plan to stop at a service station whether we need gas or not. It's at least a half hour more to Langley, and I could use a restroom. How about it?"

"Nate's the driver. Tell him."

He did then caught her gaze probing him again. He infused his voice with compassion: "I admire you, Bobbye, but honesty isn't enough for your job. DCIs also must be visionary and daring. Willing to gamble. But you've had too many bridges blown out under you, and you're tired. You avoid risk. My advice is you should move on before you're asked to."

Her voice dropped twenty degrees. "What *are* you up to, Larry?" she repeated.

He looked directly into her chilly eyes. "I'm doing my job. That's all that I'm up to. Right now I'm your DDO, and I'm damn good at it; otherwise, you really would fire me." He felt a rush of excitement as he saw a service station. "And you're wrong about what you call my sense of entitlement. All I've ever wanted was what was best for Langley. Stop over there, Nate," he told the driver. "That one will do." Then to Bobbye:

"We both want only what's best for the country."

Before she could respond, he was out of the car and heading to the restroom, where he could lock the door and call Ghranditti.

The Blue Ridge Mountains, Virginia

Gul Shah's airy hut was both an office and a communications center. Sunlight flowed in through the two large windows, illuminating equipment and creating a chiaroscuro of shadows in the corners. Four wireless computers sat on desks next to satellite phones, landline phones, and wireless radios. Maps of Asia and the Middle East covered one wall. A second wall was devoted exclusively to maps of Afghanistan — evidence that more was at work here than nostalgia.

"Naswar?"

At the sound of Shah's invitation, Ben turned. It would be impolite to say no. *"Manena,"* he said in Pashtu, expressing his gratitude.

The warlord removed a mirrored lid and extended a circular steel tin packed with moist *naswar* — a green chewing tobacco made with ash, indigo, cardamom, and water, which was popular in Pakistan and Afghanistan. Ben rolled some into a ball

460

and tucked it between his cheek and gum. Almost instantly he felt the heady kick.

"We have a saying in Pashtu," Shah said. "Perhaps you've heard it — watch the walk of a man who says he comes in peace."

Ben peered at him then turned to a map of Afghanistan. Wide arrows swept up from the southwest, indicating invasions by the Persians then the Greeks long before the birth of Christ, then the British in the late 1800s and early 1900s. Arrows down from the north meant more conquerors — Mongols and Moguls in the thirteenth and sixteenth centuries, then the Soviet Union just twenty-six years ago. Finally, an arrow up from the southeast stood for Britain in the years India was a lucrative jewel in her empire's crown. Some victors stayed centuries; still, the Pashtun never really capitulated.

Ben gestured. "Here's the tragedy of Afghanistan: Invasion. Resistance. Invasion. It's no secret the new government's on the verge of imploding, and the Taliban are regaining strength and want to retake the country." He walked to the window that overlooked the clearing. In pairs, men were practicing knife attacks. He looked back at the office, where no religious items were displayed. "You've got something planned,

461

and it has more to do with your being Pashtun than Muslim. My guess is the reason you're still listening to me is the contraband shipment involves not only my enemies — but yours."

"Jihadists." Shah's lip curled with disgust. He paced the floor. "Pashtunwali is our ancient code of laws. If you don't live by it, you're no Pashtun. But it's kept my people bickering in the mountains while others run the country, even though we're the majority. Only tribesmen such as ourselves can convince the tribes."

"You intend to convince them with M-16s?" Ben asked curiously.

"Violence isn't the first answer. But only a Pashtun with a weapon is respected. That shows how much the tribes have to modernize."

"Then it makes sense you tell me about the shipment."

"You're damn right." Shah stopped. There was fire in his eyes. "I don't have the details of time or place, or even who the seller is. But I've heard rumors. With what you tell me, I know the buyer now. They call themselves the Majlis al-Sha'b. They approached us to join about a year ago, but we turned them down. They present themselves as a combination U.N. and NATO for revolutionary groups. The vision took off like a Hellfire missile, and now the Majlis represent some twenty major organizations. Their treasury is a fat two trillion dollars."

Ben's throat was dry. That was more than the gross national product of all but a handful of countries. "Have the Taliban joined?"

Shah nodded. "That makes it inevitable the Majlis will do everything they can to stop us in Afghanistan. This arms deal is supposed to give the Majlis all the firepower they need to do whatever they want." Shah's sun-carved face was troubled. "Then not just us but the whole world really needs to watch out."

"They're buying submarines? Tanks? Nuclear missiles?"

Gul Shah shrugged. "I honestly don't know." But for several more minutes he added other details.

Ben listened carefully then asked, "Do you have any of their names?"

"The man who approached us called himself Faisal al-Hadi. He seemed to be their leader, although he denied it. He didn't take our refusal well."

Ben hid his surprise. "I'll bet he didn't." He extended his hand. "Thank you. There's no time to lose."

The warlord shook Ben's hand then nodded to the guard at the door. "Escort Mr. Kuhnert out of camp to his car."

Gul Shah dropped into his desk chair and picked up a report from his top spy in Kabul. But before he had finished two pages, a noisy scuffle erupted outside, and his door swung open. Noor Yusufzai skidded inside. Noor wore the ash-colored turban of the Wazir tribe. He was one of the oldest enlistees, nearing thirty.

"Says he has to talk to you," one of the guards who followed explained. He carried Noor's British Bullpup.

Shah repressed irritation. "Knock next time." He focused on Noor. "Speak."

Noor's face was flushed with outrage. "A few years ago I checked out the trial of the Turk who was accused of smuggling explosives to blast the Brooklyn Bridge. The man who just left was one of the CIA witnesses. I don't know who he told you he was, but I know he's CIA. He must be spying on us!"

Shah felt a chill. "You're sure he's CIA?"

"May Allah strike me dead!"

Gul Shah scooped up his AK-47 and ran.

Ben and his escort were halfway out to the road when he heard men racing toward them from camp. Immediately he slashed the rigid edge of his hand into his escort's windpipe and, when he fell, kicked his solar plexus, knocking the air from his lungs. The man scratched uselessly at his throat and grabbed at his chest.

Scanning the drive and trees, Ben confiscated the guard's M-16 and a wicked-looking Afghan knife and jumped up as eight guerrillas rounded the bend, their assault rifles at high port, ready to fire. Ben plunged into the forest.

Shots erupted, biting into the dirt and sending puffs of dust mushrooming.

Ben raced past boulders and around a blue spruce and flopped down behind a log. His heart pounded. Sunlight shafted down around him, leaving him in shadows. He raised his head. The men had hesitated over the fallen escort. Some crouched in an effort to get him to talk, to reassure them he was all right, showing how young and inexperienced they were.

Still, it would not be long before their training reasserted itself. He needed to slow them and at the same time lure them. He opened up with a long burst over their heads — but not too far over.

They dropped flat. He fired three more bursts, provoking them to scramble into the timber for cover. As he watched them vanish, he rose. They would expect him to go in the opposite direction, deeper into the woods, to escape. Instead, he checked the angle of the sun and trotted south, paralleling the pitted drive, thinking. Just eight pursuers. That meant Gul Shah had likely ordered the rest on a variety of paths to cut him off.

Soon he heard the eight again, back on their feet and running carefully, some toward him. He loped to the road's edge, fell onto his belly, and crawled to where he could check both directions. A brisk wind had risen, whistling along the route. Tree shadows wavered. The road was deserted.

Cradling the M-16, Ben crab-walked across and ran again, looking for duff to muffle his footfalls. In his mind, he pictured his goal — his camouflaged Range Rover — parked not at the entrance to the camp and not before it, but two miles beyond. He had come prepared for escape.

His strides ate up the distance, but his chest heaved, and his years began to weigh heavily on him. Tree leaves brushed his face. Briars tore at his clothes. A low rustling sounded behind him. The volume rose quickly. Men were approaching.

He quickened his pace. But when he finally spotted his Range Rover, covered with branches, a team of armed guerrillas hurtled out from the forest to his left. Praying he had time, he dove inside, fired up the engine, and gunned out of the timber, leaves and branches flying off. As his wheels hit the mountain road's blacktop, he was already turning east, toward Washington.

At the same time, another team spilled out onto the blacktop. Their heads swiveled as they took in the situation. There was an explosion of noise as bullets rained into the Range Rover's tail. He floored the gas pedal. His back tires spun, and the car shot forward like a cannonball. They raced after him, firing.

In his rearview mirror, he watched them grow smaller until at last they stopped in the middle of the road. They looked young and confused. Ben shook his head, fearing for them in Afghanistan. Then he put them from his mind and took out his new cell phone. He had calls to make.

34

Alexandria, Virginia

Frustrated, Elijah Helprin ran his fingers through his brush of wiry hair as he trotted up the spiral staircase in the darkened town house. He had spent hours on the phone and interviewing people before arriving at this pricey place. Upstairs was his best hope for information about the StarDust subminiature computers.

Elijah slipped back into the bedroom. It reeked of last night's booze. Karel Dudek flung an arm out from beneath the covers of the king-size bed and reached across to the other side. His eyes were still closed.

"I told her to leave," Elijah said. "You can send the escort service the money."

"What?" Dudek sat up, long hair a sweaty mess, eyes wide not with fright but with outrage. "My wallet's in the bureau drawer. Take what you want. Get out!"

Elijah nodded to himself. You did not rise

to be CEO of a high-tech electronics giant like Nanometrics, Inc., by being faint-hearted. "Tell me about this." He tossed the Bubble Wrapped package of StarDusts onto the bed and held up his CIA identification.

Dudek snatched up the StarDusts and stared at Elijah's ID. "These are top-secret — DoD cleared, not CIA. *How did you get them?*"

"From a killer's car. Your contract doesn't allow you to sell StarDusts to anyone but DoD. So either you've been flogging them illegally or you've had a robbery. DoD will breathe down your neck with a flamethrower — if I tell them."

The CEO seemed to disintegrate. He collapsed onto his pillows. "Someone stole them from our headquarters in Santa Barbara. My people are investigating." He rallied. "We'll find out who did it. Believe me, it'll *never* happen again."

"When were they taken?"

"Yesterday. We didn't realize it until late afternoon."

The crime might seem last-minute, but Elijah had no doubt it was planned carefully and long before. He glared. "You were at a big DoD dinner last night, Dudek. Who else has had military product stolen recently?"

"You think we talk about that sort of thing? You're crazy!" But his bleary eyes narrowed, and he looked away uneasily.

"You and your pals were drinking heavily. All of you were up until dawn. In conditions like those, people let things slip." Elijah held up his cell phone. "You want my cooperation? Or do you want me to call DoD?"

Dudek stared at the cell. He licked dry lips. "If the fed's checks weren't so goddamned big, I'd never bother. Yeah, there was another one. It was . . . strange."

Elijah leaned against the bed's foot rail. "I'm listening."

"It's camouflage material called Mirror-Me. The deal is, it makes things seem transparent by displaying whatever's behind, in front. See, nanometric video cameras record the images and send them in real time to nanometric projectors that display them on the cloth. Mike — the head of the company that makes it — had some photos in his billfold. The stuff is creepy. Of course, the Pentagon loves it because of its military potential. Fighter pilots can 'see' through the bottom of their planes for safer landings and to dodge attacks. There's all sorts of ways to use the cloth in urban warfare. The public's not going to be able to buy

Mirror-Me for quite a while — if ever."

"How much was stolen?"

Dudek looked up uneasily. "Mike said they lost enough product for a hundred thousand cloaks. No way to know what it'll actually be used for."

As a wave of disquiet rolled through Elijah, his cell phone rang. He checked the LED — Ben Kuhnert's number.

"I was never here," he told Dudek. "Clear?"

Karel Dudek grunted agreement, and Elijah turned on his heel and left.

Once outside, he answered Ben's call: "Did you get anything?"

Reston, Virginia

Palmer Westwood had spent the morning making phone calls, checking into Global Motors, Inc., the monolithic multinational that made and sold GyroBird drones. When he arrived at the office of the corporation's regional security chief, he found a cup of steaming coffee and a cheese Danish waiting.

"Hell, Palmer," Clyde Ypres told him, "I never expected a legend like yourself to call. Your favorite Danish is the least I can do." He had a horsey face and auburn hair that had lost its vibrant color, but his eyes were still as intelligent as ever.

"It's good to see you, too," Palmer said. "It's been a lot of years. I'd better skip the Danish. Show me around."

Carrying their mugs, the two men walked out into the world of modern defense manufacturing. As they passed windows showcasing scientists in white coats and goggles working over lab benches, Palmer led the conversation back to a mission that had unmasked Soviets secretly selling fissionable material to Third World countries.

"You're damn good, Clyde. I always admired the way you cracked that ring." With that compliment, Palmer changed the direction of the conversation: "I hear Global's got a hot new military product called Gyro-Bird." First he encouraged Clyde to describe the drone, and then he got to the point: "How are you handling the thefts?"

Clyde stopped so quickly his coffee mug shook. "There was only one event." He looked around. A door opened, and the noise of metal being cut whined through. Two men dressed in coveralls and gloves passed by and through another door. "I guess I'm not surprised." Clyde followed the pair. "There had to be a reason you were here."

Once they were moving alone along a

concrete sidewalk, Palmer lit a cigarette and pressed his point: "I'm doing some contract work for Langley. You know how short-handed they are these days. If you tell me everything, I'll try to keep you and Global out of it."

"Yeah, and it'll be my good deed for the year, too." There was no bitterness in Clyde's voice, just tired reality. "A week ago a shipment vanished off the dock. The next day, one of our warehousemen was killed by a hit-and-run driver. Naturally, the dead man turned out to be my prime suspect. My people are still investigating, but I basically have nowhere else to go. Not a single lead. Whoever put him up to it knew what he was doing. I interviewed the widow, but she didn't have a clue. I don't know who got the GyroBirds or where they are." His long face toughened. "If you know, tell me. I'll take care of them — through legal channels, of course."

Palmer inhaled his cigarette, studying him. "You checked with security people at other companies?"

"I did." It was Clyde's turn to peer thoughtfully at Palmer. "And, yes, a couple had thefts, too. One was called the Sky Sword. It's a missile, fast as hell — Mach 3 at high altitude; or when it's flying low to the ground, just sixty feet — Mach 2. At its fastest, it gives targets a maximum theoretical response time of just twenty-five to thirty seconds. That means it's almost impossible for anyone to employ jamming and countermeasures, let alone fire missiles and quick-firing artillery in return. It's got a guidance system you need only a laptop computer to control. But the real kicker is it's shoulder-launched, and it'll break down so small you can pack it into a music case. Once you slip into a country, you don't actually need to get any closer than a hundred fifty miles to the target before you fire. That's its range. And before you ask — their count is five hundred missing."

Palmer stared. "I don't like the sound of that."

"Terrifying, isn't it? The second one is a tiny gun. It hangs off your key chain and looks like a car's remote control but a little bit larger than normal. But if you punch the four buttons in the right sequence, it separates into a handle and a barrel. The darn thing has amazing firepower. It shoots two bullets. At the same time, aviation security machines can't identify it. You just dump the key chain into the airline's dish with your watch and pens, and it sails right through. It's called the Retaliator and was developed for undercover forays into less-than-friendly nations. Two thousand are missing."

"Two thousand!"

Clyde nodded soberly. "That'd take care of a lot of planes. Scares the shit out of you to think what terrorists could do then."

"It does indeed." Palmer thanked him and walked back to his car, mulling. As he climbed behind the wheel, his cell phone rang. He whipped it out.

"What's your report, Ben?" He could hear the deep growl of a car's big motor in the background. Ben was somewhere on the road.

"Hold on. I've got Elijah on the line, too. I'll call Frank now."

Georgetown

The leafy campus of Georgetown University was quiet, most students and teachers in classrooms, when Frank Mesa finally found the correct lecture hall. Still wearing his zippered jacket and cotton chinos, he settled into a seat at the back and hunched low, so colorless no one noticed.

From between the shoulders of students, Frank studied the political science professor — Rudi Gruhn, Ph.D. — who stood at the podium, lecturing. Rudi had acquired a basketball-size belly, pink cheeks, and a passionate delivery. He had to be in his mid-forties now. The course was called "The Merchants of Death."

"Our time's nearly up," he was saying, "so I'll close with a legendary trafficker from the late 1800s and early 1900s. His name was Basil Zaharoff. He was outgoing, a natural pitchman who claimed to be Greek when it suited him. Zaharoff was highly successful until he started repping submarines and discovered he couldn't talk anyone into buying one because of the high price. He was desperate. So he went to Greece and ingratiated himself by saying he was 'first a Greek, a patriot like yourselves, and only second a salesman.' Then he did something new — he offered to sell on credit. The result was the Greeks bought one sub. If you recall your history, you know Greece and Turkey hated each other. It was a historic feud that flamed into blood-soaked combat periodically. So, of course, Zaharoff went to Turkey next. He terrified them with stories about Greece's menacing new sub. By the time he'd finished, they'd outdone the Greeks and bought *two* submarines."

Laughter rippled through the young audience.

Professor Gruhn let the amusement ebb.

When an uneasy restlessness took hold, he spoke into it: "Zaharoff left an enduring legacy. He proved to the industry that the most practical means to maximize profit was to sell to all sides any way you could, because that bred conflict, and conflict led to war, and war meant increased demand for weapons." The students were silent. "Lying, inciting fear, and selling on credit are still basic principles followed by modern traffickers. Who can tell me which country produces the most weapons, and which country sells the most weapons, and which country makes the most profit from weapons today?"

Hands rose.

"No, no." He shook his head. "*Tell* me."

They shouted it out: "The United States."

He gave a clipped nod, slammed his lecture folder together, and stuffed it into his briefcase. There was a hesitation, then the students were on their feet and moving to the doors, quiet at first but soon talking — but not about the lecture. They had more pressing issues of a personal nature on their minds. Still, Frank hoped Gruhn had planted intellectual seeds that might grow into critical thought, perhaps even good deeds.

As the aisle began to clear, Frank pushed

against the flow, heading toward the podium. When the professor noticed Frank, his pink cheeks paled. Briefcase in hand, he hurried toward a rear door.

"Forget it, Rudi." Frank kept his voice low but made certain it carried. "You know you have to talk to me."

For several seconds the professor's stubby body was nimble. He slipped through the doorway like the athletic gunrunner he once was. Frank caught up.

"You know better than to come here." Gruhn did not look at him. "I've rebuilt my life. I'm completely out of the business."

"I don't have time to leave messages and hope you'll phone back. I need to talk to the Italian, your old boss — Tiberius DeLoreto."

Frank had been around so long he knew something the new generation of arms merchants did not — that Georgetown's renowned terrorism expert, Professor Rudi Gruhn, had once been DeLoreto's protégé, as close as a favored son. Even in those days Rudi had been smart, which told Frank he would have done everything possible to keep tabs on the dangerous and vindictive DeLoreto.

"If I tell you," Rudi Gruhn said, "I never want to see you again."

"Done. Talk."

When they were finished, Frank said, "I'm impressed with the way you've turned your life around, Rudi. But if you tell anyone about this, you *will* see me again."

As Frank headed back across campus, his new cell phone vibrated against his hip. He grabbed it and felt an electric surge of excitement — Ben's voice was on the line.

"This is a conference call, Frank," Ben announced. "The shipment's going to a highly ambitious and dangerous new terrorist network called the Majlis al-Sha'b. . . ."

35

Outside Herndon, Virginia

Something wet and cool nudged Elaine's arm. She shoved it away. It was back immediately, pushing harder. Her eyes snapped open. Bright sunlight sliced through the window glass on either side of the heavy damask curtain. For a moment she did not know where she was. Then Houri butted her arm again, ran to the door, and was back, giving the arm an even harder prod.

She leaped out of bed, still dressed. "Jay!"

"Jesus, Elaine. Keep your voice down." His warning sounded clearly through the wall.

The house's silence seemed to throb with threat. Elaine slammed her feet into socks and tennis shoes and checked the clock. It was noon. She snatched her shoulder bag and rushed into the hall, pulling a brush through her hair. Jay's back was disappearing downstairs. He had his Browning in one hand and was slinging his backpack onto his shoulder with the other. She dumped the brush into her bag and pulled out her Walther. Then she ran.

Ben Kuhnert was waiting at the bottom, looking up, his golden skin flushed. He was covered with dust. "I just got here. Company's coming." His black eyes glinted with anger.

As Jay landed and she followed, Ben backed up, pulling Houri by the collar. Panting, Houri twisted from side to side. He released her, and she ran around the room and into the kitchen.

"Who is it?" Jay asked.

"Don't know yet."

"No one drove in?" Jay showed only his usual neutral expression but radiated a heightened alertness. He looked rested, as if he'd had twice the five hours she figured. His short hair was combed, the dark circles under his eyes had vanished, and the athletic slouch had returned to his shoulders. His beard was a gray mat.

Ben shook his head. "I'm assuming they're arriving on foot because they don't want to warn us. Too late. We're warned. I've got things to tell you. We'll do it fast." He held up the front page of *The Washington Post.*

481

Elaine inhaled sharply. There was the same CIA mug shot that had been on the TV news last night. The headline gave her indigestion:

CIA OPERATIVE ELAINE CUNNINGHAM IS MURDER SUSPECT

Ben tossed the newspaper onto a sheet-draped sofa. "I put the license plates from my old station wagon on the Jag last night after you went to bed. That'll help. I've called the others, and they're making progress. Seems both the GyroBirds and StarDusts have been stolen, plus Palmer and Elijah found out about three other products that are missing, too."

"Any direct connection to Jerry and Mr. G?" Jay wanted to know.

"They're still investigating, but I've got a big-ticket item for you — the identity of the buyers. Let's move, and I'll tell you." Ben hurried into the kitchen. Houri was waiting. "I've locked the house and turned on the alarm system, but that won't be enough to stop our visitors if they're who we think they are." He opened the pantry and took out a dog's halter. Straps hung from both sides. "The buyer is a group called the Majlis al-Sha'b. In English, it's People's Assembly.

Think of it as a terrorist U.N. and military mall combined."

Elaine swore. "A 'military mall'?"

"It's as bad as it sounds." As Ben described the group, he hunched down, and Houri stepped into the halter. "Most are jihadist czars, but the rest are leaders of political extremists like the United Self-Defense Forces of Colombia, which is connected as hell, as you know." He stood up.

"With their funding and diversity," Jay said worriedly, "they could create an arc of crisis from Marrakesh and Bangladesh to Paris and New York. I hope like hell the shipment hasn't changed hands yet. What did your source say about that?"

"He didn't know the exact time, but he says it's going to be sometime tonight." Ben took sunglasses from a drawer and used a slipknot to tie them to Houri's halter. "This shipment is supposedly so big and deep it'll launch them." He unhooked the pager on his hip and attached it to the other side of her halter.

Houri's ears were raised and alert. She gave a soft woof.

"I know, girl," he told her. "I'm hurrying." He grabbed a large white handkerchief and an adhesive bandage impregnated with antibiotics. He looked at Jay. "He told me something else. A ghost from the past's involved — Faisal al-Hadi."

A shadow seemed to pass over the spymaster's face. "What about al-Hadi?"

"Al-Hadi approached my source to invite his group to join the Majlis last year. My source refused, but he kept in touch."

Houri lifted her muzzle and growled.

"She says they've arrived. No more time." Ben rushed to the sink and grabbed a thin-bladed filleting knife.

Frowning, Jay hurried toward him. "Ben, what are you —" He looked at the bandage then down at Houri, who hovered beside Ben, and nodded to himself. "Go ahead. I understand. Good plan."

There was a second's hesitation. Ben pushed his jacket sleeve up over his elbow.

"Ben!" Elaine ran to his other side. "Don't!"

Jay pulled her close and held her. "It's necessary."

Ben's jaw tightened, and he sliced the top of his arm. Blood poured.

Jay released her and used the handkerchief to soak up the blood, then pressed it against the wound to slow the bleeding. "Put on the bandage, Elaine. Do it quickly."

The cut was narrow and livid. As she taped the bandage, Ben handed her the garage key. At the same time, Jay crouched. Houri licked his cheek, and he fastened the bloody cloth into another of the harness's straps. Blood dripped to the linoleum.

"What's most critical is finding Raina." Ben rolled his sleeve over the bandage. "So Houri and I will be your diversion. Get moving. Both of you. My girl and I have work to do."

"Ben, we're grateful," Elaine said softly. "Good-bye."

As the older man nodded, Jay said simply, "Thanks, Ben."

They exchanged a long look that crossed continents and decades, their ages showing clearly in their seamed faces and thinning hair. And then it was gone.

Jay stuck out his hand.

Ben ignored it. He pulled Jay close and thumped his back. "Good luck. If I never said thanks for everything, it's only because I'm shy." As Houri loped to the door, he snagged a lightweight dog coat from a hat hook. It was the same color as the amber animal. "We're going to keep them very busy as long as possible to give both of you a good start." He fastened the coat over the harness, hiding it. He stood up and put on sunglasses that were identical to the ones he had fastened to the harness. "Go! *Bismillah!*"

He pulled out his Browning.

"He's right, Elaine. Where to?"

There was a lump in her throat. "This way."

She ran down the short hall, Jay at her heels. As they crossed the living room to the other side of the house and through Ben's office, she described Ben's hidden escape route and what both must do.

"Got it." He pushed past her and opened the glass door onto a stone walkway, a gray ribbon through the sun-splashed lawn. It led all of the way around the big main house to the two cottages. Some twenty feet distant were woodlands, lush with ferns and blue wildflowers. He surveyed cautiously and stepped outdoors.

Gun in hand, she followed. Suddenly a gunshot sounded from the driveway, and a second responded.

"Don't think about it," he ordered. "The best thing we can do is get the hell away so Ben and Houri can, too."

She nodded, and they ran toward the garages.

36

The noontime sun pulsed over Ben Kuhnert's compound. The air smelled combustible, of dust and promised heat. In quick succession, two more bullets slammed into the stone corner of the cottage where Ben hunched, Houri behind him. He ducked as shards of stone exploded. By allowing his attackers to think they had him pinned, he had figured out where they were, and how many — six.

One was at the corner of the main house near the kitchen. One was positioned between two sycamores on the driveway just before it entered the woods, to stop anyone's leaving. One darted along the driveway's low hedge, trying to close up on the far corner of the cottage where Ben was. Two were across the drive, nearly opposite him, at either side of that cottage. And the last was also across the drive, skirting the trees toward the main house where his office was located.

"That should be enough time," Ben muttered to himself.

He reached behind and patted the dog, then he made his hand into a fist and rotated his wrist, telling her they were shifting to signals. She butted the fist with her nose in acknowledgment. He pointed and closed his thumb and forefinger, indicating which plan they would follow, although he knew she already realized it from the way he had loaded her harness.

He dropped flat and rolled out around the cottage and rose up a few inches. He squeezed off two bullets in quick succession at the man who was the greatest threat to Jay and Elaine.

The man stopped in his tracks and arched. "I've been shot!" he yelled, and staggered forward.

"Hold on, Hank!" an authoritative voice bellowed. "Close in, boys!"

Automatic gunfire strafed Ben's cottage. The noise was deafening.

As the hail of bullets started back again, lower this time, chewing up the grass, Ben jumped up and used every ounce of strength in a death-defying sprint toward the woods.

Houri raced beside him, panting.

"That was Jerry's voice!" Elaine said as she and Jay ran toward the two stone garages. The Jaguar was parked inside the closest.

Two more gunshots detonated, followed by shouts ringing from the distant drive. A fusillade of fire sounded. This time from an automatic rifle.

Elaine and Jay did not look at each other as they continued their headlong rush. Framed in stone, the rear wall of the first garage was wood and faced down a grassy slope to the palisade of woodlands that encircled the glen.

As the lethal gunfire continued, Jay plummeted down the hill.

The wind on her hot face, Elaine jammed Ben's key into a hole in the wall and pulled open a book-size door. Inside was a keypad. She tapped in Ben's code and looked for Jay. He was hurrying along the trees, studying them. Ben had warned that the gate might be hard to locate — it was veiled in wild growth.

Watching all around, Elaine waited impatiently as the wall groaned and swung open at the center like wings. She jumped into the Jag and put her key into the ignition.

■ ■ ■ ■

Ben paused just inside the woods. The storm of bullets had stopped. The cottage he had used for protection was set at an angle and closer to the trees than any of his other buildings and blocked him from the view of the shooters. He took off Houri's coat and with a quick gesture sent her into action. Her tail beat swiftly once in nervous excitement. She lowered her head and hurtled onto a footpath that led deep into the forest.

As the trees enveloped her, Ben turned and crouched. Within seconds bullets slashed past. Leaves shredded and flew. He jumped up.

"There he is!"

As planned, they would know exactly where he was going.

"Get that bastard!" the voice thundered.

Smiling grimly to himself, Ben bolted onto the trailhead, following Houri. The cut on his arm did not hurt. His age did not matter. Everything was working perfectly.

Abruptly his shoulder scorched with pain. He lurched forward. Grabbed the shoulder. Blood oozed between his fingers and flowed down his arm and chest. He had taken a bullet. Another round of gunshots sliced through the timber.

With a silent curse, he moved, ordering his feet to hurry. Not thinking. Just hurrying. Feet behind hammering. Getting closer. He passed the familiar looming boulder. Then the pair of young maples. He spotted the sunglasses exactly where they should be — Houri had left them by pulling the slipknot open with her teeth. The running feet behind him were too close.

Another ten feet, and there was the sheet of granite that spread into the trees. He turned onto it, warning himself not to slide. He was growing dizzy. Three steps later he slipped and fell anyway. Breathing shallowly, he rolled and crawled under a bush.

Elaine sat behind the wheel of the Jag, slamming the steering wheel with her fist. Jay had still not found the gate. He was moving slowly now, rechecking the treeline.

At last he gave a wide wave of his arm.

She threw the gear into neutral. The Jaguar's four thousand pounds rolled down the angled floor and onto the grassy slope. The tires were a hushed whine over the thick grass. Because the Jag had an automatic transmission, and the engine was not turned on, she had little ability to guide it, but that seemed the least of their problems. If she had to, she could fire up the motor at the last minute — but the noise would notify the killers of their escape, which Ben was risking his life to protect.

Gunfire resumed. Each shot pierced her. Elaine glanced in her rearview mirror in time to see the garage doors automatically shut. Ahead, Jay hauled open a black iron gate. A maze of vines and creeping plants dripped from it, the tendrils bouncing.

The hill was graded to create a shallow, flat-bottomed, W-shaped trough so that once a car's wheels were in place, the vehicle theoretically should hurtle straight through the gate's opening and into the woods. But the grass was thick and tall, and the depressions were purposefully hard to see. Worse, she was not able to control the Jag's direction.

Jerry Angelides wiped his hand across his sweaty forehead and stared down at the sunglasses lying half open on the shady footpath. Three of his men stopped beside him. He had left the other two behind, the injured one where Kuhnert's driveway entered the clearing, and the other to investigate the house.

"Goddammit!" He picked up the sunglasses. "Where's he gone?"

"I shot him," Rink said. "I know I shot him!"

"Well, he ain't here. And I don't see any blood."

"We should check around." Derek peered into the growth. "These are his woods. He could've gone off trail onto some secret path."

"You're right," Jerry decided. "Dammit, you're right. Derek, you go that way —"

Suddenly noisy beeps sounded ahead. Jerry bolted, his men following. The beeps stopped just as he spotted a pager lying in the dirt. He snagged it and examined it quickly.

"Someone called Kuhnert," he told them. "No message. No phone number. It just says 'wireless caller.' "

"Guess he's still on the trail," Rink observed.

No one spoke. They ran again. Trees reached toward them, tearing at their clothes.

"Look at that!" Rink said. "Look!"

They paused over a blood-soaked handkerchief lying on the trail.

Rink held it up by a dry corner. "See! I told you. Blood! I got him for sure!"

"Looks like you're right," Jerry decided.

He breathed hard. All of the men were breathing hard. "Okay, let's go. If he's losing blood, he's not gonna get far."

They ran again, deeper into the forest's dark shadows.

The branches over Ben's head swayed in a light wind, making a breathy, disquieting sound. He returned his cell phone to his pocket and stumbled on. He had dialed the pager, knowing the beeps would be loud enough for the men to hear. With luck, it would persuade all of them to push ahead.

There was no trail here, but the forest was as familiar to him as an old friend. This was his home, where he had grown up. Sweat coated him. It stung his eyes. The world seemed off-kilter. His balance was chancy, and the pain in his shoulder burned like a volcano. He had no idea how much time had passed. Ordinarily, this part of the plan should have been executed in minutes.

When he finally found the towering boulder that time and erosion had shaped into the face of a sharp-beaked bird, he rolled under a sheltering lip on the far side. He had never considered himself a top-flight operative, which had made him more careful than most. He always had several escape routes. He closed his eyes and was drifting into a black, dreamless world when he was yanked back suddenly by a wet tongue on his cheek. He looked. Houri.

"Good girl." He smiled and fell asleep.

Elaine held her breath and dragged the steering wheel to the right. The Jag was going to miss the gate. As it gathered speed, she saw Jay's eyebrows rise. He backed away.

Sweat beaded up on her forehead. She kept up the pressure on the steering wheel. Finally, like a great sailing ship, the car yawed. With a burst of relief, she felt the wheels drop into the W's ruts. The Jag corrected itself and swept down the emerald carpet and through the opening and into the deep, dark quiet of the timber.

She braked while Jay closed the gate. He was in the seat beside her within seconds.

He dropped his backpack. "Let's go."

She let the car glide downward again, crushing flowers and grasses and ferns as it continued its descent on the primitive road. When the Jag reached the bottom of the long hill, about a half mile from the main house, Elaine turned on the engine. Its throaty hum was music. She punched the accelerator, and the car sailed up the next hill. Treetops twined together overhead.

They were silent, worried with their own

thoughts. When they neared the end of Ben's road, Jay hurried out and opened another pipe gate hidden by the forest's growth. She drove through. She could see the highway.

Jay jumped back inside. "Let's go find Raina."

■ ■ ■ ■

Part Four

■ ■ ■ ■

There's something about a secret that's
addicting.
— J. Edgar Hoover
former director of the FBI

What we really exist for is stealing secrets.
— R. James Woolsey
former director of the CIA

37

Montgomery County, Maryland

The long private road looped through the heart of hunt country, past bushy verges and green pastures and woodlots. Tiberius De-Loreto's large farm spread along both sides. Studying the area, Frank Mesa parked on a grassy shoulder. Across from him, a high white stucco wall extended to the horizon in both directions, protecting the death merchant's sprawling modern house.

Frank locked his weapons in his trunk. Between his memory of DeLoreto and efficient research, he had come prepared. He picked up a brown grocery sack and walked purposefully toward the kiosk that guarded the entrance.

The lone sentry had stepped outside, watching. In his early thirties, he wore tan cords and a brown work shirt. His shoulder holster held a Heckler & Koch pistol. He said nothing, his dark eyes cool, appraising.

"I'm here to see Mr. DeLoreto. My name is Jonathan Smith. From the old days." Frank pointed to the sack. "Tell him I've brought fresh orecchiette."

The guard stepped inside and repeated the information into an intercom.

There was a long pause, then a disembodied voice announced, "He wants to know where Smith got the orecchiette."

"Tell him my brother's wife made it this morning. She's from Puglia, too."

Again the sentry relayed the message.

There was another pause. "Frisk him, then send him in," the voice ordered.

After searching Frank, the guard returned to his post, and a pedestrian door in the white wall swung open. Frank walked through into Tiberius DeLoreto's expensive world. Arabian horses ambled across verdant pastures, tails switching. Crews cleaned and trimmed. Armed guards stood sentry across the expanse and into the woods.

When Frank reached the porch of the big house, a man strolled around from the rear. It was DeLoreto himself. About Frank's age, mid-sixties, he wore a straw hat and battered jeans and a new Pendleton shirt.

"You say I know you?" DeLoreto moved slowly, showing his arthritis. He had knobby hands and dead blue eyes.

"*Buongiorno, Don Tiberius.* It was a long time ago. I used to be CIA."

The arms trafficker's gray eyebrows arched. "Is that the pasta?" Frank opened the sack, and DeLoreto peered inside. "Haven't had good orecchiette since '94. Kitchen's in back."

DeLoreto led him around the house and into a large stainless-steel kitchen. A chef in a white hat was setting a copper boiling pot on the stove. He turned and bowed.

DeLoreto glanced at him. "Leave us."

The chef vanished while an outside guard carrying an M-4 assault rifle alertly checked in through a bay window and moved on. Frank surveyed the room. *The Washington Post* lay open on a wide table covered by a heavy linen cloth. A half-dozen wineglasses waited to be washed by one of the sinks. A big walk-in freezer was nearby.

DeLoreto fired up the gas burner under the boiling pot. "You got to have plenty of water and salt to cook orecchiette. My mother taught me, God bless her and keep her safe in heaven." He poured salt onto his palm and dumped it into the water. "You don't talk much, do you? I like that. Or did you already know?"

"I knew." Frank opened the sack and removed a covered plastic container, set it on the counter, and peeled off the lid. Shaped like small human ears, the pasta was symbolic of Puglia but little-known outside Italy.

DeLoreto gazed at it then at Frank. "You're old to be CIA."

"As I said, I'm retired."

"You got some wine there, too, I saw. Salice Salentino."

Frank took out the bottle of fine red wine plus a bottle of extra-virgin olive oil, tins of anchovies, and two jars of sweet black olives.

"Hey, that's good," DeLoreto said. "Everything's from Puglia."

Frank nodded. Last he removed a second covered plastic container identical to the first but three times as deep. He pried up the lid and pretended to check inside. He let the lid fall. "This is more orecchiette for some other time. She says you should cook it before it gets old. You want me to make a sauce for you? That's why I brought the wine and olives and anchovies."

DeLoreto looked up at the ceiling and smiled. "He cooks, too." Then the smile vanished, and his dead eyes probed Frank. "You come unarmed so my men don't have to embarrass you by pointing out you should've known better. You show respect by bringing gifts that matter to me. You greet me politely — and in Italian. You let me talk or not, whatever I want. And now you offer to cook. All right, ex-CIA man, what do you want?"

Frank leaned his hip against the counter and crossed his arms so that his left hand was under his right elbow, near the deeper container of orecchiette. He noted the same guard was peering in through the window again.

"There's a big shipment changing hands somewhere around here today," Frank told him. "One of the people on the buying end is a terrorist named Faisal al-Hadi. The dealer's known as Mr. G. He's been in business awhile. I'd like everything you know about it and him."

"For some homemade pasta? That only gets you in the door." DeLoreto's voice was as hard as Carrara marble. "You seem to know me. So you should know I don't give out information about my colleagues."

"I know." In a swift motion, Frank's hand shot into the pasta dish and pulled out a small Colt and aimed it at the gun merchant's heart. "Get over to the freezer."

DeLoreto looked at the weapon and frowned, unafraid and annoyed.

Frank did not have time to argue. "Move." Watching the window, he kicked DeLoreto hard toward the walk-in freezer. DeLoreto stumbled and opened his mouth to yell. Frank kicked him again, harder. As De-Loreto fell, Frank ran around and opened the freezer door. He grabbed the gun dealer by the back of his jeans and threw him inside and closed the door. Their exhalations were white clouds in the icy chill.

Cursing loudly, DeLoreto picked himself up, his face thick with anger.

"I also know the first commandment in your business is 'Fuck thy neighbor,' " Frank told him. "Now's your chance."

"Fuck *you*, you lousy scheming CIA *animale!* You'll never get out of here alive!" He raised his fist and shook it.

Frank aimed and squeezed the trigger. The explosive noise reverberated. The bullet shattered DeLoreto's right knee. The air was so frigid that pieces of flesh and bone sailed through the air almost slowly enough for Frank to watch. DeLoreto screamed and crumpled. His blood froze crimson red on his jeans and on a side of pink beef hanging next to him.

"I can phone in my report from here," Frank explained calmly. "That means I don't give a holy shit whether I get out alive. Tell me about Mr. G."

For the first time, fear showed on DeLoreto's wrinkled face. He glanced wildly around. "And if I do?"

"I leave. You live. This is your last chance."

When DeLoreto took time to consider, Frank snapped, "Your other knee's next. Then your elbows. Then I scrub you."

"It's Martin Ghranditti's deal." The trafficker talked so fast his words tumbled into one another. "That slime turd Ghranditti's come out of retirement. That's your answer. You want that sick fucker *Ghranditti!*" His lower lip quivered. "What are you — ?"

Frank had what he needed. He backed out of the freezer and locked it. He ran to the stove, pushed the pot aside, and turned all of the burners to MEDIUM. He dropped the *Post* onto the stove and threw the tablecloth on top. Smoke seeped out around the edges. He hurried to the counter and crashed the neck of the unopened bottle of Salice Salentino hard against it. Broken glass sprayed. Grabbing a wineglass from the sink, he poured into it as he ran to the door. Behind him, the fire suddenly crackled.

Taking a deep breath, he put a pleasant smile on his face, set the bottle on the floor, and strolled outdoors. Casually, he checked around, noting two of DeLoreto's sentries about a hundred yards away. He raised his wineglass and nodded. They nodded back.

As he retraced his route to the front of the house, he planned. He would lose the wineglass in the bushes by the front porch and be at the entry gate in less than five minutes, just about the time he figured the guard would return to the kitchen window. By then the smoke would be thick, and he would be inside his car, driving away.

On the road, Northern Virginia

The Jaguar hurtled along the highway among rolling hills. In the valleys, veins of fog shimmered. Traffic was moderate, allowing Elaine to push the speed limit. With luck, they would reach the rendezvous with Raina on time.

She watched Jay pick up his cell phone. "Are you trying Ben again?" There had been no answer the first time.

Jay's jaw tensed. "I am." He tapped numbers and listened. "This is my second message, Ben. Hope you're okay. Phone as soon as you can." Without looking up, he said, "Elaine, I'm going to call someone else for help. Don't ask questions." He dialed and put the cell to his ear again. Finally he cursed. "No answer." He left a message: "You know who this is. There's been a development. Send people to Ben Kuhnert's place fast." He relayed the address. "Tell

506

them to look for a saluki. Her name is Houri. If she trusts them, she'll lead them to him." He dropped the cell into his lap.

Elaine watched traffic. "What more can we do?"

"We can only wait."

The possibility of Ben's death lay between them like an open grave. They fell into guilty silence. Sunlight streamed inside, and dust motes danced crazily in it.

As Jay scanned the highway and an approaching intersection, he said, "This thing with Ben reminds me of a story Palmer told me a long time ago. It's about a famous English actor named Leslie Howard. You've probably heard of a couple of his movies — *Gone with the Wind* and *The Petrified Forest.*"

"I know the movies."

He nodded. "Howard was really too old to fight in World War Two, but he volunteered anyway, and the Brits wanted him because he traveled a lot, entertaining troops and doing radio broadcasts. Perfect cover for intelligence work. So one day in 1943, the British prime minister — Winston Churchill — was sitting in a car at the Lisbon airport. When he rolled down his window to take a plane ticket from an assistant, a Nazi spy spotted him. The Nazi investigated and found out Churchill planned to fly home to London that night. The spy told Berlin, and Berlin ordered the Luftwaffe to take out the plane. What they didn't know was their spy was wrong — the man was one of Churchill's doubles. But we knew everything, because we'd cracked their Enigma codes. This is where Leslie Howard comes in. He was in Lisbon, too, scheduled for the same flight. It was just a regular passenger plane, unarmed. The solution seemed simple — make up an excuse and cancel it.

"But the problem was, by then we'd been using so much decrypted intel that the Nazis were beginning to suspect we'd broken Enigma. If they brought another coding machine into use, our river of intel would dry up, and we needed it to win the war fast. So we decided we had to let the plane fly. The crew and the double volunteered — they were necessary for the charade. But Leslie Howard wasn't. Still, if a big movie star like him went, too, and then the Brits leaked he'd been on a secret mission, the Nazis would have to believe Enigma was secure. Howard said we couldn't take the chance. He boarded with everyone else, and right on schedule the Nazi night raiders attacked over the Bay of

Biscay." He hesitated, seeming to gather himself. "The plane didn't have a chance. It went down with no survivors."

She felt a bolt of horror instantly followed by pride. "He died to keep the secret."

"Yes. For something bigger than himself. All of them did." His expression troubled, Jay ran his fingertips along the car's windowsill. "Was their sacrifice worth it? For the 'greater good,' as the cliché goes — probably yes. But if Howard could choose again, would he make the same choice? Or would he think it was enough the others had given their lives? If so, he'd thrown his away. I don't know. Was Ben's going into danger to protect us worth it — and would he do it again? Again, I don't know. Still, considering who Ben is, I doubt he had a choice."

As the Jaguar soared onward, memories careened through Elaine's head, and somehow each ended with Rafe, the sight of him riding away on horseback across the desolate Tora Bora. He, far more than she, had understood how large a gamble it was that backup would arrive in time. But what did that mean? That she was even more responsible for his death — because she should have understood it, too?

Jay's phone rang. The noise was like a

series of small detonations. He snapped up the phone.

"Yes?"

"This is Frank. I found out who Mr. G is."

Elijah and Palmer picked up, too. Still driving, Elaine listened in to the conference call.

"The arms merchant is Martin Ghranditti," Frank announced.

"Ghranditti?" Jay repeated, surprised. "Who in hell is that? Should I know him?"

"Not necessarily," Palmer informed them. "Ghranditti wasn't good enough to be high-level. Still, he had connections and eventually got wealthy. I investigated him for a couple of situations in Belarus and the Ukraine but never found anything substantial. He was damn slippery, hungry as hell for respectability — and smart. He shielded his holding companies under a mountain of pseudonyms and kept out of the limelight so he could act legitimate. His base was West Berlin, and he was a real swashbuckler there, flashing his money. During the DEADAIM operation, I suspected he was Faisal al-Hadi's dealer — and what we've got now is another al-Hadi deal."

"Okay, it's starting to come back to me," Jay said. "Every time you think one of those gunrunners has quit or died, he turns up somewhere else, still peddling arms." He paused, thinking. "Frank, you did a hell of a good job. Dig deeper into Ghranditti. We still need to know the where and when of the shipment. What about you, Elijah? You have anything new?"

"Nothing concrete," Elijah reported.

Palmer asked, "Does anyone know whether there's a clearinghouse for thefts and robberies of national security–related product?"

"Not my end of the business," Elijah answered instantly. "But I can find out."

"No need to." Jay's fingers drummed his thigh. "Go to the Department of Homeland Security. They started centralizing the intel before I left Langley. Palmer and Elijah, since you both have pieces of that puzzle, check it out together. Anyone have anything else?"

Everyone was silent.

"Okay," Jay said. "We're finished. Stay in touch."

Langley, Virginia

For a few minutes, Laurence Litchfield was free. Bobbye Johnson had released her stranglehold on him so she could join a secure online conference with the U.S. and

Iraqi intelligence chiefs in Baghdad. Frustrated, he hurried back to his office to check for a message from Martin Ghranditti. There was none. Ghranditti's men should have found Jay Tice and Elaine Cunningham through the old DEADAIM spies by now. Angry, Litchfield dialed the arms trader's number and left a message, demanding an answer.

Restless and disgusted that he had to wait, he looked at his watch. It was time. He switched on his television then went to CNN — and smiled. Newsman John King was standing outside the ugly concrete facade of the Hoover Building, setting the scene for the forthcoming joint CIA-FBI press conference.

"It's not official yet," King was saying, "but we have word from a usually reliable source that Jay Tice escaped from prison early yesterday. . . ."

The FBI auditorium appeared on the TV screen. Litchfield smiled wider. Agency and Bureau spokesmen stood at the podium, properly serious as they took turns reading the press release. Hoping Jay was watching, Litchfield sank into his expensive executive chair, reminding himself that it was the double-crosser's own. He leaned back, enjoying that — and that the show was going exactly as he had advised the joint intelligence committee. Bobbye Johnson had lost. He had won — again.

When his phone vibrated, he picked it up quickly. *Ghranditti at last.*

"Hello, Litchfield." The voice was hollow, disguised as always.

Litchfield was stunned. It was a voice from the past, one he had given up hope of ever hearing again. "Moses? I can't believe it. After all these years . . . is it really you?"

"As always, that swift intellect of yours is impressive," Moses said in his peculiar disembodied tones.

"Where in goddamn hell have you been? There were a few times I could've used you."

Moses was an anonymous intel dealer whose reputation ran high during the last years of the Cold War. From the beginning, his modus operandi had been simple — he serviced favored clients on both sides of the Iron Curtain, in both government and private industry He charged a great deal of money, but inevitably his information had been well worth it. Some swore he must be Venezuelan and a former disciple of Abu Nidal. Others thought he was Sicilian with ties to La Cosa Nostra. Still, when anyone wanted Moses's help, they did not care who or what he was.

"I've been here and there." As always, Moses revealed nothing — unless he had a reason. "You seem glad to hear from me again."

"That depends. What are you selling — and how much is it going to cost me?"

Litchfield had mixed emotions about the peddler. Although Moses's tips had helped to propel his career, he hated paying for them, and he hated that the man had no loyalty. Plus he resented never being able to uncover Moses's identity, despite assigning top technicians to track his calls. They always appeared to have originated in Bali or Cabo San Lucas or some other offshore haven, but the numbers inevitably turned out to be shams.

"The cost?" Moses repeated. "Cheap, when compared to how much you value your career and freedom. I know you're looking for Jay Tice and Elaine Cunningham."

"Of course. It's on the news."

"As well as Raina Manhardt."

Litchfield tensed. "How in hell did you find that out!"

"I wouldn't be any good to you and my other clients if I didn't protect my sources. Now, here's the real news, and why you need me — Tice and Cunningham escaped the thugs you sent to Ben Kuhnert's place. At this moment they're driving to meet Manhardt. I can deliver that location, which means if you hustle, you can grab all three at the same time. I like the efficiency of that, don't you? In fact, I like it so much that my fee just went up ten percent."

Litchfield swore. If Moses knew Ghranditti's men had been at Kuhnert's, then he must be telling the truth that Tice and Cunningham had gotten away.

As if he were reading Litchfield's mind, Moses laughed. "They're all alive, Litchfield. Yes, *alive*. Do you want them — or not?"

38

Washington Dulles International Airport
Sterling, Virginia

Sheltered in the pack of deplaning passengers, Raina Manhardt moved out of the flight tunnel's gate, still in her Gunnar Hamsun disguise. She carried her gym bag in one hand, and a guitar case she had bought at the Milan airport in the other.

Instantly she spotted the big CIA man from Geneva, Alec, hulking where he had a wide view. His shrewd eyes moved fractionally, studying faces in the crowd like a biometrics machine. He was holding a walkie-talkie and a flyer. At least one BND photo of her had to be on that sheet of paper. At the same time, she was sure her real name was not. The CIA would be as eager as the BND to keep that secret.

Chest tight, she lifted her bearded chin and slapped on her sunglasses. She could hear Jay's voice: *Remember the power of distraction.* Annoyed, she swung the guitar case. She slouched Gunnar's shoulders and moved Gunnar's lips as Gunnar sang quietly to himself and did his own jive thing. The big CIA man focused on her face then shifted to the gym bag and the case. But then his mouth twitched, and his gaze snapped away to examine a woman wearing a chic turban.

She told herself to breathe as she kept pace with the flowing crowd, but her disquiet increased as she noted more security people, all holding flyers. All stationed at gates where flights from Europe were due. That was when she saw her old BND colleague Volker Rehwaldt. His arms were crossed, and anger showed in the thin slice of his mouth as he sorted passengers through slitted eyes. He had a walkie-talkie, too. She would pass much too near, within ten feet.

Volker caught sight of her. He frowned and stared. He and she were the same height. The exact height. They had always looked evenly into each other's eyes, an oddly strong bond. He started toward her.

Her lungs contracted, and she angled away, desperately considering options for escape. But then Volker raised his walkie-talkie but not to talk — to listen. She glanced around. Other surveillants listened to their walkie-talkies, too. She looked again for Volker, but he was striding off. The others on stakeout were leaving, too. She did not like it. Something had happened.

Washington, D.C.

The brown brick building was World War II vintage and ordinary-looking, set on a busy downtown street. The door's single glass pane, which was opaque, showed only the street number. As pedestrians and traffic cruised past behind them, Elijah Helprin and Palmer Westwood raised their CIA IDs to the glass and waited.

The DHS had grown so huge — more than 180,000 employees — that it was scattered in buildings similar to this one throughout the District, handling such myriad responsibilities as intelligence, warning, transportation security, domestic counterterrorism, and homeland defense.

A DHS guard opened the door and confirmed their IDs. With a polite nod, he let them pass. Elijah and Palmer marched twenty more feet across a weathered parquet floor and came to a clipped stop at a tall mahogany counter.

Elijah held up his ID again and announced his name. "We have an appointment in

Room 222A. George Popescu."

Slower, showing his impatience at last, Palmer displayed his identification, too.

"Sign in," the uniformed clerk ordered. He checked their signatures against their IDs and handed them visitors' badges. "Careful you don't go into any room but 222A."

Elijah gave a curt nod, and he led Palmer through a metal detector to an elevator that whisked them up to the second floor. Their quarry, George Popescu, looked up as they reached his cubicle. He was a retired CIA analyst called back to work with the rapidly expanding DHS.

"Eli! It's been a while." He stood up and shook Elijah's hand.

Palmer had no time for small talk. "You have it for us, Popescu?"

George raised an eyebrow. "Hello to you, too, Palmer. A little nervy, are we?"

"It's kind of important, George," Elijah soothed.

"Sorry." Palmer smiled his patented friendly smile. "Afraid I am a tad on edge."

George nodded. "Aren't we all. Okay, I've got it — a printout of our complete data-bank of missing national security–related material in the past month. Everything from fully confirmed thefts to disappeared computers that may never have existed in the first place. Checked, cross-checked, and rechecked according to every reference made during the investigations by anybody involved. As soon as I got your call, I ran your request through ForeTell and had it integrate everything new that's come in over the past twenty-four hours. Took only five minutes." He held out a massive printed document in a cardboard box. "Careful. It's heavy. Could give you a hernia."

Palmer grabbed it. "How's it indexed?"

"By commonality. You said that's what you wanted."

Without another word, Palmer headed to one of the small soundproof reading rooms that lined a wall.

"Great work, George. Thanks." Elijah hurried to catch up.

Once inside, Elijah took the first half of the alphabet, Palmer the second, and they checked the commonalities. The only sound was the turning of pages.

Elijah was the first to spot a hit. "Palmer! Here's a category named 'Jerry.' No last name." He flipped to the referenced pages, studying the entries. "Ten items, and each time Jerry was mentioned by someone involved in their disappearance. Our Star-Dusts and GyroBirds are among them.

Guess your security guy and my business guy decided to come clean with Homeland Security after we twisted their arms."

Palmer nodded. "Here's another — a category labeled 'Los Angeles voices.' See, your ten are there plus another eight. One of them is the Retaliator key-chain gun. Search for a Ghranditti category. I'll check Mr. G."

Elijah thumbed rapidly, shook his head. "No 'Ghranditti.' "

"But thirteen 'Mr. Gs' — and only four appear on our other category lists. The new ones include the Sky Sword missile and the Mirror-Me nanometrics fabric."

They looked for 'al-Hadi' and 'Majlis al-Sha'b.' For 'BMW' and 'limousine.' For 'bribe,' 'disgruntled,' and 'blackmail.' In the end, they had a list of twenty-two incidents.

Palmer stared at the list, then swore. "Hell, this is worse than we thought!"

Elaine parked near the Maine Avenue Fish Wharf in Southwest Washington and watched as Jay checked his weapons. His motions were controlled, precise. Gazing into the small mirror in the sun visor, he adjusted his new aviator sunglasses and tugged the brim of his baseball cap low. His skin was now the color of café au lait. The dark makeup gave him a faintly Latin look, perhaps Carribean, definitely exotic. He was no longer the lily-white man from the upright Caucasian world of most CIA spies and spymasters.

"You're excited, aren't you?" She had also altered her appearance, with oversize sunglasses and a straw hat, her hair tucked up underneath.

He did not look at her. "I suppose so."

"Oh, for pity's sake, Jay. Smile. You want to see Raina so bad you're like a kid with a hundred-dollar bill and an ice-cream truck only three steps away. Get out of the car. You're going to be late."

He shot her a million-watt grin. "She might be here already."

As soon as they were out of the Jag, she rushed to him and slid her arms around him. For a moment, his arms waved indecisively at his sides, then held her, thick and warm.

"I know you didn't do it, Jay," she told him. With each word, he had stiffened more. "Don't say anything. It's okay. I just want you to know — really know — that I know, and I'll always be your friend." She pulled back and kissed his cheek.

He hesitated then brushed a strand of hair

from her eyes. "Take care of yourself, Elaine." His smile sent something lovely and tender through her. Then he leaned over and kissed her forehead.

He strode away. His broad back grew smaller. His tread became predatory.

As the moored fish barges nudged against the Maine Avenue wharf, the rhythmic *thunk* of steel against wood resounded eerily. The Potomac River's brown tide was rising, while seagulls circled low, eyeing the fresh crabs and oysters and fish in dozens of varieties arrayed on shaved ice on the block-long marketplace. The late-afternoon sunshine washed the scene in an eerie lavender light.

In his tinted skin and baseball cap and sunglasses, Jay Tice strolled beside the flatboats, his body slumped and deliberately old-looking, his hands loose and free, as he stayed aware of his holstered weapons, aware he saw Raina nowhere. He repressed disappointment and worry.

A fishmonger's voice suddenly sang out: "Loive crabs! Get your loive crabs!"

Jay resisted an impulse to turn. The accent was the real thing with the rich inflections of someone from one of the fishing outposts along the Chesapeake Bay.

Where was Raina? He turned and retraced his steps, pretending to study the modern restaurants that rimmed the river south of the barges. He scanned the marina's houseboats and cruisers and trawlers. He surveyed the pier — busy but not overcrowded — worried something had happened to Raina.

He carried an image of her in his mind from that first dawn exchange at Glienicke Bridge. She had looked like a Prussian princess in the wintry light, so bundled was she against the cold. He smiled to himself as he recalled her rosy cheeks, her pink nose. With her fur hat squarely on her head, her blue eyes had seemed larger than ever. And at her side, her gloved fingers had flexed once, her only betrayal of nerves. There was humanity in that gesture, the ice princess come alive. It revealed the woman, real and honest, beneath the perfect sheath of steel. The Raina he loved.

The barrel of a gun rammed sharply into his back. "So, old man, why shouldn't I wipe you?" The woman's voice was a hot, angry whisper beneath his right ear.

His lungs tightened. He controlled an automatic urge to swing back and jam his elbow into her throat. "Dammit, Raina." He kept his voice low. "What the hell do you think you're doing?"

"You bastard. Because of *you*, he's dead. Where's your car?"

This was not what he had planned. "It's a block from here. Put that gun away. You're going to get us noticed."

"I'm better than that, for God's sake. Don't try anything. I *will* wipe you if you don't do exactly what I say. Come to think of it, I may anyway. You've got one more job — we may have been burned, so keep an eye out. I said *walk*."

As instructed, Elaine had been following at a distance, nearly a block away. But a young thug in Levi's and a Harley-Davidson denim jacket had just moved in behind Jay and was so close they were almost in lock-step. Jay's taut body language signaled a weapon was involved. Suddenly Jay relaxed, and the punk backed off a fraction. They turned, and Jay raised his head and gave an almost imperceptible nod in her direction. That was when she knew — it was Raina in disguise. And the reunion looked far from romantic.

Elaine stopped and surveyed the wharf, the customers lined up at glass cases of fish, couples sauntering, nannies out with babies in strollers. No one appeared threatening. She reversed direction, too, walking back to

Maine Avenue. She glanced over her shoulder occasionally, checking on Jay and Raina.

But as she closed in on the street, Elaine spotted three men in off-the-rack suits striding purposefully onto the pier. One was tall and thick. All were moving too fast to be ordinary customers arriving to barter for fresh seafood, nor did they act like jaded health inspectors. She saw no sign of weapons, but their jackets were loose. Alarmed, she gazed beyond them to a van that was rolling to a stop in a no-parking zone. There was something about the first man out of the van — he was tall, familiar. With a jolt, she remembered. He was the one she had seen slipping into a doorway behind her after she left the Reading Room and sensed she had a tail. He must have been with the operative who had tried to wipe her with the poisoned darts. *Whippet.*

Pulse hammering, she checked on Jay and Raina. They were still too far away to be noticed by the newcomers, but not for long.

With a quick gesture, Elaine loosened her straw hat and again hurried, her speed attracting the attention of the trio. Their heads swiveled. They stared. She stared back through her sunglasses and then at the half-dozen others who had exited the van and were striding toward the first three.

She let her mouth fall open in horror. She bolted away, giving a shake to her head so her hat would fall off. It did, and her hair flew. Now they would have to recognize her.

"That's Cunningham!" one said, his voice raised.

"If she's here, they must be, too," said another. "Moses was right."

"Spread out. Look for them. We'll take Cunningham!"

Elaine glanced back as the initial trio came after her while the others scattered to search the dock for Raina and Jay. *Dammit! She'd screwed up!* All of them were supposed to chase her. She slammed to a stop, drew her Walther, and spun.

39

The men's voices had carried over the shoppers and past the bargemen and burned a single phrase into Jay's brain: *Moses was right.* He was enraged — but the rat was out of the hole at last.

"Who's that woman?" Raina demanded from behind as Elaine whirled around to face the men.

"The hunter Langley sent to track me down — Elaine Cunningham." He watched, appalled, as she dropped to her heels and opened fire. "I've got to help her!"

Under the sudden spray of bullets, the men dove for cover. Shoppers screamed, pushed, and ran in every direction. The terrible noise sent seagulls screeching into the wind. Panic swept the wharf.

Raina grabbed his arm and pulled. "Come on, Jay! We have to leave while we can. It's what she wants. *Come on!*"

Abruptly the gunfire died, and Elaine

sprinted off, this time with all of the attackers in hot pursuit. She was leading them away from him and Raina.

Jay darted between two shops, the sound of Raina's footsteps behind. He led her swiftly along the pier's edge, where shops and stores shielded them. They rushed past bluefish and crabs and bargemen offering deals. The noise of boats bumping the wharf sounded to Jay like hammers on coffin nails.

At the street, he checked all around for Elaine then turned to wait for Raina to catch up. And stared. Raina looked like a man, from dark lanky ponytail and violent sunglasses to mustache and short beard and loping gait. He hardly recognized her; she still had the touch.

Raina snapped, "Left."

They accelerated. He kept surveying the busy area until finally he saw Elaine again in the distance — the team of men in a tight, determined pack, pursuing.

An online meeting with the Majlis al-Sha'b was not something to be done in a Kinko's, so Faisal al-Hadi had rented a luxury hotel room in Northeast Washington for privacy and a secure wireless communication. He stood at the mirror and meticulously combed the last of the mousse from his wet hair. His ability to blend so easily was testament to the superficiality of their world. He ran a hand over his jaw, feeling the bristles of his black beard. He longed to grow it again, and soon he would. This was his last mission; the council had insisted he stop endangering himself.

As he straightened the starched white uniform of his new disguise, he saw the message on his laptop's screen announcing his brothers had assembled. It was seven A.M. in Malaysia, just after prayers. He hurried to his laptop and sat, imagining them gathered around their simple meeting table. With Allah to guide them, the Majlis had built new headquarters where no one could find them — on the hot, lush coast along the Strait of Malacca.

Convenient to the Middle East, Pakistan, and the Philippines, and encircled by thick mangrove swamps and centuries-old suspicion of anyone who was not Islamic, their hidden cove provided security and more than enough land on which to increase their sprawling nerve center. Because of reefs, the infidels' behemoth ships could not reach them. There was no landing strip for their mammoth jets. And there had never been roads through the jungle.

He typed his code and entered it. Immediately the screen showed his brothers. As always, they had placed a laptop at the head of the table — at his place — and turned it so he could view all. At the same time, each had his laptop open to have close sight of him. There were whip-lean Afghans, squat Turks, tall Sudanese, brown Pakistanis, Iraqis, Iranians, Kurds — thirty of them and growing. Their network of networks was spreading quickly.

After the usual greetings, he came to the point. "You've studied the manifest?" He spoke in Arabic. All meetings were conducted in the ancient tongue in which the holy Koran was written.

Salim Mahfooz, whose severe countenance showed an informed seriousness far beyond his thirty years, was a new councilman. "I understand Kalashnikovs and grenade launchers and SAMs. Partnerships among us in small arms dealing and smuggling make sense, but I see no future in Western gadgets." He was from Libya, where outrage over Mu'ammar Gadhafi's "peace" with the Great Satan after its invasion of Iraq had sent a flood of new enlistees into his organization.

"I'm concerned, too, brothers," Ibrahim Allahmar said. "Remember our primary goals — set up an international network for economic and financial cooperation, exchange intelligence, and share safe houses and joint training programs and arms buys. That demands all of our resources. This deal is costing far more than we anticipated. Now that I see the final manifest, I'm worried." Small, intense, and hard, he was a Uighur from Kashgar. He had been with them a year.

Al-Hadi was annoyed, but responding was a small price to pay for the cause. "Our brother, the Sheik bin Laden, is wise above all." He waited until everyone murmured agreement. "Two days before the sacred strikes of 9/11, he phoned his mother to tell her a big event would happen soon, and she wouldn't hear from him for a while. Do you think he was being careless?"

"Laa." The voices rang out — no.

"You're correct. He called because he knew the infidels' NSA would intercept the conversation — and that their intercept-interpret-analyze cycle was seventy-two hours. By the time they actually understood what he'd said, the attack would be over. Therefore, he could phone his mother and, at the same time, demoralize them with the depths of their arrogance and incompetence. How did the sheik know about the cycle? Because he'd spent years gathering information about their intelligence systems."

Around the table, turbaned heads nodded. Some stroked their beards with approval. The two who had objected remained silent and motionless.

"If the Soviet Union and every other hostile country couldn't overcome America's strategic defense, we'd be stupid to try," al-Hadi explained logically. "Islam may be stateless, but we can still defeat nations by using fourth-generation warfare. First, we accept that the West's military machine is vast, so we ignore it whenever possible. Second, we ignore their rules of war, too. For us, there's no difference between 'soldier' and 'civilian.' Civilians fight, too, by supporting *their* war. Third, the infidels believe early warning, preventive strikes, and deterrence will defeat us. Wrong. That works only when both sides want to survive. It's erased when fighting us, because we care only about the everlasting life of the soul."

"Our martyrs are holy," agreed Imam Burra Tilkrit from Yemen. *"Man maat al-yaum salim min dhanb bukra,"* he said, offering a proverb — Who dies today is safe from tomorrow's sin.

Al-Hadi waited until the pair of objectors

nodded along with everyone else.

Ibrahim Allahmar spoke again: "Tell us why you think this shipment is necessary for our holy jihad, Sheik al-Hadi."

Al-Hadi quoted a phrase from the Koran: "The answer is because it will 'instill terror in the hearts of the unbelievers.' Each product plays a role. For instance, we'll have a thousand integrated Land Battle packages. That's their brand-new soldier uniforms. They have built-in scrambled communications gear, personal electronics, global navigation, and new enhanced fabric that's impervious to gunfire. Instead of planting bombs that inevitably destroy their outposts, our men can wear these uniforms, invade while the infidels sleep, capture them for questioning, and leave with all of the intelligence and electronics equipment and guns. If their people spot us, we'll be fully equipped to defend and attack and still escape with our plunder. Don't you agree that this is good?"

"Very good!" the once-reluctant Salim Mahfooz said enthusiastically.

"You'll like the RadioTech chip, too. It sits at the base of an antenna and instantly converts any incoming analog radio signal into digital data. With it, we can convert local wireless signals to our use anywhere on the planet. There's also the Vibraject, a new way to use ultrasound vibrations to force drugs through the skin without a needle. What makes this useful is that it works from as far away as one hundred feet. We can shoot poison into the infidels from a distance, wait until they go down, then enter buildings to plant bombs or steal information without risking that our warriors will be stopped. Another product is the HiWave high-energy radio wave. It scrambles the computer chips — the digital brains — that control the functions in a car, a bus, a plane, a control tower, anywhere, in fact, that we wish."

Al-Hadi watched the councilmen turn to one another, talking excitedly as they translated his explanations into practical deeds for the jihad. When there was a pause, he said, "I could continue through the manifest, but I'll be home with the shipment in a month, and we can talk more then. Do I have your approval for it?"

"Why do we want this ForeTell software?" asked Kilim Dekat. Born in Germany, he was Hezbollah's representative.

Al-Hadi smiled. "ForeTell brings all the aspects of our networks together to a degree we've only dreamed of. We'll know where every man, every weapon, every tool in our arsenal is, and the stage each plan has reached. With ForeTell, we can program and coordinate the details of the defenses around each target along with the advanced physics and mathematics needed to guarantee every strike is successful. . . ."

When he finished, he studied them. Like beacons in a long, desolate night, pride and belief shone from their faces. With a nod to himself, his voice rose, full of emotion and truth: "Our loyalty is to no nation — only to Islam. We'll strike at the infidels' hearts — where they live and work and play. We'll demolish their most cherished landmarks and institutions. Each time we make their people pay a high price economically and psychologically, they blame their own leaders for allowing it to happen. As our strikes continue, they'll crumble more. We'll destroy them from the inside out. And then Allah will have his kingdom on earth once more!"

40

Old magnolia trees lined the residential block of small clapboard houses in Southeast Washington. Although a scattering of people were returning from work, the shadowy street gave off a feeling of desertion. Ahead was Raina's rental car, a beige Ford Mustang with a big V8 engine — a neutral color plus good horsepower.

As he and Raina hurried toward it, Jay inspected the area. "Where did you get the steel pipe you stuck into my back?"

"You knew?" Her fury at him had quieted.

"Not at first."

Both looked around quickly and climbed into the car. She turned on the engine and drove into the street sedately, doing nothing to draw attention in the tranquil neighborhood.

"I suppose it's a miracle I managed that. But then I had the best teacher," she said bitterly. She pulled a short length of pipe from her Harley-Davidson jacket and tossed it into the back. "I couldn't carry a weapon onto the plane, and I didn't want to risk picking one up around here. Pipe was the simplest solution."

He drank in the sight of her. In his mind, he erased the mustache and wig and studied the hollowed cheeks, the smooth skin, the quiet radiance of her personality, the kindness that flowed beneath. She had a way of tilting her head when she drove that gave a sense of combined vigilance and pleasure. He studied her long-fingered hands and short nails — her practical side. She gripped the steering wheel with nonchalant control. At the same time, her lanky body relaxed into the seat as if luxuriating in it. Still, at a moment's notice she could come alert and be lethal. Her beauty and complexity seemed to enthrall him even more.

"Have you learned anything about Kristoph?" she asked.

"Nothing directly. I was hoping you'd fill me in about him first. But before you do, we'd better talk about Moses."

"I heard the janitors say his name. The intel about where to find us came from Moses."

He nodded grimly. "That bastard! For years he always seemed to be somewhere near but just out of sight, a puppeteer alternately working us, working for us, and working against us. We had to play his game — we had no choice. I tried to find him, but he was always a step ahead. When he went quiet in the late nineties, I'd hoped he was gone forever."

"Someone knows where he is and is feeding him information."

"Did you say anything about our meet to anyone?"

"Absolutely not."

"I was afraid of that." Sickened by the implications, he admitted, "I told four trusted operatives from a close-knit covert team I worked with in West Berlin. I can't believe one of them would sell us out, but it's the only answer. You knew them later — Frank Mesa, Elijah Helprin, Palmer Westwood, and Ben Kuhnert, but Ben's out of commission or dead. So it's got to be Frank, Palmer, or Elijah."

"Good Lord! One of *them* gave us away?" They were at the end of the quiet block. Raina pressed the gas pedal, accelerating. "Can you figure out which one?"

As he watched for tails, he thought about it. "The logical time for a wet attack on Elaine and me was when we were sleeping and they were out on assignment. The house was secluded. No witnesses. So something must've changed after that." He ran the day's events through his mind. "The sole piece of new intel we got was the identity of the weapons trafficker who's fueling the situation — Martin Ghranditti."

"Ghranditti? I remember him. Not exactly a small-timer, but definitely on the verge of upholstery. More swagger than muscle. A real womanizer, too." She stopped herself. "Never mind, tell me about him later. Finish your analysis."

"Frank brought us Ghranditti's name, so it's not Frank." His hands knotted into fists as he fought a profound sense of betrayal. "It's got to be Elijah or Palmer." He had never been as close to Elijah as he was to Palmer, but he had a deep fondness and respect for him. After so many years of working with both, of trust and mutual duty, of covering each other's backs, it seemed impossible either would knowingly help to terminate Raina or Elaine or him.

Raina shot him a compassionate look. "You realize both men are well sourced, or at least they used to be. It's possible Palmer or Elijah *is* Moses."

He searched his mind futilely for an argument against the idea. Finally, he nodded, defeated. "Oh, hell, you're right. We've got to be very careful. I've been running the team as I always did. They report in, and we occasionally conference on our cells. That means Elijah or Palmer could phone anytime. We don't want them to know where we are or what we're doing or anything about Elaine. Agreed?"

"Of course. But we've also got to figure out how to force the pig into the open."

"Later. Right now our top priority is to pool what we know so we can stop the weapons deal." They had left the residential area. Traffic was thickening. "Turn north at the next intersection. That'll take us farther away from the fish wharf. Tell me what you've learned, then I'll fill you in."

"I'll start with Kristoph." Raina's hands tensed on the steering wheel. "A few months ago Kristoph took a short-term job to make final adjustments on a new software program. The morning of the day he died, he called from Geneva to tell me its name was die Sehergabe and it was for the Ministry of Justice so they could improve their ability to track court dates, lawsuits, attorneys, defendants — all sorts of things — and organize and analyze data. To keep it ultrasecret, the ministry sent the team out of the country under the cover of a private German company called Milieu Software."

"Milieu is a Whippet front, Raina. Whippet is a CIA special unit. It's deep in what's been going on."

She stared. Ripped away her gaze and swore loudly in German. "That explains a lot. Kristoph asked a favor. He wanted me to find out whether the program really was for the ministry. That terrified me, and I tried to convince him to get out of there. But Kristoph had a mind of his own. He could be very stubborn." She hesitated, seeming to collect herself. "He wouldn't even explain why he was asking the question. I phoned a friend who's high in the ministry and knows what he's talking about. He got back to me with what I was afraid of — no one had heard of die Sehergabe." She swallowed. "Kristoph died before I could tell him."

She angled the Mustang onto Seventh Street and accelerated into the traffic. Expression pinched, she related a harrowing story of the phone call announcing Kristoph's fatal accident, her rushed flight to Geneva, and her investigation into Milieu. She described Volker Rehwaldt's nighttime stakeout of Kristoph's apartment and the hug that enabled her to be tracked.

"He set me up for a CIA man who said his name was Alec." She described Alec.

"That's Alec St. Ann, a Whippet op. He's very good. Been stationed in Europe for years." He watched the street warily, thinking about Alec, who could be relentless.

"Alec knew I was sleeping. He tried to reactivate me to find out everything I'd discovered about Milieu. Of course, I told him nothing, but then I knew very little anyway. But I had something else he wanted — two surveillance tapes of the Milieu building's back and front entrances for the seven days before Kristoph's death."

He stared at her. "Have you viewed them?"

"I haven't had a place to."

"We've got to see them. I'll think about where we can take them that's safe. I don't like this business of the CIA and BND working together against you."

"I'm not crazy about it, either. Once they got the videotapes, they planned to scrub me and make it look like suicide."

"Those *bastards*. Alec was protecting Whippet. I'll bet anything that Kristoph's software is somehow involved in Ghranditti's deal." He paused, realized: "Die Sehergabe could mean the Seer's Gift, right?" When she nodded, he felt a chill.

"Why does it matter?"

"A seer 'foretells' the future. Die Sehergabe is our top-secret ForeTell program. This is *very* bad. We were overwhelmed with data, six hundred and fifty million events every day, more information than the Library of Congress holds — radio and data transmissions, radar signals, faxes, satellite, cell, and landline calls, and messages in dozens of languages, often encrypted. There was no way to interpret it in a timely way — until ForeTell. We got it a few months before I was arrested. It enabled us to keep track of everything while spitting out warnings, potential targets, rising enemy and terrorist leaders, where our vulnerabilities were, scenarios we should think about, on and on. It looks for patterns and relationships, identifies hidden power brokers, people with crucial skills."

They exchanged a worried look.

As she watched the traffic, she asked casually, too casually, "So who's really calling the shots at Whippet?"

He had known this moment would come. "I'm sorry, Raina — it has to be Larry Litchfield. He runs the unit. He's been feeding Ghranditti information that's nearly gotten us killed several times. He's the only one with access to get a copy of ForeTell to give Kristoph. He's also the only one who knew you were a sleeper. And unless it was in the heat of the moment — and obviously it wasn't — any Whippet wet jobs would've had to be ordered by Larry."

Raina stiffened as if she had just been struck.

He said softly, "I figure a child's murder is about the toughest thing anyone has to come to grips with. Besides, children are supposed to bury their parents, not the reverse. Doesn't get much worse."

Fiery rage radiated from Raina. Her lips peeled back. "They killed Kristoph. Whippet liquidated him. Your protégé — Larry Litchfield — had him *liquidated!*"

He looked away. "Yes, dammit!" His body felt taut, brittle with rage and grief.

He forced himself to look at her again. Finally she glanced at him.

A well of sorrow shone from her eyes. "One of the last things I did in Geneva was pack Kristoph's things and mail them home to Berlin. Just a dozen cardboard boxes." She took a hand off the steering wheel to wipe one eye then the other. "It seemed so little for such a big life. Odd, isn't it, how death affects one." She swallowed. "My heart felt as if it'd shattered into hundreds of pieces." Tears streamed down her cheeks.

Jay fumbled anxiously around, looking for a tissue. Of course, there was none. This was a rental car.

She reached into the back and unzipped the gym bag and grabbed a box of them and wiped her eyes and blew her nose. "I'll probably never see any of his things again," she said, "or his room. Or any of the photos of him in our house. The things that he touched, that he cared about. All of it . . . all of it seems to matter a lot now."

Jay watched her helplessly. "I'd like to see everything, too. Very much."

She nodded wordlessly. Another tear slid down her cheek. He took a tissue and dabbed. He ached for her at the same time he ached for himself. Tentatively, he lowered his hand. She let him close it over the top of hers, where it rested on her thigh. Her hand was cold. Slowly she turned it over so that they were palm to palm. She slid her fingers between his, wove them together.

He was afraid to speak. He wanted nothing to interrupt this moment. It felt as if the whole world were there between their hands. He listened to her breathe. He knew it would have to end, but when she squeezed his hand and slid hers away to grip the steering wheel again, he still felt bereft.

41

Miami Beach, Florida

The ice-cream parlor was bright with sundaes and milk shakes and cones of ice cream painted across the glossy white walls. Round tables were spaced close together, with wire-frame chairs tucked around each. With effort, Marie Ghranditti smiled as the children raced to the counter to order.

"I want Chocolate Huckleberry Mound, please," Aaron announced, his nine-year-old voice piping with excitement as he rested his chin on top of the old-fashioned glass counter. "Two scoops. Jimmies on top. *Please.*"

"And what does my Mariette want?" Marie stroked her daughter's black ringlets.

"Screamin' Dreamin'— the ghost ice cream!" Although seven, she was still a pixie. The top of her head barely reached her older brother's shoulder. She had a Three Investigators book by William Arden

547

under her arm.

"And Kristoph?" Marie said. "What would you like, darling?"

His wrinkled face beaming, Armand picked up Kristoph. The two-year-old leaned over, peering down through the glass, his brow furrowed, his thumb in his mouth. He removed it and said, "Chocolate."

"Armand?" Marie prompted.

Eyes twinkling, he said, "I second Kristoph's choice. Chocolate, plain and simple."

"Dante, you must choose, too."

"I don't know, madam." The bodyguard appeared uncomfortable, his shoulders tense, his eyes nervously darting. This was hardly his usual hangout. Thankfully his pistol was only a small lump under his left armpit.

"Then I suggest a hot fudge sundae, and I'll have one, too." Her smile felt plastered to her face. "Everyone likes hot fudge sundaes."

"Whatever you say, madam."

As the teenage boy behind the counter filled their order, Marie sent the children to choose a table. Armand and Dante delivered their cones. When Armand had his, too, Marie sent the men to the table to keep the children company.

Was it her imagination, or was Dante observing her more closely than usual? It seemed to her he was, his black eyes less suspicious than Martin's but far more wary. She was dressed normally, in a sweater and skirt, but she was wearing a scarf to hide her dark hair. She resisted an impulse to adjust it, to make certain not a single dark brown strand showed.

As the two sundaes arrived on the countertop, she took out her billfold. *Your back is to Dante. Just do it.* She handed the teenager a twenty-dollar bill. When he turned to the cash register, she opened the flat pill box she had put into her billfold and sprinkled the powder over the hot fudge. She stared, willing it to dissolve.

When the powder had vanished, she carried the dishes to the table and set Dante's in front of him. "Didn't you have hot fudge sundaes when you were a little boy, Dante?"

He nodded. "Yes, madam."

Kristoph climbed into Armand's lap and nudged his forehead against Armand's crepe-paper cheek, then resumed licking his dripping cone. Armand's arm encircled him and gave him a gentle hug. Armand had arranged everything for this afternoon.

She found it hard to talk. Dante had not tasted his sundae. She wanted to urge him, but that would not be wise. She dug into hers in hopes he would get the idea. Dante still did not eat his. The children chattered and devoured their cones. She encouraged them to talk about school.

Finally she said, "Dante, do you want to hurt my feelings? Remember, this is a special occasion. My birthday. Please have fun. Enjoy your sundae."

He glanced at her, surprised. She saw a faint look of shame. She held her breath. At last he picked up his spoon and ate.

She smiled broadly. "It's good, isn't it?"

For an instant, she felt proud — then guilty. The powder was two pulverized Oxy-Contin pills. A single crushed OxyContin tablet had the power of sixteen Percocet pills. Soon Dante's respiratory system would slow, and he should lose consciousness.

The party continued as Dante finished his sundae with no apparent symptoms. The children poked each other and giggled.

She exchanged a worried look with Armand. "Let's go," she told the children. "It's almost time for the last story hour at the library."

They trooped out to her small white limousine. Above them, streetlights glowed through the dusk. She and the children climbed in back, and Armand got behind the wheel. But Dante seemed to trip. He slapped his hand on the roof, catching himself. The noise made the children jump. They looked at her with large eyes.

"It's fine, kids," she said softly. "Dante just stumbled."

She watched as he shook his head and forced himself erect. He seemed to have recovered by the time he climbed in beside Armand, who put the car into gear and drove off. But as the limo swayed around a curve, Dante struggled to reach down. Finally he managed to pick up his Uzi. He embraced it.

Marie pulled Kristoph onto her lap. "Do all of you know I didn't have chocolate ice cream until I was nearly twenty years old?"

"No!" Aaron said, disbelieving.

"Ah, but it's true. Where I grew up, chocolate was a luxury. Only the very richest people could afford it."

The limo cruised along the dark waterfront. Mariette opened her book. Marie turned on the overhead light so she could read. Kristoph sucked his thumb, and Aaron described a new boy at school who seemed to be a potential friend.

Suddenly in the front seat, Dante mumbled a slurred curse, "Shun-bish." He tried to raise the Uzi but instead slumped heavily against the passenger door, limp as a rag doll. His jaw slackened, his tongue lolled out, and drool dripped from the corner of his mouth. The powdered Oxy-Contin had finally hit him.

Marie felt a flutter of excitement. Armand screeched into a U-turn and sped off in the opposite direction.

"What's happening?" Aaron asked, his voice rising.

"Is something wrong?" Mariette wanted to know, letting the book fall to her lap.

Marie looked at the children, her voice urgent. "We're going on a little trip, darlings. Just the four of us. We'll —"

Mariette's voice shook. "Will Daddy be with us?"

"Daddy has important business to finish first," she told her daughter calmly.

"Are we going to the island early?" Aaron wondered eagerly.

Marie felt a small panic. Martin had brainwashed the children. She would have to undo that, but first she must get them safely away. "Not to the island, sweetie. Still, we'll have a lot of fun. Promise."

Aaron subsided but peered at her suspiciously. Seeming confused, Mariette raised her book, hiding in it as she often did. Kristoph squirmed on her lap, oblivious.

Armand peeled the limo off onto a side street and stopped behind a rented Taurus. He grabbed Dante's Uzi and got out as she reached across Mariette for the door. Suddenly an SUV screeched up to their rear fender, engine pulsing, bright lights igniting the limo's interior. Her heart seemed to stop. Instantly a second SUV careened alongside them, braking next to Armand. Four armed men leaped out.

"Leave her alone!" Armand shouted, raising the Uzi.

There was one silenced shot, and Armand crashed back onto the hood, head at an unnatural angle. Marie gasped. The children screamed. The Uzi fell to the ground.

Kristoph cried out, "Armand!" He reached out his arms, opening and closing his little hands as if trying to draw Armand to him.

Marie bit back a sob and cuddled him close as Martin's Ukranian guard, Karl, slid in behind the wheel, and another of Martin's armed men dropped into the passenger seat next to him. She pulled her older two children protectively close while Kristoph buried his face in her shoulder. Aaron and Mariette looked up at her with stark fear. Their little bodies trembled as Karl turned and aimed his Uzi casually at her. He smiled, showing brown teeth.

"We just in time, *da,* Mrs. G? Good thing Mr. G said keep close eye on you today. Put GPS tracker on your limo. Smart, huh?"

42

Washington, D.C.

"It's your turn, Jay," Raina said as she drove them around the darkening swath of Thomas Circle. Fill me in."

He took a deep breath. Beginning with his prison breakout early yesterday, he described what had happened and what he had learned. At last, he concluded, "So now we know Ghranditti's deal is with al-Qaeda's successor organization."

"I've never even heard of the Majlis," Raina told him worriedly. "That alone is frightening, because I oversee a lot of antiterrorism — or I did." Regret filled her voice.

"I understand." As he glanced at her, his cell phone rang. He had been sitting with it between his hands. He flipped it open and checked. "It's Elijah," he told her.

She frowned. Jay answered the call.

"Frank and Palmer are on the line," Elijah

told him. "I've been trying to raise Elaine, but she's not answering. I'll try again." If Elijah were Moses's source, he gave no indication he was surprised to hear Jay's voice.

"Don't bother," Jay said smoothly. "We dropped her off at a friend's house. She finally admitted she was in over her head."

"Really?" Elijah said, disappointed. "I thought she was tougher than that. Damn. Sorry to lose her. Palmer, you want to handle the report to Jay?"

"Absolutely." Filled with concern, the older man's voice gave no hint of duplicity, either. "It's an understatement to say we've got a nasty kettle of silverfish on our hands, Jay. Glad you're sitting down. Take a deep breath. The news is Ghranditti's shipment appears to be nothing but high-tech — which is bad enough. Far worse, it's not just *any* high-tech. It's fucking state-of-the-art. Everything — absolutely everything — is cutting-edge. The U.S. government's best, latest, most covert, most ingenious — and deadly. Plus it covers the whole spectrum — weapons to intelligence gathering, detection to communications."

"I've never seen anything like it," Elijah admitted. "I'll read you the list."

Jay turned on the speakerphone so Raina

could hear. As Elijah talked, her eyebrows rose, and she paled.

When he finished, Elijah concluded worriedly, "No one's ever assembled anything like this for even a friendly government."

Jay took a deep breath. "If the Majlis get all this, God help the world!"

Elaine pushed through a throng of tourists and dashed down the steps of L'Enfant Plaza and into the underground mall, listening to the careening noise of the Whippet operatives chasing her.

Covered in sweat, her lungs heaving, she shoved her Walther into her purse and slowed to a quick walk, ignoring the stares of shoppers and commuters heading to catch the Metro. Ducking into Harper's, a small women's clothing store, she wove among the goods until she reached a distant wall where she could see the door. With luck, her pursuers would rush past and she could slip back out and escape.

At last she saw them through the window — the big man with the broad chest in the lead, his face red and murderous. He paused to talk to the others and sent them off in different directions. Then he turned to enter the shop. Her chest tight, she dropped low and crawled under hanging racks, heading back toward the door. She watched the shoes of the big man and two others as they stalked inside, their feet heavy. They stopped occasionally. Finally their knees bent. They were going to look under the clothing.

She grabbed the top of the metal rack and pulled herself up among long dresses. She could taste her sweat as it streamed down her face. Her arms began to ache. At last she heard the feet return to the door. Again they stopped. With relief, she let herself down softly.

"You stay here," a basso voice ordered quietly. "Watch for her. She's got to be around somewhere."

Raina drove east. The sun had disappeared, and dusk had swallowed the golden light of sunset. They had received more phone calls from Elijah then Palmer, asking whether they were all right and where they were. Jay had dodged their questions smoothly.

As Raina stopped the car at a red light, she looked closely at him, feeling a strange curiosity. The geometry of his jaw had softened, and age lines etched his skin. As they always had, his hazel-colored eyes gave a sense of ice chips from a glass of fine bourbon, cold and brittle, while she sensed, as she used to, he secretly wanted to be

558

warmed by the right human hands. He was still very handsome, and there was a muscularity to him that made him seem as physical as ever. She had a fleeting memory of what a principled man she had once thought him.

After he tried to call Elaine again, Raina could feel him studying her, although he was clearly not seeing her. It gave her a strange sensation to remember his habits so well: "You're trying to figure out something, aren't you?"

He nodded. "We used to do this together. Help me, will you? Now that we know how unusually dangerous Ghranditti's shipment is, I've been trying to understand what in hell is going on with Larry Litchfield. Information is power, and ForeTell is the planet's most effective vehicle to deliver information. But he's apparently selling it to the Majlis al-Sha'b despite knowing as much or more than we do about how dangerous they are. Has he gone insane?"

"Maybe the answer is more complex than madness or greed." The light turned green, and she drove off.

Suddenly Jay sat up straight. "I think you're right." He peered at the traffic then at her. "Back in the eighties, the White House ordered NSA to 'penetrate banks to combat money-laundering and other criminal activities and illegal sales of high technology to the Soviet Union.' I remember one of NSA's solutions was to install a backdoor in a forerunner of ForeTell. A backdoor is a few lines of code hidden inside hundreds of thousands of lines of programming instructions. Then no matter where the software is used, Baghdad or Paris or Timbuktu, all you have to do wherever you are is hit the right keystrokes and you can track employees, take money from bank accounts, manufacture records — even change the trajectory of missiles or download everything in their database. And you can do it without leaving any footprints, no audit trail at all that you were there.

"In those days, it was the most powerful software in the world. So Langley created front companies to peddle the backdoor version. A lot of nations snapped it up — France, Canada, Germany, Bulgaria, the Soviet Union, to name a few. So did a lot of multinationals, including *all* of the big wire-transfer clearinghouses in America and Europe. Mossad got into the game, too, with their own backdoor. The intel was so extraordinary that we stopped assassinations and savage attacks. Then somehow word leaked out, as it always does eventually, about what we were doing. The news spread like an epidemic among IT people. When no one could find the backdoor lines of code, everyone destroyed their software. And suddenly our ocean of intel went dry."

She had an awful feeling. "There was no reason to bring in Kristoph to make 'final adjustments' on ForeTell — it was already finished. So you think Litchfield used him to design a backdoor!"

Jay clasped his hands in his lap, weaving the fingers into a knot so tight his knuckles turned white. "Bin Laden's people knew about the first backdoor, because he had one of the versions. That means al-Hadi and the Majlis would immediately suspect anyone who wanted to sell them ForeTell. Their prejudice that we're all just greedy, godless infidels would work in Litchfield's favor if he offered it to them for a large amount of money — but it wouldn't be enough for them to take the risk. That's why I figure Litchfield's working with Ghranditti. Ghranditti's shipment is such a threat to us that the Majlis have to believe Litchfield wouldn't gamble on letting them have it *and* the software — unless all he really did care about was the cash."

"Good Lord. Litchfield *is* insane. The Majlis could find out tomorrow the software's dirty and never even use it, and they'd still have the high-tech shipment!"

He grimaced. "They could kill tens of thousands, if not millions, of us."

Shocked, they fell silent. As the lights from other vehicles flashed into the car, she tried to find a solution.

Suddenly Jay's eyes narrowed. "We've got to take the fight to Ghranditti." He dialed his cell.

His fingers hammering the keyboard of his wireless laptop, Frank Mesa sat alone on a park bench under a towering maple tree in Lafayette Square, across the street from the White House. Cloaked in evening shadows, just outside the rim of one of the park's lamplights, he had been making phone calls, collecting information about Martin Ghranditti.

His cell phone lit up. He noted the number and answered. "Yes, Jay?"

Jay's voice was taut. "What's the latest about Ghranditti? Are you getting close to finding out where the shipment's going to change hands?"

Frank frowned. He had not made nearly the progress he wanted. "Ghranditti's done a damn good job of hiding himself. I've got nothing new about the shipment. For a while I thought I was getting close to finding at least one of those shell companies Palmer thought Ghranditti had, but it turned out to be just a realty firm in Northern Virginia he's done business with. But through it, I was able to track two residences. He owns one in Miami Beach with so much security it could be a bank vault. The other's here in D.C., a penthouse. It's up for sale in one of those quiet, hoity-toity arrangements where there's no sign on the door, and any parties interested in purchasing it have to prove they've got a million bucks in the bank even to view it."

"Sounds as if Ghranditti's planning to disappear after the deal closes. If we don't get him now, we may lose him forever."

"That's my guess, Jay."

There was a pause, and Frank could almost hear the wheels in Jay's brain spinning with ideas. "You've got a suggestion?" he prompted hopefully.

"Get me a key to that penthouse. Maybe I can find something there about the shipment."

Frank smiled to himself. "I'll give you a call when I have it, and we can arrange for you to pick it up. Bye, Jay."

"We're not finished." Another pause, and Jay's tone grew heavy with warning: "I'm going to say something that might not make a lot of sense, Frank, so you'll have to trust me. Something's brewing, and Palmer or Elijah might be part of it. Don't breathe a word to either of them that we've talked."

The minutes passed slowly where Elaine hid nervously beneath the dresses in Harper's clothing shop. Her sweat dried, and her skin itched. The man continued to lurk in the doorway. Finally his feet shifted more and more frequently. He was restless. When he called a thank-you to the clerk and stalked off, Elaine sighed with relief.

After five minutes she crawled under the clothes toward the door. Evening shoppers passed intermittently in the corridor. But there was also a man's shadow, cast by the underground mall's strange illumination. He was still on guard but positioned on the other side of the door from the store window.

Cursing silently, she scuttled to another rack, where she grabbed brown trousers and a matching jacket and a black T-shirt. Still hidden, she changed, then crab-walked down the aisle and pulled a black slouch hat from a display pole and tucked her hair up underneath. She removed the paper funnel she had zipped into a side pocket of her purse and carefully unfurled it on the floor, wary of the tips of the darts inside. It seemed incredible that it was only yesterday afternoon in Franklin Park that the Whippet operative had shot the darts at her, trying to scrub her.

Holding one of the darts by its flight, she rose until her eyes were above the dresses. The clerk had moved to another area and was helping a mother and daughter.

Elaine stared then dropped down and crawled toward the door. The shadow was still there. She eased out. He was a man of medium height with an almost boneless face and a look of intense boredom, but the tension in his body told her he was also on high alert. Suddenly he noticed her.

As he looked straight at her, she rammed the tip of the dart into his calf. He grunted. In an instant, his arms uncrossed. His weapon, with its long sound suppressor, pointed at her. As she fell back inside the doorway, he pulled the trigger. The *pop* was loud in the quiet mall, reverberating from tiled and concrete surfaces.

"Get down!" Elaine yelled at the women in the shop.

She rolled under the clothes and ripped her Walther from her purse. Then rolled back toward the door in time to see the man stagger inside. His eyes were crazed with fury and poison; his skin gray. But as soon as he spotted her, he aimed again. She sprang forward and crashed her shoulder into his knees. She heard one snap. He grunted and went down like a tower of blocks, his finger reflexively pulling the trigger. The shot splintered the floor next to her. Within seconds she was up and out the door. She looked both ways and ran.

43

Near the Mall, Jay Tice trudged through yellow pools of lamplight toward a concrete sidewalk planter, limping slightly. His shoulders were rounded, his lips down-turned in a grimace, emphasizing the elderly age he pretended. Pedestrians flooded past as he sank onto the planter's wall. He checked around carefully then slid his hand back under the decorative rock Frank had described. His fingers probed. At last he found the freshly made elevator key to Martin Ghranditti's penthouse and retrieved it. Staying in character, he limped away.

The Mustang stopped at the curb. He climbed inside.

"It was there?" Raina asked anxiously as she drove back into the traffic.

"Exactly where Frank said." He pulled out his SIG Sauer and handed it to her. "You may need this. It's loaded."

She glanced at it and slid it inside her waistband. A neutral mask settled over her face, a mask that reminded him of his own.

As she turned the corner, heading toward Ghranditti's place, he studied her. Her eyes were cool and intelligent in the shadowy interior, completely professional. Still, the undercurrent of towering sorrow and rage was also there, tangible.

He might never have another chance. "You're still very angry with me."

Her brows shot up. Her wide-set eyes were the color of lapis lazuli — and now flaming with fury. But her voice was controlled as she said, "Of course I'm angry. You broke our agreement. You stayed CIA, and not only wouldn't you let me out, you turned me into a sleeper. I was trapped. Kristoph was trapped."

"Langley came to me —"

"I don't want to hear it. It doesn't matter anymore."

"Yes, it does, or you wouldn't be so damn mad. If it's any comfort, I was just doing my duty —"

"Kristoph's *dead.* In effect, you killed him! Was that your duty?"

Pain knifed through him. In a way, she was right. He gathered himself. Then: "We both know you're here for Kristoph, not for me or you, although I wish you were. This Ghranditti and Litchfield situation is too big for either of us, but together we have a chance." When she started to object, he shook his head hard. "We've got to settle things between us."

And he stopped talking. Waited. Felt her peer at him a moment. He looked just in time to see it was not at him she stared but off through the cocoon of the car, past the hum of the engine and the clotted street and Washington's grand buildings and into the distance, as if searching for another time, a better world, another chance.

"The past isn't sacred," he said. "Don't let it dictate the future."

Like a gun, her gaze homed in on him. "You're doing it again. *Words.* 'The past isn't sacred.' Of course it is — to *you.* You've always been so noble. The great spymaster. The man of a thousand faces, a thousand eyes, a thousand wiles. Trusted, honored, revered. But you broke our agreement without consulting me. You dictated our future and put Kristoph and me in a position neither of us ever wanted!"

A queasy feeling slid through him.

"You talked me into being a mole for you," she continued more calmly. "Then you talked me into being a BND mole, but it wasn't just so I could work for democracy, for the future of Germany. You'd studied the economic intelligence of the Soviet Union and realized it was collapsing. So you prepared. You maneuvered and manipulated me as only you could do. Your real goal was to make sure I'd be taken care of later, in case you couldn't."

"I don't understand why you're so upset —"

"Be quiet and listen! Yes, that meant after the Wall fell I'd have a job, a place in the New Germany, while everyone else in the Stasi would never be able to find legitimate work. But that set me up for Erich Eisner to turn me into a national symbol. I hated it because it was a lie. Kristoph hated it because he was young, and the glare of my celebrity was so blinding he couldn't see who he was. He had to take my mother's name to try to make his own way. You even denied him his own name! And now it's led to this. He's dead, and I can't go home if I want to live."

He started to speak.

She waved a hand dismissively, silencing him. "All you had to do was keep our agreement." Her voice brimmed with disgust. "All you had to do was quit. It was that simple. *Retire.*"

"I couldn't." He was holding the car's armrest in a death grip. The only thing he had left was the truth, but it was a truth he did not want to tell.

"Langley needed me. No, wait. Let me finish. Just because the Cold War was over didn't mean my work was. The world was heading into uncharted political territory, and I had institutional memory. I had experience and expertise and the sort of reputation that reminded the Oval Office of Langley's tremendous value. So of course the seventh floor came to me. By then the DCI and DDO knew about you. I told them you wanted out. When their silence stretched, I flew back to Langley to convince them to release both of us. That's how I discovered they planned to turn you into a mole, spying against Germany, and if you resisted, they'd expose your Cold War work for us."

As she continued to drive, her eyebrows shot up with shock. "They'd blackmail me? Use the help I gave . . . the terrifying risks I took . . . to *blackmail* me?"

He could not look at her. "The only way to protect both of you was to bargain them into making you a sleeper. That was the best I could do, and that's why I pursued the promotion to DDO. I needed to be right there at Langley to make sure you were allowed to continue to sleep."

"Oh, dear Lord. I had no idea."

A hush filled the dark car, and an ocean of regret.

"And Moscow?" she said. "Why did you turn? How could you go against everything we worked for? Everything we believed in!"

He hesitated. He pressed a fist against his chest, felt the beat of his heart. His mouth was dry as he said, "I didn't turn." He looked at her.

She blinked several times as if unable to comprehend. "What happened?" she asked softly.

"Bobbye Johnson got a call from Moses that he had a client who was going to expose you. He was going to tell the media you'd worked for us during the Cold War and were sleeping for us with the BND now — and that you were behind Pavel Abendroth's assassination. Plus he'd give details to the Mossad." As a renowned dissident and Jewish refusenik, Dr. Abendroth had been a particular hero in Israel.

"Mossad never forgets or forgives." She breathed shallowly. "It would've been my death sentence."

He nodded. "That's why I had to give Moses what his client wanted." His mind touched gingerly the cold edge of that moment Bobbye had delivered Moses's message. "The offer was that I could buy his silence if I'd set myself up as a traitor and go to prison for life. The client didn't want me to be executed but instead to live in a limbo of nonexistence, essentially erasing my past and whatever pleasure I took from it, and guaranteeing me no future." His voice sounded matter-of-fact, surreal. "So that's what I did. I fabricated evidence to justify arrest and conviction. Obviously the Kremlin knew it was a lie, but it made them look good, so they never disputed it. Bobbye did the best she could to make sure I was comfortable in the penitentiary. I had a few more privileges than the other inmates."

Raina stared at him. Her voice crackled with revulsion. "I don't believe you agreed to that."

He was stunned. "It was my duty to take care of you and Kristoph. There were risks to you that —"

"Your damn duty!" she snapped. "I never wanted nobility. *You* did — it was all for you, always about you. *Your* duty. *Your* choices. *Your* noble causes. Duty is blind, Jay. Duty's only loyalty is to the concept of duty. Any fool can be dutiful. If someone asks why you're doing this or that, and you say, 'It's my duty,' you haven't really thought it through, have you? You're lazy! You're fulfilling others' expectations. You're doing what you've been told to do. Here's something that's tough: Do you really think I'm so incompetent and stupid that I was incapable of participating in all of those crucial decisions that were life-changing not just for you but for me?"

"No, of course not. I was protecting —"

"Protecting? *Bullshit.* We both know how well that's worked out. Talk about the pornography of power. You had the power, and because you had it, you thought it gave you the right to use it however you damn well thought best. You and your stupid, stupid ideas and games. You owed Kristoph and me because you loved us — and we loved you. You owed yourself. That was your *real* duty!"

Yearning swept through him, followed instantly by a sense of great loss. He wondered what their lives would have been if he had vanished with them as she had wanted. He had seldom allowed himself to really think about that after Langley had convinced him he was irreplaceable and must stay. Then Langley had decided he *was* replaceable — by Raina.

"You're right," he said simply. "I was

wrong. Very wrong. I just didn't see it." He let the admission hang there, naked, raw. When she still said nothing, he nodded to himself. "It's inadequate, but I want you to know I'm sorry. Truly sorry."

"I've never heard you apologize for anything."

He sighed heavily. "It's long past time."

A strange quiet filled the car. Suddenly she lifted her chin and stared hard into the rearview mirror.

Before she could speak, he jerked himself erect. "I see it."

A District police cruiser was speeding up behind them. The temperature inside the car seemed to plunge. The traffic light ahead turned red.

"Damn!" She slowed and stopped behind a Mini Cooper.

Neither moved. He studied his side-view mirror, watching the police car draw closer. It pulled abreast in the next lane. He waited for some indication the police had made them.

When the stoplight switched to green, Raina hesitated then drove smoothly forward. The police car angled away and was out of sight as soon as they crossed the intersection.

He exhaled. "It's a reminder of how

vulnerable we are."

She seemed to think about that. "You're right, Jay. We *are* vulnerable, and I'm sorry for being so hard on you." Finally she asked, "Did you ever find out who the client was who demanded you set yourself up for treason?"

He shook his head, feeling weary. "Our closest link was Moses. Bobbye and I tried everything to identify him. We're still trying. No one she or I questioned had heard from Moses for a couple of years before then, and no one's heard from him since."

"The client could be anyone. But how did the client find out about me and the CIA? I never told anyone, and it sounds as if you didn't, either. You kept the information controlled at Langley?"

"I sure as hell did. It was need-to-know. That meant only four people — the DCI, Arlene Debo; the DDO, Greg Stephens; the ADDO, Palmer Westwood; and me. Arlene, Greg, and Palmer were retired by the time Moses called to blackmail me, and frankly I can't imagine any of them would say a word to anyone. But clerks and secretaries and data techs have some access — if they figure out how to work the system. So it also could've been someone else at Langley. Believe me, Bobbye and I investigated thoroughly. We could never pinpoint the informant."

"You don't think it was Larry Litchfield?"

He shook his head. "He didn't find out about you until he took over as DDO. That's when he had need-to-know. He still has no idea I'm anything but a traitor. Bobbye and I — and now you — are the only ones who have all the facts."

"The client has to be someone you know personally," she persisted. "The 'offer' was a vendetta. Revenge — very personal revenge."

44

As Elaine hurried toward her Jaguar, she surveyed the busy street near the Maine Avenue wharf. She had dry-cleaned and felt reasonably sure she was safe. Breathing deeply, she pulled out her cell phone.

There was another message from Jay, no doubt anxious about her, plus three from Elijah Helprin and three from Palmer Westwood. Something urgent must have happened. Since Elijah had been the first to phone, she dialed him first then jumped into the Jag. As she turned on the engine, he answered.

"Have you heard from Jay?" he asked worriedly. "We're getting no information out of him. For some reason, he's cut us off."

With one hand, she spun the Jag into the street. "He's with Raina. They have a lot to talk about."

"True. Where have you been?"

She filled him in then asked what he and

Palmer had learned.

"We had luck with Ghranditti's shipment."

She listened to the items, staggered by the chilling implications.

Finished with the list, Elijah sounded particularly weary. "Palmer and Frank and I are finally together, waiting for orders from Jay. We still don't know where the shipment's being held — or when it's transferring. Come join us. That way at least we'll be ready when Jay needs us, or maybe we can figure out what to do next on our own."

"Good idea. Where are you?"

He gave her the address of a motel in Southeast Washington, and she turned the Jag, heading toward it. She dialed Jay. She was relieved to hear his voice. She could hear the sounds of an engine and traffic, too. He and Raina were also driving.

"Thank God," Jay breathed. "You're alive. Tell me what happened."

Elaine described the long chase and hiding in the dress shop. "I liked the poetic justice of using a Whippet dart to down a Whippet operative. I just talked to Elijah. Everyone's concerned about you. I know they'd like to hear from you. They're in a motel, waiting for me."

She heard Jay's sharp intake of air. "Don't go there."

As she listened to his explanation, fear then rage swept through her. "I can't believe Elijah or Palmer is Moses. It must've happened some other way!"

"Don't go to the motel," Jay insisted. "I can't get over there to protect you unless I drop following up a good lead. Drive someplace else and lie low — but don't tell me where. I'm not going to say where we're heading, either, but I'll phone as soon as we have something useful. I won't cut you out of the action, Elaine, but for now, please do as I say."

She mulled. "But if Elijah or Palmer really *is* Moses, then we've lost an opportunity to find out which one. And if they're both clean, I'll be with them when you call and are ready for support."

"Dammit, Elaine." There was a long pause. When he spoke again, there was resignation in his voice: "All right, go if you must, but report every hour."

As Martin Ghranditti's elevator door opened onto the sweep of polished brass and carved wood in the elegant lobby of his small apartment building, his cell phone rang. He answered as he marched across the marble tiles.

"Yes?" He passed a scattering of other residents, ignoring them.

"We got a problem, boss." It was Karl, his Ukrainian chief of household security.

Ghranditti knew at once. "Is it Marie? The children? What's happened? Where's Dante?"

"Dante is unconscious," Karl reported gloomily. "The hospital says it was an overdose of OxyContin. It is touch and go. Boss — Mrs. G was stealing the kids."

Ghranditti dug the cell into his ear. "Tell me." Ahead of him the uniformed doorman opened one of the two monolithic glass doors.

"Armand was behind it. He got them passports and airline tickets, rented a car, and put many suitcases of the kids' toys and clothes and her jewels and clothes into the limo's trunk. They were going for sure."

Ghranditti walked out into the roar of Washington's traffic and exploded, filling the dark air with curses. The old-fashioned concept of loyalty was dead, even from his own wife. As his limo appeared at the curb, he demanded, "Armand told you this?"

"Oh, boss. It is very sad. Armand ran into a bullet. He is dead. Oh, one more thing.

Mrs. G dyed her hair dark. She hid it under a scarf."

Ghranditti swore again. For a moment he wanted to murder her. How dare she, after everything he had done for her. He took deep breaths.

As his chauffeur ran around to open his door, Ghranditti ordered, "Don't let Mrs. Ghranditti out of your sight. Drive her and the children to the airport. Tell Jock to take the nanny there. Fly all of them to Washington in one of the company jets. There's a doctor here I want her to see." Obviously, new medical care was the only solution. Marie must regain control of herself. "She'll need to have her hair color returned to normal tonight, too. Someone will phone you with the details of both appointments. I don't want her with me until all of that's handled. Then as soon as my business is finished, I'll take them to the island."

Bearing his burden with dignity, Ghranditti ended the call and sank into the limo's luxurious interior. He pulled out a cigar, and the door closed with a whisper, shutting out the gaudy blare of the metropolis. He was worried about Marie's instability. She was lucky he had taken her in hand when she was still not much more than a child. The poor woman. Well, with proper medication, she would be fine again. He had tried to do the same for his first Marie. . . .

Before grief could rise in his throat, he stopped himself from thinking about her. He put his cell phone away, but it rang again. This time it was Jerry Angelides. As his limo blended into the bright lights of traffic, he listened to Angelides's sober report.

"Cunningham and Tice are still on the run, Mr. Ghranditti, I am sorry to say. But there's a bright side — they haven't screwed up the deal."

"Has everything arrived at the terminal?" Only when the ship left Baltimore for the high seas would his mind be at ease. Its destination was Port Muhammad bin Qasim, Karachi, Pakistan. For six months he had been sending furniture and other large items to a wholesaler in Karachi to establish a pattern. Baltimore was a foreign-trade zone, where goods could leave without fees, but U.S. Customs was supposed to inspect all shipments. Still, they had too many containers and not enough time, so they relied on patterns. In the beginning they had checked his containers closely, finding that the items accurately matched his manifests. This time, Angelides again e-mailed the manifest. As they had for four months, Customs matched it against the earlier shipments and approved it without looking inside the containers.

"Yes, sir," Angelides said firmly, "all the stuff's there, safe and sound. The stevedores are almost done loading the ship. Your big deal's going off without a hitch."

Ghranditti's rage at Tice was bottomless, but he could not let it stop him from enjoying the future. He owed that to Marie and the children. He warned in a steely voice: "That does *not* release you from your responsibilities. You must still find Tice and Cunningham." He told Angelides the latest news about Raina Manhardt. "My contact says she's arrived in Washington."

"I'm keeping part of the boys out on patrol everywheres," Angelides assured him. "I'll tell them to look for her, too. Then I'll refresh all my contacts and sources. They'll get back to me the second anything turns up. Hell, the cops could be arresting Cunningham or Tice or both right now."

"They're trying to make a fool out of you, Mr. Angelides," Ghranditti growled.

"No way are they going to do that. I will get those people and make them dead!"

Hiding their uneasiness, Jay and Raina sauntered across the elegant lobby of Martin

Ghranditti's building, past the suspicious glances of the valet and the few residents sitting in stately chairs and sipping their evening tea. But as soon as Jay slid the copy of the key into place and Ghranditti's elevator gave a soft chime of acknowledgment, the glances changed from suspicion to acceptance tinged with curiosity. He and Raina boarded and gazed at each other.

"So far, so good," she said as the door closed.

The elevator rose and at last opened onto an expansive vestibule where funnels of soft white light shone down from the ceiling. Weapons in hand, they stepped out, and the lights brightened, showcasing opulent furnishings and a snow-white carpet that seemed a foot deep.

A melodic artificial voice inquired politely, "Welcome to Martin Ghranditti's residence. Would you like music this evening?"

Raina looked at Jay. "I wonder if it asks the maid that, too, when she arrives."

"My bet is it's a crew of maids." He raised his voice: "No music."

As they split up and searched the rooms, lights preceded them. Voices inquired about temperature, quality of lighting, and music. When Jay approached a wall, a fully equipped bar swung out. At a long expanse of aquarium glass, a glass door slid open, and fresh breezes gusted in. He slipped outdoors and around a wraparound terrace decorated with a manicured jungle of flowers and small trees.

Then he found Ghranditti's office and walked straight past a mammoth desk and a sofa-and-chairs grouping to the computer. He turned it on and left for the kitchen. It was a stainless-steel monument to food preparation — refrigerators, stoves, microwave ovens, regular ovens, freezers, counters, cabinets. He studied the food in the Sub-Zero refrigerator and pulled out beluga caviar and chopped boiled eggs and sour cream and Gala apples. He found a box of large soda crackers in a cabinet and bottles of water in another.

He put the food he had taken onto a gilded tray and went to look for Raina. He found her on the far side of a recreation room armed with video games, a professional Foosball table, a full-size billiards table in dark walnut, matching tables for chess and checkers and card games, a well-equipped bar, and an oversize liquidlike television screen hanging like a fine painting on the wall.

"Look what just revealed itself." Raina gestured at a colossal entertainment complex worthy of the Kennedy Center. "Let's check out those surveillance tapes I brought from Geneva. I've loaded one into the VCR." She picked up a remote control.

They settled uneasily onto the sofa. With a weary sigh, she took off her wig, beard, and mustache. She ran the fingers of both hands through her matted hair again and again until the jet-black locks shook free. Jay smiled, soaking in the face he remembered so well, the fine bones, the clear skin. She had aged but in a way that somehow made her more beautiful.

He set the tray on the cocktail table. "We need to eat."

She nodded mutely. When the TV screen came alive, she said, "What we're seeing is the building's front lobby. Milieu had the entire fifth floor. So anyone who takes the elevator to it or from it is of interest to us." She put the speed to fast-forward.

They watched people stream into and out of the lobby, most taking the elevators, a few the stairs. Then Kristoph appeared. They froze. The counter in the lower right-hand corner of the screen said the time was 7:38 A.M.

She backtracked and slowed the tape so they could view every moment he was on screen. They stared silently, hungrily, absorbing his jaunty walk, his ruffled golden hair, the sprinkling of freckles, the large shoulders and narrow waist and hips, and the concentrated expression with a hint of a smile.

"He looks remarkable," Jay said softly. He brushed his eyes.

"Yes. I'm . . . I'm so sorry I kept you apart. It was a terrible mistake."

They viewed the entire tape, slowing each time he arrived or left the building. They saw nothing that indicated anything about the shipment. By the time she started the second tape, which showed the rear lobby, they had finished their food.

Again she fast-forwarded. Kristoph did not appear, but Laurence Litchfield did — just four days before Kristoph died. He looked the way Jay remembered — trim and wiry, eyes deeply set, a straight line of black eyebrows, an aquiline nose, a square chin. As they watched, Litchfield slid his pipe into the breast pocket of his sports jacket, and Alec hurried up from behind and stopped next to him. As they waited for the elevator, they talked intently, heads together, each looking around for eavesdroppers. Whatever the topic was, it was important — and secret.

Raina leaned forward. "I wish I knew what

they were saying."

She fast-forwarded again. Litchfield and Alec left together the same day. Litchfield did not appear again. Finally the video was finished.

"I have an idea about how we can listen to Litchfield and Alec's conversation. Let me see that remote."

She handed it to him. He studied it, then went to the entertainment center. "I'm going to burn a copy of the parts with Litchfield and Alec onto a CD. Then we'll try something on Ghranditti's computer."

45

In notorious Southeast Washington, drugs and violence ruled the night. The motel where Elijah, Frank, and Palmer were waiting was not far from the Anacostia River in a less seedy but still treacherous area. As Elaine drove past, she noted the sign — MELODIE MOTEL — but the lights for the *Me* and *I* were broken. It now announced itself as the LOD E MOTEL. The VACANCY sign shone brightly.

She circled the block and pulled into the motel's lot alongside four other cars. She recognized two from Ben Kuhnert's place — Palmer's was not among them. All four appeared empty.

Turning off the engine, she studied the one-story motel. It was built in the shape of an L. The operatives' room — 1D — was on the long wing, at the angle where the two parts of the motel met. Outdoor lamps were turned on above most of the doors, although the lights were feeble. Nothing illuminated 1D — either the bulb had died or someone had unscrewed it. Curtains were drawn across all of the windows.

She listened as she speed-dialed Elijah's cell number. It rang and rang. No answer. She speed-dialed Frank's and Palmer's numbers. Again no answer. Finally she left a message on Palmer's, telling him she was at the motel. She had heard no sound of ringing phones from the room. That could be because their cells were turned off or because the walls were extra-thick. She liked neither answer.

Cautiously she emerged from the Jag, but she did not lock it. Key in left hand, left elbow pressing her shoulder bag to her side, Walther in right hand, she approached the angle of the two buildings. Room 1D was on the right side. Traffic growled past behind her. A boom box set at high volume showered heavy metal music into the night.

Her senses burned with wariness. She knocked, heard a small sound to her left.

"Don't turn, Elaine!" It was Palmer Westwood's voice. "You can look at me, but *don't turn.*"

Repressing a shiver, she gazed over her shoulder. Terror shot through her. Palmer was aiming a 9mm Browning with a sound suppressor at her, standing in the doorway of the room that was theoretically next to 1D but was actually ninety degrees away — a perfect angle to ambush her.

He closed the door quietly behind him. "I was right. Jay did warn you that you might be walking into trouble. I knew he'd figure it out. Lower your weapon — there's no point in your shooting a hole in the door. You might wipe Elijah or Frank. Stop thinking! You don't have a choice. Just do it! There's a good girl. Lower it nice and slow."

Jay sat at the computer in the big penthouse office, put on his glasses, and tried to read Ghranditti's e-mail. It was password-protected. No surprise.

Raina pulled up a chair beside him. "What are you going to do?"

He loaded the CD of Litchfield and Alec's conversations, copied it onto the machine, then into a file. "Contact someone who can tell us what they said." He created a new Hotmail address and composed an e-mail to another Hotmail address — SundayRedBurma@hotmail.com. He attached the video of Litchfield and Alec then typed into the message box:

I need the time and place of an arms shipment. Need it yesterday. Check the attached conversation for it. I'll try to wait here. Phone if I don't respond to e-mail. We could already be too late.

As he sent it off, he dialed his cell and told Raina: "Don't ask who I'm calling. Other people could be hurt."

"Jay, please. You're contacting Bobbye Johnson." Surprised, he stared as she continued: "She's the only other one who knows the full story."

He gave a curt nod and spoke into the cell as soon as Bobbye answered: "You know who this is. There have been more developments." He related the highlights of the high-tech shipment and what they had learned. "Raina's here with me now," he said. "Do you have anything on Larry Litchfield yet?"

"He's a sly sonofabitch," Bobbye said, clearly angry. "He wants to fry my ass and steal my job. So far he's doing a damn good job of both. Did you see yourself on the news this afternoon? Don't bother to find a TV if you didn't — it'll only depress you. Larry forced me to go public with your escape."

He swore, covering a stab of anguish. "I've e-mailed you video that Raina brought from

Geneva. No audio. On it is a conversation between Larry and Alec St. Ann — he's a Whippet op. I'm hoping they said something you can turn into gold. I don't need to remind you to handle everything yourself."

"No, you don't, Jay. You can drop the spymaster crap with me. As far as I'm concerned, I'm still your boss."

"Wishful thinking. No matter what happens, my government career is over." Still, he found himself smiling at her gruff kindness.

"If I get something out of it, I'll assign a team," she said.

"No! Don't make a move yet. Let's make sure we know what we're dealing with. So far, it looks like only Larry and Whippet, but we have no guarantee. We want Ghranditti's deal to hold together so we can roll up everyone at once."

Controlling her fear, Elaine peered up into Palmer's face. The raptor features were unemotional, but the faded eyes were bright and alive. His thick mane of white hair, always immaculately combed, was disheveled.

"You did miss the game, didn't you, Palmer?"

"More than you'll ever know. Lock your car."

With a swift motion, she angled her wrist and punched the button. The flash of the car's answering lights reflected off the motel's window glass.

"Give me your cell. Carefully."

She pulled it from her bag and handed it to him. "Going to call Jay? Going to tell him you're Moses?"

He laughed and slid the cell into his pocket. "Open the door and go inside."

She glanced at the door then at him.

"Do it!"

She turned the knob and pushed. A jolt of horror paralyzed her. As if from a great distance, she heard Palmer laugh again. Elijah lay in an ocean of blood on the bathroom's cheap linoleum, the light glaring down as if showcasing him in some depraved department-store display. She swallowed bile. There was so much blood she had to believe he was dead.

Her gaze shifted. Frank sat on an upright wood chair beside the more distant of the two beds, trussed to it by duct tape tight across his chest and hips and thighs and legs. Another strip sealed his mouth. His eyes were savage with rage. He shook his head and struggled to speak, but all she heard was a mumble.

"Go in," Palmer repeated. "Move!"

She stumbled over the threshold.

Palmer shoved her farther into the room and quickly locked the door. "See, Frank? I was right," he said. "I told you she'd come. There was no way she'd be able to resist. Did you tell Jay where we were, Elaine? Come on, fess up."

"Of course I did. He'll be here soon."

He cocked his head, considering. "Not soon enough. Sit on the bed! No, this one. You don't need to be close to Frank. Where's Jay?"

"He wouldn't tell me. That's the truth, Palmer. You know how he is. But I told him where *I* was — and where I was going to meet you!"

Palmer considered again. "Dial Jay's number. Now!" He tossed her the cell.

She caught it. "No."

He aimed his pistol at Frank's heart. "I'm a crack shot. Say the wrong thing, and Frank joins Elijah on the bathroom floor. Tell Jay you weren't able to find the motel. That you must've gotten the address wrong. Ask him where he is and what he wants you to do. If he doesn't answer, leave a message."

She stared at Frank, at his helplessness.

As if in slow motion, she laboriously tapped in Jay's number. "It's busy," she told Palmer.

"I said to leave a message!"

She did: "Jay, I couldn't find the motel. Please call back. Where are you? What do you want me to do now? I keep thinking about Palmer's Leslie Howard story. You know, Palmer —"

He was at her side in an instant, snatching the cell from her hand, the gun steady on Frank. He punched the POWER button, turning it off. "I may be old, Elaine, but my brain works just fine. Stupid of you to try to give Jay a clue. And that was a stupid damn story about Howard anyway. I told it to Jay to make the point that grand gestures waste lives. Howard threw his life away." He moved sideways toward Frank and ripped the duct tape off his mouth.

"Goddamn you Palmer all to hell!" Frank bellowed.

Palmer slashed the pistol across Frank's mouth. Blood erupted. "Shut up!" As Elaine sprang off the bed, he swung the weapon around and pointed it at her. She sank back, and he glared. "Don't count on a coronary getting rid of me, either. My heart's as sound as Fort Knox. Sounder. Now, Frank" — he checked the seething operative — "this is your chance to save Elaine's life.

You made me wipe Elijah. Are you going to make me wipe her, too?" He peered at Elaine. "According to Frank's cell, he and Jay were on the line long enough to actually talk. The cell also told me Frank phoned household security services then a keysmith. Ergo, he made a key for Jay." He raised his voice only slightly, but it sounded like a cannon's roar in the small room. *"Where are Jay and Raina, Frank!"*

"Don't tell him!" Elaine said quickly. "They might be able to stop the shipment!"

Palmer sighed. "I don't have the patience for this." He fired. Elaine's left hand was resting on the bed. The tip of her little finger detonated. Bits of flesh and bone sprayed her face and clothes. She screamed and grabbed her hand to her chest. The pain blistered. The end of her finger was gone. Hot blood poured down her arm, soaking her sleeve.

Palmer tossed her a handkerchief. "I said I was a good shot. And don't think that scream will bring anyone. Around here, they'll think someone's just having good rough sex."

Frank's face was pale. Sweat coated it. He said nothing, but the fire was gone from his eyes.

Elaine tried to press the handkerchief

against the wound, but the nerve endings sent black pain to her brain. She swallowed a sob. "I'll scrub you, you fucking bastard, Palmer. First chance I get! I'll scrub you myself!" Tears of pain oozed from her eyes as she wrapped the handkerchief around her hand to catch the blood. The raw flesh and exposed bone flamed and throbbed.

Palmer said calmly, "If Frank tells me where Jay and Raina are, I'll let you take one of Elijah's shoelaces to make a tourniquet. Still, I doubt you'll bleed to death." His icy glare landed on Frank, while the pistol remained trained on Elaine. "All right, Frank. This is it. If Jay is really on his way here, I've got no more time. How many corpses do you want me to leave in this room? Answer me! *Where are Jay and Raina?*"

Frank had the look of a man condemned. "All I know is I got a key to Martin Ghranditti's penthouse for them." He looked into Elaine's eyes, pleading for her to understand as he told Palmer the address. "Go ahead, Palmer. Shoot." He nodded.

"Thanks, Frank, but I hardly need your permission." Palmer raised the silenced pistol and fired straight into the old operative's heart.

Again blood geysered. Frank's chest

turned red as he jerked, his chin lifted, and he and the chair crashed back onto the thin carpet. His legs twitched and stopped.

"God, what a mess," Palmer said. "All right, Elaine, kick your shoulder bag over here, then go get that shoelace. I've got a call to make."

46

Ghranditti's penthouse was quiet now except for the sound of Raina's footfalls as she stalked around the office. As Jay ended his cell call with Bobbye Johnson, he turned in the chair to watch her stare out the wall of windows then turn toward the desk. She was as restless as a cheetah. She stopped beside Ghranditti's contoured leather chair, her attention captured by something on his desktop.

She gave him a startled look. "Did you see this, Jay?"

He was beside her in an instant. She was focused on a photograph framed in sterling and standing on Ghranditti's desk, her hand outstretched but apparently unable to make herself touch it. The photo was the only one there, and it showed a woman who looked so uncannily like Tice's wife, Marie, that a sickening moment of déjà vu swept through him. But Marie had been dead nearly twenty years, and those were not their children. The man was about fifty, heavyset, and sleek in an oily sort of way.

Shaken, Jay said, "They're posed like the last formal portrait Marie and I and our kids sat for." The girl was leaning across her mother's lap and peering up adoringly at her father. Between the parents and slightly behind stood a son. The third child was a little boy about two years old who played with a blanket at his father's feet and looked into the camera with a sweet smile.

He could not tear his gaze away from the woman. The features were almost identical to Marie's. The same height and age and even body build and eyes — green. Slightly unfocused, but definitely sea green, and the longer he studied her, the more sense it began to make in a completely insane way, because the woman sat as stiff as a piece of furniture, just the way Marie used to be the last few months of her life. She was drugged, as Marie was all of the time.

Jay dropped heavily into the desk chair and turned over the photo. Raina put a reassuring hand on his shoulder and leaned close so she could see, too. On the back was a date six months ago and names neatly printed in a list:

Martin Ghranditti
Marie Ghranditti
Aaron Ghranditti
Mariette Ghranditti
Kristoph Ghranditti

Rage seized Jay. His hands shook as if from palsy. He flipped the photo over and stared again. His family. But not his family. A charade, a farce, a travesty of the living and the dead. His eyes felt hollow. The feeling of violation was as sharp and deep as razor slices to his marrow. He wanted to terminate Martin Ghranditti. If Ghranditti were there, he would be dead.

Raina grabbed the picture and turned it over once more and looked at the list of names as if she could not believe what she had seen. "Kristoph! *Kristoph* is on his list. Ghranditti named his baby after Kristoph!"

"For some obscene reason that bastard has tried to steal our lives."

"What does this mean!" she demanded. "Why did he do this?"

They gazed at each other. Bright red spots of fury radiated from her cheeks. Her eyes snapped. But there was a sense of illness around her mouth. She was sickened, too. It was not only thievery, it was a violation so intimate and cruel that it was almost unfathomable.

"Come here." Jay stood and wrapped his arms around her.

She burst into tears on his shoulder. Trembling, he buried his face in her soft hair. They stood that way a long time, their grief for what they had lost and rage for what had been taken by subversion and violence felt like a bottomless pit, unassuagable.

In the shabby motel, Elaine gritted her teeth to keep from crying out in pain and from the sight of poor dead Elijah and Frank. Sitting on the bathroom floor, she worked to undo Elijah's shoelace with her uninjured hand.

After calling in an anonymous tip to the police that Jay Tice had broken into Martin Ghranditti's penthouse to hide, Palmer phoned Laurence Litchfield on a cell equipped with a compact voice modifier.

Dragging on a Pall Mall, he stalked back and forth. "Face it, Litchfield. Your people were incompetent. They couldn't handle a simple job like capturing an old man and two women. Tice has been out of commission for three years. Cunningham's no operative. And Raina Manhardt spends most of her time behind a desk now. Your failure doesn't relieve you of your obligation to wire me the first half of my payment!"

Finally she had the shoelace. With her teeth and hand, she wrapped it around her pulsating finger and struggled to tie it, hoping to ease the raging hurt.

"What? Because Ghranditti's people failed, you knew it wouldn't be easy, so you weren't going to pay me until yours succeeded?" His words were cold steel: "You're smarter than that. You don't want anyone to know you welshed on a deal with me. Here's what you're going to do. First, you'll send people to make a couple of corpses look as if they died in a fight over drugs." He gave him the motel's name and address. "It's Elijah Helprin and Frank Mesa, and you can thank me that they're no longer trying to turn you into cat food. Second, Cunningham's with me, so if you want her, you're going to send that first payment to the account number I gave you, and you'll do it while I'm standing here talking to you. Otherwise, I'll let her go."

The shoelace tourniquet tied, she looked up in time to see a triumphant smile on his face. He was getting what he wanted.

"All right, I'll check. Hold on." He lowered the cell, touched buttons, watched the LED, and smiled more widely. He inhaled his cigarette. Then: "It's there," he told

Litchfield. "Third, I've sent the police to arrest Tice and Manhardt. They're at Ghranditti's place. . . . I know, but it'll be more amusing if the police succeed. If they do, you'll wire me the second half of my funds. Since there's risk attached to that, tell me where the shipment is, when ownership's being transferred, and all of the details I need to get in. I'm going to do you the great favor of delivering Cunningham so you can dispose of her as you wish. We don't want her found dead here, do we? That'd trigger questions that might lead back to you. A strong suggestion: If Tice gets away from the cops, you can damn well bet that one way or another the bastard will figure out where the shipment is leaving from, and he'll go there. With Cunningham, you've got a hold over Tice. He's crazy about her. Treats her like his own kid. Jealous, Litchfield?" He chuckled.

She staggered to her feet, judging the distance to her shoulder bag.

"Why will I deliver her? Because I can't afford to leave details like Jay Tice living. But then, neither can you. I'll phone just before we arrive. Have a couple of men waiting. I'll drop her off. She won't give you much trouble — she's injured. Once all three of them are on the premises, I want

606

the rest of my money. Agreed?"

She advanced awkwardly. The unrelenting pain was making her dizzy.

He frowned at her, dropped his cigarette, ground it out on the carpet, and lifted his Browning, aiming it at her again.

She paused. As he listened to Litchfield, she pointed to her bloody finger then to her purse. "I may have my little med kit in there. I want antibiotic cream." And her remaining poisoned darts.

He gave a violent shake of his head. *No.* "Good, Litchfield. I've got it. And don't try to get a look at me when I arrive. That's worse than welshing. In fact, you have my personal guarantee that none of the top intel merchants will ever do business with you again. Your sources will dry up like autumn leaves."

Watching her, he snapped his cell closed and crouched over her bag. He unzipped the compartments, then dumped out the contents.

"Hmm. No med kit. Why am I unsurprised? So, what did you really want?" He pushed through the pile. His fingers paused over the paper funnel. "Everything looks ordinary except this." He looked up quickly, caught the expression on her face. "Ah. So this *is* what you wanted."

She said a silent prayer that he would stab himself with one of the tips.

But he unfolded the funnel cautiously. When he saw the darts, he peered up at her through slitted eyes. "Bitch."

"You're carrying a Browning just like Jay's. Trying to imitate him, Palmer? Your protégé became your competitor, didn't he? We both know Jay's better than you ever were. Probably the best of his generation. Elijah and Frank knew it, too. Two seasoned ops like them — they not only trusted him, they worshipped him. They took orders from him — not from you."

He laughed loudly and rolled the darts back into their paper shell and slid it carefully into his sports jacket pocket. He shoved everything else back into her bag. "No, my dear. I carried a Browning first. Jay imitated *me*. Time we left. You've got a date with destiny, as the cliché goes. We'll take your car. I've always been fond of Jaguars."

47

The hush in Martin Ghranditti's penthouse seemed charged, like the hot, stifling air before a storm. Jay gave no sign of his unease as he sifted through the papers in the death merchant's massive desk. Raina was sitting at the office computer, checking Internet history and trying to crack the e-mail password. Her black curls shone like sable in the overhead lights.

"He doesn't visit many Web sites," she said. "Mostly real estate. Whatever his password is to his e-mail, it's not the usual family names. I also tried *money, guns, high-tech,* and a lot of others." She spun in the chair and gazed at him. "Don't you think Bobbye Johnson should've e-mailed or called by now?"

"I'm worried, too. As for this desk, my verdict is that it's mostly for show. Ghranditti did almost no work here. There are household bills and orders from caterers and florists, that sort of thing." He leaned back in the chair and laced his fingers behind his head and yawned.

She paced across the carpet, leery and restless, and picked up Ghranditti's family photo again. "That bastard. I suppose he's to be pitied."

"Probably. I still want to tear out his throat. Personally."

"Me, too. Why did he do it?"

"Each of those names has 'Ghranditti' carefully printed after it. There was no need for that. He did it to put his stamp of ownership on them as if they were pieces of property. Land. Cars. Dish towels. He owns them. He's paying me back."

"He is? *Why?*"

Suddenly he felt old. "I'd suspected Marie was having an affair, then I decided I must be wrong. I told myself I was overreacting because I had a beautiful wife. Still, there were afternoons I'd get home early and find the kids with a sitter — or alone. They were too young to be left alone. Marie had never been like that." He was silent. "Marie and I grew apart somehow. We both knew the marriage was dead. Then I found you."

She skinned off her denim jacket, tossed it onto a chair, and sat on the desk, facing him. "You may not know this, but there's

610

another link between Ghranditti and Marie — he used to sell black-market pharmaceuticals, so it's likely he was her supplier."

His jaw clenched. "Makes sense. He could keep her dependent that way."

"It's also likely he knew she'd signed up for drug rehab. At the same time, you said Palmer thought he was the trafficker in the DEADAIM operation. So those were two very large bad events for Ghranditti — he'd just lost a fortune, and he was threatened with losing his girlfriend, too, because if she cleaned up, she might want nothing more to do with him. On the other hand, if he wiped you, he'd get revenge, and he could keep your wife. So I'll bet Ghranditti's the one who had the bomb planted under your car. When the wet work went bad, it would've driven him nuts knowing he'd liquidated her, and he's been stalking you in his own weird, crazy way ever since. All you have to do is look at that family portrait to know how much he wanted her and hated you. It's got to be him who blackmailed you into prison."

Repressing a shudder, Jay inclined his head and studied his hands, remembering the feel of death between them. "It's logical." He looked up. "There's at least five years between his second child and his baby,

Kristoph. That's a big gap for a man who plans everything, and it tells me that if he'd known about us earlier, he would've blackmailed me earlier — and had the baby then. His Kristoph must be about two years old now. That means he was conceived a few months after I was arrested — after someone told Ghranditti about us."

Raina leaned forward. "Palmer was one of the very few who knew about us. As Moses, he told Ghranditti. Then he blackmailed you into prison."

He could hardly feel his heart beat. He had modeled himself after Palmer — Palmer's sharp intelligence, his wise habits, his common sense. They had decades of trust between them. When he was young, he had often wished Palmer were his father. It was unthinkable the older man would betray him — or anyone.

He sighed heavily and closed his eyes. When he opened them, he admitted the truth: "As soon as we found out Ghranditti was handling the Majlis shipment, Palmer would've been nervous as an elephant with a bellyache that if we captured Ghranditti, Ghranditti would let something slip, and eventually I'd have to realize he was Moses."

"That means Palmer was the rat inside DEADAIM, too."

His jaw flexed angrily. "Yes, he has to be Moses. He hadn't had a big operational success in several years, so not only did he look like a hero for thinking up the idea of cutting his gold medallion into pieces, it appeared he'd enabled us to keep going so we could pull off the triumph Langley wanted."

"The pig betrayed both sides to get what *he* wanted — renewed prestige and the job of ADDO."

"And plenty of reason to continue being Moses. He had the experience, the contacts, and the brains — and the ambition for money."

"I'm so sorry, Jay. This must be awful for you. You cared about Palmer."

"Not anymore." He gazed away.

She held his face in both hands and stroked his cheeks with her thumbs until he looked at her. Her eyes probed, and in them he found an odd kind of solace and perhaps even love. "You never told me what happened when you vanished for those three days after your family was wiped."

He sighed and took her hands and kissed the palms. "You have beautiful hands." He stared at them, remembering. He looked up. "I still love you, you know."

She nodded. "I know. Tell me." She waited.

"Two Libyans planted the Semtex. I cornered them in Tripoli, and they admitted it. But they wouldn't tell me who'd hired them, and they denied it had anything to do with the shipment. Hell, they probably had no idea about the shipment. They were terrorists for hire, and they were far more afraid of their employer than they were of me." He paused, trying to find peace with the unforgivable. "If I'd gotten up early that morning and moved my car myself, the kids and Marie would still be alive."

"But you'd be dead. And I'd hate that. Tell me what happened to the Libyans."

His life rushed over him in a cold wave. He recalled slipping into Tripoli. Finding the killers. Interrogating them. With sudden insight, he saw it all — who he had been, what he had done, why he had done it. He was among the elite. That was how you felt. How you had to feel. The Clandestine Services had to attract the highest quality of people, because it expected them to pay the highest costs. You began to see yourself as so crucial to America's survival that you were above the law, ethics, and sometimes ordinary decency. Old values faded. Unsavory ones took root. To his shame, he had been seduced. In the end, he had seen it all, done it all. There was a sour taste in his mouth.

He confessed in a low voice, "I executed them."

She nodded, surprised but not surprised, and sat on his lap and held him close. Slowly he wrapped his arms around her and rested his head against her breasts.

"The life of a spy is corrosive," she murmured. "None of us escapes." She hesitated. "Do you want to talk about the exchange at Glienicke Bridge? About Dr. Abendroth?"

He listened to the pain in her voice and said nothing. Abendroth's liquidation had always stood between them, solid as an executioner's wall, the true cause of their first breakup. Finally, by the time he knew she was pregnant with Kristoph, he had realized he could not stay away from her, no matter the cost.

"Not yet," he said.

They tightened their grip on each other, clinging in an eerie hush. He did not seem to know quite what to do. The feeling of his head upon his shoulders was wrong. His legs looked unfamiliar. Confused, he listened to the steady beat of her heart, hoping in it he would find a lifeline to a better world.

The penthouse's melodic voice shattered

his trance: "You have visitors. To view them, please turn on any television set to Channel 100."

She shivered and jumped up. He grabbed the remote off the desk and switched on the TV. The channel showed an interior view of Ghranditti's private elevator. Six policemen in body armor and helmets stared stonily ahead. They carried M-4s and had pistols and grenades on their belts.

"Oh, God," she murmured, her voice tight with fear. "It's an antiterrorist unit. That elevator doesn't stop on any other floor but this one!"

He blinked. Thought. "Quick. Grab all of the remotes. Anything with batteries. We want batteries!"

Langley, Virginia

Laurence Litchfield was feeling lucky. Bobbye Johnson had released him again to do some sort of important business, so he had been free to answer Moses's call. And the news could have been worse. One way or another, he would at least have Cunningham.

He grabbed his briefcase and left his office, checking the door to make certain it self-locked, and hurried toward Bobbye's. He needed to deliver the copy of ForeTell to Ghranditti. The hall was quiet. Most of the office personnel were gone for the day except for Connie, her number one secretary. Excellent. He would make his excuses to her and escape Bobbye's questions.

He leaned against the doorjamb, feigning a weariness he did not feel. "Hello, Connie. Or rather, good night. I'm taking off. Let the director know, will you?"

"Of course, Mr. Litchfield."

He was suddenly curious. Since they had spent the day together, he knew what Bobbye was working on. There was nothing new that had to be addressed. "She's got you here late. It's time you demanded combat pay."

She was a large blonde with a full figure and coquettish eyes. "*You* tell her." She chuckled.

When he was DCI, he intended to keep her in the job. With her institutional knowledge, she would be hard to replace. "Why haven't you gone home? For that matter, why hasn't she? Is there some new emergency?"

"Nothing big. She got an e-mail that needed to be handled by the techs. I think it had some kind of conversation that had to be lip-read. She asked me to call down while she picked up her other line."

"Glad it's nothing big. We've had more than enough excitement for one day. Good night again, Connie."

Uneasy, he peeled away from the door. He took the elevator down to Decryption. As always, the room was littered with fast-food wrappers and cans of soda. He found Bobbye sitting beside Hiram Kukkahameni in his cubicle, both wearing earphones. She was bent over, her back intense, as she wrote on the pad in her lap. Litchfield was riveted — Hiram's computer screen showed Alec St. Ann and him talking in front of the elevator in the Milieu building in Geneva. Instantly he knew — it had to be from Raina Manhardt's copies of the surveillance tapes, which was a strong indication Bobbye was in touch with Jay Tice.

A bead of sweat rolled down his temple as he backed away. When he was out of sight, he exhaled and circled back through the maze.

As he approached the cubicle a second time, he called out, "Has anyone seen the director?"

Bobbye appeared in the cubicle's opening. "Yes, Larry. What can I help you with?" She seemed unfazed.

"I just wanted to let you know I'm leaving and thought you might go with me to my car. Something has come in." He looked around. "Probably we should have a quiet discussion about it."

"Oh?" She took his arm casually and guided him back to the big room's entrance. "And what's that?"

"The elevator trip to the basement is short. Mind indulging me by coming along? I'm dead tired."

She seemed reluctant. "Fine, but talk fast. I've got a project to wrap up."

He punched the elevator button. "What's the project?"

"I'll let you know soon." Her eyes were bright with a wicked light. Then the light vanished, and she was her usual boring self. "Tell me what's so important." The elevator landed in the garage.

He held the door so she would be sure to walk out first. "It's Moses. I got a call from him tonight."

She turned swiftly. "Tell me!"

He strode past, carefully checking the quiet, well-lit area. He could hear her footsteps speeding to catch up. By the time she was at his side, he was halfway to his car, and no one was in sight. Still, there were video cameras.

"He's up to his usual tricks." He took out his keys and punched the remote, unlocking the car. "And, of course, it will cost us a fortune. He claims to know where Jay and Raina Manhardt are."

"And you're going home?" She frowned. "This is unlike you, Larry."

He opened the driver's door. "Climb in, Bobbye. You should drive."

"To see whom? Moses? Jay?" She planted her feet, and her eyes narrowed. "What in hell's going on? What are you up to?"

She did not have her purse. She was dressed in a blouse and skirt. It was clear she was not carrying a weapon. He slid his hand inside his suit jacket. "Get in, Bobbye. You wanted Jay. I think I've found him. Get in *now*."

Her eyes remained narrow, and she cocked her head slightly as if she suddenly had an insight she did not like. Her gaze settled on his hidden hand.

"Get in the fucking car. I don't want to put a bullet in you here where your death will be immortalized on film. Still, Jay always said to do what we had to do and worry about cleaning up later. See how much respect I have for the man? I'm still quoting him." He tossed her the keys.

Her expression furious, she caught them and climbed into the car.

48

Washington, D.C.

As Jay sprinted off through the bright kitchen, Raina threw batteries from remotes, two digital cameras, and four mobile phones into the microwaves.

"Set the timers for five minutes," he told her. "Make sure the temperature is on high. Turn the gas burners up as far as they'll go. One good spark, and our visitors will have something a lot more immediate than us to worry about. Meet me in the recreation room."

He tore down the hall and back into the large room. Rushing past the entertainment center, he dumped the battery out of the laptop and shoved it into the microwave on the bar. He punched buttons, setting the microwave on high. Raina arrived just as he turned to look for her. He hit START, and they ran toward the big glass door. In the foyer, the elevator chimed faintly.

At his side, Raina swore in German and glanced behind as the recorded greeting played.

"We might still make it." *Always have a good backup plan,* he muttered to himself.

The glass door opened automatically, and they dashed onto the terrace as a strong voice snapped orders from deep within the penthouse.

The terrace was rimmed by a solid low wall. Treetops and the lights of the city spread to the horizon. Jay gestured, and they raced around the penthouse. As the police searched, light spilled out from room after room. At the master suite, Jay swung a leg over the wall. There was a slight sound of metal rubbing metal. He reversed direction, grabbed Raina's arm, and yanked her behind potted ficus trees.

As they crouched, the barrel of an M-4 appeared at the bedroom door, followed by a helmeted head and armor-encased policeman. The M-4 moved from side to side, searching. Jay breathed slowly, waiting.

A bellowed warning sounded inside. Orange light flashed. An explosion thundered. The building trembled under their feet. Blue and orange light blasted into the night from the rec room. The acrid odor of smoke gusted out the door of the master suite.

Loud detonations rang out in a series of bursts.

As the policeman on the terrace bolted back indoors, Jay touched Raina's arm and ran back to the wall. The escape ladder was riveted into the building, only a few inches for the toe of a shoe. The ladder looked as old as the building and was none too safe.

Jay was ten feet down when he looked up. "Come on, Raina!"

"It's six stories!" The glittering night sky framed her pinched face.

"I know. But it could be twenty. Come on!"

Her face disappeared, and a leg appeared over the wall.

"Goddammit, Raina!" he said in German. "Would you rather die from being ripped up by automatic gunfire or go fast with a nice swift splat on a brick driveway? You don't have any fucking choice! *Hurry!*"

She gave a brisk nod and started down.

"Keep your feet sideways," he said more calmly. "Don't look anywhere but the wall. Concentrate on that, and you'll be fine."

"Right. Sure."

"Are your eyes open?" *Keep her talking.* He moved slowly and said a silent prayer that she did not freeze.

"*Nein.* I like it better this way."

"You're missing a great view."

"Shut up, Jay!"

Two stories down, he landed on an antique fire stairway. "I've got a nice surprise for you." He watched her feet test each rung. "It's a staircase. You'll like it."

"I'll like anything more than this. It's like hanging from a kite tail."

"You sound like a Soviet," he said. "Remember what a *kaputnik* is?"

"A pessimist. Someone who shoots himself in the head, and his legs fall off."

"You can start being an optimist any moment now."

With a groan, she landed beside him.

He hugged her. "Will you marry me?"

"It's too late."

"I'll take that as a maybe. You first this time."

Like a gazelle, she scrambled down.

When they reached the driveway, they backed off and looked up. Gray and black smoke billowed from the top of the aged building where Ghranditti's very modern penthouse had been built. They smiled into each other's eyes, relieved, and hurried toward the sidewalk, straightening their clothes, smoothing their hair. A police van was parked in front. People had gathered around to stare up at the clouds of smoke.

As they walked swiftly off, Raina said, "Check your cell phone. Maybe Bobbye Johnson called."

He dialed and listened, then accelerated. "Only one message — from Elaine. She's got trouble. She started to talk about the Leslie Howard story, and she used Palmer's name twice. It was the last word she said before she was cut off."

In the motel's dingy parking lot, Palmer scrutinized the street while keeping his Browning trained on Elaine. She stood stubbornly beside the Jag, holding up her mutilated finger, refusing to get inside. The handkerchief around her hand was red with blood.

"I have to take care of my finger so I can drive. The pain's so bad I can't even think." She bit her lower lip. She was exaggerating but not by much.

She eyed her Walther in his waistband as Palmer watched three teenagers pimp-walk along the sidewalk side by side, rap music throbbing from a chromed boom box on one's shoulder. In a line, they looked over and stiffened as they caught sight of Palmer's pistol and Elaine's bloody hand. They hurried onward, eyes averted.

Palmer studied their backs suspiciously.

"Open the trunk. Hurry."

She punched her key unlock, and the red lid rose.

"Stand back!" He opened the med kit and checked inside, removing small sharp scissors. "All right, have at it."

She grabbed a bottle of Vicodin and swallowed a pill. She squirted antibiotic cream on the open wound and fought off a wave of nausea. Even the weight of the cream made the nerve ends shriek. She took out sterile gauze and used her teeth to open the packet. With one hand, she folded the gauze into a thick square. Biting her lip again, she moaned as she used the gauze to brush a flail of skin over the top. She took a deep breath and exhaled and laid the gauze over it.

Tears of pain spilled down her cheeks. "Help me!"

Annoyed, he tore off a length of hospital tape. "You've still got quite a bit of finger left. I don't know what you're complaining about."

"You son of a bitch." She snatched it from him and taped the gauze square around her finger tightly. She loosened the shoestring tourniquet and watched the gauze. As it filled with blood, she put more tape over the top.

Finished, she grabbed gauze packets and tape and the bottle of painkillers and put them in her jacket pockets. "Close the trunk and bring the med kit." She marched to the driver's side door. She would definitely fucking scrub him as soon as she found out where the shipment was. There had to be a way to wipe him, and she sure as hell was going to find it.

She climbed in and started the engine, propping her left hand at the top of the steering wheel to elevate the finger. As Palmer dropped in beside her, she noted he sat clumsily. Palmer was the type who gave no quarter, not even to leather upholstery and lush padding. She was beginning to have an idea. She threw the car into gear and gently backed out. She wanted him to feel safe in the car.

"Where to?" she asked innocently.

"Get on the Anacostia Freeway heading north."

"That's hardly an address. Where are we going?" She paused the Jag at the street.

The barrel of the gun pressed into her neck. The chilly steel sent a shock of warning to her brain.

"No need to concern yourself," Palmer said smoothly. "Just do what I tell you. As you've no doubt discerned, I'll shoot again.

627

I'll give you directions as we go along."

She drove off, sliding into traffic. Buildings were dark. The dusky light of streetlamps shone down to the pavement. "You're proud of being Moses, aren't you? Why in God's name did you betray us?"

He shrugged. "Nothing ruins a relationship like shared failure. My relationship with Langley and my colleagues had become a bore. The assignments were repetitive, the goal ludicrous. The best we could hope for was a stalemate with the Communists. There was no longer any point. We were outspending them, so naturally we'd win."

She understood. "*You* were bored. And now you're in big trouble. Your cover's blown, and you're cornered. Jay got you again." She turned onto Pennsylvania Avenue, heading toward the John Philip Sousa Bridge.

"Jay's my creature," he said easily. "I invented him. Without me, he'd be nothing."

But when she glanced at him, she saw bitterness. "Every chance you got when we were at Ben Kuhnert's, you stepped in to prove you were still the éminence grise. Jay kept handing you compliments, but never once did you say anything about his abilities or accomplishments. You must've been livid when he rose to be DDO, but you never did. Even in the official hierarchy, he outranked you. You're so jealous it oozes from you."

"Elaine, child, you've spent far too much time enjoying your talents and too little acknowledging the limitations of them."

"I love the way you patronize me. 'Child.' 'My dear.' You're consistent. I'll give you that."

Tired of her, his shoulders turned and he looked away. She studied the broad boulevard, feeling a frisson of excitement. At last there was a long clear stretch. She had been driving slowly, allowing cars to pass. A pack of headlights was approaching from the rear. She had a minute before they overtook her. She dismissed a torrent of doubts. If she was going to make a move, it had to be now.

"On the other hand, you're probably right about my limitations," she continued. "But more likely you said that to divert the argument from yourself. Oh, no, Palmer. Look! My finger's bleeding badly again!"

As she had expected, he peered over, disgusted. His shoulders were still angled toward his window, while his head was turned to look at her. His butt had never been anchored properly in the seat, and his twisted body created far more space than was necessary inside the seat belt.

Before he could speak, she rammed the gas pump to the floor. The Jag shot forward, tires squealing. Swearing, Palmer arched against the seat then the seat belt, fighting both in a losing battle to straighten his spine and find equilibrium against the powerful G-forces of acceleration.

She slammed the brakes. The Jag's high-performance tires gripped to a shatteringly fast stop, forcing him helplessly forward. As his head lashed the dash, she snatched his Browning and her Walther. His skull smacked his window. He groaned.

She released a long stream of air. Left hand on the wheel, she aimed the Browning at Palmer and pressed the accelerator, climbing toward a modest thirty-five miles an hour. Horns blasted as the herd of cars hurtled past.

Palmer stared silently at the muzzle of his gun. His tan seemed to pale, then his eyelids slitted and his gaze darted as he searched for a way out. He was wily — and danger-ous — still.

She wheeled the car off onto Potomac Avenue. "I want to empty your own gun into you, Palmer you asshole traitor." She bit off each word. "But I'll give you a chance to redeem yourself. *Where's that shipment!"*

49

As Raina sped the car south through the glare of Washington traffic toward the motel where Elaine was to have met Jay's ops, he called their cells. No one answered. He left a message on Elaine's and dialed Bobbye Johnson. No answer again. He left another message.

They were silent, worried. Traffic was congested. The din of engines and tires was constant, irritating. When Jay's cell phone finally rang, Raina shot him a hopeful look.

It was Elaine. "Where are you?" Jay demanded. "*How* are you!"

"Frayed but alive. I need you. I've got a gun on Palmer. I guarantee you he's Moses." She did not wait for a response. "I can't get him to tell me where the shipment is — and he *knows!* I'm parked at the entrance to the Congressional Cemetery."

"Be careful," Jay warned. "He has more tricks than a coyote. We'll be there in ten minutes." He gave driving instructions to Raina then told Elaine, "I'm putting you on the speakerphone so Raina can hear. Tell us everything that happened. Then we'll fill you in. Stay on the line until we're together." He lowered the cell from his ear.

Elaine cleared her throat and hesitated. Then she talked in a torrent, her voice full of anger and grief. As they listened to the horror, Raina slid her hand over Jay's, holding on tightly as she drove with the other. Palmer muttered occasional disagreement in the background. The report was graphic, from Elaine's discovery that Palmer had wiped Elijah, to the brutal interrogation of Frank and her, and finally to Frank's execution.

"Palmer called Litchfield," she said. "That's how he found out where the shipment is."

Jay controlled his rage and asked calmly, "How's your finger?"

"It's handled. I took a Vicodin. I'm seriously considering more."

"Take them. We just left Martin Ghranditti's place." He described the surveillance tapes and the conversations he had sent to his contact to be lip-read. As Raina turned the car north on Seventeenth Street, he said,

"We're almost there, Elaine. Just two more minutes."

He related their escape from the penthouse, and Raina accelerated the car along the Congressional Cemetery's old brick wall and then northeast on Potomac Avenue, where the wall stopped and an old-fashioned wrought-iron fence began. The burial grounds spread in a vast sea of black punctuated by toothy nineteenth- and twentieth-century tombstones, ragged gray teeth in the wash of moonlight.

"I see the Jag," Raina said, relieved. "They're inside."

"We see you," he told Elaine.

Raina pulled into the entryway beside the car. Wrought-iron gates set into brick pillars blocked the road into the graveyard. Before she could park, Jay swung open his door and shoved his Browning into his shoulder holster. His strides were long and angry. He yanked open the Jag's passenger door.

Palmer looked up, offering his most engaging smile. "Good to see you, Jay. I must say I doubted I'd ever have the pleasure again."

Jay yanked the old spymaster out by his lapels and hurled him to the ground beneath a tree. "You piece of human trash. Stand on your feet!" He pulled out his Browning and aimed.

Propped up on his elbows, Palmer seemed to be reclining casually. His snowy hair was in shadow. His leathery face was dark, almost skeletal. He gave no sign of contrition. "Be reasonable. Forgive and forget. Remember, we did win the Cold War. I simply made a few extra shekels along the way."

"Right. Let's talk about your first wet job — Trent. Our colleague and friend. And let's talk about your most recent — Frank. A good man who respected you, who served his country well. And all the others in between."

"Unfortunate events like those were infrequent, I'm happy to say. Alas, they were necessary."

"Necessary? You soulless bastard!"

"On the contrary." Palmer climbed to his feet and dusted off his trousers. Except for his crepe-paper skin and gnarled fingers, there was little sign of his advanced age — his movements were resilient, his features animated.

Without a glance at Elaine or Raina, who stood guard with their pistols, he solemnly considered Jay. "As Moses, I have the ethics of a priest. I minister to my flock, collect appropriate tithes, and protect all of you from one another. And I never reveal any-

635

thing about my sources. Don't forget how many times Langley found me more than useful. In fact, I always gave Langley preferential treatment. I'm going to have a last cigarette, Jay." He spread his empty hands. "See, no tricks. My cigarettes are in my pocket, along with my lighter. Do you mind?"

Jay made a curt nod. "Go ahead. Do it slowly."

Palmer removed the pack then the lighter. With a sigh, he took out a Pall Mall and let the pack fall to the ground. His lighter snapped, and he inhaled.

"Drop the lighter," Jay ordered.

It fell from Palmer's fingers.

They stood facing each other, both nearly six feet tall — Jay robust, short prison haircut, pointing his gun; Palmer thin and gangly, his thick white mane disheveled, arms crossed nonchalantly as he lifted his hand to smoke.

"You're no goddamn priest, Palmer." He stared, not quite recognizing the man. "How could I have let you fool me for so many years."

"Love is blind." Palmer smiled widely, displaying his large white teeth. "And I've known exactly what I was doing from the beginning. I'm sure you remember the first

Moses was the founder of Israel. It's no coincidence he was a spymaster, too. 'And the Lord spake unto Moses, saying, "Send thou men, that they may search the land of Canaan."' So Moses picked twelve, one from each of the tribes, and ordered them into the Promised Land on an undercover mission to collect intel about whether the Canaanites could be conquered. That's the earliest recorded espionage assignment. Appropriate, isn't it?"

Disgusted, Jay said, "Ten of the spies reported the Canaanites were too strong, while the other two argued that their land of milk and honey had made them fat and lazy. Moses didn't check into which of his spies was self-serving, and he didn't send another round into Canaan for a more thorough investigation. He took the short-sighted majority opinion and made it policy, and the Israelites didn't invade. That's why they spent the next forty years living in the desert — God's punishment. The truth is, Moses was a rotten spymaster." He aimed his Browning at Palmer's forehead. "But I'll give you a chance at redemption. Tell me where the shipment is. You owe us at least that."

"That's what I intend to do. Elaine has

her points as a diversion, but I wanted to see you."

Jay frowned. "You can't be serious."

"But, my boy, I am." For an instant, Palmer seemed to glow with genuine sincerity. "And to prove it, here's everything I know. Ghranditti owns an international transportation company called Cross-Global, although I doubt you'll be able to document that. It has docks around the world, including at the port of Baltimore, which is where you need to go. Look for the *Mango Blossom* — a delicate name for what must be a weighty lass. She's a container ship, very big, very modern. Larry told me she's almost loaded. The deal transfers ownership at ten o'clock, and then the tugs tow her out to the Chesapeake. You'll have to hurry. You don't want to be late for the festivities."

Jay stared, astounded. He had expected the old bastard to be difficult, impossible. "Come on, Palmer. You're going with us." He gestured with his pistol.

"Not even a thank-you. Oh, well. You once told me there were three corruptions, Jay. You're wrong, though; they're compensations. As I recall, the first two are ambition and ego. Mine is the third — money. Personally, I found it to be the only salve for disap-

638

pointment. So that's your answer — no. You'll have to have your adventure without me. I never much cared for Martin Ghranditti — or Larry Litchfield, for that matter. I never much cared for anyone, certainly not enough to end up dead from a fool's bullet or, God forbid, in a cell in Allenwood for the rest of my life. Felt bad for you about that, but that's the spy game, isn't it? I meant it when I said I wanted to see you. You do tend to get under a man's skin."

Before Jay could respond, Palmer gave a crooked smile, and his jaw clenched.

With a sickening lurch, Jay jumped forward. "Palmer, no!"

Raina and Elaine were instantly at Jay's sides. They stared at Palmer.

"Too late, son." Palmer staggered a step and forced himself upright again, struggling to maintain his dignity. He still clutched his cigarette. "I taught you everything. The only reason you got where you did was me. Without me, you'd be nothing. I never got the credit I deserved, but I had to watch the world pin medals on you. It was disgusting."

"What happened?" Elaine asked.

Raina was breathing shallowly. "He bit into a poison pill of some kind."

"Cyanide." Palmer gave a crooked smile.

"In my molar. A large dose. I hated retirement. Had it put in a few years ago. Remember, Jay — it was me who taught you to have a backup plan."

"You're right, you did teach me a lot." Jay looked at his weapon and then at Palmer. "But I was the one who always had a *good* backup plan."

Palmer's knees buckled. His cigarette fell from his fingers, and he pitched onto his side and gasped. His chest heaved as he struggled to breathe. Jay stayed with him, trying to understand what he had missed. How he could have so badly misjudged Palmer — and himself. As Palmer seemed to shrink, Jay felt for a pulse.

"He's dead." Jay looked up at the two women. He picked up Palmer's cigarette lighter and stood and wrapped his arms around their shoulders, clinging to them, and let his gaze roam over the gently rolling hills of the graveyard and then around the modest residential area on the other side of the street where signs of children were everywhere — swings, bicycles, baby seats showing in the windows of cars.

Raina touched his cheek. "I'm sorry, Jay. He wasn't who you thought he was."

"Me, too," Elaine said softly. "Very sorry. But he was really such an awful man."

Jay straightened. "Yes, he was. But now we have to move. We'll leave him here. Do you want to go on, Elaine?" He examined her worriedly. "There's no shame in stopping. You're not in the best of shape."

"You can't leave me behind now." She lifted her chin.

He nodded and checked his watch. "I understand. We're going to be badly outnumbered, so we need to figure out a plan and pick up supplies. Follow us in the Jag."

50

Baltimore, Maryland

Across the wide Port of Baltimore, the Patapsco River spread like black ink, ripples chromed by moonlight. At a cove, the long wharves of the Cross-Global Sea Center jutted out into the sheen. Tonight only the *Mango Blossom* was anchored, and only Jerry Angelides and his armed men — dressed in Cross-Global's smart blue guard uniforms — were on duty on the terminal's one lit dock.

A cigar clamped between his teeth, Ghranditti paced high above, along the *Blossom*'s railing. Trimmed in brilliant blue and gold, her hull was the creamy white of a mango flower, his first Marie's favorite scent, while inside was stored a fortune in shipping containers, including those destined for the Majlis al-Sha'b. Beside him, more containers extended in a towering steel flotilla from bow to stern. As his gaze swept over his kingdom, he felt a moment of rare pleasure. Someday the world would know about his triumph. It was his legacy, and a legacy endured forever.

He turned on his heel and glanced down at the pier. Laurence Litchfield was striding toward the ship's gangplank, a woman beside him. Ghranditti slowed to study them. They were an odd pair, Litchfield lean as a wolfhound, the woman short and rounded. As they climbed the ramp, Ghranditti swore loudly. It was Bobbye Johnson.

As a tugboat whistled in the distance, Ghranditti pulled his cigar from his mouth and glared at Litchfield. "Explain!"

"I don't like this any more than you do." There was bite to the CIA man's tone. "Is the ship loaded?" He and Bobbye Johnson stepped aboard.

"Just finished. Pilot and tugs will be here in an hour. You have the DVDs?"

"Of course. But nothing happens until I know you'll handle our problem."

"*Our* problem?"

"Her." Litchfield nodded brusquely at the DCI.

The DCI's eyes snapped. "Do you really think you're safe? If the Majlis get their hands on so much state-of-the-art technology, you'll go down with everyone else. You may be their friends tonight. Tomorrow you'll be like everyone else — prey."

Litchfield ignored her. "She needs to vanish when the ship's out to sea."

"The cameras caught you kidnapping me, you son of a bitch." Her chin jutted. "If I disappear, Langley will come after you!"

Litchfield told her calmly, "There was no sign of a kidnapping. You got into the car of your own free will."

Smoking, Ghranditti considered the situation. The ship's officers were American, the crew mostly Filipinos. All civilians. None was armed, which was the rule in case pirates attacked; they were more apt to survive if they did not resist. He had kept them on for the voyage because the *Blossom* must appear to be like all others, with nothing unusual to attract authorities in the ports at which she would call.

Still, there was a solution. "Yes, I have someone. He'll enjoy scrubbing her."

Sweat beading on his forehead, Jay rowed through the dark night toward the tip of Ghranditti's dock in an inflatable boat with a glass-reinforced plastic hull. Its diesel engine was high-powered, but now they needed silence — so he rowed. To the left loomed the *Mango Blossom,* a massive piece of machinery more than three football fields long. From the waterline, her gleaming hull and superstructure rose fourteen stories to the bridge and monkey island above.

Raina sat at the small boat's prow, SIG Sauer ready, her upturned face vigilant. As Jay shipped the oars, letting the craft skim silently ahead, she holstered her pistol and grabbed a rope. When they neared a tree-trunk piling, she threw the rope around, and he caught it. Pulling on the rope, he angled the boat until it slid into the deep shadow of the wharf.

He looked at Raina. Both were dressed completely in black, from special microfiber pants and waterproof jackets to backpacks filled with supplies. As in the old days, warmth passed between them, then acceptance of their fate. One way or another, they must stop Ghranditti's cargo.

As their boat rocked and Raina gripped its sides, Jay reached up. Muscles complaining, he grabbed the dock and pulled himself up and over. Drawing his weapon, he lay flat on the planks and studied the men who were patrolling under the radiant illumination of tall pole lamps. Jerry and Rink were in their usual sports jackets, guns concealed, while the other guards were uniformed and carried Uzis.

Jay followed the line of the gangplank. Shocked, he stared as Bobbye Johnson wrenched herself from Laurence Litchfield's grasp, and they and Martin Ghranditti headed along the deck toward the wheelhouse.

He scrambled back to the edge and looked down into Raina's questioning face. "Come." He reached down a hand.

She shook her head, stood, and pushed off the balls of her feet. As she leaped, the boat swayed and thumped the piling. He peered across the dock. When he turned back, she was pulling herself up and over.

Gripping their pistols, they dropped to their bellies to study the situation. On their right stood the terminal building — a three-story warehouse opening onto the pier. A shadowy interior showed through the giant doorway. To their left was the ship, and alongside it were two cargo cranes that looked like colossal four-legged spiders. The cranes were dark, confirming the shipment was loaded. Beyond the pier spread a parking lot, and farther yet a double-wide truck gate with a kiosk in the center.

Whispering, he told her about Ghranditti, Litchfield, and Bobbye Johnson. "If we can free her, she'll call in her shooters."

"If she's still alive."

It was what he had been thinking, too. The situation seemed to grow only worse.

"No sign of al-Hadi?" she asked.

"Not yet."

They watched longer. As guards drifted across the dock, converging to talk and smoke, Jay speed-dialed his cell phone: "Elaine, we're here. Where are you?"

"Arrived a while ago. Sitting in my car now. There are two guys in the sentry kiosk, both carrying Uzis. I've got a clear view of the ship, wharf, and warehouse. The complex is fenced — heavy wire mesh, rolled concertina wire on top. No surprises."

Raina interrupted by touching his arm and pointing up. "Ghranditti's back."

"Hold on, Elaine."

Smoking a cigar, Ghranditti was marching alone along the deck as if he owned not only it but the world. He was an imposing figure tonight, radiating self-confidence. Stopping at the rail, he rested his forearms on it and leaned over, attentively watching a limousine roll toward the gangplank.

"Bastard," Jay muttered. Still, the limo offered possibilities. "We may have a better way to do this, Elaine."

"Jay! You promised not to cut me out!"

"I'm not." Keeping the cell at his ear so Elaine could hear, he told Raina, "As soon as we have a distraction, we duck into the warehouse and wait for a couple of guards. We overpower them and take their uniforms." Then to Elaine: "This is a safer opening to accomplish what we want. They've got Bobbye. Try to help her." He ended the connection.

Inside the plush limousine, Marie Ghranditti stared straight ahead, feeling ill.

"It's okay, Mom." Aaron patted her hand as if he were the adult and she the child. "Dad told me he'd be waiting for us here. Remember?"

Marie nodded mutely. She had felt sick as soon as the doctor's needle punctured her skin. She had no idea what the new drug was. She glanced at the nanny, Bebe, young and pretty, who cuddled the sleeping Kristoph on her lap. Little Mariette dozed, her shoulder sunk into Bebe's side. She wanted to tell Bebe she would take care of her children, but that was not going to happen for a while. Not until she figured out how to get them away from Martin.

Turning her head, Marie saw Jerry through her window. He opened the door and offered his hand. She grasped it and heaved herself out as a bustle of activity erupted. The limo's trunk swung open.

Suitcases emerged. More suitcases from the front seat. Children awakened and yawned.

From the gangplank, her name floated toward her. "Marie! Darling, you're *here!*" It was Martin.

She straightened. She must not embarrass Martin. She stretched her dry lips in a smile. Jerry held her arm, supporting her. They made their way around the limo.

Controlling his emotions, Jay watched Marie Ghranditti. He studied her rigid movements, the apparent weakness in her joints. She sagged against the rear fender when Jerry released her to help with the suitcases.

In other respects, the scene was touching. As soon as he reached the bottom of the ship's ramp, Ghranditti crouched and enveloped the children in his arms, delivering kisses to little cheeks. He took Kristoph's and Mariette's hands and drew the children up the gangway. Both feet together, Aaron enthusiastically jumped up the ramp after them. Jerry returned to Marie, and she leaned heavily on his arm as he escorted her next, followed by a chauffeur pushing a dolly loaded with suitcases. Last was a young woman, probably another employee.

"What a happy parade," Raina whispered angrily.

As the arms dealer's troops gathered in a loose circle, transfixed by their employer's beautiful family, Jay gave a sharp nod. "Now."

Bent low, they sprinted across the swath of open space toward the warehouse. The illumination from the outdoor lights seemed to pulse. As he followed Raina through the door, Jay checked behind.

"Jay." Raina's voice was a warning.

He whirled back around. She was motionless, surrounded on three sides by high loads of crates. An S&W pistol leading, Alec stepped briskly out from among them, his broad features cool and shrewd.

"Hello, Glinda." He seemed to fill the warehouse with his bulky presence. "So we rendezvous again. Fortunately, I remained here to observe Ghranditti's Pied Piper act. Family occasions hold no charm —"

As if she were elastic, Raina spun on the ball of her right foot and, using her hips for power, shot back her left foot in a *yoko kekomi* thrust kick that landed hard against the big Whippet operative's solar plexus.

Jay was already around her. As Alec staggered, Jay ripped away the S&W.

But the barrel of another gun rammed

into Jay's side. "Jay Tice. At last. You and Raina have been such trouble. I will have that." Volker Rehwaldt yanked Jay's Browning away while Alec retrieved his weapon and grabbed Raina's SIG Sauer.

Hardly breathing, Raina glared at Volker.

His pocked face was severe. "To the ship," he ordered. "Go now."

Jay peered around.

"Forget it, Jay!" Alec snapped. "You're not going to get out of this one. Move!"

Jay and Raina exchanged a look then walked slowly back out into the harsh lights, their two captors close behind. The Ghranditti family had vanished on board, while the limousine cruised back toward the terminal's gates.

"We've got them!" Alec bellowed to the men on the docks. "We goddamned well got them at last!"

The Jaguar was parked against the curb that arched into the terminal, where the approaching limousine blocked Elaine's view for a few seconds. When she could finally see again, the throbbing pain in her finger vanished. She leaned forward, alarmed.

Jay and Raina were crossing to the container ship, herded by two men with guns. She recognized the shooters — they had led the pack that had chased her from the fish wharf. She must do something quickly.

As she judged the limo's speed and distance, she pressed the switch that kept her headlights dark. Turning on her engine, she touched an overhead button, and the sunroof opened. Damp air drifted down.

Keeping herself calm, she watched the gate slide open. She would have only seconds to slip through before it closed. She studied the limo's headlights as they grew larger. In the kiosk the guards were watching the vehicle, too. As it nosed through the opening, Elaine snapped the Jag's gear into DRIVE and slammed the accelerator.

With a squeal of tires, the car took off. The entry's ornamental bushes seemed to fly past her window. Turning the steering wheel, she sped around the limo. Metal screeched against metal as she sideswiped its tail and rushed on. Guards leaped out of the kiosk, a blur, too late. She sideswiped the gate's steel post. Shimmying, the Jag burst through into the Sea Center, speeding over the pavement toward the wood dock.

51

Atop the *Mango Blossom*'s towering deck-house, the bridge was intense with activity. Voices crackled from the shortwave radio while officers plotted the ship's course, checked charts, and tracked weather patterns.

Martin Ghranditti stalked onto the bridge first, followed by Faisal al-Hadi, wearing cheap eyeglasses and a white steward's uniform and carrying two martinis on a silver tray. With his Mediterranean skin and slick black hair, he looked as if he had been serving at sea for years. Ghranditti hid his annoyance. Al-Hadi had demanded Laurence Litchfield be present for the transfer, a personal guarantee against duplicity.

Ghranditti nodded at the captain then at Litchfield, who was waiting alone in an alcove, hands clasped behind, apparently admiring the scenery. A laptop computer sat open on a ledge beside him.

"I thought you might like a drink before you go." With a timbre of excitement in his voice, Ghranditti spoke loud enough to Litchfield for the crew and pilot to hear, then he disappeared into the alcove with al-Hadi.

His deep-set eyes emotionless, Litchfield looked the "steward" up and down then nodded. "It's ready for you to inspect." He stepped aside.

Al-Hadi set down the serving tray. "You have the decryption disc also?"

"On me."

As al-Hadi's fingers flew over the laptop's keyboard, the arms merchant and the CIA official drank and watched data and point-and-click interfaces flash across the screen. At last al-Hadi removed the DVD from the laptop and stood back. Without a word, he pulled out his cell phone and tapped numbers, signaling his approval.

Ghranditti and Litchfield took out their cells, too.

Within minutes, al-Hadi transferred $6 million into Ghranditti's account, and Ghranditti wired half into Litchfield's. When Litchfield confirmed his had arrived, he handed the decryption DVD to al-Hadi. The simple gesture completed the transaction.

Pride surged through Ghranditti. He had never felt so alive. "We've just created history!" He touched the rim of his martini glass to Litchfield's.

The CIA man chuckled loudly. "To a better future."

They drank and smiled.

Ignoring them, al-Hadi slid the ForeTell and decryption DVDs inside his shirt, propped the empty silver tray on the ends of his fingertips, and strode away. His starched white back was erect, his tread triumphant and sure.

Summoned by Alec St. Ann's announcement, the guards on the dock grinned and shouted in celebration. Like big-game hunters, they converged on Jay and Raina.

"You got them!" One pounded Alec's back in congratulation.

"Shit, it's about time," said another.

While Alec and Volker silently accepted the men's praise, Jay used his peripheral vision to scan the complex's entry. Raina's head moved slightly; she was looking, too.

"Be ready to move," he told Raina quietly.

"Shut up!" Jerry Angelides's voice boomed from the top of the gangplank. "Both of you, shut the fuck up!" He pulled a Colt handgun from inside his sports jacket and trotted down the ramp. His flat, stony gaze never left Jay.

Rink called out, "I knew you'd get them, Jerry. I knew it!"

Jerry nodded. "I knew it, too, Rink. It was only a matter of time." He landed on the dock, his bristle haircut flicking artificial light, and stalked to Jay. "Don't you say another word." He raised the Colt inches from Jay's mouth.

"Volker!" Raina twisted to peer at him. "You can't let —"

"Be quiet!" the German operative ordered. "It is none of our business."

Jay stared into the deadly muzzle, hoping like hell it was not Jerry's personal weapon, but it probably was — a shooter liked to work with his own gun.

Thinking quickly, Jay allowed terror and indignation to radiate from him. "That's not Billy's Colt, is it?" he pleaded. "It's bad enough you're going to scrub me, but it wouldn't be right to do it with that poor kid's gun!"

"I was training him good until you tricked him," Jerry snapped. He stuck his Colt back inside his holster and slid the other from his waistband. "Yeah, Billy's the one who should take you down!"

"Watch out!" someone yelled.

The growl of the racing Jaguar pierced the hush. Heads whipped around. Showered in the dock's lights, the windshield displayed Elaine's small face, angry and intent, as the car accelerated directly at them.

Alec and Volker spun and fired. Their wild bullets made explosive sounds as they slammed into the car. The pair ran backward, firing sporadically, while the rest of the men scattered. More erratic gunfire split the quiet air.

Jerry swore loudly. "Gotta ice you fast, buddy." He squeezed the Colt's trigger. But it did not shoot. There was no sound, no bullet, nothing.

The car's motor was a roar. The dock shivered. Jay controlled an urge to bolt.

"What the fuck did you do to Billy's gun!" Yelling, Jerry squeezed again then tossed the Colt and reached for his own weapon just as the car was about to smash them.

Before Jerry's weapon was fully out, Jay rammed his shoulder into the killer's chest, carrying him away. At the same moment, Raina sprinted for the gangplank, and the Jaguar slashed past in an eruption of dust and grit, shielding them from the janitors as it hurtled on toward the end of the pier.

Jerry fell hard. Jay stumbled but grabbed the good Colt and kept moving, picking up velocity, until he was tearing full speed up the ramp. At the top he dropped flat beside Raina. Her backpack open beside her, she had uncoiled thin, flexible detonation cord.

In unison, they looked out in time to see the Jaguar sail off the end of the wharf, a streak of red. The air was hushed, the guards staring after it. Then there was the shuddering noise of a huge splash. The river's black water geysered up, moonlight turning its rippling surface into mercury. There was no sign of Elaine. Jay said a silent prayer.

On the bridge Ghranditti and Litchfield were finishing their martinis when gunfire sounded. They dashed out of the alcove just as the first officer, who was working at the navigation station, froze and turned. Two young officers leaped to their feet, shocked. The captain reached for the satellite phone.

"Don't call the Coast Guard!" Ghranditti ordered. "My men will take care of this!"

As the captain nodded, Ghranditti and Litchfield hurried out onto the portside wing. Far below, their men were running toward the gangplank.

Ghranditti stared. "There's Tice and Manhardt! What the hell are they doing?"

Jay and Raina exchanged a worried glance.

Then she resumed pressing the detonation cord into the gap between the platform and the turntable. The det cord had an explosive core, while the turntable allowed the ramp to swing out to accommodate the distance between ship and pier. If it were severed, the steel gangway would collapse, isolating them on the ship — until Jerry found another way to get his men on board.

As Jay attached the blasting cap to one end of the det cord, a hail of Uzi fire erupted around them, biting into the hull, slamming into the platform. When it paused, Jay heard the ramp creak. He leaned out quickly.

His heavy face determined, Alec was halfway up the incline, leading Volker and a line of guards at a fast pace. Jay fired and dropped prone again. More bullets thudded around them, sending jagged pieces of steel whining past.

As Jay set the cap's timer, Raina used det cutters to sever the other end of the cord. A bullet ricocheted off the post, burning inches from Raina's skull. Dragging their backpacks, they slithered backward. The echoing sound of running feet on the ramp suddenly stopped.

Crouched for protection between sheer cliffs of containers, Jay and Raina slung on their backpacks and waited. The seconds ticked past like hours.

Abruptly there was the loud *bang* of an explosion. Seagulls screeched and took flight from the ship's rail. The gangplank dropped and crashed against the hull with an enormous *thud.* The ship trembled. Men screamed. There were noisy splashes.

Jay and Raina peered out. The stink of melting steel was noxious. Brown smoke plumed. Smiling grimly, they jumped up and ran.

On the outdoor observation deck high above the action, Litchfield straightened up from the railing, furious. Alec St. Ann and Volker Rehwaldt were in the drink along with two of Ghranditti's men, while Tice and Manhardt were not only on the ship, Tice was armed. For the moment it was up to Ghranditti, al-Hadi, and him to stop them.

"Call al-Hadi. Tell him I need help!" In the lead, Litchfield shoved open the sliding glass door and rushed back onto the bridge.

Behind him, he heard Ghranditti tell the captain, "The ramp's down. Two terrorists have boarded. My men will handle them, but first they've got to get on the ship. Figure out a way to do that — fast. I'm going to make a cell call."

Pulling out his Browning, Litchfield jumped onto the elevator, mashed the button, and descended, cursing. He did not have time for this. He stretched and breathed, trying to relieve his disquiet. He grasped his Browning in both hands and tucked against the wall next to the door. When it opened, he rolled out into the base of the deckhouse.

Swinging the gun from side to side, he checked the enclosure. Coils of rope rose in piles. Gear and equipment stood neatly stacked near the stairwell. The place had a hollow sound and stank of salt and metal.

Warily he pivoted again, listening, watching. But when he finally hurried around the elevator toward the door, cold steel pressed into the back of his neck.

"That's far enough, Larry."

It was a voice he had never wanted to hear again.

52

As the Jaguar dropped through the chilly river, heavy silence settled around Elaine like burial cloth. She reached up and grabbed the open sides of the sunroof and propelled herself straight up, aiming for the moonglow that glistened far above. Pulling the water, she climbed higher, one stroke after another, fighting a desire to inhale. Finally she entered the river's silvery light — but the surface seemed to recede.

Stroking faster, she shot through to the air and gasped. As she treaded water, she breathed deeply and peered around until she spotted the inflatable boat where Jay had said he would leave it. She swam and heaved herself over the side and lay there in a stunned kind of wariness — until footfalls sounded on the wood planks above.

Chest tight, she scrambled up to her knees and paddled with her hands. The boat slipped silently out of sight under the wharf.

Controlling her nerves, she waited.

When the footsteps finally retreated, Elaine examined her wounded finger, covered first by a special antibiotic gel that hardened then by latex — no cracks or holes in the latex. She pushed the pain from her mind, stripped off her wet clothes, opened the waterproof package waiting for her, and dressed in black microfiber turtleneck, pants, socks, and sneakers. She strapped a holster at the small of her back, checked her Walther, and fastened it inside. And put on her backpack.

Feeling more in control, she untied the rope and rowed around to the distant side of the *Mango Blossom.* As she approached, the river quaked from the vibrations of the ship's idling engine. Tightening her grip on the oars, she pulled hard through the prop wash. She had two options to get aboard — shinny up one of the anchor chains and squeeze through the hawseholes, or if she was lucky, the captain had ordered preparations for the pilot boat, and she would find a ladder draped over the hull.

As she skirted the ship, she looked up. The white hull was a precipitous wall, at least eighteen feet from shuddering waterline to deck. With relief, she saw a rope-and-wood ladder. She pulled alongside. As she looked up again, she swore a string of silent oaths, cursing her short height. Her boat was lower in the water than a pilot boat, which meant the gap between her and the bottom rung was too great to jump. Suddenly she heard Jay's voice inside her mind: *Use what you have.*

She attached a magnetic grip to the steel hull and tied the anchor rope through the grommet. She crossed the oars over the prow in an X and lashed the intersection. Pushing the boat out until it was at the end of its tether, she braced the oars' paddles on the far side of the prow's bench and leaned the top of the X against the ship. Scanning around, she clambered up the oars, grabbed the ladder, and climbed. At the top, she drew her Walther. Part of the plan was that Jay and Raina were to have blown the gangplank. So far, the plan seemed to have worked — none of Jerry's thugs was in sight.

She opened the gate and rushed along the mountain range of containers, checking through the stacks to the other side of the ship. She paused only to peer inside three lifeboats that looked like small space capsules, completely enclosed except for igloo holes for entry. All were empty.

As she straightened, she looked along

another steel ravine between the containers. On the other side, one of the multistory cranes that had loaded the ship blazed with light, and its elevator cage was rising. As she studied the glass front, her throat tightened. She recognized the faces — they were Ghranditti's people. She bolted.

Surrounded by the gray bulkheads, Jay took Litchfield's gun, stepped back, and slid it into his waistband. He tried to stop the image, but for a moment he imagined Kristoph lying broken and alone at the bottom of the Swiss gorge. This bastard, Litchfield, had murdered Kristoph. His muscles pulsed. Rage rolled through him.

"He's mine! *Mine!*" Feet pounding, Raina ran out from the stairwell. As she closed in, her furious breathing resonated with his own.

Litchfield's back went rigid. "You don't understand —"

"Like hell we don't!" The thunder in his own voice jerked Jay back from the edge.

But Raina was like a wildcat, all sinew and revenge. Distancing himself from his emotions, Jay watched her holster her pistol and slam Litchfield into the steel bulkhead.

"You fucking monster!" Fists knotted, she hammered Litchfield's kidneys. "I want to see your face before I erase you. Turn around. You goddamn killed Kristoph!"

As Litchfield grunted with pain, Raina smashed the ball of her foot into his knee. He staggered, recovered, and rammed an elbow back, connecting with her ribs. She gasped, but in seconds a HideAway knife — short, easily concealed, and lethal — materialized above her knuckles.

In midturn, the CIA man froze. He stared at the glinting blade.

Jay focused. "Stop, Raina. No!"

"I'm not finished!"

But when she glanced at him, Jay saw she had worked off enough of her fury.

He glared at Litchfield: "Tell us where Bobbye Johnson, Ghranditti, and al-Hadi are, or I'll let her carve you."

Raina's voice was suddenly soft, almost caressing. "Think about a Thanksgiving turkey, Larry. Skin, meat, joints. That's you. One slice at a time — until I dismember you. I'll make sure you live to the end. My pleasure."

Litchfield's expression smoothed, grew neutral, the experienced covert operator. Ignoring Raina, he addressed Jay: "The Majlis al-Sha'b is your enemy — not me. Kristoph's death was unfortunate but unavoidable. We didn't know he was yours."

Raina's voice rose. "You think that's an excuse?"

Jay kept his focus on Litchfield. "We've figured out about the backdoor. That's why you needed Kristoph."

For a moment Litchfield seemed surprised. "Should've known you would. It's just what America needs. Sun-Tzu said it best — 'If you know the enemy and know yourself, you need not fear a hundred battles.' With the backdoor, we'll learn everything about them — who they are, what they're planning."

With effort, Jay made his voice reasonable. "The rest of the shipment is too damn dangerous. You've got to help us stop it."

Litchfield shrugged. "In our business, risk taking never ends — it just gets more zeroes behind it. You taught me that, Jay." Bitterness flashed across his aquiline face. "Besides, you're nothing but a goddamned asshole traitor. How could you have sold us out? Didn't you think about us? You were a giant. We looked up to you. We wanted to be you. But now you don't have to matter anymore — because I've *topped* you!"

Pain washed over Jay, the pain of failure. Espionage's corrosive forces changed one in ways one did not see and then could not look at. It had happened to him, but he had never guessed Palmer Westwood and Larry Litchfield would sink so low. Now Litchfield was the real traitor.

"Where are Bobbye, Ghranditti, and al-Hadi?" Jay demanded again.

The CIA man checked Raina's blade, then homed in on Jay. "By now the captain's figured out how Ghranditti's men can swarm the ship. You'd be smart to jump into the river and swim for it, Jay. You used to take my advice — do it now. Let the operation alone. It's for the good of Langley."

Jay stared. Litchfield no longer understood a damn thing. "Where are they!"

There was a small, satisfied smile on Litchfield's lips, and his eyes glittered, radiating an odd kind of achievement. "The bridge," he said simply as he clasped his hands behind his back.

Jay frowned, sensing something was wrong. He studied Litchfield, saw his shoulders adjust. And then he knew —

Litchfield's arm swung around, a pocket gun in his fist, trained on Jay.

"Watch out!" Raina shouted and leaped.

As Litchfield pulled the trigger, Jay dove to the steel deck.

Raina slashed the HideAway knife deep across Litchfield's throat, rotating it to rip the flesh. A torrent of blood erupted. Litchfield hesitated, then his black brows beetled in puzzlement. He opened his mouth to speak, but blood poured out, and he sank cross-legged against the bulkhead, dying.

Pain ricocheted through Jay's mind from the searing bullet that had gashed across his temple and scalp. He tried to blink away the burning pulses. A hot wash filled his ear and flooded his neck.

In a shocked reverie, he watched Raina drop beside him, opening her backpack. Her hair was a wild confusion of black curls. Her blue eyes were pools of worry.

He rallied. "I'm okay. I've seen him put his hands behind his back like that a thousand times. Stupid of me to miss what he intended. I guess he learned something from me after all. Good work."

"You scared me to death." Watching over her shoulders, she unscrewed the tube of special antibiotic gel and squeezed. "You've got a furrow a mile long. This will sting, then it'll set and stop the bleeding just as it did on Elaine's finger."

The deckhouse door banged open, and a gust of fresh air burst in. Elaine leaped nimbly inside, a furious cyclone in black. Her gaze sharp, she crouched, her Walther in both hands, as she checked cautiously around.

"You made it!" Jay said.

Raina smiled warmly at Elaine. "I knew she would."

Elaine ignored their welcome. "Jerry's men are boarding!" she warned.

Jay nodded. "Let me up. Lock the door, Elaine. We're going to the bridge."

"Not me." She spun and ran back outside.

Marie Ghranditti awoke with a start, fear oozing from her veins. She focused on the moonlight streaming in through the portholes of the ship's stateroom, then on the children and nanny, sleeping shadows on sofas and the other bed.

Now she remembered — Martin had brought them here while he finished business, scheduling everything as he always did. She wondered whether all men who craved danger were like that, finding compensation in controlling others since they could not control themselves. Now he was back in the weapons game with some new deal that was making him nervous. Tonight she had made herself pay attention.

She struggled up, gingerly testing her body. She felt better, stronger. She swung her legs over the side of the bed and walked quietly to the door. Cracking it open, she heard only the muted rumble of the ship.

She hurried down the corridor, reading numbers. At last she found the right door. Someone had attached a padlock to it.

"Hello," she whispered. "Are you in there?"

"Who are you?" a voice answered.

"Marie Ghranditti. If I free you, will you help me take my children away from my husband?"

"He'll never bother you again."

Marie ran to the deck's axe and fire extinguisher, but the glass-enclosed case was locked. There was a handle, but if she pulled it, the ship's alarm would sound. She looked around desperately. The officers' quarters were on this deck, just beneath the bridge. She listened at a door, heard snoring, and moved on, listened again, and opened it. The cabin was dark, quiet. Praying, she flicked on the light. The cot was empty.

She rushed to the closet, studying the clothes then two shelves of mountaineering equipment. She tore through everything, discarding rock-climbing boots and ropes and pulleys and pitons and a peg hammer . . . and stopped, frustrated. Then focused on the hammer. Gripping it, she chose a sharply pointed piton and ran again.

"I'm back," she whispered at the door.

"I'm going to break the lock."

"Hurry."

Looking around anxiously, Marie inserted the piton and hit it until the padlock snapped. Inside the cabin, the woman was waiting, petite and furious, fists on hips.

"I need a cell phone," she ordered. "Pronto!"

Marie led her at a fast clip back to the stateroom. Sliding inside alone, she rummaged through the nanny's purse and carried her cell back into the corridor.

The woman snatched it, dialed, and spoke swiftly into it: "Is the forward deployment standing by at Warrenton?" She listened. "The target is a container ship, the *Mango Blossom*." She described the location and problem. "I need rapid insertion!" She snapped the cell closed and gazed appraisingly at Marie. "Where did you find that hammer and piton? Maybe there's something else I can use."

Again they raced off. But as they passed the cabin where the woman had been jailed, they heard catlike footfalls. They glanced back. Marie fought terror as she stared at an M-4 and then up into the cold face of the steward who aimed it at them.

53

Jay and Raina pressed back against the bulkhead, she on the step below his, both out of sight of the corridor. As they had ridden the elevator up from the deck, Jay had pulled the faceplate off the terminus buttons and installed a delay timer on the wires while Raina set more det cord. Exiting at the officers' deck, they had padded up one flight to this position just beneath the bridge level.

The bridge emanated a threatening hush, palpable. They heard no voices, not even the shortwave radio, only the mechanical clicks and whirrs of the navigation and other technical gear. It was eerie — a ship's bridge was always manned. Ghranditti or al-Hadi or both had cleared it and were probably nearby, planning something. There was perhaps another minute before the elevator would arrive.

He cocked his head, listening to gunfire

on the main deck, the noise muted by the bulkheads. "Elaine's trying to hold them off down there." He kept his voice low.

Raina's glance was compassionate. "She has a chance — she's like a foal finding her legs. She's on her way to being very good."

He nodded. "I hope she makes it, Raina. You did."

"You and I also made a lot of mistakes. And paid high prices."

"I know. But Elaine was already headed into field ops. She just didn't know it yet." He studied her, drinking in the smooth lines of her face, the curve of her chin, the glow in her eyes. If he did not survive, at least he'd had this time with her.

"But now neither of us can go back," she reminded him.

"Do you mind?"

"Not at all." She smiled, her love for him naked.

A lump formed in his throat.

A bell rang once, announcing the elevator's arrival. Their trance broke. In unison, they raised their pistols in both hands, tucking them against their pectorals, ready. They breathed in for a count of four, held their breaths for a count of four, and exhaled for a count of four.

As they repeated the drill, Jay felt his heart

rate decelerate and his nerves quiet while his senses grew more acute. He tracked a single set of feet hurrying from the opposite direction of the navigation center toward the elevator. He checked, saw a square, heavy back pass by.

He mouthed the identity to Raina: *Ghranditti.*

As the elevator doors clanged open, there was the loud clap of an explosion from inside. Ghranditti yelled in surprise. Smoke stung Jay's nostrils as a second set of feet pelted toward the elevator, this time from the navigation center. It would be al-Hadi. The two men would take only seconds to absorb the fact that the elevator cage was empty.

Jay and Raina hurtled out of the stairwell, firing, raining bullets into the deck, the bulkheads, the elevator — purposefully missing al-Hadi and Ghranditti. The pair plunged to the floor. As the hail of fire continued, Ghranditti covered his head, but al-Hadi was already rising to his elbows, positioning himself.

Jay kicked away al-Hadi's M-4 and pointed his Browning, while Raina snatched Ghranditti's Beretta and aimed her SIG Sauer.

675

Jay scooped up the M-4. "Where's the software!"

Al-Hadi's black gaze blazed hatred. *"Khaibar, Khaibar, Ya Yahud, Iaish Muhammad Safayood!"* Khaibar, Khaibar, O Jews, the army of Muhammad is coming for you!

Jay lifted his head, listening again. Gunfire had resumed below. "Your threat is empty, al-Hadi. Your weapon's gone. Where's the damn software!"

Al-Hadi seemed to think about it. "All right, I'll show you." Slowly, making certain each gesture was seen, the terrorist rose. The youth from Berlin had grown into a good-looking man, with the same high-bridged nose and olive skin, but now a more muscular body. His eyes were intelligent, piercing — and frightening in their certainty.

Ghranditti got cautiously to his feet, too, barrel-chested, his silvered black hair still perfectly arranged. His jowly face was dark with rage. He glared at Jay.

Al-Hadi rotated his hand, showing his palm, where his thumb pressed a wedge-shaped piece of electronics. "Bobbye Johnson is wired with plastique. If I release my thumb, she dies."

Elaine paused where she had a good view of the cargo crane. With a sinking feeling, she saw the crane's elevator cage had risen to deck level and the boom was lowering a steel-mesh ramp from the crane to the ship. Ghranditti's janitors would be aboard in minutes.

Quickly analyzing the supplies she had in her backpack, she hunched low and sped along the railing, alternately scanning the content lists attached to the containers and checking the deck for the plugs that looked like large manhole covers and allowed the crew to check the refrigerated boxes — "reefers" — stored belowdecks. When her brain finally registered the word *propane*, she turned on her heel and doubled back until she found a container isolated from the others. Inside was highly flammable propane.

With the butt of her Walther, she smashed open the strip-and-bolt seal and yanked open the door. Inside, two-pound propane cylinders wrapped in thick buffering material were packed to the ceiling. She slid a cannister out carefully, left it on the deck, and ran again, at last spotting a reefer cover. She opened it, scrambled to the side, and fell next to another. She opened it, too.

"There's Cunningham!"

She looked up. In the distance, men in guard uniforms were racing toward her.

Jerry was in the middle of the pack, his sports jacket falling wide open. As they lifted their weapons, she plunged to her belly. Bullets splintered into the steel deck around her. She rolled, pulled a flash-bang grenade from her backpack, yanked the pin, and heaved it a dozen feet beyond the open reefer holes — just where she wanted it.

Retreating in a fast zigzag, she dove out of sight into a steel chasm just as a loud *bang* smacked the air. Thick ocher-colored smoke billowed past her hiding place. She held her breath and threw herself into it, continuing back toward the deckhouse.

"It's a just a smoke bomb!" someone yelled.

The feet resumed their pursuit. She scooped up the propane cylinder and pelted onward, tearing off the buffering material. When she was safely away from the container where the rest of the propane was stored, she slowed and looked back. The smoke was thinning into gray.

Four men blasted through. Two dropped from sight feet first down the reefer holes, their eyes wide with surprise. As their angry obscenities rang out, more men appeared, slower, cautiously examining the deck. Elaine smiled to herself.

"Move!" Jerry ordered. "We've got to get

her. There she is!"

Elaine set the propane in the shadow of a container and sprinted. As the men resumed the chase, she slid into another steel canyon and checked out around the corner. They were closing in. She counted her breaths, keeping herself calm. Jerry, burly and determined, his flat eyes cold with rage, was leading. When he was almost on top of the cylinder, and she could see the sweaty slick on his face, she squeezed her trigger.

The propane exploded in a firestorm of flames, swallowing Jerry Angelides. One arm was visible, the sleeve of his sports jacket a burning torch, the hand in a fist. Men screamed. The deck trembled. The rail melted and sagged.

Elaine nodded soberly to herself. *Distract. Demoralize. Defend.* As a wave of heat rolled past her, she leaped up and raced away again. Some would survive, and they would come after her.

On the bridge level of the deckhouse, Jay and Raina followed al-Hadi and Ghranditti down the corridor. Suddenly a noisy blast sounded from below.

Raina grimaced. *Elaine,* she mouthed.

Jay frowned and nodded. They entered the bridge with its long row of windows that framed a dramatic view of the glittering nighttime port. Two radar screens glowed. Data tracked across monitors. And Bobbye Johnson sat immobilized — duct-taped to the captain's chair, more tape holding a roll of plastic explosives to her belly. The detonator was visible. Her mouth was taped, too, but her gaze shot lightning bolts at al-Hadi and Ghranditti.

Al-Hadi turned beside her. His lips skinned back in a smile. With his free hand, he opened his shirt, then a black Kevlar vest, showing a black T-shirt with two front pockets. In each was a DVD.

"As promised — your very fine ForeTell software." Al-Hadi closed the vest and buttoned his shirt.

Ghranditti marched across the room and pushed aside a curtain that concealed a small galley. Inside, Marie Ghranditti was taped to an office chair, her platinum hair tumbling around her shoulders. Her green eyes were wide with horror as she gazed up at her husband.

"Marie, darling, forgive me for keeping you safe." Ghranditti ripped the tape from her mouth. "That's better, isn't it?" He straightened up. "See, Jay? She's *mine*." Then to Marie: "This is Jay Tice, darling. I thought you'd enjoy meeting him."

Marie's face grew haggard with understanding. She peered at Jay. "I'm sorry."

"*Sorry!*" Ghranditti bellowed at her. "He had everything! He came from a monied family. He had the best education. The government pursued him and handed him a career. But *I* started with *nothing!* I had to fight my way up from the gutter. I had to work like an animal for every penny. For him, respect was automatic. I had to buy it!" He turned on Jay. "Marie was quality. I wanted her, so I figured out what I needed to do, and I took her. She told me about you, where you came from, who you were. *What* you were. She would've left you eventually. Instead, you fucked up one of my big deals — *and you wiped Marie!*"

"*You* terminated Marie and our children!" Jay took a menacing step toward the death merchant.

When Raina touched Jay's sleeve, warning him to control himself, envy at the intimacy flashed in Ghranditti's eyes. Jay inhaled two deep breaths and gave Raina a stiff nod of acknowledgment. But as Raina squeezed his arm reassuringly and dropped her hand, Ghranditti's fury seemed only to deepen.

Watching all of them, al-Hadi laughed loudly.

Ghranditti glanced at al-Hadi. Cursing

Jay, he exploded off the pads of his feet and ran across the bridge at him, his arms outstretched. His features were twisted with hate.

"Stop!" Jay warned. Quickly he lifted the Browning, aiming it at Ghranditti's head while keeping the M-4 on al-Hadi. "If you want to live, get the DVDs from al-Hadi!"

Ghranditti stared at the gun. He slowed, then froze. His gaze shifted to the terrorist.

Al-Hadi laughed louder. "You forget, Ghranditti, I have the trigger for the plastique. If I release it, all of us die. Do you want a martyr's death? Will you join me at last, my brother?"

Ghranditti's heavy face sobered. One hand drifted down to his side; the other took out a cigar.

"That's better." Al-Hadi considered Jay. "What stupid drama that was, but typical. Put down your weapons or I *will* detonate the plastique."

"Disarm it," Jay countered. "If you do, you'll have a fair trial. You can spout your fundamentalist rhetoric from the witness chair. Think of the press coverage." He saw Raina adjust her stance, casually move closer to the terrorist while Jay kept him occupied.

Al-Hadi shook his head. "The software

and shipment are a far greater prize. Be sensible, Tice. I could've ordered your death long ago, but I always planned to take you myself. Now you'll escape even that — simply give me your guns, the ship will sail, and you can have a lifeboat once we're on the Chesapeake."

Jay kept his face expressionless. No matter what he promised, al-Hadi would erase all of them as soon as they lowered their weapons. Their one chance was to use the man's self-serving beliefs against him — if Raina could move swiftly enough, and al-Hadi would move his hand away from his body. From his peripheral vision, he saw her inch closer and her free hand slide into her pocket. He hoped like hell she was within striking distance.

"Remember Imam Husayn?" Jay began evenly, "He said it right — 'Death with dignity is better than a life of humiliation.'" Husayn had died bravely with a sword in one hand, a Koran in the other, when he was ambushed in the desert. As al-Hadi's anthracite gaze on him intensified, Jay put a sneer in his voice: "If you're a true believer, Sheik al-Hadi, how could you have lived two long decades with the humiliation of knowing you took freedom that day on Glienicke Bridge rather than execute a world-famous Jew? You're nothing but a coward and a traitor to your people!"

Al-Hadi's eyes blanked from a thunderstorm of emotions. His body trembled. He raised his hand, slowly unfurling his fingers, showing his thumb massaging the trigger button.

"Death to you!" he shouted. He extended his hand.

Instantly Raina whipped a thin cord with a special adhesive end across the open space, lassoing al-Hadi's fingers tight around the trigger button.

As al-Hadi tried to jerk free, Raina ran at him. At the same time, Jay threw himself at Bobbye Johnson, yanked the detonator from the roll of plastic explosives, and hurled it away.

Al-Hadi turned to flee, but Raina kicked his right leg. He staggered, grabbing for Bobbye Johnson's chair. Jay shoved a shoulder into his chest. Al-Hadi fell, and Jay landed on top, wrestling to hold him down while trying to yank open his white jacket.

As Raina tore at the duct tape on Bobbye's chest, al-Hadi slammed a fist at Jay's cheek and rolled away. Jay shook his head, fighting dizziness, and slowly lunged for the terrorist. Al-Hadi was already on his feet and rushing toward the glass door that led onto the starboard wing. Ghranditti was right behind.

As Bobbye leaned over, tearing the tape from her legs, Marie nodded frantically and shouted, "They're escaping!"

The terrorist yanked open a drawer and snapped up an M-4 and slammed out through the door.

Ghranditti grabbed an Uzi and whirled to face the room.

The cool deliberation in Ghranditti's thick face was chilling. Intelligence had returned, and so had competence. He pointed the Uzi at Jay. "You've ruined me!"

Jay ducked and aimed his pistol. Their weapons fired.

As Ghranditti's bullets whined into the galley inches above Marie's head, a black hole appeared between his eyes. Blood spurted out. He staggered back. The Uzi clattered to the deck. He dropped onto his knees beside it. His gaze lifted, and he glared accusingly at Jay. Abruptly, the light vanished from his eyes, and he pitched forward, motionless.

"Get that bastard al-Hadi!" Bobbye Johnson ordered as she jumped off her chair and ran to free Marie. More gunfire sounded from below, louder through the open door. "I'll hold the damn thugs off.

I'm going to enjoy this."

"Call in the paramilitary first!" Jay left the M-4 for her on the chair.

"I already have!" Bobbye snapped.

Jay and Raina rushed out onto the balcony and down the outside staircase, following al-Hadi, whose feet seemed to have grown wings.

54

Elaine was pinned at the corner of the tall stack of containers nearest the deckhouse. Blood dripped from wounds to her scalp. More blood pooled on the top of her firing hand. She hurt in places she had no idea could hurt. But when she leaned out to shoot, she spotted another load of men pouring from the cargo crane across the steel-mesh ramp onto the ship.

She ducked back as more bullets struck the steel container and deck. She could hear men running quietly down the canyons among the stacks, circling, closing in. With her free hand, she shakily wiped sweat from her face.

The propane tank's fiery explosion had killed or removed from action eight in the first pack of twelve. The two who fell into the reefers had crawled out but had not rejoined the firefight. She was certain her bullets had injured an additional two, and there was a possibility she had hit another one. But she had not permanently downed anyone since she detonated the propane. With the addition of the new group, that meant fourteen were out there far more healthy than she liked.

Elaine stuck her head out and shot three times in fast succession. Suddenly bullets blasted at her from her unprotected side. The only cover left to her was inside the wheelhouse, a long twenty feet away.

She dropped to her stomach and opened fire across the width of the ship at her two new attackers — uniformed guards who crouched on the starboard side near the rail. Then she rolled and fired along the railing next to her, on the port side. But as she rolled back to shoot across the deck again, she heard the faint *chop-chop* of powerful helicopter blades approaching far in the distance.

Her throat swelled with hope. It was the distinctive song of a Black Hawk, and there were at least two.

Warning shouts filled the air. Suddenly there was the loud noise of multiple pounding feet. She looked to her left. The two new shooters had vanished. Then she checked along the railing. A herd of uniformed guards was hustling as fast as they could toward the cargo crane's ramp, glancing back over their shoulders at the sky behind her. The Black Hawks had persuaded Ghranditti's rats to abandon ship.

She felt a surge of gratitude. Aching everywhere, she picked herself up and walked toward the wheelhouse — and stopped. A flash of white was descending the outside stairs from the bridge's starboard wing. She was riveted. It was a man in steward's dress. It was al-Hadi!

Her gaze traveled upward. Two black shadows were pursuing.

Al-Hadi leaped down onto the top of the fleet of containers, stumbled, and took off across them, out of sight. The two shadows — Jay and Raina — bounded after him, firing.

Adrenaline shot through Elaine. She put on a burst of speed, racing toward the port staircase. She climbed, forcing energy into her exhausted body. As her eyes rose above the tops of the containers, she could see the three figures again, silhouetted against the stars. The terrorist had a good lead. Gunfire slashed back and forth.

As Raina ran alongside on his left about forty feet away, Jay hesitated his pell-mell pace just long enough to aim over the distance at al-Hadi. In quick succession, he squeezed off more bullets, missing. Al-Hadi turned and crouched, his dark face gray and angry.

Listening hopefully to the noise of approaching Black Hawks, Jay fell flat. So did Raina. Gazing at each other, they pressed their cheeks against the cold steel roofs of their containers as al-Hadi showered bursts of M-4 fire at them. In their dark clothes, they made lousy targets. The bullets screamed and punctured metal.

The moment the violent storm ceased, they jumped up and ran again, firing as they followed the terrorist across the flat tops of the jumbo boxes. The containers were stacked and packed in ranks of a dozen, some twenty ranks in all, extending in a steel sea toward the bow. In between were five-foot-wide openings that plunged straight to the deck.

Curling from side to side, al-Hadi shot bursts back at them. Suddenly he was in the air, cresting one of the chasms. He landed and spun around again, searching for his targets.

Instantly Raina and Jay dropped flat again — al-Hadi had a semiautomatic weapon; their pistols were no match. His bursts sliced into the containers. When silence descended, they looked up. Al-Hadi had peeled off his white jacket. He hurled it away, eyes peering into the sky toward the helicopters. He careened off. His black undershirt vanished against the night, while his white trouser legs pumped.

They chased again, sprinting, hurdling canyons, sprinting again, firing. They dumped empty magazines from their pistols, reloaded, and continued to fire. They needed to be much nearer al-Hadi. Luckily, he was short-legged and no speed-runner. They were closing in.

Jay's lungs heaved. He glanced at Raina. Thick sweat glistened on her face. He was covered in sweat, too. Both of them gave every indication of tiring.

When he gestured to her, indicating al-Hadi was angling toward starboard, she nodded. She was near that side of the ship. Firing less frequently, she hurried to intercept the terrorist's escape.

Of the three, Jay was the most experienced runner. He bounded over a ravine, caught his balance, and hurtled onward, herding al-Hadi.

At the same time, al-Hadi glanced back more often, seeming to recognize that they were wearing out. But then, they had been in action more than twenty-four hours; he had not — and he was younger. He squeezed off a battery of bursts.

Almost simultaneously, the three sprang over chasms. Like pincers, Jay and Raina closed in. They were almost near enough. . . .

Raina breathed heavily, her exhalations noisy. Her eyes were glazed. Jay gasped for oxygen. But al-Hadi's steps were still light.

As Elaine rushed headlong across the containers, trying to catch up, she realized Jay's and Raina's bullets were becoming erratic, often wild. Frightened, she fired past them at the steward, hoping for a good-luck shot.

At the sound, Jay turned to look at her, breathing hard.

Raina's head was drooping, but she raised it and turned, too.

With the speed of the healthy and impeccably trained, al-Hadi spun around, threw himself onto his belly, and raised his M-4.

"Jay!" Elaine bolted. "Raina!"

Jay and Raina were not only standing still, they were only a few arm lengths apart, perfect targets for semiautomatic fire. Al-Hadi swept bursts across them. Running with a speed she never knew she had, Elaine watched Jay give her a weary look that somehow announced he was going to die.

His back arched, and his arms flung upward. Blood sprayed out behind him. Blood showered from Raina's back, too, and she pivoted, crumpling.

Elaine shrieked, "No!" She pulled the trigger, shooting again and again at the prone al-Hadi while Jay and Raina fell out of sight between the stacks.

Laughing, al-Hadi slithered toward the edge of the containers and slipped over, vanishing.

At the same time, three Black Hawks swooped past overhead, their sleek fish bodies blocking the stars. In the doorways, feet dangling, sat CIA paramilitary team members in uniforms, black boots, helmets, and thick gloves. They bristled menacingly with gear and weapons.

As Elaine closed in on the void where Jay and Raina had disappeared, the Black Hawks sank gracefully toward the wharf. Their noses rose thirty degrees, and they stabilized at eighty feet. Thick ropes plummeted from their doors. Within four seconds, teams of seven fast-roped down and spread out. Shouts of fear sounded from the docks.

Hot tears streaming down her cheeks, Elaine fell to her knees and leaned over the container. Angrily she brushed her eyes so she could see Jay and Raina lying splayed faceup at the bottom in shadows, motionless.

She shook as if from palsy. At last she gathered herself and holstered her gun. Then she slid over the side and dropped softly to her feet. There was an engine noise near the rail. She duck-walked toward it, praying it was al-Hadi so she could empty her Walther into him.

Instead, a motorized hoist for one of the podlike life rafts was rising. The raft was gone. Al-Hadi had escaped. She bellowed a curse and hurried back into the steel-lined passage, yanking out her cell phone to tell the paramilitary where al-Hadi was.

She did not understand it. Jay had broken every rule he had ever taught her. So had Raina, who seemed to know the rules equally well. There was no intelligence in their behavior — no use of the supplies in their packs, no deception. They had even turned their backs on al-Hadi. It was almost as if they *wanted* to die.

Her throat tightened as she peered at their corpses lying ahead. Then she frowned, her thoughts repeating — *no deception.* With a jolt of anger, suddenly she understood.

She marched toward them. "Dammit all to hell, Jay. You're not dead. Get up." Furiously she wiped her sleeve across her face, drying her tears. She raised her gun. "Damn you, I said *get up!*"

With a chuckle, Jay sat up.

"I'm a hunter, remember?" she snapped. "I'm taking you in. I *know* you're no traitor. We'll get this straightened out. How dare you fool me!"

As Elaine reached Raina, she saw "blood" pooling out from beneath her. "Squib bags of red dye!" she accused, glaring at Raina. She pointed her Walther at her. "I didn't know you had Kevlar protection. Your jacket's as thin as mine!"

"You're a smart one," Raina said approvingly as she stood and slid off her backpack. "They're made out of a new fabric combining Kevlar and some state-of-the-art protective material our troops will be using next year. After we left you, Jay and I made one more stop to pick up the jackets and squibs."

Elaine shot Raina a scorching look. Then she picked up Raina's SIG Sauer from where it had fallen, tucked it into her waistband, and closed in on Jay. "Al-Hadi has the software, doesn't he? Now that he thinks he killed you, he'll be sure it's clean. Langley will be able to track the Majlis through the backdoor. That's what this was all about!"

Still sitting, Jay grinned up at her. "A last-minute operation, you might say." He rotated his Browning and offered it to her butt first. "Glad to know you made it through the firefight on deck, Elaine. You did a damn good job of protecting us. You're turning into a first-rate covert operative. How did you get on board in the end?"

"I found a pilot's ladder on the starboard side." She grabbed his weapon. For a moment she felt uneasy.

"You left the inflatable boat there by the ladder?" Jay climbed to his feet.

There was something wrong. "Yes."

Pain stabbed her back near her shoulder pad. She tried to whirl, but her body responded slowly. She finished the turn as Raina put an empty hypodermic syringe into her pack. Elaine looked into Raina's smiling eyes and started to swear but could not seem to find the right word.

"You'll be excellent in the field, dear," Raina assured her. "You'll never let this happen again." She reclaimed her gun from Elaine's waistband.

Jay walked around Elaine, smiled down at her, and hugged her warmly. Then he helped her to stretch out on the deck.

"Raina injected you with a fast-acting seda-
tive. You won't be out long. Ten minutes —
at the most, fifteen. Confirm for Bobbye
about al-Hadi and the ForeTell backdoor,
but don't tell anyone else." For a moment,
his gaze misted. "I'll miss you, Elaine." He
took his Browning.

Her eyelids growing heavy, Elaine watched
Jay pull Raina to him. She seemed to melt
into him. As they clung together, he stroked
her cheek and looked deep into her eyes.
She lifted her lips, and they kissed for quite
a while. Her fingers curled into his back. At
last, they walked away. He slung an arm
around her shoulders; she wrapped an arm
around his waist. Their strides matched.

As they disappeared, she thought she
heard Jay chuckle and his voice float back:
"Remember — always have a good backup
plan."

EPILOGUE

Three Years Later
Aitutaki, Cook Islands

As Jay Tice walked home, carrying supplies and groceries, sunset arrived with the tropical languidness he loved, dusting the South Seas horizon in soft gray that deepened into tangerine and brilliant gold. The vibrant colors reflected off the darkening ocean as if it were a mirror and painted the powdery white beach a blushing rouge.

In his shorts and sleeveless shirt, Jay passed houses big and small, built of pink coral or weathered wood, surrounded by vegetable gardens, fenced pigs, and chickens running wild. Palm trees swayed in the frangipani-scented air.

One of their friends, British expat Denise Cumberland, was leaning her bicycle against the beech tree outside her bungalow. When she noticed him, she grinned. Her tall height and sun-carved face were impressive.

"Kia orana," Jay greeted her in Maori. May you live long.

"Kia orana yourself, Phil. You're walking fast today. Definitely not your usual amble." Her eyes twinkled.

He held up a manilla envelope. "Mail!"

"Wonders never cease. How's Kitty doing?"

"Busy as can be. Me, too. It's more fun than we'd ever thought. Stop by for a drink soon, okay?"

"You really should wear shoes, Phil. You've gone native."

Jay laughed and continued on, increasing his pace. As his gaze swept the ruffled ocean, his thoughts drifted back to his escape with Raina from Martin Ghranditti's container ship. They had rowed to a spit of land where their hidden packet waited and begun a peripatetic journey that had taken them through Mexico then on to Australia and finally here — to this remote Shangri-la in the southern Cook Islands chain where neither had ever been, no one knew them, and they could start over.

Bobbye Johnson had covered by alerting the Coast Guard to look for his drowned corpse in the Baltimore river. When no corpse was found, she declared Jay Tice dead and good riddance. In Germany the

BND issued a formal statement that Raina Manhardt had gone into seclusion and retired — which told him Bobbye had twisted BND president Erich Eisner's arm hard.

As a reward for her outstanding work, Elaine received a commendation and an open ticket to whatever she wanted to do for Langley. Of course, she chose undercover work, with Bobbye's blessing — and Jay's misgivings, but no one asked him, which was the way it should be. In congratulations for her help and obstinance, he arranged a brand-new red Jaguar be delivered anonymously to her town house. He was sorry to have missed the expression on her face.

In the unfortunate way of the world, today's news quickly became toilet paper. More often than not, the lessons of the past were worse than ignored; they were forgotten. And the events of those difficult days were no exception. Ghranditti's death and his dangerous shipment held international attention for several weeks, then evaporated. The perilousness of undermanned inspection teams at ports and the thriving underworld of death merchants continued without change.

Still, Langley reaped a flood of intel from

the backdoor Kristoph had created. Within six months, Elaine led a NOC team in cooperation with the South Korean government and arrested Faisal al-Hadi outside the National Bank of Pakistan in Seoul. Al-Hadi made no attempt to fight; instead, he angrily denied his identity. At the same time around the globe, teams attempted to capture thirty-two other Majlis al-Sha'b leaders. Some of the terrorists survived and were arrested; others opened fire and died. No one escaped.

With its leadership decimated, the Majlis was out of action. Al-Qaeda had swarmed down on the group's secret headquarters on the pirate-infested Strait of Malacca to confiscate records and technology. It made him smile to think the bastards took Kristoph's software and were using it.

Jay stared ahead. Raina was standing on their porch in a gauzy white dress, holding two chilled drinking coconuts. The light of the setting sun illuminated her tired but happy face and the mop of dark ringlets that had grown out, flowing down to her shoulders in a silky cloud. She seemed to shine, glow with femininity and allure.

"Hello, darling," she called. "Denise phoned to let me know you were on your way home. We have mail?"

He dropped the sacks onto the porch and held her, inhaling the natural perfume of her body, feeling her firmness and warmth. Heat coursed through him.

"Later," she murmured, twining one bare leg around his bare calf while balancing the two coconuts.

"Honey, believe me, you're worth waiting for."

Laughing, she sat on the porch swing and handed him his coconut. Their photo album was open on the table next to her.

She noticed he was gazing at it. "It does me good to see them," she told him.

"Me, too. I'm glad to have had those children as long as we did."

He picked up the album and turned the pages. They had put it together from pictures from her Berlin house and those he had saved in his storage space in Washington. It chronicled the short lives of Aaron, Mariette, and Kristoph, who might be dead but were still very loved. At last he closed it and laid it on the table. As he drank from his coconut, he grabbed the sack that contained the newspapers, magazines, and manila envelope he had picked up in the village.

She watched alertly as he opened it.

"It's from Ben," he told her unnecessarily.

Only Ben knew where they had settled. Thanks to Houri, Ben had survived, and Bobbye had cleaned up after "David Oxley" so that Ben and Zahra did not have to go into hiding. A few months later Ben and he devised a series of forwarding drops so they could stay in touch.

He took out a letter and another envelope.

"Read it, darling," Raina said.

He nodded, put on his glasses, and read aloud:

Dear Kitty and Philip,

Things are good here. Hope they are good there, too. You'll be glad to know al-Hadi is finally going to trial. His damn lawyers don't have any more delays left in their legal quivers, thank you, Allah.

Last week, I got an e-mail from Marie Ghranditti — she calls herself Emmi Ghranditti now. She and the children are still in Miami Beach and doing well. In fact, she's getting remarried, this time to a real financier. He sounds like a good man.

As for the envelope I've enclosed, it's in response to the letter you asked me to forward a few months ago. Sorry this took so long. I finally had to go to Bobbye to find out where the family was liv-

ing — in Tel Aviv, as it turns out. Bobbye said Pavel Abendroth's widow is
dead now. I didn't read your letter or
this one, of course.

Stay in touch!
Ben

Raina was sitting as wary as a cat at a
snake hole. "You didn't."

"Of course I did." Strangely, his hands
trembled as he opened the blue vellum
envelope. The stationery was also blue vellum, which somehow made it all the more
personal, more affecting. The words were
written in a feminine, strong hand:

I won't use your name, because I
understand you still need to maintain
your security, but please know I address
this to you with all respect. My brothers
and I always believed our father was assassinated, and we were angry about
that. We loved him and needed him. But
more important, he was a hero, and the
world needs its heroes to live as long as
possible.

Last year when our mother was dying,
she called us together and told us what
really had happened and made us promise to say nothing unless we had your

permission. Since you haven't given it, we'll keep the secret.

You might like to know that she said he admired the way you risked your life to slip into East Berlin to talk with him and that you knew what few others did — that he was dying of cancer.

Since he'd dedicated himself to stopping totalitarianism, he felt it was only right to sacrifice himself so the identity of your mole — your wife now, you say — wouldn't be uncovered and she could go on feeding information to the West. You were both continuing the fight he couldn't.

It was kind of you to write with your apologies and to let us know you regret the "assassination." But Mother said he never had any regrets. You and your wife made a great contribution and no doubt sacrificed a lot as well.

Mother liked to quote the historian John Shedd, because it reflected my father's philosophy, too — "A ship in harbor is safe, but that is not what ships are built for."

Sincerely,
his daughter

Jay silently folded the letter and returned

it to the envelope. He glanced at Raina and admitted, "I could never do enough to earn the right to be happy. Dr. Abendroth paid with his life so I could have you."

She took his hand and pressed it against her cheek. "I know, darling."

The swing creaked. They drank their coconuts. The sun set in a dramatic flash of hot light, and twilight settled in a violet mantle over the palms and bougainvillea.

Jay glanced at the house several times.

"Check on them, darling," Raina said, smiling. "I know you want to."

He nodded and padded indoors. Their one-story bungalow was glassy and usually full of light, but now soft shadows draped the simple furniture and wood floors, somehow adding a sense of enchantment.

He went into Michael's room, crouched beside his bed, and gently brushed back his black hair, as glossy as his mother's. Michael had just turned two, an energetic child who ran nonstop while awake and fell quickly into deep slumber at the end of the day. He was lying on his side, his chin tucked, his long black lashes shadows on his cheeks.

Suddenly he opened his eyes and looked up. "Daddy!"

Jay grinned. "Shh. Don't tell your mother I woke you. I'll be in trouble."

Michael grinned back. "Our secret." He puckered his lips.

Jay kissed him, and the boy's eyelids drooped and shut. Jay lingered, studying the miracle of life — that he and Raina could have created this miracle together.

At last he went into Jennifer's room. She was two months old. After sleepless nights of taking turns to be up with her through the usual crying jags and hunger, Raina and he had privacy again, because six days ago Jennifer seemed to decide that was enough of that and slept a solid six hours every night. Now she had graduated to her own room, too. She smelled wonderful, of baby powder and moist sleep.

He dropped to his heels beside her crib, soaking in her sweet expression and milky skin and fiery red locks. He smiled, thinking about what a challenge she was going to be to raise. He pressed a finger against her tiny palm, and she curled her hand around it. Joy flowed through him.

When he returned to the porch, Raina was swinging slowly, the album again on her lap, opened to a photo of Kristoph. She glanced up guiltily. "About Kristoph — I tried to tell you a long time ago in Dubrovnik when we met after my husband died, and you found out I was pregnant with Kristoph.

Then I tried to tell you several times later —"

"Don't worry, darling. I've always known he was Kristoph's biological father."

"Jay! But why didn't you —"

He sat beside her, feeling again his happiness in Kristoph, his love for the boy. "Because I didn't care about any of that. Because I loved you, and Kristoph needed a father. But mostly . . ." He hesitated. "Mostly, I needed him. I desperately needed something or someone good to believe in. Kristoph and you gave me all of that — and far more."

As a tear rolled down her cheek, he pulled her close. "They're asleep," he confirmed.

"I told you." She kissed his ear and snuggled into his side. After a while she asked, "When they grow older, what will we do when they realize there's a huge world out there? They'll ask questions and probably grow restless. Our safe haven may not be enough for them."

He thought about it. "Let's let tomorrow take care of tomorrow."

ABOUT THE AUTHOR

Gayle Lynds is the bestselling author of several thrillers, including *Masquerade* and *The Coil.* With Robert Ludlum, she authored three of the bestselling Covert-One novels: *The Hades Factor, The Paris Option,* and *The Altman Code.* Before becoming a full-time novelist, she had a varied career, including stints as a journalist, an editor, and at a military think tank where she held a top-secret clearance. She recently cofounded the International Thriller Writers (ITW). She lives in Santa Barbara, California. Visit her Web site at www.GayleLynds.com.